AS
THE EARTH TURNS

AS
THE EARTH TURNS

GLADYS HASTY CARROLL

New York
GROSSET & DUNLAP
Publishers

TO
H. A. C.

CONTENTS

WINTER

WINTER

I

OUTSIDE the house it was storming, a busy downfall of flakes that the wind blew lightly across acres of old snow left from December. Drifts piled up over the steps and over the sawdust banking that covered the sills. Fence posts were hidden, and the rails; only a few apple trees in the back field and the pine in the corner at the end of the lane struck black lines on the whitening air, while other pines and scattered hardwood trees surrounded the farm at a little distance, a smutted circle darker than the heavy, late afternoon sky.

Inside, all the rooms but one were cold and closed, the comforters in stiff heaps on the beds, the windows of the parlor and sitting-room thick with spiralled frost. The women and children sat in the kitchen. Here night came earlier than to the rest of the house for the barn shut out the sunset light from the ell, but it was not yet lamp time, and the girl at the dark end of the cookstove peeled and sliced her apples with swift, firm strokes to finish them before it should be. The little woman in the rocker by the north window held her sewing high and twitched at it, her sunken mouth pinched with concentration. The children, one fat with red braids and big new front teeth, the other, younger, a sober small boy in overalls, sat on their heels before the couch cutting figures from a mail order catalogue and assembling them into families.

"Shutting down awful early to-night," the woman said. "Time they was getting home, ain't it? Lois May hadn't ought to be out in this night air, her throat the way it is, after that cold."

"They'll be right along," the girl answered.

She rose to put wood on the fire. Flames, shooting up brightly toward her face, showed it round and serene with gray eyes and light hair pinned in smooth braids about her head. Her arm, crooked to shake the lid into place, was bare to the elbow and stout, her hands quick and sure. She went toward the sinkroom for a saucepan. The apples were ready for stewing.

"That's pretty, ma," she said. "I don't see how you ever do it so fine."

"Well, I've always been called a very good hand at tucking," the woman said. "I know when Lois May was born folks up to Kezar Falls thought she had the prettiest things of any young one round. I'm different from some. I take a little pride."

She stroked the strip of white rayon smooth across her lap, regarding it with anxiety, her eyelids swollen, her heavy, pale red hair sliding low on her neck.

"What's all that commotion down the road?" the girl asked.

She stopped by a window and peered out, holding the basin of apples balanced against her hip. Through the snow which whirled between the house and the road and the damp flakes clinging to the glass, it was not easy to tell what passed by at this time of day. Still, anything that stirred, except the snow, was a wonder and had not escaped her as she glanced out.

The children came running and squeezed in between her knees and the low window ledge.

"Is it a shanty, Jen? Is it a Frenchman's shanty being hauled?"

Sometimes the choppers moved their houses from woodlot to woodlot two or three times throughout a winter, often with women nursing babies by the windows as they rode along. At these wanderings the farmers and their families looked on with curiosity and high contempt.

"There, I can't see," the mother said, standing too, "enough to know!"

"It's not a shanty, Bun," Jen told the little girl, "but it's probably Frenchmen's folks on the move. It looks like a load of furniture. It's pretty big for that one horse in this going, ma. He'll never get far to-night."

"Well, that's the Frenchman of it all right," the woman said grimly. "That's as well as they can plan. ... Yes, now I can make out some chairs tied on the back without a mite of covering. I guess this wet will start the rounds in them!"

"I guess so," Jen agreed.

The caravan had passed. She went on into the sink-room and came back, glad she was not travelling. She had never slept in any but this house in her life, nor been more than a few miles away from it. Deftly she transferred the apples, poured water from the teakettle over them, and set them on to cook. There was nothing better than warm applesauce for supper, and these

bellflowers held their flavor the best of any she had
ever used. She set the table with big black and white
plates, yellow bone-handled knives and forks, new
aluminum teaspoons, and a red glass sugar bowl and
pitcher. She brought in a frypan with ham already
placed in it and, while it was heating, lit a tall lamp
with a clear base that the white wick and grayish oil
showed through.

"I'll bet the old horse will balk," Bun was saying
with narrowed, prophetic eyes and much satisfaction.
"I'll bet he'll balk and the man will be lost and they
won't know where to go. So he'll holler to his wife
and young ones that's under the blanket and they'll
get down under the cart to sleep and the snow'll drift
over them tight and they'll freeze to death right in
the road."

She sat on the couch, rocking and swinging her
feet. The room was warm and light and smelled of
supper and she had enough paper dolls to last out any
storm that ever blew. She even had colored ones; and
in the sitting-room cupboard there was a bag with
seven pieces of candy in it, heart-shaped wafers with
printing on. She hoped the storm would last and last.
She would not mind if the snow should cover the
windows, for Jen could light the lamps, and there was
oil enough, for her father had brought home a great
can full only yesterday from market. Ed might have to
dig a tunnel to the well, and she and John could play
in it. Her face shone with anticipation.

Jen chopped vigorously in the sinkroom. Her father
liked his warmed-up potatoes cut very fine.

"They won't, will they?" John asked behind her.

"They won't have to stay outdoors all night, will they, them Frenchmen?"

"Land, no," Jen said, looking at him quickly. "They're probably just going up to Cherry Swamp. There's a mill set up to saw in there, Ed said yesterday. They're maybe there by now."

John turned his back on her, rubbing his forehead against the cupboard door very hard.

"You s'pose they got beds?" he wanted to know. "Beds to sleep in, up there to Cherry Swamp?"

"Land," said Jen again, "yes. And hot beach rocks to put in them, like enough, just like we have. And stoves to cook suppers on. Why, they'll be snug as a bug in a rug in no time."

She chopped again and then lifted her head to listen.

"I believe I hear old Bob. . . . Yes, that's them. You put on your jacket, John, and I'll light the lantern and you can take it out to father. I guess it's dark enough in the tie-up to-night. . . . Bun, you go with John and carry the milk pails down."

Cora Shaw had taken a hand lamp and gone upstairs to put away the white rayon, and for a minute Jen was alone in the kitchen. She took quiet steps between the stove and table, cellarway and sinkroom, wasting none, a stocky figure in a dark wool dress and bright pink apron. Many things she reached for without looking at them, so accustomed was she. Now and then her glance slid about the room, not aware and yet not unaware of the year-old tulip paper on the walls, the faded border around the new calendar, the black stove with a fat baby engraved on the oven door, the steeple clock on the shelf over the table, the sagging couch with its flowered pillows, the worn, reddish chairs, the tall woodbox, the geraniums in the windows, the smoky fragrance of the fried ham, the yellow shine of the lamplight on the dishes. There was still more here which she could not even see, much more describe, but of which she was not unaware, much that was a part of the room and also a part of her. She had been mistress of this house since her ninth year, and she was nineteen now. The coming of a stepmother six years ago had changed nothing. This was Jen's kitchen. She brought a pitcher of milk from the cellar, briskly stirring in the risen cream with a big spoon, and set it on the table.

"Jen! Jen, can you open the door?"

She let in a slim, dark girl in a red crocheted cap and short brown corduroy coat, with a plaid shawl worn over all and pinned under her chin, and her arms full of books and boxes.

"Well!" Jen exclaimed. "I guess you're loaded, Lois May, scuppers all in under!"

"I've got the darlingest hat," the girl said in a husky, excited voice. "It's that brown straw of Margaret's but we steamed and shaped it over to-day, and Mil had a yellow feather she gave me to put on it. They said it was lucky for me feathers had come in again, for they've got quite a few were their Aunt Grace's. And Margaret gave me some silk to make a scarf. That's yellow, too. Look!"

She threw the shawl and coat and cap on the couch and rummaged through the boxes to produce a narrow length of yellow crepe and twist it around her neck. She was taller than Jen, but younger, not over sixteen.

with small, well-made features and a long bob that
had been waved with an iron. Her eyes were deep
blue, narrow and slightly slanting, her skin smooth
and dusky, and she had brought a smell of perfume
into the room.

"Now you're fine, I must say," Jen declared admiringly. "Ma! Ma, come along down before you freeze
and see what the girls give Lois May! It looks as if it
would pay to send her visiting every day."

She went back to her supper and while the other
two fingered and nodded and talked, she set on
biscuit to steam and tasted the applesauce to be sure
it was sweet enough. Lois May had also four yards
of lace, three fancy handkerchiefs, a string of amber
glass beads, and a new tablet of scratch paper in her
boxes. She displayed these with an air of triumph.

"Well, now, I'm sure Mil and Margaret went to a
good deal of pains," said Mrs. Shaw. She added, "If
your own folks was all as interested to see you get
ahead as George's wife, and Margaret, too, even if
    ain't married to Ed yet, you'd be in business
school by spring all right. Folks has to work together
and kind of figure when money's as scarce as 'tis
here."

Sometimes the Shaws were Lois May's kin, and
sometimes not. It rested with her and Mrs. Shaw to
decide to fit the occasion whether the fact that her
name had once been Webster carried any significance
With Bun, Mrs. Shaw's other daughter by her first
husband, the point was never disputed. She was Bun.

"That's right, ma," Jen said now, cheerfully. "What
is it they sing in school, Lois May? A long pull and
a strong pull? You'll be educated yet!"

"If I could only get hold of a decent spring coat anywhere," sighed Lois May, "I'd have clothes enough to do."

"Yes, but you've got to have money for that tuition fee," her mother said. "And your board's got to be paid some way. I don't know. Sometimes I can't see any hope at all, but I'm bound you'll go, that's all. I'm just that set. Seems as though I'll get down sick, though, studying over it."

"There, now, don't do that," Jen said. "For goodness' sake. That's no way."

"I'll have to have some new stockings, of course," suggested Lois May. She sat down on the couch and ran her finger delicately up two long, mended runs in her cheap, pale silk stockings. "These are as good as I've got."

"There, that's another thing!" her mother exclaimed, bending over to look. "I ought to have caught them sooner."

Jen set the steamed bread on the table, the ham and potatoes and applesauce, and began to pour the tea. John came panting up the shedstairs.

"They're coming, Jen," he told her in his grave, five-year-old voice. "They're just right behind."

"That's good," Jen said. "Everything's ready."

She looked up and smiled at Mark Shaw, her father, a big stooped man with light hair graying at the ends and a broad, brown face; at Ed, her brother, tall and lean, in a blue frock coat and overalls over his heavy winter clothes; at Bun helping Ed to carry a basket of wood, her full, plain face twisted with the effort, and her red pigtails bobbing into her mouth.

"I can carry as much wood as Ed can, Lois May. Jen, look! I did, didn't I, Ed? I'm getting stronger and stronger. I guess I'll be awful strong when I grow up."

"Yes," Jen said. "I don't doubt we'll have to put you in the circus. . . . You just leave the milk there, father. I'll tend to it right after supper. Everything's ready now."

The two men hung sheepskin-lined coats and visored caps behind the stove, and laid wet mittens on the shelf to dry. They sat down, one in a chair, the other on the end of the couch, and pulled off their felt boots, grunting faintly as they did so. John scrambled under the stove and brought out slippers, Mark Shaw's of green carpeting, well worn and run down at the heels, Ed's of leather, new and shiny, a Christmas present from the sister of his brother's wife, the girl he would marry in the spring. They stood up, spreading their arms to take in the heat of the supper fire, and after a minute went together to the sink, washed, and took their places at the table without speaking.

The others were already there. Jen waited on them, tied John's napkin, filled Ed's cup again when he had gulped down, hot and clear, the tea she had poured for him, pushed the biscuit toward her father. The men ate heartily and bent their minds upon their plates. Mrs. Shaw took a bit of meat, a taste of applesauce. "My tea," she said, "is all that keeps me going. I don't know when I ever had a mite of appetite for anything." Lois May sat upright, her hands held daintily, aware of how she used her fork and spoon.

The fire in the stove licked birch sticks, and a coal snapped out on the rug, making the cat jump. The children twisted in their chairs to see, and laughed. "Come, finish your suppers," Jen said. "Drink your milk, John." He drank fast, gurgling, and emerged from the glass with a white rim on his upper lip, his eyes triumphant. The heads of the Shaws made shadows on the wall.

Mark, his knife and fork now crossed upon a cleared plate, looked around at the family from deep, colorless eyes. He had known winter nights when only he and Minnie Foote sat at this table, Minnie Foote, his first wife, young then, thin and gay and red-cheeked, quick at figures and wrote a pretty hand. They drew up more chairs as the children grew. George, the first boy, fat and always hungry; George had been a great one for baked beans and brown bread from a baby. Then Ralph and Lize, the twins, thin and far looking like their mother; and Ed here, and Jen; and then Olly. After Olly, Minnie Foote had never used her chair much, and finally not at all. The frost was going out of the ground when the men dug the grave down in the pasture, Mark Shaw remembered.

Then George was married and went up the road to live. And Ralph went off and joined the army, strange enough to think of, and Lize to a job in the city; it was a wonder what they wanted of that life out there. Ed worked on the neighboring Searles place as long as Caleb lived, and the old man had made it cheap to him to buy it; it was as good a farm as any around; Ed had done well. His father's slow thought dwelt with pride on this third son. Jen, there, she kept the house going, and for a year or two they two had been alone, except for Olly, the boy who was all Foote, with a head for books and nothing else; she was a good girl, light on her feet and handy at her work.

Then he brought Cora Webster here from Kezar Falls, the year fire went through Burke woods and took two houses at the edge of it. That was a bad fire and nothing but a week's rain could have put it out. Cora was never much contented; she had a nervous way with her, and all the drugs she wanted him to get never had much effect. But she had brought two children with her, girls, to help fill up the kitchen that was growing empty; and she bore John. Olly, too, had gone away now, to a college down east, but Cora Webster had borne John, a stout, steady boy already. Mark Shaw's deep eyes stayed longest of all on John.

"Can't you eat anything more?" Jen asked. "Any of you?"

She looked at Ed. He shook his head.

"See your new neighbors go up by to-night, ma?" he wanted to know, tilting on the back legs of his chair.

"We see a load of Frenchmen's stuff," sniffed Mrs. Shaw, "if that's what you mean."

Ed made no reply but crooked the corner of his mouth, staring at the ceiling. He had a hard, ruddy, handsome face.

"Did you meet them, Lois May?" Mrs. Shaw pursued.

"We didn't meet anybody," Lois May answered. "Not coming home." She added, "Margaret's afraid this storm'll make it so she can't keep school to-morrow. She says they've missed enough time this winter as it is."

"Gee, I hope it will," Bun cried. She wriggled joyfully, for she had paper dolls and seven pieces of candy.

"It's been a terrible winter," sighed Mrs. Shaw. "I know that. How did you find Mil?"

"All right, I guess," Lois May said. "The baby's cute." She wrinkled her nose. "If *only* she would scrub her kids once in a while!"

"I guess you'd have your hands full, Lois May, if you had four to tend to and a house to keep," Jen said. "Did you see George, father?"

"We didn't go in," her father answered. His voice was heavy and he used it with care. "We just stopped in the road there when we come out of the woods and Lois May come right along. George was lugging water to the barn. He swung his hand."

"It makes it bad for George in winter," Jen said. "The way he has to go outside to get to the barn, so. It would be worth everything to him to have a shed between."

She began clearing the table as she sat there, reaching for the plates and stacking them before her.

"No, that wasn't any Frenchmen's stuff you saw, ma," Ed took up his topic where it had been left. He still looked secretly amused. "That was Polack stuff."

"Polack!"

They all turned toward him sharply, except Mark Shaw who only listened, warm, filled, comfortable, finished with one day many hours before the next would begin. He liked his supper table.

"Yes, you've got Polack neighbors, ma. Or so I hear. There's Ondia Janowski, and Rozia Janowski, and some fifteen or twenty little Janowskis, and they're all going to live right over here on the Old Joe place, or so Bill Carpenter said to-day, and I see there was tracks over in there when we come by to-night. And you say you saw the furniture go up, so I guess they're here all right. *Now* you've got neighbors, ma, and we don't want to hear any more fuss about you not being able to see anybody's smoke in the daytime nor anybody's light at night."

He had been thinking this up as he sat there, while the others talked, or it would not have come so easily.

"Polacks!" said Mrs. Shaw again bitterly. She knew nothing of the Polish, but they sounded even more foreign than the French. "What right have they got on the Old Joe place? Tramps, are they?"

"Folks say they've bought it," Ed said. "From the heirs. Old Joe's daughter, is it, lives up around Boston somewhere, father?"

Mark Shaw cleared his throat.

"It's Joe's brother's girl," he said. "Henry's girl. She married a Peters from down Portland way. Hattie Peters, her name is."

"Yes; Hattie Peters," Jen agreed. "I've heard her spoke of."

She looked again at Ed.

"Well, she's sold the place," he was saying, "to Ondia Janowski and Rozia Janowski and all the young Jan——"

"And where," demanded Mrs. Shaw, "are they going to live? In their cart?"

"Why, ain't you familiar," Ed asked in mock surprise, "with the Old Joe mansion? Situated right down under the hill in the edge of the swamp, bounded on the west by the brook, on the north by a boghole——"

"Ed!" Jen gasped, for the first time stirred out of her waiting. "You don't mean they're going to stay in that old barn!"

Ed flung back his chair and reached into a box behind the stove for a match to light his way upstairs. He had had his fun and was through. This was his night to go up the road to call on Margaret.

"Well, all I know is what Bill was telling," he said. "You womenfolks will have to find out the particulars for yourselves. I've got other business."

"Well, so have I," rejoined Jen. "My land!"

She sprang up and carried the milk and butter to the cellarway, coming back for what was left of the meat and potatoes. Mark Shaw withdrew to a chair by the back window; he often sat until bedtime looking out on the dark. His wife brought her mending close to the lamp, pushing up her back hair wearily with one hand. Lois May dallied with the dishes, her head full of imaginings of life as it would be in the city at the business school where a girl learned how to make high pay with which to buy a fur coat and a wrist watch and silk underwear. She had never worn anything richer than rayon next to her, and only two sets of that, for very best. The children broke bread into the cat's dish behind the stove and poured milk over it.

"Now if you want to go practicing on that shorthand Margaret's teaching you, you go ahead," Jen said to Lois May.

When Ed came downstairs, dressed in his brown

suit and light shirt and tie, he found her turning hot water into the dishpan. Steam rose from it in a white cloud. It was never quite warm in the sinkroom in winter. He fumbled in the cupboard and took a long time about brushing his teeth.

"It's an awful dirty house over there," he said. "Lord knows how it'll ever be got dug out."

He meant the Searles house which he had bought and would take Margaret to live in in the spring.

"There, I suppose it is," Jen said. "Poor old Mrs. Searles wasn't fit to take care of herself, even, for long enough before she died."

Ed put away his brush and cup noisily. Jen had to press against the edge of the sink to leave space for his big body in the narrow room.

"I can't put the roof windows in until the attic's straightened out a little," he said. "That attic's the worst hole there is, too. It's going to be one awful job."

"I'll bet it is," Jen said. "I'd like it though."

She rinsed the cups and began wiping them.

"Wouldn't want to do some of it, would you?" Ed mumbled. It cut him to ask help, though he did not mind accepting it.

Jen looked up at him in disbelief.

"You don't want me to!"

"Why not?"

"Well, I thought—" Jen flushed. "You know, Ed. Margaret'll be helping you. You folks wouldn't want me——"

"Oh, go on," Ed told her. "I can't hang around waiting for her to get out of school. She wouldn't have an hour before dark anyway. . . . Besides, you could

clean a whole house while she was wiping off a look-
ing-glass, and you know it."

It was true. Though Jen understood that Ed loved
Margaret so much it did not matter to him how well
she could work, it was good to be favorably compared.
Margaret was prettier than Jen. She was wiser. She
could teach school, and play the organ at church. But
when Ed wanted his house cleaned, he needed Jen.

"All right," she said meekly. And then, with conviction, "If there's anything I like, it's cleaning something awful dirty!"

"That's dirty enough," Ed assured her.

A minute later she heard his boots crunch across
the snowy porch. He was going to Margaret's. Every
Tuesday and Thursday night he went to see her, where
she lived with George and Mil, and Sunday afternoons. It took more than a storm to keep him away.
Jen smiled, rinsing her dish towels.

"You _can_ see a light up on the Old Joe place," she
said. "Even through this storm. High up. It must be
from a window in the loft."

There was a rustle as those in the kitchen turned
to look.

"I never heard such works," said Mrs. Shaw. "Living
in a barn! . . . Well, they'll be moving on again in a
month or so, just like Frenchmen!"

Jen went in to help the children out of their clothes
and into the flannel nightgowns she had hung to
warm over the oven door. The beach rocks were so
hot they scorched the cloths in which she wrapped
them, but the beds would cool them off. It would be
a cold night.

"Now scamper, you two! You're all but asleep as it is. Hold the shawls around you tight."

At nine o'clock only she was still awake in the house, and sat by the table studying a letter that had come from Olly that day. He did not write often, but he made his words round and plain; some said he had a hand like Minnie Foote's, with the curls and scrolls left off, as his hair was like hers, except that it was short, and his build like hers, as much as a boy's could be.

"You needn't tell anybody else," his letter said. "The folks would probably think I am wasting my time. But when I got an A in the Argumentation quiz, the coach asked me why I didn't try out for the debating team. So I tried, and I made alternate for the next debate. There are three regular fellows on the team, speakers; and the alternate works with them to help get out material, that's all. Of course, if one of them couldn't speak, I would take his place, but that hardly ever happens. No freshman ever has debated for Hathorn yet. Of course, it is going to take a lot of work and time, but I figure it will be worth it. You see, I think some of going on to study law when I get through here, and debating is good experience for a lawyer to have back of him. It gives you confidence in speaking and makes contacts and you kind of get the hang of that kind of thinking. If I ever should have a chance to speak, I'd have to hire a dress suit, and that would cost about $3.50, but I could manage it. Don't say anything though. I guess I just told you so you would know what a smart guy I am——"

Jen stared past the letter. Of all the children Olly had had the worst sicknesses and been the hardest to take care of, done puzzles quickest, felt it deepest when his clothes were patched and outgrown, kept the most to himself, and on occasions poured it out the most shockingly of all the Shaws. The other boys had laughed at him, his books, his glasses, his violent opinions, his thin, tense, jerky body. But now he was doing what none of them would have dared to do, working his way through a four-year course at a college away off down east. He even looked beyond that, and meant to study law. This debating would help him be a lawyer, he said. Lawyer Shaw. And Jen knew more than he had told her. She knew lawyers made good governors and presidents.

Whistling softly under her breath she tucked the letter behind the clock, and laid a big stick of wood on the fire. She carried the plants, two by two, from the windows to the table where the frost could not reach them, and took a pail of water into the cellar to keep the chill off the potatoes. The outside thermometer had reached ten below zero already.

As she came upstairs recipes were running through her head. She knew how Olly saved money for dress suits and other things, and it was not right; it was contrary to nature. She could send him baked beans in a glass jar, and a fresh johnnycake, and some pickles, and a big box of doughnuts and tarts. She could boil a half dozen eggs; there was a good deal of nourishment in eggs, and they kept well.

She turned down the lamp and set it in the window where it would light Ed across the icy stretch by the pump. Peering out, she could see it still stormed. Winter, she thought, had its back up.

II

Upstairs Bun gave a mighty leap and plunged from her right side to her left.

"You shut up!" she roared defiantly in her sleep. "You shut *up!*"

Lois May, lying beside her, stirred and shivered. The comforters had been pulled out from under the mattress on her side and the cold was striking in. It was a penance, she thought sleepily, to have to share a bed with Bun.

"*You* shut up," she said. "And keep still."

Then she smiled. It was pleasant to hear her voice in the quiet of the night. It sounded young and clear. She snuggled into the clothes and lay with her cheek on her palm, feeling the smooth firmness of both and the slim lines of her body among all the spongy mass of cotton batting and feathers. One hand slid down and encircled a half of her waist, though it was a small hand. She was little and young and lovely, and by and by she would go to live in the city of Rumfret. The blue serge suit and the sweaters and plaid skirt would do for classes at the business school but when she went out in the evenings she would wear the green velvet her mother had just finished making, unless it was a very special occasion; for such she had a yellow crepe de chine and a wide brown taffeta sash.

"Who's the girl in yellow?"

"Oh, is that the Shaw girl you've raved so much about? Well, I don't wonder."

Lois May heard these remarks, but no one knew that she did. Whirling past a corner in her partner's arms she looked only at him and smiled, a tantalizing smile. "You're glorious to-night, my dear!" She laughed skeptically. "Oh, am I!" He whirled her faster and faster, but her feet never missed a beat of the music and she kept on looking at him, provoking him. "Lois May, will you come into the conservatory, just for a minute? I can't stand this. I must speak to you." Then she caught herself up. She could not risk the scent of those flowers and the white lights beating down on his curly brown hair. "No, Paul. It really isn't any use. Perhaps you didn't know—but I've been appointed secretary to an ambassador. I sail in the morning for the Orient. I'm sorry, Paul. I've liked you."

Lois May slept beside Bun, hugging the comforters tight to her chin, and her breath showing on the air.

III

All night it snowed and for three days steadily, the worst storm of the winter. There was no passing on the road. If a man could not live without a doctor he must die. It was for times like these women bought medical books of agents who called in the spring, and kept top shelves well stocked with syrups to loosen a cough, peppermint for the colic, nitre and ammonia for the heart and nerves, stick salve and ointments and goose grease. Drifts grew higher and higher. Jen carried a lamp into the cellar even at noon to light her to the pork barrel or the potato bin. Bun had her wish and played on the floor with John all of every day; they cut out still more paper dolls and looked the family album through and made a tea-party of cookies and six of the heart-shaped wafers; the seventh wafer Bun held in reserve against the storm lasted a week. Jen had to keep sharp watch not to step on fingers as she went about her work. Mark Shaw and Ed took the good of the covered passageway between the house and barn.

George, who must go outside to tend his cattle, was up at every daybreak, an old sweater tied over his head and across his mouth, shovelling a new path where twelve hours had blown the old one full. And by mid-afternoon he was at it again.

Mil, glancing out of the window behind her cake-board, saw only an indistinct blur leaning hard to the wind. She could not tell whether he kept the sweater tied well, but hoped so. He ought to have some warm knit things if she could only get to making them, out, as he had to be, in the worst weather. He took a bad cough when a cold was on him, and it meant a long stretch when a cold started through a family of six. Then it would be a shame if Margaret should catch it; keep her from her school, and in a winter like this, every school day counted.

Mil drew herself up wearily, straining her shoulder blades in to ease the pain to the right of her spine. It was a strange thing about that pain; it always came on when she had the most to do, as if it knew, and meant to plague her.

"Let me cut out the cookies, mum!"

"Oh, *I* want to cut out cookies too. You let Esther cut out cookies last time, mama. It's my turn."

"It ain't either. Is it, mum?"

"Mama, she's hateful to me. She's *always*——"

"Betty!" Mil exclaimed. "Don't you dare to do that again! You know what happened the last time you

kicked your sister! I never saw such a bad girl. Now
you both get out of this pantry and don't you come
near again until I'm through."

That would be a long time, she thought grimly.
She was never through. When the weather or sickness kept the children in, the work dragged more than
ever. She was always dead tired before night, and
never quite rested even in the morning.

"But it don't do any good to think of it," she told
herself.

She rolled the dough very smooth and thin and
pale brown on the floury board. She ought to be
patient. She ought to be thankful she could do as
much as she did. Some women with month-old babies
were still flat on their backs. As she cut out neat
round disks and laid them in a pan, she heard Margaret helping little George with his counting, and reflected that big George should get twenty dollars
apiece for his calves; they were fine, fat calves.

IV

The morning that the sun came out Mark Shaw
and Ed and Charles Grant and Allie Walker, the
four men who lived along the lane, were busy with
their shovels before seven o'clock, having milked by
lantern light. By nine they joined the men from down
the main road, their lane open behind them but the
snow on either side piled three feet higher than their
heads.

"Quite a storm, Mark."

"Yes. Hung on some time."

"No trouble at your place?"

"No. No trouble."

Fred Bartlett had lost a horse from pneumonia. The medicine he kept on hand had done no good. The other men leaned on their shovels to listen to the story of it, and shook their heads. You lost a creature now and then, they said, the best you could do. Only Mark Shaw kept steadily at work. He never lost a horse or a cow or even a pig except to market or when it grew too old to chew its food and wanted killing. Fred Bartlett's barn was no fit place for stock; wind and cold came in from somewhere every foot or so.

"Seen anything of the folks on the Old Joe place, Mark?"

"No. Not yet."

"Polacks, ain't they?"

"I've heard so."

"There's quite a lot of them got in down the lower part of the town. It seems as if they can live anywhere, any way; you can't kill a Polack without a gun. That's what folks say down there. They're tough."

"That so?"

"They're bad ones to beat at marketing, too. They get an awful lot of produce off their places and sell for little or nothing. They're getting all the trade from the village folks. We need to look out. Yankees have to make a living. We got here first."

"We kind of figure," Grover Harrison said, spitting, "we ain't no call to be too friendly with this crowd. That is, until we see. They've took a hard row to hoe, coming here this time of the winter. Now let 'em hoe it."

Mark Shaw said nothing. He did not approve of so much talk on the town's time. Shrewdly he guessed the talk had not just begun when the men from over the lane joined the others. Those from down the road had been mulling this over among them since early morning, and now it had reached him, but here it would stop. He had nothing against them that could raise a big crop and sell it cheap; they must be good farmers. Let them hoe their row, to be sure. Let him hoe his. Let men who took town's money stop leaning on their shovels and start to dig with them. But he said nothing of all this, nor was it in his face. He lifted great blocks of snow easily and tossed them over his shoulder in the sun. Mark Shaw was not known as a neighborly man.

When the crew passed the Old Joe place on their slow advance up the road, they saw two stove funnels issuing from the south end of the gray barn in the meadow. A cheerful smoke poured out of both, and that was more fire than any of the shovellers had in his house. Several children played on the incline before the big door, and a man was leading a horse down a neat path to the brook. The sound of a hammer and saw carried plainly on the clear air.

Mark Shaw looked and listened with the rest, but not for long. He was here to shovel snow.

v

"Teacher, can I get a drink?"

It was eleven o'clock but the sides and front of the schoolroom were not yet warm. Margaret had brought down her chair from the platform and sat by the stove, holding little Gertrude Austin on her lap. The other children had ranged themselves at the two rows of desks in the very center of the room, under the stove pipe, and there were barely enough seats for them. Added to the eleven old scholars there were now five new ones. There was Manuel Janowski, a twelve-year-old with a wide body, generous grin, dark, good-natured eyes, and thick, black hair. There were his four little sisters, Maria, Ellena, and the two with American names, Louise and Marian, all sturdy, bright-eyed, radiantly friendly. The Shaws, the Austins, the Forrests, and the one Carpenter regarded the new arrivals gravely, and rhythmically squeezed fingers under warm armpits. It would be no easy matter bringing young Poland and young old-New England together, Margaret supposed.

But she was glad to be back. Watching Mil so long had made her anxious and irritated, for Mil did everything the hard way and never had less to do because anyone helped her. Here at school Margaret kept to a system. One finger for brown paper, two for white, and the whole hand to ask a question. Writing and arithmetic and history in the morning; reading and spelling and geography in the afternoon, with music, sewing, and drawing each once a week. The place for chalk and crayon was on the top shelf where the younger children could not reach and waste it. The globe stood on one corner of her desk, the dictionary on the other, where she could keep an eye on those consulting them. Arthur Forrest's free-hand sketch of New Year bells had been replaced by the picture of George Washington which Esther Shaw had traced on tissue and transferred to drawing paper by pressing hard with her pencil, for it was February now. Everything ran smoothly.

Margaret, a tall girl with smooth chestnut hair and brown eyes, sat for an instant relaxed and secure. Here was the fire burning brighter in the rusty box stove. Here were the painted yellow walls shutting out the cold and snow and the wind that howled beyond them, shutting in the shabby desks, the books, the blackboards, the snuffly noses, the mischievous eyes, the bitten apples that rolled into the aisles, the voices that broke, the feet that wriggled, the smudged papers, the dark heads, the light heads, the whispers and shivers and checkmarks. Here was everything that Margaret knew and could deal with.

It was not so sure how she would do as Ed Shaw's wife. She did not know a recipe for mincemeat, nor how it was Jen saved the small pigs from their mothers. Her floors might grow dingy, her sheets gray, however much she scrubbed. She did not know the kind of seeds it was Jen sowed in boxes early in the spring and carried from window to window, following the sun. Mil never did these things, and when Margaret had lived with her father and mother she had been too thoughtless to notice. But she hoped Ed would teach her what he knew; she would coax him. And the rest she would learn somehow. She would not be like Mil.

"Yes, Tom," she said. "But remember to use a paper cup. Don't drink out of the dipper."

She smiled at Tom, and Tom smiled back, sidling toward the water pail.

VI

"Yes, sir," said Jen as she climbed the last fence that separated the Shaw from the Searles place. "When you get that house cleaned and papered and painted, and your chambers finished off and the roof windows on, you'll have a big job done."

"I got to be through by planting time," Ed said.

It stood before them, an old house of fourteen rooms, lowposted, widespread, and weather-beaten. The shed merged with it, and the little old barn with the shed, making a stand of buildings that loomed up against the birches and pines of the pasture. A wisp of smoke curled out of one of the three big chimneys from a fire Ed had laid earlier in the morning. Cows, hearing footsteps, made a melancholy movement in the stalls. Wind whistled icily across the low ground and broke against them as they climbed the brow of the hill.

"My, I always forget, 'til I get here, what a mansion it is," Jen said. "No girl in Derwich ever went to a finer place than this will be. Fourteen rooms, didn't you say, Ed?"

"It'll be fifteen with the chambers," Ed told her.

He was proud of it. His would be the largest house for miles around.

They went inside. From off the little hall with an enclosed staircase lay a great parlor to the left and to the right a greater kitchen with a sealed fireplace and brick ovens. A later addition built on at the back provided a guest room behind the parlor, a little sitting-room and a pantry behind the kitchen; and the milk rooms were in the ell.

"My," Jen marvelled. "Seems as if there's no end to it, Ed."

It was a wonder Caleb Searles had wanted to buy such a great house, stingy as he was, and solitary-minded. But when he bought he had been in his young days. There was no telling what he might have expected then in the way of a big family, and people coming to dance at his daughters' weddings.

"We'll start at the top."

Upstairs was all open chamber with one window in each far end. It seemed that Caleb had used it as a place to throw things all the forty years that he had lived here, and never once cleared it out. The loose boards of the floor lay deep under old clothes, fishing tackle, hornets' nests, broken dishes, traps, nuts, and wire. The sides and corners were lined with half-empty barrels, storm windows, screens, and boxes of mice-eaten newspapers. Spiders had spun their webs everywhere undisturbed, and the dust of years had made their fine handiwork into cord as thick as Ed's little finger.

All day and all the next day they sorted and packed. Ed carried boxes to the window and turned them out in a cleared space on the floor. Spiders, fat and black, scampered out of folds and crevices. Hornets woke to the warmth that crept up from the open kitchen door and beat themselves in a frenzy against the rafters. Five small white mice with pink eyes blinked out from the sleeve of an old coat. "Oh, Ed! See! Wouldn't John love them?" Jen saved old underwear; Margaret would find knitted stuff good for scrub cloths. She folded strips of shirting and burlap neatly on her knee; they might do for a quilt some time, or for a rug. It was not a bad idea to start housekeeping with a piecebag. At last she swept joyfully, proud of the barrels and boxes stacked in their place under the eaves at one end, and the rest of the floor bared to her broom.

By the afternoon of Tuesday Ed had started work on his roof windows, and Jen downstairs, singing, dug and tore at seams of the old parlor paper that stuck fast. Behind the door a bit of the design was still plain, a bunch of red grapes with big green leaves in a wreath around it. She wondered what pattern Margaret would choose. The sample books were full of pretty papers. The one she liked best was cream color with a little vine running over it, and a narrow gilt stripe. It had a nice look, like a parlor.

"When the *roll*," sang Jen, "is called up *yonder;* when the *roll* is called up *yonder,* when the *roll* is called up *yonder*—" She liked songs better than hymns, but she did not know so many and the hymn-tunes were easier to carry.

About two o'clock she saw her father coming. He had been up in the hills for wood that day and now, his load off, had driven over on his horsesled. Bob pulled staunchly through the deep, soft snow, his head swinging from side to side. Behind him Mark Shaw sat huddled on a folded blanket, his big knees drawn up, jerking with every step. He had ridden like that for ten miles now, and his hands were stiff and cracked from handling icy logs; but if he felt tired, he was not thinking of it. Jen knew this as she watched him. She knew the firm lines in his cheeks and chin, the way he stared ahead and let Bob guide himself. It meant he thought of seed and grass and crops, and laid his plans. *Much snow, much rain to follow; this is the year to plow the hills. Cold winter brings a hot summer; plant early for frosts will be light; a good season for corn.*

"When the roll is called up yonder, I'll— Well, father, what does this mean?"

"I just thought I'd see how you was getting on."

"We're coming fine. Ed's started finishing off his upstairs."

"That so?"

Mark Shaw stood in the doorway, plastered with snow, and looked around the room.

Then he said, "The mailman brought you a letter and I got it here. Olly's hand, I kind of thought."

He drew it from among his buckles and straps and suspenders, his eyes on her face. Letters made him apprehensive. They had not come often in the days when the children were all under his roof. There had been no need of them then, when trains were nothing in his life but a whistle in the distance and a roar and a rush that frightened his horse on market day. It was a strange thing how so many of the children had wanted to go off, as if farms were not good enough any more. He puzzled over it sometimes when nobody knew what he was thinking.

Jen tore open the envelope and read, her fingers leaving stains on the white paper.

"How is he?" Mark Shaw asked. "All right?"

"He's fine," said Jen. "They had a debate Saturday night. One of the boys that was supposed to couldn't speak and Olly took his place. He was the first freshman ever did."

Her voice was quiet and matter-of-fact. She folded the letter and put it into her pocket.

"That so?" asked Mark Shaw. He stood looking at her, not knowing what a debate was, not liking to ask.

"He stood up in front of all the people and told

how this kind of government is better than the kind they've got over in England," said Jen. "Some other ones said it wasn't, but Olly maintained it was. He won it, too."

"So," said Mark Shaw, satisfied now. "Well, Olly's a smart one at his books. He'll likely go far."

"I shouldn't be surprised," said Jen, taking up her knife. She thought again of governors.

But Mark Shaw moved toward the stairs, toward that other son who used a saw and hammer. Olly was well; he felt relieved. He must warn Ed not to grain his cows too much at first, when Caleb had always skimped them. And then he must get back to his own place; a man had tinkering to do around his barn when he had been away and nobody left at home to take a thought for cattle, more than to throw in a little hay to them at noon.

"Better call it off for to-night," Ed told Jen, some hours later. "The fire's down and it's coming towards dark."

The two went out together into the evening, the only life abroad. Hills and meadows, pastures and swamps and marshes lay silent under the snow. Each single pine needle hung encased in ice, and the thin, black branches of walnut and fruit trees looked brittle and dead, as if only the cold kept them from crumbling. Sun glittered along the crust and the moon hung pale over the alder thicket to the east.

Ed walked with long, easy strides. He was taller than any other Shaw, and broader. He did not mind the cold; even his threadbare sweater was not fastened. His skin was tough and his blood warm. He let down heavy bars with one hand, negligently. Jen's breath quickened with pride in him, and with the effort she made to keep up.

They left his land behind and started up their father's pasture lane.

Ed looked down and put his big fingers around Jen's arm, giving it a quick, hard squeeze. Jen smiled at him.

"Say, I s'pose you'll be starting a hope chest before we know it," he said, laughing. "You're a big girl now."

"Hope chest!" Jen sniffed. "I'm not hoping for anything. I've got all the family I can tend to."

The air was crisp and bright and she felt happy. They bent to go under the sprawling, laden branches of the maple tree.

"Gosh, what a pile of dewdabs Margaret's got worked up in that box of hers," Ed chuckled. "Ever see 'em?"

"Yes," Jen answered. "She's got a fine stock, and all her work is pretty too. So neat and fine. It's a wonder she knows how to put so many colors in just right."

Ed had forgotten her already, Jen knew. It was only natural. Margaret would be his wife in March. She ran ahead of him into the house. Lois May and the children were doing their best with supper but it had not progressed very far. She laughed at them, and took it over, slicing and chopping with sure, accustomed rhythm. "How does it look now, Lois May? That's good. Bun, you better turn your lamp down a little. It's going to smoke the chimney. Set the chairs up, John." She turned huckleberries from a frosty glass jar into a big yellow bowl. They were round and

firm and had kept their color. She had had good
luck with all her canning last fall. Mark Shaw came
in with the milk. "Back, are you." She caught up John
and when he was settled, saw all the others in their
places.

"I need a smaller bit," Ed was saying.

"We'll see what we can find," her father answered.
"Come morning."

Jen saw his glance rest on the huckleberries. They
were his favorite preserve.

"Eat your bread," she urged John. "Look. It's good."

Later, the dishes done, she sat at the kitchen table
writing a letter to Olly, her mouth twisted with the
effort. It was not long; she never wrote much; but
she told him she thought he had done fine. She said
she had heard it said her mother's Uncle Jeff was a
lawyer, the one that lived out in San Francisco. She
added she guessed he had not needed to go so far
away.

VII

Through February the weather held cold but
bright. There was a stiff crust on the snow; the
children dragged their sleds all over the fields and
skinned their noses but left no mark to show where
they had been. Mark Shaw went every day into the
woods, sometimes two trips, carrying an axe to make
footholds for the horse. The days grew longer. It was
not so hard now to leave bed in the mornings. Jen
had her washing out by eight o'clock at latest. No
woman in the place could get her washing out so soon
as Jen. "Ma gets the breakfast, Mondays," Jen excused
herself. "It makes a sight of difference." But as she

rinsed, her fingers always flew the faster if she could
see anywhere a steady chimney smoke that meant a
steaming boiler. She was not needed at the Searles
place now. Ed worked alone except for an odd day
when George could help him. New partitions
and dormer windows appeared upstairs, new sills
and hearths and cupboards down. People said they
would not have guessed Ed was such a hand at car-
pentering; that boy could do anything, it seemed; he
was a handy one. Ed laughed, twirling his hammer
into the air and catching it neatly. When all the nail
holes had been filled with putty and the ceilings
plastered, Jen would go back to paint and paper. It
was a little early and cold for that work yet, in any
case. She put her own house straight, and dyed the
muslin of an old dress her mother was making into
nightgowns for Lois May. It took a soft, clear pink
like Flowering Almond blossoms. Jen thought of
spring. Sometimes it seemed she smelled it in the air.
When her father was late in getting home, she put
on his frock coat and went into the barn to milk the
cows and bed them down. As she sat beside them,
her fingers stern to their bags, her cheek pressed
against their warm brown sides, it seemed to her they
had their own kind of feeling that winter was nearly
done. They did not stand so still, were not so patient,
but stretched their necks and coughed and shook the
chains against the stanchions. The hay was old and
stale, and the air in the barn was thick with dust, and
the floor had grown hard to their feet. All these
things would be different in the spring.

And then one day the dry goods peddler came. Bun
spied him first—it was a Saturday—and ran in from

where she played with John among the piles of cord-
wood in the yard.

"Jen! Jen! Ma! Say, here comes Mr. Keele. Mr.
Keele's coming down the road. He's 'most here."

"He's 'most here," panted John, behind her.

"This early!" Jen exclaimed. He hardly ever made
his rounds before March. "It can't be."

She glanced out of the back window and saw for
herself the familiar blue, covered cart that usually
rode on wheels but had sleds under it to-day. And
little Mr. Keele sat upright in front, holding the whip
high in one hand and the reins high in the other as
if he drove a coach-and-four instead of one bony white
mare.

"Well, it is," Jen said. "Quick, you young ones,
sweep out that snow you tracked in while I lay some
newspapers on the table. He'll want to set his cases
there, the first thing he does. The floor is never good
enough for *them*."

"Oh, my land, what a mess I'm in here," her
mother cried. She sprang up from her chair and bent
over to brush her hair and pin it up smoothly. "Lois
May, get me out a clean apron. There's no need of
anybody's thinking we're slacker than we are . . .
John, let me wipe your mouth. You're all stuck over.
I believe I never saw you young ones such a sight——"

"They're all right, ma," said Jen. "Don't fret so."
She flung open the door and leaned out. "Hullo, Mr.
Keele! Will your horse stand? If she won't, hitch
her right to the barnyard fence. It's good and stout."

She did not mean he should hitch to the maple tree
as he had one day last fall, and let his horse gnaw a
great hole into the bark.

"You going to ask him to stay to dinner, Jen?" Bun whispered. "You ought to ask him to stay to dinner. We've got enough, ain't we?"

Jen thought swiftly as she watched Mr. Keele hopping about his horse's head and dragging suitcases off his cart. Her beans would not be done; Mr. Keele was very fond of beans; but she had some beets and cabbage left from yesterday, and it would not take long to fix a hash. Usually when he came in the spring it was dandelion green time; he liked greens too; but since he was here so early, he must take what he could get. She had dried apple turnovers just hot out of the oven, and nearly a bowlful of sour milk cheese.

"Well, seems you're kind of forcing the season, ain't you, Mr. Keele? Come right in. You look cold. Set up to the stove and thaw out. It's been quite a winter, hasn't it?"

Mr. Keele's name was not really Mr. Keele, but something unpronounceable that began that way; nobody remembered what, unless he did, though when he had made his first trip through here, twenty years ago, it had been painted in black letters on the side of the little wagon he drew by hand. Now that he had progressed to the fine blue cart he did not need his name on it, for everybody in the county knew Mr. Keele. He always trotted, never walked, a dark-skinned, wiry little man with a bald head and a broad, wide-lipped smile that revealed how few teeth he had left. He trotted, now, into Jen's kitchen.

"My, my, now it is cold. Hello, hello, Miz Shaw. How you to-day? How the nice girls? My, so many nice girls you got, I bet you don't know which one

is the nicest, eh? My sakes, I don't either. I bet the
boys round here is all dizzy in their heads, and who
would wonder at it? My, my! St, st, st!" Rubbing his
hands above the stove, he beamed around at them, his
admiration including Mrs. Shaw, as if he had never
seen the like. "Well, how you been, anyway? There's
a lot of sickness round. Oh, my, it's been a sick winter. I thought about you folks when I was in the city,
how some them storms they must block you up. That's
bad, too, in times of sickness. My, that's bad. And it's
been a sick winter, too."

"Well, now, we've been real well," said Jen. "I'm
surprised to hear it's been bad. It's always a green
winter I mistrust."

"Oh, yes, it's been bad," Mr. Keele said dolefully.
He dropped into a chair and spread out his hands.
"I was up Cornish way last week and my, such
changes! One my customers, a nice maiden lady name
of McIntire, she bought some cloth of me last fall to
make her wedding dress, and this spring she dead.
Oh, my . . . And lots of old folks gone. And one
little boy how tall as this one been sick in bed all
winter. My, too bad. They good people up in Cornish,
too."

"Well, did you go through Kezar Falls?" asked
Mrs. Shaw, bending forward, her hands under her
apron.

"Kezar Falls? Oh, yes. Yes, I see that lady you
always ask about. That—that——"

"Carrie Webster," Mrs. Shaw urged him anxiously.

"Oh, yes, Miz Webster. Oh, she's fine." Mr. Keele
beamed again, and began unbuckling his suitcases.
"Yes, she's fine and all her folks. She speak of you,

say she never can get round to write, but she'll have
more time when the little girl go to school this spring.
She's got fine little girl seven years old now."

"Evelyn seven? Why, I can't hardly believe it."

"Oh, yes. She grow up fast. Tall like up to here.
Miz Webster say she outgrow everything she got. I
sold Miz Webster six different pieces to make that
little girl some dress." He chuckled. "I guess she be
fixed out fine, uh, Miss Bun? Here. Look. One piece
for that Miss Evelyn was off this. How you like a
dress like that, uh? Or here. How you like this blue?"

"You got any candy this time?" asked Bun. She
did not so much as look at the cloth.

"Candy? Well, I say so," Mr. Keele cried, snatching out a pasteboard box. "My, yes. Just you see!
Chocolate bars! Every kind they is, I think. This one
is chewy, and this one has got nuts inside——"

"She can have one," her mother said. "And so can
John. Now you two go along outdoors so we can
think. What you got in cotton lace, Mr. Keele?"

"Oh, my, cotton lace! Miz Shaw, I got the handsomest cotton lace this time ever I carried!"

Mrs. Shaw hitched her chair closer as Mr. Keele
shook out the lace, unrolled blue gingham and draped
it over his arm, tipped up the corner of a remnant of
yellow satin and clucked reverently, looking at her as
if he thought she would bow her head. "My, that
would make a pretty bit of something. And here. I
thought the lady with red hair for this—there!" He
snatched up each material as if it were a nugget of
gold he had come upon unexpectedly. His face shone
with joy, and as he talked, he kept breaking off to
tip his head to one side and listen, hushed, for the

gasp of delight he thought it must surely bring. Jen had turned her vegetables into a wooden bowl and was chopping them quietly, the steady sound of her knife an accompaniment to the display. Lois May leaned over the back of her mother's chair, her eyes more attentive to the goods than the others' were, and less to Mr. Keele. She knew the yellow satin would fade; it was too cheap, even as a remnant; she had seen Mr. Keele's bargains put to the test before. But the lace was fine and firm, and she saw a roll of green wool under the ginghams that might do for a coat, if anyone was buying stuff for a coat.

"Blankets?" asked Mr. Keele. "I got nice blankets. Pink ones. Blue ones. Brown."

"I need some close-wove cheese cloth for my strainers," Jen said. "And if you've got some pretty cretonne, I'll take enough to line a quilt."

Searching for this, he spilled out a shoddy brown linen, some sheeting, and the green wool. Lois May reached down and felt the wool between her fingers.

"How much is that?" Jen asked.

"The wool? Now let me tell you. I sell that cheap, so long it getting spring. Six yard in the piece. I sell for six dollars."

Jen felt it, too, and nodded.

"That's cheap enough," she said. "Too much for us, though, ain't it, Lois May? And I guess ma's sewed all she can stand, without a coat."

"Oh, I could make it up all right," said Mrs. Shaw. But she figured and shook her head.

Mr. Keele looked from one to the other.

"No," said Jen. She rose, laughing. "We can't do everything we want to this spring, Mr. Keele. There's too much going on. Lois May here thinks of going to school in Rumfret and Ed is getting married. Money can't go every way."

"To school? Oh, my! And married!" marvelled Mr. Keele. This would be news to take to Kezar Falls, and elsewhere, as he went. "Well, well, the Shaws change, too, don't they? Not a thing stays like it was! My, my."

"Except my biscuit, Mr. Keele," Jen said. "They're just the same. You go out and feed your horse and by the time you're back I'll prove it to you."

"Oh, my, you needn't, now——"

"No beans to-day! No greens either! You're too early. But I'll have something got together here that you can stomach, I guess."

She was not quite so quick as she had said, but nearly. The dishes set smoking on the table, the biscuit and the hash and the pot of coffee. There was the bowl of cheese too, and pale yellow butter, and clear sweet pickle made from ripe cucumber rinds. Mr. Keele rubbed his hands together as he sat down. He often had his meals along the way and spent the nights with customers unless he slept in his cart, but nobody could cook like Jen Shaw. He had always said so since she was little, before her mother died. He eyed her admiringly. Now there was a girl.

"You make yourself at home, Mr. Keele. We don't stand on ceremony here."

As he ate, he talked more of Kezar Falls, and neighboring towns. Cy Plaisted's barn was burned. The Jewett girl had started working up in Buxton somewhere. Old lady Morse was feebler every spring.

"Oh, I wanted to ask you," Mrs. Shaw broke in.

"Did you call in on this family that's moved onto the place next to here? The one above to your right?"

Mr. Keele turned his eyes on her.

"Mr. Janowski's house, you mean?" he said. "Oh, my, yes. I stop there. They Polish peoples." He laid down his knife and fork and spoke impressively. "They fine peoples. Oh, my. They got their place all fixed pretty snug, for what it is. They going to build them a house in the summer, they say. Oh, they get on fine. They got good stuff in them. That Mrs. Janowski she keep the house end of that place just like a shiny pin. Her man and that big boy they got, they make a good farm in the spring. You see . . . I Polish too."

"You Polish, Mr. Keele?" Jen asked. "Well, I didn't know that . . . Can't you eat another turnover?"

"But not that kind Polish," Mr. Keele admitted sadly. He did not take another turnover. "It is the right kind Polish stick to the country. We know how to farm, but we don't do it; we want too much the money all the time. We don't stay still, over here; we keep going. It is the right kind Polish takes to farm. He knows the way to do. That Mr. Janowski and that grown boy, Stan, they know the way. Take to farm. My, my, that's the only way, for Polish."

Mr. Keele rose with tremendous dignity. He looked very old, and as if he might be going to cry.

"Well, I guess they're smart folks," Jen said reassuringly. "I hear the young ones try real hard at school, and there's business going on up to the—where they live, all day long every day. I see the young man go by with a load of boards every once in a while. I guess they're fixing up to one great rate. It seems as if you didn't eat much, Mr. Keele."

"They're fine folks," Mr. Keele repeated, jerking nervously at the straps of his suitcases.

Suddenly he threw open one of them, snatched out the green wool, and tossed it, the whole roll, in the direction of the couch. Going hurriedly through the door he nodded his head backwards at Lois May. "You wanted it," he said. "You have it. I pay for my dinner so."

He had gone. The Shaws stared after him. Mr. Keele was a niggardly little man. He charged more than things were worth and had been known to give short measure. He was a man to watch, and even then, if you were not very sharp, he cheated you.

"Quick," said Jen. "Lois May, bring up some cans of anything you see down cellar. Some corn and peas and some berries. Get a jar of jelly." She halved four biscuits, laying cold ham between them, and packed them into a box with a paper separating them from the turnovers. "You young ones take this out to Mr. Keele. Don't fall now. Tell him we thank him very much and we'll do something for him some time."

"We thank you very much and we'll do something for you," said Bun, standing in the snow of the yard and holding up a paper bag and two cans of string beans with an angelic smile, her cap awry and her mouth crumby.

"My, my," Mr. Keele said. "My, my. We'll put it here under the seat. My, my." He took John's offering, too, and stowed it away. "Now ain't this nice. My, my."

Then, sitting high on his cart, he called down,

"You be good now 'til I come back again. In the fall I come back again. You be good. And you play nice with them kids, them new ones. They nice kids. You see."

As he drove down the lane only the top of his brown felt hat showed above the snowbanks, and the tassel of the whip he held so high. Bun stared after him.

"Say, what's eating him," she wanted to know, "about the Janowskis?"

She did not appreciate being told whom to be "nice" to. That was her affair. All those Janowski children had black eyes.

VIII

Washington's birthday fell on Monday that year, bringing both Lize and Olly home for the week-end. The house was a flurry of preparations for days before. Mrs. Shaw hurried to finish Lois May's new coat and matching beret to have them ready for Lize's critical inspection; Lize always knew what was being worn. Jen cleaned the bedrooms and the parlor, brought in an old heater from the shed and polished it, kept a fire in the sitting-room to dry out the walls and shrink the doors. On Saturday morning she was up at four o'clock starting her baking. Lize liked one thing, Olly another, and there must be enough of everything to go around. She made dough-nuts, dried apple, pumpkin, and lemon jelly pie, fruit cake and molasses cookies, and a great Indian pudding in a brown crockery dish. Then there were her beans besides, and brown bread, and a smoked shoulder boiling. She was still hot and floury, with a stove cloth flung over her shoulder, when she heard her father drive into the yard at five o'clock in the afternoon. By the time she could reach the door Lize was running up the path, and Olly had gone on to the barn to help unharness; Jen glimpsed only the line of his felt hat and dark hair under it.

"Well, old lady! So you got here. Well, if you ain't a stranger! Just walk yourself into this kitchen . . . Say, you're half froze. Set up here. I declare I wonder sometimes if you've got a cupful of blood in you. Thin as a rail!"

Lize was thin, short and thin and not small-boned. She had a narrow, pallid face, and light hair like Jen's but worn in a long bob with a deep, perfect permanent wave which Lois May and the iron she heated over a lamp had tried in vain to imitate successfully. Lize's dress was Roman red, though Jen did not know it, a wool material with black fur at the neck and wrists, and it hugged her breasts, waist, hips, knees, and Lize wore it well, but self-consciously here, aware that Jen and the others would wonder at it. She seemed excited to be home, talkative, chilled, restless; her eyes were tired; she was twenty-five and might have been thirty or more.

"Oh, there you are, ma! How are you? Hello, Lois May—you *sugar!*"

She always made much of Lois May. The two regarded each other with appreciation, both noting every detail of the other's hair, face, and clothes. They were not related and yet in a sense they were sisters, one only waiting, breathless, to begin the glamorous life the other lived and still thought glamorous.

"Oh," Lois May said softly, "I love your dress, Lize. I love it; I *love* it."

"Well, you'd better take her upstairs if it's warm enough," Jen broke in, "and see she changes it. She'll be catching it on a nail or the woodbox if you don't, first thing you know."

She stirred another great lump of butter into her Indian pudding, and as she finished, saw that Olly had come in. She had thought from the step that it was Ed; Olly must be growing heavier, but still he looked the same. Crouched before the oven, she watched him taking off his outside coat, a new gray one, too thin for this weather; she hoped his underwear was heavy; she must see to it before he went back. He was still slight and very dark, smaller in every way than any of his older brothers, smaller than John would be at his age, quick, quiet, sensitive. He felt her eyes on him now and was turning. The others had not yet even noticed him in all the hullabaloo over Lize. It was always like that when they came home together.

"Well, there you are, Jen!"

"Yes, here I am. Into the oven, same as usual. Well, how've you been?"

She was matter-of-fact, did not offer to kiss him. The Shaws never did much kissing. But Olly pulled her to her feet and hugged her well. It made her burnt color deepen.

"Old stick-in-the-mud," she said.

"Why, here's Olly!" the others cried.

They gathered thick about the stove, Lize and Lois May with their arms around each other, Mrs. Shaw stepping here and there aimlessly, smiling, the children

sober, watchful, Bun waiting greedily for whatever
had been brought her; surely, she thought, something
had, but they took their time about producing it. Ed
came in from the barn and shook hands awkwardly,
cordial but not certain what to say to these two he
had used to scorn for lack of muscle, now that they
had gone where muscle was not needed. The clock
ticked gravely, the tall, brown steeple clock that
Minnie Foote had brought here as a bride; and Jen's
pudding bubbled in the oven.

Conversation darted back and forth.

"Well, listen; when are you coming down to Rumfret, sugar? McIntire's starts a new term the first of
March."

"The first of March? Oh, ma——"

"There, Lize, I've got her clothes all ready, but I
can't make money. That's all there is to it,—I can't
make money where none is!"

"Well, Ob, they work you hard, I suppose?"

"Ssss. John. Did they give *you* anything? They
never give *me* anything, either one of them!"

"Oh, bless your heart, kid. Where's my bag? Here.
Here, John——"

"Now don't you young ones spoil your supper!"

"Ma's made up that yellow crepe you give me, Lize.
It's real long. It's lovely——"

"Oh, dear, I don't know what you'll think of what
we've got together, Lize, I'm sure, but I done the best
I could. Off out here in the country so——"

"You ought to go over in the morning, Ob, and
take a look. It don't hardly seem like the same place.
Come to get on some paint and paper——"

"Stop, Bun. Don't eat it. Jen don't want us to eat it."

"You shut up!"

"Now you young ones over there——"

Mark Shaw came in. The family din was never so unrestrained when he was by. It softened now, though the children still counted their candies on the couch, and Mrs. Shaw continued enumerating what Lois May had ready to take to Rumfret, and Ed joked Olly as to whether there were girls at college. Above it all the sounds Mark Shaw made as he took off his boots and washed his hands and felt for a comb in the steel case were very plain. When he spoke he did not lift his voice, but all his children heard him.

"You boys," he said, with narrowed, speculative eyes, "will be about the same height when Olly gets his growth. Let's see now. How tall are you, Ed?"

"Six foot two," Ed answered briefly, as if he did not care.

"Yes," Mark Shaw said. "Well. Olly'll make it. Another year or so. That kind shoots up fast."

Olly burned with gratitude, but did not speak. His father did not need a word. He, too, had been small at eighteen, smaller than his brothers, but now was tall enough, with heavy shoulders and stout arms to do two men's work. He went on slow feet to his place at the table, seeing it was laid.

"Come along, the rest of you," said Jen. "Everything's piping."

They made the kitchen crowded, and there was hardly space for her to squeeze between their chairs and the stove, but she liked that. It had been so before. She knew the way to take short steps moving sideways.

A little later George came over bringing Margaret

and his three oldest children. Mil could not leave the new baby, he said, nor take it out so young. She sent her love. Little George shrieked with fear of so many strangers all in one small room; he had not seen another woman than his mother since the fall. His sister Esther took him up and held him capably; he was more or less her creature now the new baby had come. His big head lolling back on her small arm, he felt safe again and smiled engagingly. Jen asked if he ate better lately, and Esther said not much; he played with food until she had to slap him. "Olly was the same," said Jen. She wondered if he remembered it. "I wouldn't force him much, though, Esther. Some young ones come by delicate appetites real natural. He's a good stout-looking boy for one as sickly as he used to be." Esther looked down at little George, her round face plain and pale. "We think he gains," she said. "When spring comes, daddy's going to take him with him after grain some day, and get the man to weigh him." She glanced about for Betty, to be sure no one of the family was in any mischief. Her father did not always notice everything he might.

The children played with catalogues and crayons on the floor, eating cookies Jen had given them and the candy Lize had brought. Jen stepped among them carefully, setting the supper food away and stacking the dishes to be washed before anyone else would be up in the morning. She thought about the beds. Bun should come in with her, for Lois May would want to sleep with Lize and talk. Olly could have the couch in the parlor, or share Ed's bed. It was warmer two together this time of the year.

The women gathered near the lamp, eager and

friendly. Lize must hear what Margaret would wear to be married in. Margaret must feel Lize's dress and hear the strange name of the black fur. They both must see what Mrs. Shaw had made, and how it looked on Lois May. Esther leaned forward over little George's drowsy body, trying to catch what they said and peek between their shoulders.

The men sat on the dark side of the room, their chairs somewhat separated each from the others. George was nearest the stove, with thought of his pipe; he was the only Shaw who smoked. (Unless Lize did; Jen had turned out her bag one day and found brown crumbles in it.) George's build was like his father's, not so tall as Ed, and he was getting fat, as Mark Shaw never had. It showed across his chest and the backs of his hands and at his belt line. He lounged in his chair and talked more than all the other men together, holding his pipe by the bowl and waving it.

"I tell you, father, this town ain't going to touch a road that ain't a state road if they can help it. They've proved that, ain't they? Now when we got Dave Worster in road commissioner—and he's a good man for the job if there is one—he couldn't do nothing any more'n the rest of them. I tell you, Sullivan's got everybody right where he wants them, and he knows it. But he ain't got me, and I'll haul voters enough to put him off the ticket this spring if I break a blood vessel doing it. He's had a noose around this town long enough——"

When Mark Shaw spoke it was of Ralph.

"Ralph ought to be here," he said.

"That's one feller," Ed laughed, "we don't see much

of. If he drifts in once a year, it's more than we expect."

"Hear from him?" George asked.

Ed shook his head. "A card sometimes. Right now we don't know where he is, even. He drifts around from place to place. He does what they call commercial piloting, you see. Jen wrote a letter a while ago, telling him he'd better come home for the wedding. Never heard anything, did you, Jen?"

Jen shook her head. "Give a boy like Ralph an airplane," she said lightly, "and he might be *anywhere*. All he needed was wings."

She did not want her father to get to thinking to-night on the only one of them all who had no ties here. Twelve years ago Ralph had run away, and the strangeness that had made him do it still lay between him and his father. The place where Mark Shaw lived and worked, where Minnie Foote had lived and borne her children and died, was hateful, it seemed, to this second son. He had run away from it at thirteen, and now when he came back, never stopped long. He wanted always to be going somewhere, high and fast. It was odd where Mark Shaw and Minnie Foote had got this boy.

"Bring out the graphophone, Ed," Jen said. "Why don't you?"

"Oh, go ahead," Lize cried. "I used to be crazy about some of those pieces. Remember the one about the ball game, George? That was the one you liked best. 'Take me out to the ball game; if they don't win it's a shame—' Remember, George?"

"Gosh, I don't remember a thing, Lize," George said. "I don't have time. If you had four kids——"

"The Lord forbid!" Lize exclaimed. She crouched before a box that Ed brought out. "Oh, *here's* a good one! 'The Preacher and the Bear'! Put it on, Olly."

She held the black cylindrical record by the very edge as she had been taught years before. Olly took it from her on two fingers carefully and slid it over the steel roll of the little machine on the table. Ed set up a three-legged rack and attached the big green horn fluted like a petunia blossom. "Whirr," the needle sang. "Whirr-whirr-whirr. The Preacher and the Bear. Edison record. Whirr-whirr. The preacher went out hunting upon a Sunday morn——"

The phonograph and its music seemed to fill the room. The Shaw family sat in a circle around it with winter and the Maine woods at their backs. In the small spot they enclosed was all the sociability they had. It was as it had always been, the same songs and jigs and hymns and marches, the same crackling in the stove, the same howling of the wind outside, and children, if not the same children, growing sleepy among their playthings on the floor. "Columbia record. Columbia Military Band. Whirr-whirr." The faces of the Shaws were sober and respectful, and tilted back a little, as when they sat in church and waited for the Elder's words to fall on them.

Later Jen moved about the kitchen, setting it right, the only one still up in the house. She had a tranquil look. No doubt these radios were fine, though she had never happened to hear one, but it was not likely they could play "Annie Laurie" any sweeter than that old graphophone. It was a good machine, people had always said; it had a rich tone to it. She put the records in their boxes, brown ones and black. The brown were wax and made a fainter sound than the others when they were played. The black were better quality. As she bent over one to see if it was scratched, Olly's voice surprised her.

"Here's your oilstove, Jen. I thought I'd better bring it out. It's smelly. The room's warm enough in there."

He stood just inside the sitting-room door, his shoes and collar off, looking young in the dim light. Suddenly Jen thought of him as he had been at twelve, a very thin boy with a long nose and a big Adam's apple. The cows he milked were not milked dry, the horse he rode for cultivating made a crooked track; he could not drive a nail straight, nor handle any tool as if he knew what it was for; he was awkward on the ladders and grew sick at the butchering and could not split a cord of wood in four days. Farmwork had been hard for Olly. And he had tried. Ralph had not tried, but Olly did; Jen knew this. George and Ed made fun of him, mocked the way he tied a knot in a hitch rope, the way he built a yard for his rabbits by directions given in a magazine, the way he turned a grindstone even.

"He'll show them yet," Jen thought. "He'll show them."

"Come over here," she said. "Tell me how it was at that debate. If you're not too tired, that is."

The fire was low and she replenished it. He came and stood beside her. They had often stood like this when he lived at home, and watched the flames through the cracks in the stove after everybody else had gone to bed. There were shadows on their faces.

"There isn't much to tell, more than I wrote."

"Did you feel scared?"

"I don't know. I guess so . . . Oh, yes, I was scared enough at first." He laughed. "By the time I got to the rebuttal I wasn't though. I had too much to say and too little time to say it in. It was funny how that second speaker from Mowry played right into my hand . . . I guess I talked a blue streak."

Jen pictured him standing before a crowd of people, and talking a blue streak. No other Shaw could do that. Not one.

"He said a king was better than a president to have, did he?"

"Well . . . Sort of . . . You see, Jen, the idea is, the British government really is so much like ours it made the question a pretty delicate one to get at. It made the decision hang on the way a few little points were turned. You see, I was second speaker on the affirmative side——"

Jen listened. She wondered how it was that a government with a king could be much like one with a president. It did not sound possible, but Olly must know. He knew all about governments now, it seemed, while she knew nothing. It counted so little here in Derwich. Only the weather and the seasons were important. Even when George spoke so loud about the road commissioner, it was mostly to have something to say. However good the roads were, the snow would come and block them.

"It must have been fine," she said. Suddenly she added, "I'd liked awful well to heard it."

"Would you?" Olly asked her. "Would you, honest?"

"Of course I would," Jen said. "You'd ought to know."

"What if you were to come down some time? I might speak again, you know."

"Oh, well," Jen said. "I guess I couldn't go that far off."

She could not imagine herself there. Neither could he. They both wondered a little at his suggesting it. Olly stood for a minute tapping the leaf of the stove with his knee, and then yawned and stretched.

"You'd better take this lamp to light you in," said Jen.

He went away silently in his stocking feet. The sitting-room door closed behind him, and the front entry door. Jen shut the draughts of the stove and tiptoed across the dark kitchen toward the back stairs. She did not need a light in this room; she could see it full as plain without.

IX

The next morning Ed took Lize and Olly and Lois May and the children to see what he had made of Caleb Searles' house. Mrs. Shaw had gone back upstairs to sleep off a headache. Jen, left alone, made her work go fast. She finished the dishes and swept the floor. She cut bits of cookie dough in the shape of hatchets and put them in to bake. In the cellar, pork waited in fat white chunks in the covered barrel of icy salt brine. She reached in quickly and sliced off a square. Pork was what made a boiled dish good. Olly would want a boiled dish before he went away. Olly was not much for beans. She came upstairs with dripping hands and began scraping beets and carrots.

"My halter broke," her father said, coming in. "Short off."

Jen filled a big needle with a stout thread and sewed through the holes he made with his awl. Their heads were close together over his knee. He smelled of barns and she of spice and wood smoke. They worked in silence, carefully.

"That'll hold now for a spell," he said at last.

"Yes," said Jen. "Till you can get a new one."

He went out. She washed her hands and looked in on her cookies. They were done. She took them out and set them by to cool. The iron kettle on the stove began to sing. She brought the cabbage and the pork and tucked them snugly in. The wood was low. She brought some from the shed-room and filled the fire-box. A minute later the cover of the kettle was bouncing over the steam. She mixed frosting in a bowl and dropped red stain on it. Humming to herself, she spread a cookie with a crimson teaspoonful. It had a gay look; the children would like it. The rich, strong smell of cabbage was creeping through her quiet house. She placed a second frosted cookie carefully on the plate beside the first.

Then she heard Lize's voice in the yard, teasing.

"Oh, come on, Ed, you might as well. We're only going this way once. What's the use of hoarding every cent? Be a good fellow."

They were on the steps before Ed answered.

Then, "What I do is my business and what I don't is the same," he said. "See?"

"Oh, good lord, Ed!" Lize exclaimed pacifically.

Lize never could remember that Ed was different from the men she knew in the city. He could not be won in the same way. He could not be coaxed. He would not be teased. He was Ed; she ought to remember. But nearly every time she came down they quarrelled, for she was quick to speak and he to take offense. It seemed a pity. Jen sighed, and looked around smiling.

"Well, how did you like Ed's place?"

Lois May went straight through the kitchen and upstairs, her chin lifted, her mouth trembling. There was heartbreak in every step. A door slammed behind her. Lize took off her coat with elaborate carelessness. The boys lingered in the entry, leaving the door ajar and letting the cold air in.

"Oh, it's a nice place all right," Lize said.

"I think so," Jen agreed. She thought also of the tracks Lois May's snowy feet must have left all the way between the door and her bed, and perhaps even on the white spread if her feelings were hurt bad enough. "Margaret ought to be pretty proud going into a house like that to live. And I guess she is, too."

The boys came in as she was speaking. Olly sat down astride a chair before the oven, his arms folded across the back and his chin resting on one wrist. He did not look at Lize but watched Jen moodily. Ed splashed at the sink, washing and drinking.

"Cold out, I guess," Jen said. "It's been a cold month right through. Father said when he wrote down the Christmas rulers in the almanac, old February would give us a try."

Ed strode in suddenly. Jen glanced up, saw the dull red of his face and the ugly set of his jaw, and went on spreading her frosting smooth.

"Yes," he said, "I've got a nice place. It's a terrible

nice and valuable place all of a sudden, and anybody'd
think to hear the talk that it'd been willed to me, and
everything on it, and two or three thousand dollars
besides. I worked and earned that place, same as I've
worked and earned everything I ever had. I never see
anything of any big-hearted sisters hanging round
offering to give *me* a living and begging money for
me. Whatever I've got, I've got myself, and the rest
can do the same. I don't owe anybody atop of the earth
one red cent, and if anybody thinks they've got any
strings on me, just let them try to pull them, that's all
I've got to say. Just let them try to pull them."

Ed could make speeches too, Jen thought. The
cookies were finished. She gave the frosting bowl to
the children and brought beets and carrots and turnips
from the sinkroom to be fitted into separate kettles.

Lize had whirled from where she stood by the
window, her hands behind her back, her eyes hot.

"Nobody's going to pull any strings on you," she
was saying scornfully. "Do what you please. Nobody
cares. It's a funny thing, though, that if I can afford
to offer Lois May her room and board for six months,
you can't even come across with twenty-five dollars
for her fees at school. Hang on to your money, if you
want to, and a lot of good may it do you. I might
have known how you'd act. You've always been just
the same, squeezing every cent. I don't know why you
couldn't have acted decent about it, though, as long
as I was fool enough to ask you before Lois May.
You've put her in a fine hole, poor kid."

"Oh, forget it, Lize," suggested Olly. "Have a
hatchet and forget it."

"Yes," Ed carried on. "Poor kid,—that's what *you*

think. Well, there's a whole lot of kids in worse holes than she is. I've been in mine. Now I'm getting out nobody needn't think I'm going to saddle myself with all the troubles of everybody in sight. Let her get up at four o'clock in the morning and put in fourteen hours' work a day like I did for about ten years, and then maybe she'll have enough to put herself through school. If she did, though, I suppose everybody'd say she had squeezed her money! . . . What's more, I ain't getting married to start some kind of a charity. How about Margaret being a 'poor kid'? You might think about her while you're being so soft-hearted. *She's* had an awful easy time of it, ain't she? I ought to send Lois May to school and let Margaret live in a barn, like the Polacks up here, I suppose. Well, I ain't any intentions of it, and that's flat."

"Attaboy," said Olly. "Have a hatchet."

Jen went into the sinkroom to get the potatoes. Ed's face had taken on a gentler, slightly mollified expression with Olly's words and he ate a cookie whole, snapping another in two between his fingers. Lize had turned back to the window and was swallowing tears of rage. It looked as if things might quiet down now. Jen hoped so. It was like trying to get dinner in a crazy house.

But Mrs. Shaw's hurried, shuffling step fell on the stairs, and in an instant she was among them. Her dress was only half-fastened; her shoe laces trailed behind her; her face was crumpled with crying. She looked nothing if not old and untidy and plain, and yet there was her hair, masses of it, a smooth, soft shimmering red.

"You're awful good to her, Lize," she said choking.

"You're just as good and sweet as you can be, and don't you think we'll forget it. All the women folks in the family has done a little something, and you've done the most; it's the men can't see a foot ahead of them. It's the men that don't care what lives or dies as long as they're kept comfortable and get what they want. And they don't want anything for anybody but themselves. That's the way they're built in this family——"

Olly, with one hopeless glance at Jen, jerked his cap and jacket off a nail behind the stove, and walked out of the house.

"Now that'll do," Ed said evenly. "I've heard all I'm going to. I've heard enough. It's all done."

He gave a slow look around, including each one, then sat down, pulled on his boots and buckled them deliberately, stood up again. He buttoned his sweater, settled his cap, and dipped a small pail of hot water from the tank on the back of the stove before starting to the barn for the noon feeding. Nobody spoke, not even Lize. Bun and John sat, frozen with awe, on the couch. It was the spell the male on the farm had the power of casting over his women when occasion demanded it. The rooster swelled up, stretched his neck, and crowed, when he had done it. The bull threw back his head and roared. Ed only buckled his boots and dipped water but it was with the same certain air of dominance.

He had scarcely gone when Mrs. Shaw disappeared upstairs again, sobbing aloud. Now that the kitchen was quiet Jen could hear her, through the half-open register in the ceiling, crying with Lois May. Lize walked into the sitting-room, her back very straight, and shut the door.

Bun and John came out to Jen in the sinkroom.

"What we going to have for dinner?" Bun asked in a hushed voice.

"There," Jen exclaimed, passing her hand before her eyes as if to brush away a veil, "the Lord only knows, but it started out to be a boiled dish!"

x

By mid-afternoon all tear stains had disappeared. Ed was in the barn cellar helping his father build a new pig pen, the children were out sliding from the doorsteps to the well, and the house was in a state of great and very pleasant excitement. Lize had asked Lois May to go back to Rumfret with her for a few weeks' visit.

"I've only got one room now, of course," Lize explained at dinner, not looking at Ed, "but another girl and I are hunting for an apartment and Lois May can be a lot of help to me moving in. It will give her something to do days, and help her get onto the town so in case she ever does come to stay— And we can amuse ourselves evenings, can't we, sugar?"

Lois May nodded, smiling mistily, her eyes following Lize's every movement with adoration.

"Can you afford it, Lize?" Jen asked later, confidentially. "It'll cost you something."

"I can do it, sure," Lize answered with pride. "I can get along without something else. I'm no *hog*."

She would spend more than she ought to now, just for the effect, but only Jen understood this, because she knew Lize. The others thought Lize could do whatever she liked, for she earned twenty-eight dollars every week as regularly as Saturday came around.

"Now I expect you'll have a time of it," Mark Shaw said indulgently when he came in to warm his hands and found Lois May trying on her yellow crepe to see if Lize thought it long enough, and just where the sash should be tied.

"It's lucky there's as much stuff ready as there is," said Mrs. Shaw. "I guess she won't shame you, Lize. If they're made right, that is. The goods is all real pretty and real becoming. Now I'll mend up these stockings the best I can, and I've got money enough of my own for her to buy her a new pair when she gets there. Now, Lois May, don't you make Lize no trouble while you're gone."

Lois May shook her head. She had scarcely spoken since morning. Tilting her chin she glanced at herself in Mark Shaw's shaving mirror. Her face was a little pale from so much crying; shadows under her eyes made them look large. She thought she seemed older, suddenly, perhaps eighteen. She smiled at herself, in very much the same way she usually smiled at Lize. Perhaps her mouth was a bit large, but her teeth were perfect. She moved her body gloatingly inside the yellow dress.

Only Mark Shaw had commented on the fact that Olly did not appear for dinner, and when Jen explained that she supposed he was taking his favorite long walk up the brook, even Mark Shaw did not speak of it again. Whatever Ed thought during the rest of the day, he kept to himself, and the others were absorbed in talk and packing. It was left to Jen to keep the dinner hot on the back of the stove, and glance out now and then for sign of a moving figure on the frozen landscape.

When he did come in, about three o'clock, it happened that she was alone in the kitchen. He paused at the door, and glanced about. His ears were brilliant red with the cold, and his nose a purplish-blue. It would be a wonder if he was not frostbitten.

"Safe to come in?" he asked, grinning.

"Safe enough," Jen said. "I don't look dangerous, do I? You must be froze through and starved to death. Where've you been, for heaven's sakes?"

"Went up the brook," he answered.

She did not say she had known he would, though they both remembered he had always fled to the trout brook when he wanted to be alone, in season or out. She took up a great plateful of steaming vegetables and placed a chair for him, brought bread and butter from the cellarway, and a glass of milk and a piece of pie. Her step was as light as if she had not already been up and about for twelve hours, and her face smooth and young. Jen Shaw had a knack, people said, of looking rested, even when she sat up with the sick for two or three nights running.

"The Janowskis over here are thinking of cutting ice off their pondhole," Olly said. "The young one was down there when I went along, looking it over. They meant to start to-morrow, but I told him the ice there would be pretty grassy. I asked him why they didn't cut with the rest of the neighborhood over at Pratt's Lake. He said they didn't know anything about it. Nobody had spoken to them."

Jen listened, leaning on the back of a chair.

"No," she said, "I don't suppose they did. I guess nobody around here has much to do with them. Ed and George and all the rest of the men, they seem to feel kind of suspicious."

Olly flung down his fork.

"Well, I should like to know what of. A name they can't pronounce, I suppose. Well, it's a heck of a place when a fellow like that Stan Janowski can't come into it and make friends and have a chance to live and get ahead like other people. It makes me sick. I must have talked for an hour with that fellow and he had more ideas in that time than Bill Carpenter and Grover Harrison have in a year, or George and Ed either. He's got a good head and he's using it. He means to build by next fall, and he's laying all kinds of plans for bringing back that old land. I'll bet he'll do it, too. It sounds as if he was really running things over there, and I'd like to see any Yankee do it better with what he's got to do with. They make me sick around here, feeling so superior. Don't they think the Polish have got as much right here as the English?"

"There, I don't know what they think," Jen said. "I don't know as they *do* think. You talk as if this was a debate. Could you eat a dish of that Indian pudding?"

Olly thought he could, and she brought it to him. He grinned at her as she set it down. Jen certainly knew how to cook. If she ran a boarding-house in a college town, she would make a fortune. And it was funny how nothing ever really went under her skin. He would give something to be able to accept life as she did. And still he would not want to, for he had liked swinging along through the cold, and feeling the

heat of impatience going out of him; and he liked
appreciating this young Pole when no one else did;
he looked forward to knowing Stan Janowski better in
the summer, if only to set his judgment against that
of his brothers.

"Good pudding," he said.

The next noon Mark Shaw drove up to the door
with the two-seated sleigh, and Ed, with ill grace,
came out to swing in the girls and their suitcases.

"Good-by, ma," Olly said. "So long, Jen."

Mrs. Shaw clung to Lois May's hand.

"Now you be a good girl. You take care of yourself and don't make Lize any more trouble than you
can help. You let us know when you get there."

"Be good, Olly," Jen said. "And you write!" She
stepped up on the runner and kissed Lize and Lois
May. "You be careful of her now, Lize. See she keeps
her throat covered up when she's out. And if she gets
homesick, you bring her right back."

"Get up, there, Bob," said Mark Shaw. "Come."

Bob pulled his load slowly out of the yard, his broad
white back spreading and arching with each step. Olly,
sitting straight, was as tall as his father who bent forward to his reins. The girls, tucked under the old fur
robe, looked almost of a size, very young and smart,
like city girls. They turned and waved their gloved
hands and shiny pocketbooks.

"Good-by."

"Good-by."

"Come home when you can, Lize!"

"Good-by."

Jen and Mrs. Shaw were left alone, for the children
had run after Ed to close the barn door. The air was

growing damp. The sun waded in gray banks and there would be more snow before morning. The outhouses and the trees looked already half-buried under the crust.

Jen glanced at Mrs. Shaw and thought how seldom she observed her. She wondered if the others did more often, if even Mark Shaw did. She stood there now, thin and small, shivering under her shawl, her face old because she kept it so strained into worried lines, her hands young, white, blue-veined, with bitten nails, her hair a soft, pale red, and heavy, but disordered. Her eyes were streaming tears. Jen knew she loved Lois May more than any other thing and that Lois May, whether at home or away, did not have much love to give back. And Cora Shaw hated the winter; she was afraid of the snow that was coming, and of the snow that had come.

"We'd better hustle in," said Jen briskly. "Or we'll freeze. Spring's right around the corner now but it's looking the other way."

Jen herself did not mind that winter lingered, nor that the house was very still. She knew of a good supply of canned things remaining in the cellar, of vegetables and apples in the "arch" by the chimney, of pork and cider vinegar in barrels, of shovels that could make paths through the snow, and of axes that could break the ice. They had dry wood and tight roofs and clean, whole clothes, all of them.

"Well, now I guess it's up to us to get our rug finished, don't you say so, ma?" Jen asked. "That is, if we're going to have it ready for the wedding. After Washington's Birthday it ain't long to the middle of March."

The snow that fell was dry and fine and the wind
had blown it off by morning. Jen took up all her
rugs and swept them on the porch. The sun came out
at noon; the mercury climbed higher than it had any
day in the month. Mark Shaw made ready for another
trip into the woods; sledding would not last much
longer.

"I'll tell you, ma," Jen said. "Why can't you take
John and ride up to spend the afternoon with Mil?
She'd be pleased to have you, and it would make a
little change."

Faint anticipation crept reluctantly into Mrs. Shaw's
face. She had sat all the morning braiding rags, her
shoulders bowed and her lips compressed.

"Why, there," she said. "I suppose I might. It seems
a little warmer, don't it?"

"Fifteen above," said Jen. "It's fine. You change
your dress and I'll get your coat to heat it through."

"I ain't been out of this yard since Christmas Day,"
said Mrs. Shaw, fumbling to put away her work. "It
was bare ground then and I stepped up to speak with
Mrs. Hale. And I ain't been out since."

"That's so," Jen told her. "It's a shame. The air'll
do you good." She washed John's face and hands and
buttoned on his leggings. "You might let Bun stop
with you after school, and play, and father can bring
you all home. Tell him not to get too big a load this
time."

"Anybody don't get sight of a neighbor here week
in and week out," said Mrs. Shaw, pinning her collar.

"To think I ain't laid eyes on Mil since before she had her last baby!"

"Can I take my sled?" asked John. "Can I take my sled? I'm going to take my sled."

"All right," Jen said. "And while you're off I'll make you a pair of overalls. Keep wrapped up good, ma."

She settled down to work as soon as they were gone. She cut and basted and stitched, glancing out contentedly now and then at the little new snowdrifts huddled against the fences, at the apple trees in the field and the pines in the pasture, and at the Janowskis' chimney smoke rolling straight upward and promising fair weather. The hands of the clock went round without her notice. It surprised her to find she had to sit nearer to the window, and to see that it was four o'clock.

"My," she said aloud. "School's been out a half an hour. The children must be sliding up and down North Hill for all they're worth. I hope Esther's with them."

Then she heard a step on the porch and looked up to see Margaret coming in. With a movement of her foot she pushed a suggestive rag bag into the dark corner beyond the cellar door. It took figuring to keep a secret in this family.

"Well, Margaret! What you doing down here? I guess for once you didn't have to make Bun stay after school." She pulled out a rocker with her toe and nodded toward it. "Hang your coat right over the oven door so it'll be nice and warm, and set down. My, this wind's give you quite a color!"

"I wanted to have a talk with you about my parlor paper," Margaret said. "Ed and I were looking through your sample book last night, and I suppose it's getting time we ordered."

She sat down, rid of her coat, and looked at Jen. Her quiet brown eyes were large to-day, her mouth soft and sweet and uncertain, her skin and nails and clothes very neat.

"Well, didn't you think they've got some handsome patterns?" Jen asked. She rested her square, chapped hands for a minute on the folds of blue drilling.

"I like them," Margaret said. "I about decided on the one in blue and white with the George and Martha figures, for the hall. And you know Mil had enough of her green left over for my kitchen; so much of it is doors and windows and brick ovens and high baseboards it won't take much. So all I have to think of is the parlor, for Ed says he doubts if we can afford to do the bedroom this spring. Of course we don't mean to touch the upstairs yet awhile."

"No," Jen agreed. "You wouldn't need to. But that parlor couldn't be left, anyway. It won't cost you much. It don't seem I ever saw pretty papers so cheap. One I liked was only twenty cents a double roll."

"Was it any of these?" Margaret asked.

She took several samples from a book in her brown Boston bag and spread them on the leaf of the sewing-machine. Jen bent over them attentively, pulled one after another aside with the point of her needle, absorbed in remembering.

"Jen," Margaret said, bending forward, pleating her coarse tan jersey skirt, "has there been some trouble about Ed helping Lois May to go to school?"

Jen did not look up, but seemed to concentrate more firmly on the samples.

"There was a few words over it," she nodded absently.

"Well, Jen!" Margaret persisted, and then paused. "I'm not quite sure—was it just the registration fee Lize wanted him to pay? Is everything else but that taken care of for her?"

Jen nodded again, setting aside two bits of paper from the rest and critically regarding them.

After a minute or two Margaret said in her low, troubled voice, "Well, honestly, Jen, it seems as if he could spare that. It's only twenty-five dollars. He could if he'd be willing to let something go about the house. And he needn't think of me. I told him so. I mean, I told him I'd rather we helped her a little now and had our parlor furniture later on. We shan't have much use for a parlor anyway . . . And it's too bad for Lois May to stay on at home now she's finished school. She's bright and ambitious and she'll get ahead if she has a chance, but no knowing what she might be up to if she stayed here these next few years. I mean, you know what girls will do sometimes when they don't have any better way to use their time."

Margaret broke off, coloring. Jen would guess she was thinking now of Mil who had been only seventeen when she married George, and still only seventeen when Esther was born too early.

"That's right," Jen said. "I've thought of that myself. Yes, I guess this was the paper I took such a fancy to, Margaret. This cream-colored one with the gilt stripes."

"It seems to me as if we really had to," Margaret said miserably. "That's the way it seems to me. There's nothing Ed and I could get for twenty-five dollars that we need as much as Lois May needs an education."

"Well, it's all in the way you look at it," Jen returned cheerfully. She went back to John's overalls, pulling out baste threads with vigor.

Margaret watched for a minute and then turned away her face.

"What I can't bear," she said. She bit her lip. "Ed wouldn't listen to a word last night when I tried to tell him how I felt about it. I know I haven't any business to talk about him to anybody, but I'm so—surprised at him, Jen! . . . He didn't act like himself . . . I wouldn't believe it *was* Ed, the way he talked to me. . . . It makes you feel sort of queer when you're going to be married to a man in a month or so—and you can't tell him how you feel about anything—but what he talks to you as if—as if——"

Jen fastened her stitch firmly and straightened up. She did not look surprised, or even concerned.

"I'll tell you, Margaret," she said. "You take it all too serious. When you've lived with Ed as long as I have, you'll know him better. He's mostly pretty quiet, but when he gets to talking, he says a lot too much. The only way is not to argue with him. Just let him work it out himself. It's harder for him and everybody else but it's the only way he can get a thing done. He's that bull-headed, but there's worse things. You mustn't remember all he ever said, that's all."

"I think—so much of him," faltered Margaret.

"He's a good boy," declared Jen roundly. "You keep right on. He's worth it. There isn't a better boy alive." She bent again over the wallpaper samples. "Here he comes now . . . I liked this one myself, Margaret. This one with the little vine and the gilt stripe. Maybe it wouldn't be to your taste."

"Why, that's just the one we picked out last night. Wasn't it, Ed?"

He stopped short in the sinkroom door and stared at her. His expression did not change, but remained surly and faintly contemptuous.

"Did you walk down here, icy as it is? You'll break your neck going back, now it's getting dark. Mil ought to known better, if you didn't yourself."

"I came to talk with Jen about the papers," Margaret told him with her uncertain smile. "You said you wanted to order them to-morrow."

"Well, I didn't say I wanted you to hike all over town with the going like it is. I've got my horse here, so I can take you home, but that's your good luck. Come on now, before it gets any darker."

"All right," Margaret said in a small voice. She looked wistfully at Jen. "I'm ready."

"Good-by," said Jen. "Maybe you can come to see me in the spring, if Ed isn't too afraid of quicksands and sudden freshets for you. I'm beginning to think having a man in love with you must be an awful nuisance. They're so fussy. Now Ed wouldn't care if *I* tumbled all the way from here to Boston."

She stood at the window to wave her hand, feeling mature and benevolent.

All the next week Ed stayed in his mood. His father watched him covertly. The children grew afraid of him. Jen came and went about her work as usual. She cooked the food that he liked best, put cloves in her apple pies, left whey in her sour milk cheese, and opened the last can of raspberries. He ate gloomily.

They papered two rooms of his house with only a word or two between them.

"Higher, Ed. That's it."

"It don't look bad."

"Looks fine."

One night after the others had gone to bed she sat making the shirt he would wear at his wedding. She had made all his shirts since he had grown too old for blouses, but from now on Margaret would make them, or he would buy them at the store. She thought of this, setting very small stitches, as he came in and flung himself down in a chair across the table from her.

"What's that?" he asked suddenly.

"Your shirt."

"I don't need a new one."

"It's for your wedding."

"Oh . . . What's the difference?"

"Lots."

He took up the daily paper and spread it wide, his long legs sprawled under the table. Jen moved her work closer to her elbow, and tucked her feet under her chair to give him room. She smiled to herself. Next month Margaret would be doing this, unless the table they were going to buy was very large indeed.

"What you thinking?" Ed demanded.

"How I'll miss you."

"That makes you smile, does it?"

He crumpled the paper and thrust it away from him, knocking her thread onto the floor. His eyes were cloudy and narrow.

"Well, I can't blame you. I should think you would . . . I should *think* you'd smile."

"Might as well," said Jen philosophically.

He did not seem to hear. He lifted his head to gaze dejectedly around the room and let it sag again, brooding on the upturned palms of his hands.

"Yes," he said. "I should think you'd laugh out loud."

"Next thing," Jen said, "you'll expect me to cheer."

He sprang up and walked to the window, his fists jammed into his pockets until he strained the seams. His mouth was puckered for a whistle that did not come. Jen's eyes twinkled at his back and she sewed with industry.

"That's all right," Ed told her bitterly, staring out into the dark. "You needn't think I don't know how hard it is for anybody to get along with me . . . Growl all the time I've got anything on my mind . . . Act like an ugly dog, that's what I act like . . . Oh, I know it. Too bad Margaret don't. You ought to tell her. Ever think of that? You ought to tell her what she's getting into."

"Oh, for goodness' sake, Ed Shaw," Jen said. "You're no pig in a bag. She don't have to be told. You couldn't hide anything from a blind man."

He saw that she was laughing at him and strode over to her. He looked suddenly excited, and pleased with himself, and tried not to let it show.

"You think you know a lot, don't you? Well, there's quite a few things I could tell you about me yet. One thing in particular would surprise you a whole lot."

"What?"

"Well." He took a turn about the room and stopped beside her again. "Well, I've got that money Lize is so crazy about for Lois May. I had the cashier down at the bank make out a check to-day."

"Pooh," said Jen, whirling a thread round and round a button to fasten it. "I've been expecting *that* since Washington's Birthday."

"Since Washington's——"

"Since the first ever I heard it mentioned."

Ed drew in his breath and caught her head roughly, one hand on top of it and one under her chin, to turn her face up. It was pink with serenity and quiet pride.

"You did, did you, smarty? Well, why didn't you say so?"

"Oh," said Jen, "I thought I'd let you."

He chuckled, touching her cheek with one big finger, and let her go. She gave her head a brief shake, like a cat, and set to hunting through her button box. He brought a bottle of ink and a long yellow pen holder from the mantelpiece behind the stove.

"I suppose you know the address," he said. "I won't write anything. I'll just put the check in an envelope."

Jen reached up behind the clock.

"Here," she said. "They're in the new apartment now. Lois May thought to come back yesterday, but I told her she'd better stay a little longer. So now she's saved carfare, coming and going again. Every little counts."

Ed grinned sheepishly and Jen smiled back. Beyond his shoulder she could see how dark the night was. The wind blew hard and crept in around the windows. The room was growing chilly. Ed's slow pen scratched across the paper. Jen's fingers lingered on the threading of a needle. One more button and the shirt would be done.

SPRING

SPRING

I

RALPH came home for the wedding, though no-body expected him.

Mark Shaw was in the yard at five o'clock, as usual, among his wood. Two weeks ago the sand of the roads had begun to eat up through the snow. There followed warm, wet, twinkling days that stopped the sledding, though drifts still clung to sheltered places; it was time now for sawing and splitting. At his left hand stood the ragged stacks of dry pine and maple and oak just as he had unloaded them when he came from the woods, long, high stacks, nearly cutting off his view of the house; he could have seen above them only the pitch of the roof and the chimney and the smoke of the fire he had built to heat Jen's teakettle. At his right hand lay the small pile of stovelengths his morn-ings' work had so far amounted to. Before and behind him, carefully separated, were the unsplit chunks for the sitting-room stove, the straight pine sticks, three or four inches through, which he would sharpen into fence posts, and the smaller limbs he had put aside for bean poles.

But Mark Shaw did not look high or far in any direction. He stood, a broad man in overalls and a black cloth cap, and took a maple limb in his mittened hands, laid it across a rude sawhorse he had made himself, lifted his foot to hold it firm, and bent and straightened rhythmically, the teeth of his saw in the heart of the wood making a singing sound.

He did not look high enough to see the smoke, nor far enough to see the new grass pushing up wherever it could find room, but he knew of both, perhaps from the smell, perhaps from the time of day and year. The sun was beginning to brighten the air; at sunrise Jen always came downstairs to her boiling kettle; and a kettle does not boil without smoke in the chimney. The tenth of May was first pasturing day, and if the cattle were to get their teeth on something then, the roots must be stirring now. But he did not think of these things. He thought of reaching and placing and sawing and reaching again. His ears did not even remark the sound his saw made; it was only the sound of a saw.

But a stir in the sky caught his notice. He heard it first as a humming to the south; it might have been a train except that it was too high up. Over the lower marshes it became a roar, and Mark Shaw hurried out into the field. By then he could see a small black speck, and he took off his cap and waved it in solemn circles round and round his head. It was Ralph, he knew, and this was the place where Ralph liked best to land. The boy might have forgotten, it had been so long since the last time he came, but Mark Shaw had made the field smoother than ever. He had ploughed and harrowed and seeded it down last fall, and never

crossed it now the snow was gone without pocketing
a rock or two that might trig a wheel a little. He
raised himself on the balls of his feet, waving his cap.

The plane circled and came down at a smooth slant.
It threw up a flurry of dirt as it struck the ground and
bounced along until it stopped suddenly on the brow
of the hill. Mark Shaw hurried over to it. This was a
strange thing to be in his field.

"Hullo, pa! I bet you thought you were going to get
bombed!"

Ralph swung his long legs over the side of the cock-
pit and came toward his father. He was big, like Ed,
but thicker set, and had a round, fair face like Jen's.
His eyes were pale and narrow as he took off his
goggles.

"No," said Mark Shaw. "No, I knowed it was you."
His tongue thickened with pleasure and embarrassment. "I knowed it was you all right, soon's I heard
your engine. I was there a-sawing——"

"Father!" cried Jen from the window. "Is it—why,
it's——"

She came running, her hair still in a braid as she
wore it at night.

"It's Ralph," her father told her. "I knowed it was
him. I was there by the wood pile——"

"Well, Ralph! Why didn't you let anybody *know*?
Well, now won't Ed be tickled, father?"

"I knowed it was him all right," said Mark Shaw.
"I can tell that engine quick 's I hear it, some way——"

As Jen looked back upon that morning, she always
seemed to see it through a blur. The milk must be
strained and the pans washed the same as always, the
oatmeal must be measured out and stirred, the coffee

poured, the chickens fed and the plants watered. Beside that, new dresses must be altered and pressed, blue suits sponged, and cuff links found where they had been hiding since last summer. Jen must make a cake, a snow-white one with three layers. She saw the shells of nine brown eggs toppling on the cooking table, and the iridescent froth of many whites in the bottom of her old blue bowl; but it was only odd minutes like these that stood out plainly, and voices calling back and forth across the yard or between the rooms.

"Do you know where Margaret got her dress?"

"She made it, Lois May. It's nice too."

"Is it white? Is it silk?"

"Yes, it's white. But it ain't silk. It's voile. It's quite long and has ruffles on the skirt and the collar is wide and full and comes out over her shoulders like a little cape."

"Must be pretty."

"Oh, it's awful pretty."

Somewhere Olly paused beside her and spoke low.

"I wanted to tell you, Jen. I'm going to be alternate again, against Wesleyan this time."

Jen could not think what alternate was, or Wesleyan. But she had a sense that Olly felt insignificant beside his brothers to-day, since he was not being married and had not come home by airplane.

"You are!" she cried. "Why, *Olly!*"

After that whenever she looked at him she made her eyes proud. It was not hard, if she stopped to think. She did not need to remember just what alternate was, in order to be proud of Olly. He was growing fast now. It made his sleeves and trousers short and stretched his coat at the seams, but he looked well.

Out in the yard Ralph's strange, careless voice said,
"I'll tell you how it is, Ed. How'd you and your lady
like to fly to Boston on that honeymoon?"

"Huh? Well, gosh, I—I'd like to, myself, but——"

"So'll she, once you get her started. Big thrill.
Honeymoon in the air. What do you say? I'm going
to Hartford to-night. It'll be right on my way."

"Well—by gosh, I'll do it!"

A sickness went through Jen and passed off. She
realized she was stroking Lize's white fur jacket in
the front room; it felt fine and soft to her fingers. Ed
and Margaret would fly to Boston, then, and have
something to remember all their lives.

"Oh, my, it's nice," cried Bun. "Out, I mean. It's
almost *hot!*"

"The only thing," said Lois May, "it ought to be
June for a wedding."

"It ought not," Jen contradicted her. "If it was, they
couldn't take a honeymoon at all. March is the best
month there is for a farmer to get married. The snow's
gone so you can't haul wood, and the weather's good
but it isn't planting time."

She hummed softly, pulling John's blouse over his
head. Everything came right for the Shaws.

At one o'clock Ralph took Olly to look down on
Mount Passy from the sky. They would try out
George's field for landing, Ralph said, and be there
when the others came.

At two o'clock Mark Shaw drew up his horses before the door and waited, sitting hunched and sober
on the front seat of the democrat wagon. His black
coat lay smooth and only slightly green across his
shoulders and the shoes braced against the dashboard

shone with polish. He held a new whip with a yellow
lash in one big fist. Jen regarded him with satisfaction
from where she was brushing Ed's felt hat on the
porch.

"They about ready?" he asked her.

"Yes," Jen told him. "They'll be right along. Here,
your necktie seems kind of twisted . . . There."

She stepped down from the wagon carefully, holding the hat and her skirts well away from the muddy
wheel. Her father eased his neck back into the stiff
white collar.

"You riding with Ed, are you?"

"Yes. He wants me here to look him over the last
thing."

Mark Shaw nodded. They did not meet each other's
eyes. Ed would not be coming back with either of
them. He would never live in this house again if he
turned out to be the kind of man who could take care
of himself. And he would. Of course they wanted him
to.

"Here they come," said Jen.

She lifted her youngest brother and settled him
safely close to her father. Mark Shaw did not look
down, but he moved his shoulder to make a place for
John to snuggle into. Jen knew what he was thinking;
he would still have John.

Mrs. Shaw climbed up to the front seat, her eyes
bright with excitement. Her coat was two years old,
but clean and neat, and Lois May had taught her how
to pin her hair so that it would show beneath her hat;
it made her feel conspicuous but modish. Lize and
Lois May and Bun sat together in the back, Lize in
the white fur jacket, Lois May in the green velvet dress

and wool coat with a new dark fur, a gift from Lize, slung rakishly across her shoulder; Lois May had changed in these few weeks though no one had time to notice it just now; she was older, secure in her experience with streetcars and revolving doors, but a little subdued, a little watchful and speculating. Bun's collar had been turned and her short hair done up on rags the night before. She wore becomingly her serious, angelic look between the red curls, and held the package which contained her own personal gift for Margaret—a dozen russet apples rubbed hard.

Jen came out bringing the cake.

"Now you can keep this right on your lap, can't you, ma? There's nothing can get through the box to stain."

Mark Shaw spoke to the horse.

"You'll have to drive slow so as not to splash, father," laughed Jen. "You're carrying ladies to-day."

She let her apron slide off and hang from her hand as she looked down at herself. Her dress was new. It even smelled new, a brown crepe from Sears and Roebuck. It had yellow wool lace at the neck and cuffs, fitted neatly about her sturdy waist and hung nearly to her ankles. Her last year's straw hat would match it well enough. Even she would do credit to Ed on his wedding day. She drew a long breath, smiling.

Early spring sunshine lay pale and thin over the yard. The branches of the tree by the well were bare but restless, as if life quickened in them. New grass grew among the old by the step. In the chip dirt surrounding the wood pile Jen could see the rocky outline of two small gardens she and Ed had made years before, hers for flowers and his for vegetables. None of the others had liked keeping gardens.

Beyond the pasture and the marshes the east end of the Searles house rose above the trees. It had been the Searles place ever since Jen could remember, but would be the Ed Shaw place from now on. It was waiting for Ed and Margaret, a house with tight roof and walls, a barn stocked with cattle, a shed for the wagons and riggings, and a chicken coop with a big yard. Margaret would go inside the house and keep it, while Ed worked for her in the fields.

"The Shaw place," thought Jen. "And the Ed Shaw place. And the George Shaw place."

"Jen!" Ed called from the sitting-room. "Come fix this thing, will you?"

It was a collar button he needed to have worked through the neck band she had starched too stiff for his clumsy fingers. His thick, untidy hair and stout, wind-reddened neck bowed humbly before her.

"I couldn't seem to get it any way."

"It does go hard . . . There you are."

"All right. I'll be right along now."

"I'll harness."

The barn door rumbled open and Ed's horse turned his head. Jen leaned her shoulder against him for an instant in the stall. The warmth of him and the weight and feel of the straps and buckles were welcome to her. She led him out into the yard and left him standing free, his coat shining in the sun.

Ed stood in the kitchen, taller and broader than ever in his new blue suit. Behind him was the couch where Jen had doctored him for croup and dressed swimming-boils on his knee; and the table where on winter nights they had studied seed catalogues together, planning for the spring. She brushed a hair off his shoulder and adjusted the loops of his watch chain but her hands did not linger.

"You look fine," she said. "Now we'll have to hustle."

"S'pose I'll forget my piece?" he asked her.

"If you do, the Elder'll tell you how it goes," said Jen, putting on her hat. "That's what he's there for."

She spoke as if she knew very well what it was to get married.

They went out and stepped into the wagon and rode away. Ed handled the reins gently. He would not drive his horse again for nearly a week.

"Better see he gets an extra pail of water around milking-time," Ed said.

"I'll look after him."

"He takes a good deal of water."

They turned out of the lane into the main road and crossed a swampy stretch known as The Flats.

"Margaret like my Easter lilies?"

"Fine. She's going to—carry them, I guess."

"That'll be pretty. I'm pleased they bloomed so soon. That plant is always early, though, I've noticed."

George's place came into view around the next turn. It was a small, story-and-a-half house badly in need of another coat of yellow paint, and a thirty-foot barn that had never been painted. Riggings stood about in the orchard on the hill, a plough leaning against a tree, a haycart off its wheels, and a horse rake, its prongs red with rust; George had no room for them in his barn and never found time to build even a lean-to; he used what days he could spare from his seasonal work to earn cash pay from the town or his neighbors.

But the front yard had been cleared of wagons and tubs and toys and a new gravel walk laid between the road and the front door. The car, still wet from washing, set neatly at the end of the house; it looked almost like new. The clothes-lines were free of laundry, and Mil's parlor windows were gay with the plants she had grown from some slips Jen had given her. Ralph's plane waited in the north field and someone had tied it with white crepe paper ribbons. The automobiles and carriages lined up by the fence numbered nine or ten in all.

"My!" said Jen proudly. "There's quite a crowd!" She looked at Ed. He was staring straight ahead.

"You better hitch at the end of the house," she said, "so Tommy won't see the plane go up. Then you go in the front door, won't you? That's what Margaret said . . . I'll just run in this way to see if ma got the cake over without crumbling it."

She smiled at Ed encouragingly and went in.

A few minutes later Mil sat down at the organ in the parlor and began to play a march. The organ was one that had been left to her and Margaret by their Aunt Grace, and she had learned the march from her Aunt Grace as a little girl. She could play it perfectly still, for on Sunday evenings the children were always coaxing her to try it over; they seemed to like it better than the more difficult selections Margaret could play, perhaps because Mil was their mother. They stood behind her now, Betty and little George and Esther holding the baby, for they felt shy and did not know where else to stand, and their being there concealed her from her collar down. Nobody could see that she was stooped, though not yet thirty, nor that her best dress had worn thin across the shoulders. Her dark hair was coiled smoothly and she held her head high, letting it sway softly as she pressed the pedals.

"Taa-ta-ta-taa; taa-ta-ta-taa——"

No one would have guessed that this room had been a nursery for the last three years. George had helped yesterday to carry the girls' bed and little George's crib up into the open chamber, and had taken the linoleum rug off the carpet. Now the library table, the wicker chair and the oak rockers stood in their old places as George and Mil had arranged them when they first came here to live. Mil remembered the day, a hot, sweet one in early July. Mil had been as straight as anyone then, and George slender and good-natured. "Say, you think I don't have any haying to do this summer?" "But, George, we can't stop without our parlor pictures hung!" "All right, all right; you're the boss! Where'll we put the lady with the hoop around her head?"— St. Cecilia still looked down from the north wall where they had placed her then, and a mirror in a gold frame hung over the library table. The carpet looked almost as fresh and new as ever, and the dotted swiss draperies were snowy and whole. Mil had made all the yellow paper chrysanthemums and white jonquils herself by directions in a magazine. Nobody else Mil knew could make paper flowers that looked like real; George and Ed were always pretending to smell of them.

"Ta-ta-tata, ta-ta-tata——"

The mirror reflected Margaret's gifts as they lay upon the table. Three patchwork quilts, a blue lustre tea-set, a wooden salad bowl and fork and spoon, a glass sugarbowl and cream pitcher, a gravy ladle, a half dozen silver teaspoons, a pair of sugar tongs, three framed watercolors, a braided rug, a book and apron and a sweetgrass basket, white napkins, and several odd china dishes. In the center set Jen's cake, very high and round and glistening.

The mirror reflected, too, the company that had gathered to hear the vows taken. An elderly cousin of Mil's and Margaret's was there, Miss Esther Kingsley of Haverford, very tall and thin in her black silk dress with ruching at the neck and wrists; and Evelyn Schroeder, with whom Margaret had roomed at normal school, a trim girl grown hard-looking from four years of keeping discipline in a city school. Aaron Hale and his wife stood near the door; Mrs. Hale had made herself a new green cloth dress and put a fresh ribbon on her hat. Old Mr. Neale and his wife, who were past their eightieth years and hardly ever left their own bounds, had driven down from Neale's Ridge; it was a wonder to everybody as they sat together, a wizened, keen-eyed pair, on Mil's gray velvet sofa. Margaret's pupils were there, every one, even Manuel Janowski and his four chubby, black-eyed little sisters. Mil had not quite liked the idea of including the Janowskis in the school invitation but Margaret had insisted, and they did seem to have washed themselves clean and dressed as well as they could; Manuel's suit had been pressed and all the girls were neat enough, standing hand in hand. Bill Carpenter had come to see Ed married off, looking flushed and awkward in his best clothes. The Grants and the Walkers were there, and the Grover Harrisons from down the road, and Arthur

Forrest with his ten-year-old girl and six-year-old boy in loose-fitting, homemade gingham frocks; Mabel had been kept at home with a new baby. Edith Faraday, who taught in the upper district, stood with her mother, prettily aware that the next wedding would be hers, and wondering who else was thinking of it; she lowered her eyes modestly. It was almost possible, by looking first at the group and then at the table, to say which of the gifts each one had brought.

Mark Shaw, his wife, and eight of his children stood together. The mirror caught the brown faces of the men and Jen, the white faces of the others. Even George stood there instead of near his wife and children. Mil did not resent this. If she had not been playing the organ, she and the children would have been there too. It was the place for all of them.

"Taa-ta-ta-ta; taa-ta-ta-ta——"

The third Shaw son stood beside the Elder between the windows. He looked steadily at the floor and the color surged dark under his skin; his hands hung big at his sides, strong enough to make their hold felt whatever he gripped but weak when put to no use. The old Elder regarded him kindly over his open Book; he had married Shaw men before and none of them was at home in a parlor. He could remember when he, too, as a young carpenter of twenty-three, had turned sick at thought of being looked at and listened to, but the call of the Lord had changed all that. "In the twinkling of an eye," thought the Elder happily, behind his white beard and crisp piqué waistcoat, stroking the worn page with a blue-veined finger. "In the twinkling of an eye."

Margaret came down the stairs and across the room

to Ed, not slowly as she had read that brides did, but easily and firmly, her natural step. She wore her white voile dress with its wide, filmy collar and clinging skirt, and carried three Easter lilies and a small black Testament, but otherwise she did not look very different from the way she did when she walked down the aisle at school, glancing over the children's shoulders at their figures. She smiled around quietly and when she reached Ed, tucked her hand in his arm and held the lilies and the Testament idly in the other hand. It was not the Lord who had changed her from the timid child she had once been, but long experience of being on display before her little public. Four years had passed since she cried all night in Evelyn Schroeder's arms because she dared not try to teach a practice class the causes of the American Revolution.

The Elder began to speak. Ed answered him gruffly, Margaret softly. No one heard much of what was said. A few words now and then, that was all.

"—take thee——"

"—to serve——"

"—to cherish——"

"—any reason——"

"I pronounce you——"

The Elder raised both hands and prayed in his old voice.

The sun came in, lying across Ed and Margaret, across Mil and her children by the organ, across Mark Shaw and his family; and it was the same sun. Beyond the window it lay across ground that waited to be turned, and across budding trees in the orchard and the pines of the woods beyond the Ridge; still it was the same sun. Jen knew of it, though her eyes

were closed. It felt warm to her, and full of promise.
The season was early. Crops would be good. It was a
fine time for a farmer to be getting married.

"The first kiss for your husband, Mrs. Shaw," said
the Elder. "The second for your minister. And may
the Lord bless and keep you both."

He drew back and wiped his eyes unashamedly.
The Elder always cried at weddings of late years.
Evelyn Schroeder and Lize and Lois May and Edith
Faraday rushed forward to seize Margaret and kiss her,
to shake Ed's hand and congratulate him. They knew
how to do these things. The others followed more
slowly, touched but shy.

"I hope you'll be happy, I'm sure."

"Come cut your cake, Margaret," Evelyn said.
"Come cut your cake now."

She cut it and it was soft and light on Mil's bluebird
plates. The company ate it standing about the room,
trying not to drop crumbs on the carpet. Esther and
Bun brought in lemonade teeteringly on a tray. Everybody drank and none was spilled.

"Well, what do you say, Ed?" asked Ralph. "Shall
I warm her up?"

Ed nodded.

"Yes," said Jen, "you want to give yourself time
enough. You want to get there before dark."

Evelyn and Lize and Lois May and Edith went upstairs with Margaret to help her change her dress. The
men and children followed Ralph and Ed toward the
plane. Mil and Jen cleared the parlor of dishes, but
still it had the faintly bitter taste of something left over
when the best is used and gone, with the desolate
little heap of gifts on the table, the yellowed sheet of

music on the organ rack fluttering in the cold wind from the open window, and Mrs. Shaw and Mrs. Hale and Mrs. Neale and the other older women speaking together in low voices with nods and sighs.

"Good-by," said Margaret suddenly, in the doorway.

She looked strange in her tan cloth coat and brown hat and figured silk scarf.

"Good-by," said Jen. "Now you take care of yourself up there to Boston, and Ed, too."

"We'll be all right," smiled Margaret. "Good-by, Mil. You've done such a lot. I only hope you don't get down sick."

Ed loomed up behind her.

"Come on, Peg, we're leaving. So long, everybody."

They ran through the yard and across the field, the women following. Ralph handed them into the back seat and sprang into his own place. Ed swung his arm and Margaret waved gaily from behind the glass that closed them in. The motor made such a din it was no use to speak a word, though Mil could see that Margaret was crying, "Good-by. Good-by." The sisters had not yet been separated a night since Margaret came home from normal school four years before.

"Good-by," Mil called back, smiling stiffly. For once she did not feel little George pulling at her finger, or think of big George's supper. "Good-by, dear!"

The plane bounced away on its small wheels and rose smoothly into the air. It was a strange way for a Shaw to begin his married life. It had been strange enough for George to take Mil for a three days' trip in his second-hand automobile, nine years before. Mark Shaw and his first wife had gone in a buggy, the third of a parade of horse-drawn vehicles carrying

four Derwich families for a Saturday and Sunday in a
beach cottage; they marked their initials on a flat rock
to show those coming behind that they had passed,
and young Mark cut the letters so deep he could still
see them now whenever he went that way with
chickens and fresh vegetables for the summer hotels.
M. F. S.; M. B. S.

The little company stood looking up, shading its
eyes as the plane grew smaller and smaller, travelling
back over the marshes.

"Well, if they git on," said Mrs. Neale, "like father
and me, they'll be all right. And I guess they will too.
They're a nice, smart young couple."

There had been no wedding trip for the Neales. In
their time a man took his new wife home to his
father's house; they spent the evening with the family
and later occupied the big bed with goose feather
pillows in the West Room. Mrs. Neale could remember the stale air of that room, sweet with lavender and
spices, and the glow of the fire on the uneven brick
hearth better than she could remember where she had
put her darning cotton yesterday.

"Yes, they be," said Mr. Neale. "A smart couple
and no mistake. Both of 'em."

II

That night Jen, as often happened, was the last
to go to bed. At ten o'clock she was still going
about quietly through the rooms, putting away things
that Lize and Lois May and Olly had used, but would
not be using again, perhaps for months. It seemed that
there was more and more of this work in her life,

getting out clean sheets and towels and bringing down comforters from the open chamber, and after a night or two carrying them away again. She patted a pillow smooth.

The sound of a knock on the side door startled her. She lifted her head and listened. After a minute or two it came again very quietly. She took up the lamp and went into the entry. The key stuck briefly in the lock and she shook it.

"Who is it?" she asked of the dark as she finally pulled the door open.

"It's Janowski from over on the next place. Stan Janowski."

He stepped into the range of her lamplight. She had never seen him near-by before and even now saw him only vaguely, a broad, stocky figure, bareheaded, with thick dark hair. His voice was deep and smooth, and he spoke almost in a whisper.

"It's too bad to trouble you this time of night. If your light had been out I wouldn't have. But one of the children over at the house is sick, and my mother thinks she'd better have a doctor. You see, we haven't got our telephone put in yet, and I thought maybe you'd be willing to call him. Or let me. If it wouldn't be too much trouble."

"Well, now, we haven't got a telephone either," Jen began.

"You haven't!" He sounded incredulous. "I wish I'd noticed that. I wouldn't have disturbed you."

"Disturbed me!" laughed Jen. "You're no disturbance. It's a wonder I heard you at all, coming as easy as you did . . . No, father's never got around to having a telephone put in. We don't seem to see much need for it. They've got one up to my brother George's, though, third place up on the left, and at Hale's, and several places down along."

He hesitated.

"Well, thanks. They're probably all in bed by now. I don't believe I'll get them up. The baby'll be all right by morning. Thanks very much."

He was turning away. Jen held her lamp higher.

"What seems to be the matter with the baby?"

He looked back, one foot on the step, one on the ground. Every word he said he spoke so slowly it seemed to Jen he drawled, but otherwise he had no accent. She saw that his face was long and earnest, with a full, gentle mouth and bigger eyes than those of any of the men she knew; but they were blue eyes, or at least not black like Manuel's and the little girls'.

"Well, I don't know. He's been fine all day, but my mother says he all of a sudden can't get his breath to-night. It's probably just a cold."

"Probably the croup," Jen said. "If you'll wait a minute I'll run over with you and take a look at him." She would have gone to any other neighbors, she thought; she would go to these. "If that's what it is, you don't need a doctor. I'm an old hand at croup."

"Oh, I wouldn't ask you——"

But Jen did not wait to listen to him. She was back in the kitchen writing on a torn strip of brown paper, "Gone over to Janowski's. One of the young ones is sick," and tucking the corner of it under the lamp. She collected a kettle, a basin, some clean cloths, mustard and flour, and the bottle of ipecac; there was no telling what Polacks might or might not have ready. When she came out of the house she carried the kettle in one hand, a lantern in the other, and wore one of her father's coats and a cap of Bun's; these had been the first things her hand touched in the entry; there was no need to keep a croupy child waiting.

"My," she said cheerfully, "it's an awful warm night for March."

"Here, I'll take your things," Stan Janowski said. "Give me the kettle too. We'd better go across the field, the road's so muddy."

"All right," Jen answered. "Hold the kettle careful, so you don't break anything in there."

"But I don't feel as if you ought to come," he insisted.

"There," Jen silenced him, "I always go when there's need. It's our way in the country."

But she knew no one else here would have gone to help the Janowskis in the night, and so did he. She felt him glancing at her often as they went down over the hill to the east, across the main road, and into the Old Joe field. It was a still night, and the air was full of fog from the river and marshes, but she could see the pricking of the stars through it, and of lamp-light at one high window in the end of the Old Joe barn.

"We haven't got much of a place to live in yet," Stan Janowski said as they went up the incline under the light, "but it's warm, anyway, and fixed so my mother can keep it clean. We're going to build a house as soon as we can."

"Things take time," Jen answered. "You can't do everything at once."

He set down the lantern and kettle to open a small

door that had been cut in the center of the big one,
and stood back to let her go in.

The whole end of the barn was one great room with
a stove on two sides of it, high, shining black cook-
stoves that had no legs but set flat on a new hard pine
floor. Jen saw at a glance that everything was spotless.
The walls had been covered with reddish sheathing
paper studded with brass nails and there was a high
ceiling plastered white. The new chairs, the long, bare
table, the stoves, and even the three beds full of children along the back wall did not nearly fill the room,
but left it still big and clean and the smell in it was
sweet from fresh air coming in at what had once been
a row of mow windows. It did not look like any living
quarters Jen had ever seen, but she found nothing to
complain of in it. The only sounds she heard were the
crying and hoarse breathing of a child somewhere behind the partition and the creak of a rocking chair.
She took the kettle from Stan and set it on the table
beside a turned-down hand lamp.

"If you'll sit down," he said, "I'll call mother. I had
her take him in my room, not to keep everybody
awake."

"I can go in there," Jen said.

But a minute after he went through a door and
she heard him speak, a woman came out carrying a
baby over her shoulder. Nobody in Derwich had ever
seen Mrs. Janowski before; some had doubted that
there was a woman, doubted if even a Polish woman
could really live in a barn. She was short and very
fat, with black hair and eyes like the children's, a jolly,
red-cheeked, dimpled face, and dressed in coarse, black

stuff with the feet of felt boots pulled over her shoes so that she scuffed when she walked.

"Now ain't t'is nice," she demanded heartily. "Now t'is what I call nice. Seem t'at I ain't seen no face but t'ese—," she moved her free arm in a generous circle, "—for how long, I don't know t'at. My, my. I guess you got big heart, great big heart. My, now I am please; you come out t'is time of night for me, one you don't know. You got ver' big heart."

"Oh, we always give and take round here," Jen said. "That's how we manage." She took the child capably and flung off a half dozen blankets from about his cheeks and neck. He had black eyes too; Jen did not expect them in a baby and they seemed to pop out at her; but he had the same raspy breath, the same distorted mouth, hot face, and restless head of all the other croupy children she had known. "Yes," she said. "Well, now, we'll get right after this. It's croup he's got."

"Croup, is it?" Mrs. Janowski asked respectfully. "My kids, t'e ot'er ones, t'ey not have t'at croup."

"It's common in these parts," Jen said. She laid the baby on the table and threw off her coat and cap, stilling him with one hand. "First thing, we'll need this kettle full of boiling water. If you've got other kettles, set them boiling, too. The more steam the better. Start up your fire good. And while we're waiting for it, we'll get some of this ipecac into him."

She shook the bottle.

"It isn't a very nice job," she said, "but it's the only way, he's filling up so fast—to use the ipecac, I mean."

Mrs. Janowski, back from putting on the kettle and

stuffing wood into one of her stoves, stood with arms akimbo, her head on one side.

"My," she said agreeably. "I s'pose!"

And she continued to stand by, still agreeable, still helpless, while Jen dosed the child and made him lose his bit of supper and part of the phlegm that had caught in his throat, while wet hot towels were bound on his neck and chest, and while steam crept slowly through the big room. Jen was not surprised that she had no help; not only Polish mothers stood aside to let her have her way with ailing babies. When the attack was over, she asked for clean, dry clothes and blankets, and dressed the little patient with as deft, sure movements as if his eyes, now growing sleepy, had been gray or blue. She was smiling as she held him out.

"*Now* he's coming," she said. Her face looked young and smooth. "Just keep him warm. He'll be all right. If he ever has another spell, you do like this and he'll come out of it. If you start soon enough, you may not need the ipecac, but it would be as well to keep some handy. When a young one goes to bed all right and wakes up hoarse and barking, you can be pretty certain it's the croup."

"My," exclaimed Mrs. Janowski, staring in admiration, only half listening. "Ain't t'at t'e great big heart you got. So good, I cannot t'ank you. Sometime maybe you come in again, I t'ink so."

"Oh, yes," Jen answered. "And you come over and see us." It was the way she would have replied to any other neighbor. She put on her coat and cap and took up her kettle. "It'll soon be good going now, and we womenfolks won't be kept so close."

Stan Janowski came out of his room, still in his corduroy trousers and high leather boots and plaid lumberjack, still with no hat. His shadow lay black across the path of lamplight. Jen had forgotten him. His coming reminded her of the children and she glanced about, seeing them all asleep in the beds that lined the wall. It was a wonder so much commotion had not roused even one of them. She supposed Mr. Janowski must sleep in the loft. After all, a barn was a strange place to live.

"My Stan take you home okay," Mrs. Janowski was saying, jogging the baby across her elbow. "You got t'e good heart. I ain't forget."

"Take me home!" Jen jeered. "There isn't a foot of the way between here and the house I don't know like my own sinkroom."

"I'll just go along," Stan said. "It's so muddy."

"He take you," nodded his mother proudly. "My Stan."

"Well, there," Jen agreed. "Just as you say."

They went back through the fields and it was foggier than when they came down. Jen had to lead the way, carrying the lantern, for she knew the lay of the land and could skirt the low spots. Stan's step was deliberate and patient behind her.

Once he said, "You don't seem old enough to know so much what to do."

"Some people always know," Jen said. "And other ones never do." She had no thought of bragging, only speaking the truth, more to excuse herself. "Anyway, I've brought up a big family. You learn things when you have to."

"That's right," Stan said. "That's what I think. I

don't know much about farming, but I'm learning.
Now I have to."

"That's it," Jen answered. "It works out so."

She turned the key in the lock of her own door. Stan
handed her the kettle. For an instant the lantern lit up
their faces, shining dimly between them.

"If you get stuck," Jen added, "maybe father can
help you. He's called a good farmer."

"I'd say he was a fine one," Stan told her. "It did
a lot of good, your coming over. Mother didn't know
much what to do. We sure appreciate it."

"You need steam to beat off croup," Jen said. "And
hot rags bound on wet. And ipecac if it's bad. She'll
get the hang of it. It's doubtful if it'll come on again
now until next winter, anyway. You folks go to bed
and get some sleep."

She nodded cheerfully, went in, and shut the door.
In her kitchen all was as she had left it. No one had
awakened to wonder where she was. She hung up the
coat and cap and set the kettle and its contents in the
sinkroom to be washed. Minnie Foote's clock on the
shelf still awaited winding. Jen reached up and felt
for the key where she kept it tucked under the paper.
She turned it with long, slow movements, glancing
about contentedly. This room felt good to her, returning. It always did, for it was hers; with all that it held
and all that it ever had held, it was hers. Even what
she saw from the back window seemed a possession.
She paused there, passing on her way to the stairs,
having blown out the light. Always she saw the same
woods and fields and sky; always felt the same gust
of cool air stealing in around the frame whenever she
stopped to look out. She felt it now, and drew a short,

quick breath of satisfaction. This was something which she had and could keep, her kitchen and her back window.

Softly she opened the stairway door, and softly crept up to undress in the dark.

III

One morning Jen and her father and John sat at breakfast before Mrs. Shaw and Bun were up.

"John, you can drink more milk than that," Jen said. "You set still now and drink your milk."

"He's in a hurry this morning," Mark Shaw explained, glancing at John gravely.

"What for? What's your hurry, John?"

"I got something," John answered.

"What?"

"Something out in the barn."

Jen studied him. Her face brightened slowly and she looked at her father.

"The heifer's come in!" she said.

"Got a heifer calf too," Mark Shaw said. "A big one for a young cow. Marked just like its mother; that streak down her back."

"Father give it to me," said John. "It's mine. I'm going to milk her when she grows up. Father says I can. I guess she'll give good milk. She's a Jersey."

"Why," said Jen, "I don't doubt she'll be the best milker on the place. When did Polly come in, father?"

"Some time in the night. Late, likely."

"She's all right then?"

"Seems smart."

Later in the morning Mark Shaw came out of the

shed pushing a wheelbarrow loaded with posts. The
fence that divided the upper field from the pasture had
to be built all new this year and because it crossed a
high sandy stretch of land it could be done early. John
ran ahead of his father to let down the bars, glancing
back now and then anxiously toward the barn. It worried him to go so far from the calf, but he could not
miss seeing the fence built; it might be that he would
even drive some of the staples for he was much bigger
now than last spring and could feel a lump on his
upper arm.

"It don't seem possible," Jen thought, "it's fencing
time again."

A shout from the field called her back to the window as she was turning away. Her father had put
down the handles of the wheelbarrow and stood looking at the sky, his hat on the back of his head. John
stood just so, too, his hands tucked inside the suspenders of his overalls. Jen saw the dark triangle they were
watching and ran out into the yard.

"My, ain't they early?" she cried.

"You won't see much more cold weather now,"
Mark Shaw said from the top of the hill. He stooped
to his load.

Jen twisted childishly from side to side within her
apron, her fists stiffened against the seams of her pockets. It was a great day when the wild geese came back.
No more winter; no more frozen water, shovelling
snow, frostbitten toes, blocked roads, snapping nails,
croup, colds, or hot beach rocks in the beds. She could
take off the blankets soon, and put on sheets; they
were much easier to wash. Wild geese brought the
spring. As the flock passed, Jen could see the leader

followed in perfect formation by ever-lengthening rows of his kind, and, after the last, spring blew along lightly like a blue train on a black gown, filling the sky.

"Well, now I know what I've got to do," she said aloud. "I've got to sow my seeds."

Bun and John had filled eight wooden boxes with sand days before. Jen brought them down from the shed chamber and put them on newspapers on the kitchen floor. She knelt among them and spread out small paper packages flowering with pictures of firm white heads of cabbage, of curly green leaf lettuce, of a smooth big tomato with skin as red as blood. The colors excited her, and the thought of how fresh, raw vegetables smell and feel, and the wild, woody taste of them. She tore off a corner of one envelope and sowed the contents in little rows she had made with her forefinger. The seeds were very small to mean so much. She tucked in the envelope at the edge of the box when it was empty, to show what variety these plants would be. The Crisp-As-Ice lettuce was the best, she thought, but Ed liked the Boston Market; it did grow ranker, but the leaves were not so tender. She worked intently, and when she had finished, lined all the sunny windows in the kitchen and shed-room with her boxes. Her finger nails were rimmed with black, her face smudged, as she stood looking down at them.

"They'll be ready to be set out towards the last of May," she thought. "That's full soon enough, the way cool nights hold on late years. They'll get a good start."

She must sow her zinnias and pansies before long

now, too, and repot her geraniums. Slips should be rooted for the box on the porch railing. After the wild geese came back, there was no time to waste.

"Did you ever see the wild geese back as early, father?" she asked him when he came in.

"Not for years," Mark Shaw said. As he wiped his hands on the roller towel he remembered another spring that they had come as early. The spring he built this house the wild geese went over almost as soon as he was able to break ground for his cellar. It brought an early season and a long hot summer, with a good second crop of hay and a big corn harvest. It did not cost him a cent to winter eight cattle and a pair of horses that next winter. "Not for years," he said.

"I never did," said Jen. "It's not common."

She put a dish of fried salt pork on the table, and potatoes in their skins, and steamed biscuit. There was not much in the house for a change, but in a few months now they would be having lettuce and peas and cucumbers. It did not seem long to wait.

That night she knelt beside John on the rug before the stove and rolled him out of his stockings and undershirt, rumpled his head in her lap, and stood him on his feet naked and pink and shaking with laughter. She liked to make him laugh.

"Look, father," she cried. "Look how John's shooting up! See the muscles in his legs and arms. See how broad his shoulders are. Here's a boy can load two bags of grain at a time before long, and throw an ox if an ox needs throwing. Here's a boy for you. Look at that!"

Mark Shaw, bent to unlace his right shoe, spreading

the toes of the other foot inside the brown stocking,
looked out under his eyebrows at the small body
lately grown so lean and hard. Yes, here was a boy
for him, a fifth boy. One like this would not want to
fly the sky nor bury his nose in books. One like this
would not leave his riggings out to rust, nor talk of
buying tractors, incubators, separators. One like this
would house himself and all he owned snug and
watertight; let horses draw his ploughs, hens hatch
his eggs, and time divide his cream from his milk;
watch the seasons as they passed and know from each
one what to expect of the next. A boy like this would
listen, not too smart nor too impatient nor too proud
to learn what his land could teach him as the earth
turned slowly round the sun.

"Stout hands, too," Mark Shaw said approvingly.
"And it takes stout hands to milk a Jersey clean."

IV

Friday afternoon when Mark Shaw came from
market he brought Ed and Margaret with him.
Margaret sat in the middle on the edge of the seat like
a little girl, and Ed drove the horse; he had not held
reins in his hands for more than a week. Mark Shaw
took up as little room as possible, still a lion's share,
one leg dangling outside the wagon to leave space for
the suitcases crowded in among the egg buckets and
butter boxes and the shorts bags in which he carried
vegetables to his customers.

"Hel*lo*, there!" cried Jen, running out, stove cloth
in hand. "Hello, *Margaret!* Did you have a good time?
Did you go to the theater? Hello, *Ed,* you old nui-

sance! . . . How are you liking him anyway, Margaret? Is he going to do?"

"Oh, he's fine," said Margaret, looking up at Ed as he dragged out their bags. Jen had never heard her speak so proudly before.

"Don't trust her," Ed grinned. "She wouldn't dare say different."

They glanced about them with a kind of relief. Jen, sprinkled with flour as usual, Mark Shaw leading the horse away, the children hanging about eager but shy, the house, the barn, and the dip and lift of uneven ground reassured them. They had finished with the strange excitement of new clothes, weddings, and cities, and were at home again.

"Something *smells* so good," cried Margaret.

"It's apple dumpling," Jen said.

"Oh, is it for supper? I love it."

"Of course it's for supper."

Ed interfered from where he was attending to the small matter of John's shyness with movements of his arms and prodding fingers.

"Don't you go spoiling my wife," he said. "She's got to make her own apple dumplings."

"Not to-night, I hope," laughed Jen.

"No, not to-night. Please, Ed!" Margaret begged him.

They looked at each other. Ed pulled her toward him, smiling across her shoulder at Jen.

"What do you think? Shall I let her off this time?"

"Oh, settle it between yourselves," Jen exclaimed. She flounced away good-humoredly. "You big sillies!"

When she had gone, Ed kissed Margaret. He turned her around until she could see the chimneys of their own house, black against the sky over the hill. He whispered something, kissed her again, and took up the two suitcases in one hand so that the other would be free to hold one of hers as they went into the house. They seemed to have forgotten the children.

"Well, is it settled?" Jen asked with amusement, closing the oven door.

The kitchen smelled of food as it always did, and of smoke and soapy water. The couch cover and pillow tops were stiff with starch. Mrs. Shaw came hurrying from upstairs, smoothing back her hair, wearing her best dark blue dress. The skin of her thin face seemed stretched with her smile. She enjoyed company in the house, and even Ed, always her favorite of Mark's children, had become company now.

"Well, you got back all right!" She kissed Margaret self-consciously. "You must have had a lovely time up there. I'm in hopes you're going to stop to tell us all about it."

"Of course they are," Jen said. "Take her right into the front room, Ed, and leave all your nice clothes where they won't get scented up."

When a Shaw first came home after being married, he always slept in the front room. Mark Shaw and Cora had, and George and Mil. Jen glanced after Ed curiously. She had to put her mind to getting used to him this new way, this older, better-natured, faintly triumphant way. It was good; she liked it in a man; but it was new in Ed. She hurried to bring out hog's head cheese made from a winter butchering, to test her applesauce cake with a toothpick, to whip the cream and thicken the gravy and slice the meat and fry the carrots all at the same time. Mrs. Shaw brought out

her own silver and the blue glass dish from the sitting-
room cupboard, trying them first one way and then
another on the table. Bun scrubbed her face and John's
and brushed their hair, so unrelenting to the knots
that both their eyes were filled with tears, but neither
objected. They must look neat and clean for Teacher;
that she was now Ed's wife, too, concerned them little;
she was certainly Teacher.

That night the Ed Shaws told what they had seen
and done in Boston. Margaret described the churches,
the Park Street, the Phillips Brooks, Tremont Temple;
she had never imagined so much stained glass, such
great organs. Bunker Hill monument looked just like
the pictures; it was quite a climb to the top; and it
was strange to see the Old North Church and think
of Paul Revere and his lanterns. Ed had been most
interested in the water front, to watch the shipping,
and in the Charles River Basin; when people could
make land out of water, they were doing something.
You saw big crowds on Washington Street late in the
afternoon; folks were packed as thick as they could
stand; it was no wonder a man had to keep his biggest
roll of money pinned inside his shirt. Trains went
overhead and underfoot and every which way; the
streets up there would cave in before long, have to, for
the ground they stood on was nothing but a honey-
comb. The Harvard Bridge was a fine bridge, though,
over the Charles River; white cement, handsome; you
could see it from the train. Margaret liked the college
buildings over in Cambridge; some of them had been
standing a good while; they had a collection of glass
flowers, too, that you could hardly tell from real; Mil
would have liked them.

Mark Shaw, in his chair by the back window, cleared his throat and said, "I never been up to Boston."

"You ought to go, father," Margaret told him. She said the last word shyly. "You ought to plan to go up there some time. It isn't far as distances run nowadays."

It was as far as it had ever been to Mark Shaw. It was ninety miles. He shook his head, his arm lying along the window sill in its blue flannel sleeve.

"No," he said. "I never was one for travelling around."

"You and I are old stick-in-the-muds, father," laughed Jen. "Whatever comes or goes, you and I stay right where we started."

She rose to set back the singing teakettle and stopped by the couch where John lay asleep flat on his stomach with his face buried in the pillow. She turned him over to see if he had suffocated, and he drew away from her, snuggling down again.

"Stick-in-the-mud," he mumbled unexpectedly.

"Yes, you're a stick-in-the-mud, too," said Jen. "They can't even get you to go to the village unless father and Jen and the cows and the pigs and the hens will go. I never saw such a boy. Father, you take him along to bed now. It's time we was all asleep."

"Well, now, I don't know whenever I've had such an interesting evening," Mrs. Shaw exclaimed as they all stood up. "It ain't often anybody comes in with as much to tell over. I could listen to it for a week."

"There, you see you've got to stay a week anyway!" Jen said, handing Ed a lamp, smiling at Margaret.

Ed shook his head.

"No, we're going over in the morning."

"Well, come back nights——"

"No, we might as well get settled in. It's well enough to be there handy. I've got spring work to do."

"He's going to take to-morrow and Sunday to help me get started in the house," Margaret added. She lifted an eyebrow at him saucily. "He's promised, and I won't let him off."

"Don't you get fresh with me, young woman," he told her. "Or I'll put you into the field to work to pay me back."

He laid his free hand on her shoulder, urging her toward the front entry door. She laughed back her good-nights over his arm, and they went away together.

Yes, Ed was married now. He had his own wife, his own house, his own spring work to do. He could not waste his time here, now that he was back from Boston. Mark Shaw lifted John off the couch, shook him gently, and led him upstairs.

"Come," he said. "You've got to get to bed if you're going to be up betimes. That calf of yours'll need tending."

"She can stand up a long while now," John mumbled, "and she's only three days old. She'll make an awful good cow."

"If she's tended," Mark Shaw insisted. "They need tending."

V

The sun rose farther toward the north and set farther toward the north every day. Jen watched her cabbage, lettuce, and tomatoes, saw the first and second leaves push up through the sand, the cabbage round and milky, the lettuce crinkled, and the tomato jagged like a two-edged saw. When the fourth leaves came she mixed the richest soil she had with dressing from the stanchions and set out the little plants in other boxes, each plant two inches from the next. They had a brave look now.

John tied a rope around the new calf's head and led her, gangling, wondering-eyed, about the yard. "Hold up," said John. "Hold up, Stripey!" If she had had a white spot on her face he would have called her Star, but as she was, her name was Stripey; she liked it well enough, and liked the feel of the soft grass under her feet. It made her want to prance, and John held her tightly, trying to be at once firm and gentle.

Mark Shaw took a basket and went into the woods on a Sunday to get wild cherry bark. His knife slid under it carefully, swiftly; he knew the way; he had learned to gather wild cherry bark for his mother forty years before and laid in a stock every April since. The stout, bitter smell of it crept into the pores of his hands with the brown stains. Half-grown trees, now in new leaf, were all around him, with a small patch of threatening April sky overhead, and rough ground underneath for his feet to find their way by. "You got to learn the lay of the land," he had told his boys. "You can't always depend on the sun to get you home." He trod his unmarked path complacently, the basket on his arm, his head bent. White-blooming thoroughwort and pennyroyal from last fall hung, dry and brown, from the rafters of the open chamber. Jen would steep the three together in a kettle and set the tea away in two green bottles that had been his mother's. The tonic had a bitter taste, but it was good for blood that got to running too thick in the spring; it helped the liver, too, and even one dose was sure to start the winter stiffness out of joints. Most people nowadays had no time to search the woods and nobody knew the herbs, which to use or where to find them, but went to drug stores, and likely paid a dollar for nothing half so good to clear the blood as thoroughwort. Mark Shaw could remember the time when the herbwoman in a town was busier than the doctor. "Thoroughwort for the blood," old Miss Mindwell Holmes had told her neighbors, not stingy with what she knew. The Charles Shaws and the Abner Joys and the William Willys used to go together for wild cherry bark in the spring and made a picnic of it, but late years it seemed that only Mark Shaw went; he never found a tree disturbed. All the woods had now was left for him, though they had as much as ever. It seemed a great waste. He settled his basket more snugly on his arm.

"Hullo, Mark," said Orrin Hale from his barn door. "What you been after?"

"Yarbs," Mark Shaw answered, pausing. "They can't make nothing that tones anybody up like cherry bark and thoroughwort and pennyroyal. Christina steep it for you, does she?"

"No," Orrin said. "We don't have it here. We used to."

"I wouldn't pass a spring without it," said Mark Shaw doggedly. "It ain't like that you buy in drug store bottles. You know what you're getting."

He started on, but Mrs. Hale called to him from

the window where she sat rocking in her pink plaid gingham dress, out of respect for Sunday.

"They didn't serenade Ed and his wife, did they?"

"No," Mark Shaw answered. He looked at Orrin Hale, a gray, thin little man who used to play the fiddle at serenades and parties. "No, it takes more young fellows than we've got now to get up a serenade." He explained, "The city takes them off." He did not know why, but he knew it was so.

"A good thing," said Mrs. Hale, "they didn't have a serenade. The works they used to have around a woman's house was past all bearing. I never forgot the night twenty or more of them carried on here."

Mark Shaw remembered it too. He had been one of the twenty. "I hear Orrin and his mother's boarder's got spliced. We'd better drop in there Saturday night and see what's going on." They brought their crosscut saws and washboilers and guns and waited in the woods across the road until the Hale house went dark. They crept under these front windows here, sat on the door rock, climbed the apple tree, and began to make a thundering noise. Gus Larribee galloped round and round the house with a cowbell tied to his neck and the others whooped, "Orrin! Orrin! Your cow's out!" They climbed up over the windows to the roof and shouted down the chimney. "Ain't you coming out? Ain't you coming out? If you don't come out and treat us right, we'll be troublesome all night." It had been fall, Mark Shaw remembered now, still and cold; it almost seemed he could hear the voices. He shifted the basket of bark again.

"I don't know," he said. "We didn't do no harm, did we, Orrin?"

"God's sakes, no," answered Orrin cordially, as if his serenade had been only yesterday and some of his treat of cigars and candy still remained in the kitchen cupboard.

Mark Shaw went on. As he climbed Old Joe's hill a glittering trickle came running down the wheel track to meet him. He regarded it soberly, and its source when he reached it, a spring that bubbled out from under a rock and made a basin for itself in the reddish clay of the ditch. It was springy land all through here.

At the top he found the two Janowski men laying a culvert between the road and the gate that led into their field. It was as well to have a culvert there and so keep out of the ditch mud in the rainy seasons, he thought. Old Joe had tipped off loads of hay and wood here, time and again, for Old Joe was built a shiftless fellow, one that left all his problems to Providence and his wife. It was no way to get along, Old Joe's.

"Laying you a culvert, be you?" he asked.

The Janowskis looked up and straightened their backs. The old one was breathing hard and his little dark face looked pasty, but the young one grinned, pushing back his hat and wiping sweat with a muddy hand.

"Trying to," he said. "Been at it since early this morning. It's quite a job when you're not handy at it, but we can't haul through this ditch."

"No," Mark Shaw agreed. He added, "You tuckering your father out?"

The young one grinned again.

"You lost your wind, pa?"

"I got wind," the old one cried. "I ain't got t'at

great arms you got. I ain't got t'em big shoulders. I
ain't do t'is heavy work in my life, I don't." He looked
at Mark Shaw fiercely. "I am tailor, one good tailor.
T'is boy he bring me out here in t'is place. All he
t'ink, farm, farm, farm. All he want, farm, farm, farm.
I tell to you—" he took a blundering step.

"You set your father on that rock there," Mark
Shaw told the young one. "He's beat out. I'll give you
a lift on them planks."

"You don't—" the young one began.

"I've laid a good many planks," Mark Shaw said,
"in my time."

He took firm hold of the end of one and, when that
was in place and nailed, of another. Together he and
the young Janowski laid a firm, smooth culvert that
would last, that would be saving horses' backs twenty
years from now; they laid it slowly, silently, with care,
while the old one leaned against a boulder, panting.
When it was done, Mark Shaw took up his basket.

"I'm certainly much obliged to you," the young one
said.

"It won't cost you much to put down a well anywhere here, when you're ready," Mark Shaw said. "It's
springy land all through. Early fall's a good time to
put down a well; before fall rains set in."

He nodded and went into his own field. It was late
enough in the year now so that grass was dry by mid-
day. He would soon turn his ground, ploughing the hills
this year for he expected rain, and sowing an acre or
more of corn for he counted on a hot season. The
stock would be in the pasture before long; May the
tenth was the day. Mark Shaw walked briskly into his
yard, his left arm bent across his back to grasp the

elbow of the right which carried the basket of herbs.
He liked to see a culvert where a culvert was needed,
and the planks laid well.

One afternoon Margaret hurried along the path
through the meadows that cut off more than a half
mile of the distance between her house and the school.
She was later than usual about getting home for
Bobby Carpenter had been kept after hours for his frac-
tions; his spelling, too. Poor Bobby seemed slower than
ever now that he had two Janowskis in his class. Maria
and Ellena were not only quick; they were eager and
attentive and ambitious; they craved approval and
would work tirelessly for it; they were different in
that way, as well as others, from any other children in
the school. She hoped Louise would soon shake off
that dreadful cough. Every pupil but two had come
down with whooping cough three weeks or more ago,
and since Bun and Tom Austin had had it before, the
school had not been closed. It seemed to Margaret that
she heard more coughs than recitations lately; somebody was always running to the window and being
sick.

It was restful to be walking out here by herself, to
be going home, her footsteps on the path the only
sound except the singing of the frogs. The sky was
soft with a pale sunset and the air very still.

Suddenly Ed stepped out of the bushes before her.
She spread her hands and uttered a cry before she could
stop herself, though she knew it was Ed and that he

had no patience with such silliness. She saw his smile drop away.

"Why—" She tried to laugh. "You startled me for a minute . . . What are you doing? Fencing? I—see you've got an axe."

"I was just looking them over," Ed said shortly. He fell into step beside her, staring ahead.

"How are they?" Margaret ventured.

"Pretty stout."

His face did not relax. She tucked her hand in his arm, but he made no place for it. They walked on silently. Margaret swallowed her breath, for Ed always glanced at her sharply when he heard her sigh, but it seemed hard that she could not have a pleasant evening after a long day; it seemed as if Ed never forgave her anything, even what she could not help; she was noticing this already. She thought a month married was too soon to begin noticing things.

At last Ed said, "I guess you're tired out."

Then perhaps he was forgiving her, excusing her. She could not be sure from his tone.

"Well, it isn't the easiest thing in the world to hear lessons and erase blackboards and hold heads all at the same time," she began ruefully, half laughing.

But Ed shook off her hand. Margaret looked at him in despair. His face was taking on a surly expression, the profile hard and sharp against the sky, the skin of his forehead wrinkled.

"Yes; well. What are you doing it for then? Who *asked* you to do it? Anybody would think I couldn't keep a wife, and when I got one she had to work out to help support herself. It's something I never thought

I'd come to, having to let the neighbors believe I couldn't feed my family——"

"Oh, Ed, you know it isn't that," begged Margaret. "Everybody knows I don't have to teach. It's only just to finish out the year. You know how it was. The School Committee couldn't get anybody else that had taught before, and I *didn't* want to see Bert Forrest have to repeat his grade now he's just getting long division straightened out— Oh, Ed, you know how it is! . . . And it doesn't really tire me. I like it. . . ."

"Yes," Ed said. "You like it. You want to see that Forrest tribe learn their figures. And you want to see all them Polacks get through whooping-cough without turning themselves cross-eyed. And you want to help Mil do her spring sewing and cleaning. Besides that you want to make hot biscuit here three times a day, and mop up every track from off the floors, and God knows what else. Oh, no, you don't want much beyond reason; any man could see that."

They rounded the end of the house; Ed set off toward the barn, his axe jerking sullenly at his side. Jen, who had lived with him all her life, would have smiled to see him, but Margaret, who had lived with him only a few weeks and was his bride, sank down on her doorstep and looked after him miserably. In the barn Ed spoke curtly to his horse. Margaret hid her face on her knees with a small, hopeless sound. The dark thickened. Wind clouds hid the stars.

The kitchen clock struck six and half-past six. Margaret rose and went inside with sober steps. As she lit the lamp and tied on her apron she thought of her mother, wished her mother were alive. A mother was the only one who could be depended on to understand. Then Margaret smiled. She remembered that when she was small, she always turned to her father when her mother failed her, or seemed to fail her. That was a difficulty with having a husband; he was the only one. Whatever he said or did, it could not be admitted to anybody else; not by Margaret.

She laid the table with her prettiest cloth and the yellow plates and green glassware. She fried potatoes in thin slices, very brown, and the meat separately, as Ed preferred it. The night was damp and cool; she made cocoa with whole milk and whipped some cream to top it. She cut gingerbread in squares; that should have dabs of whipped cream on it, too, when it reached the table. Margaret liked to bring in the dessert when the rest had been finished, not as Mil and Jen did.

She paused to look at the gay table in the center of the warm, neat kitchen. She sniffed the rich, toasted smell of frying food. So far she had not failed as a housekeeper even if she was teaching. She could do both and do them well. If she did not wash so much as Mil or bake so often as Jen, still she kept clean clothes on hand and nobody went hungry. Besides, she did things *nicely,* as she had learned at normal school. The pea and onion and olive salad, now, on green glass plates in lieu of lettuce—Jen never would have thought of that. Any old bowl would have done for Jen. And Mil almost never had vegetables. That was why the children caught so many colds.

Margaret ran upstairs, feeling suddenly light and happy again. In hers and Ed's room she lit a lamp and brushed her hair before the big old maple and cherry bureau that had once been Mattie Searles's. On it were arranged many things of hers, and a few of Ed's; beyond the half-open closet door their clothes hung together. Behind her was their bed, their one window where the ruffled white curtain blew in like a dancing ghost at night; sometimes she lay awake and watched it. She liked her own house, not only this room but every room in it. She blew out the light and let her fingers trail along the wall all the way downstairs. It was sweet to be married. It would be sweet to be a mother. Already there was this possibility. She felt rich in sweetness and excited by a faint, not unpleasant fear of life; it was a wonder she could ever have been dully miserable.

When Ed came in, she stood by the stove, tall and pretty in a yellow apron and not unaware of it.

"You sit down as soon as you're washed," she said. "I have to run down cellar after the cream at the last minute. It whips so much better when it's cold."

She was flushed when she slid into her chair. Stairs always made her breathless. She smiled at Ed.

"I made some gingerbread," she said. "I hope it's the way you like it. It's Jen's recipe. It seems light and good to touch."

Ed passed his plate for macaroni and cheese, looking at her with a reluctant lighting of his eyes. Qualms had assailed him at his milking but he had beaten them off, and left his hair uncombed to irritate her because she liked him neat at table; a lock of it stuck out now like a brown horn in the middle of his forehead.

"Ed," said Margaret, holding the plate, "I wasn't going to teach after June, dear, but I'll stop now if you really want me to. I'll stop this week. I'll let them get any kind of substitute they can . . . I won't do *any-thing* you don't want me to."

He came around the table and took the plate away from her and took a spoon away and pulled her up by her hands. He was grinning now, playing with her.

"Sure of it?"

She rubbed her cheek against his chest, nodding.

"Say it."

"Yes."

"All right, then. You can finish the term, but not another day after June. You're my wife and you're going to act like it, too; see?"

"Not another day after June," repeated Margaret.

Her fingers lay quiet under his. She could feel his arms hard against her shoulders, his heart beating under her chin, his mouth grinning against her hair. It would always come to this in the end; she must do as Ed wanted and do it happily, not complaining; she must see things as he saw them; for Ed there was only one way. It seemed easy now when he brought her to it by pretending he would force her if she did not yield, but still being gentle; it was exciting while it was part of love. She shook away the thought of what it would be to live with Ed if love were lost and there were no pretenses left between them. That was nothing she need ever know.

"Not another day after June," she said again, earnestly.

VII

Mark Shaw ploughed his fields. Ed came one sunny morning, left his wagon in the shade beside the road, and led Tommy through the yard with the

clink and rumble of a whiffletree dragging behind.
Bob was brought out of the barn and joined to
Tommy by buckles and leather straps. "Get up," said
Ed. "Come." The horses plodded away, their big feet
sinking into the turf, the plough on its side at their
heels. "We'll start in here," Mark Shaw said, "and
break clean to the fence." Ed nodded. "Come. Get
up." The horses surged forward. The point of the plow
crept in, superficial at first but probing deeper. Mark
Shaw held it firm. The trail stretched back behind
him, straight and dark, a grayish darkness not rich
but faithful, running east and west over the hill. He
would plant sweet corn on the high ground, and potatoes down below. He walked with steady step, there
and back, there and back again. Ed's eye was true; he
had done well with horses from a boy; the piece
would be a hundred straight rows wide. John brought
cold water in a can and stood by while they drank it.
"Come. Get up," said Ed. The blade of the plough was
shiny now. It glittered, sliding in. John watched it fas-
cinated, and followed after, seeing the pale roots of
turned-under grass, the curling up of worms strange
to the sun. Dirt filled his shoes, and Ed's shoes, and
Mark Shaw's, seeping through their stockings, damp
and gritty to their feet. The opening of the ground
had changed the air. It had a heaviness, no longer clear
and sweet, but thick with an opulent, fertile smell.

"My, it's going to be a great big piece this year,"
thought Jen, glancing out. "They'll be hungry enough
when it comes dinner time."

She cut dough into dumplings for her soup.

George ploughed alone. He always did. When he
helped his neighbors he wanted pay for it, not their

help in return. He held the plow with the reins looped around his neck, directing the horse with a pull now and then, and with his voice. If the edges of his piece were not quite straight, it did not matter; the stuff would grow as well one way as another He had had enough of this trying for straight lines when he was a boy at home, before Ed grew old enough to drive the horses; his father took too much pains with everything. The horse panted, lingered, stopped. George gave her her head and sat down under a tree to fill his pipe. Ploughing was too much for one horse, and Kate was old; her teeth were getting bad. Kate would not last much longer, and he ought to have a new horse, ought to have a pair, but where they would come from was a question. There was no money to be made by farming these days; a man showed himself a fool to try it.

George leaned against the trunk of the tree, resting on the small of his back, smoking. Here he was, thirty years old, with ten years of his life gone into this farm. The land had been run out when he took it, and it was not much better now. He needed more stock to fertilize it, but he had no money for more stock, and if he owned more stock he could not tend it; he had all the chores he could get through with now. His father said a farmer could not afford to spend time off his place, but it took money to pay doctor's bills, buy shoes and tools and gasoline. It was all the farm could do to run itself and feed them and pay up the interest on the mortgage.

"Let's see. When is it that comes due again?" George wondered, pressing down the tobacco in his pipe.

He glanced briefly toward the house. Mil knew

about such things and kept the figures. It seemed to
him a woman's business, doling out the money here
and there. He could not see why it was some men
took such a pride in keeping what they had. Like Ed,
now; Ed said his money was his own, but if a woman
wanted some, she had only to ask. George puffed contentedly; he had no time to bother with the figuring;
Mil would know. She would not cheat him either; she
knew better than that. He stretched and studied the
sun, wondering whether it would pay to start the
ploughing again until he had had his dinner.

"George! George! . . . GEORGE!"

It was Mil calling. She stood in the back yard with
the baby in her arms, waving something white over
her head. George crawled to his feet and went toward
her without answering. Something was the matter or
she would not have called him, but whatever it was,
he could not raise his voice to shout that distance; only
a woman could manage that. It must be the baby had
swallowed something, but if she had, George could
not help it.

"George, hurry up! Hurry up, quick!"

Mil was running to meet him, stumbling over the
stones George never had time to pick out of his grass,
the baby held carelessly under her arm. It was not the
baby, then. It might be little George. Big George's
breath quickened; not the boy; if it was the boy Mil
should not have left him to run off down here. Whatever it was, there was nothing he could do. Mil ought
to know it.

"George, *can't* you hurry a mite? One of the cows
is down,—Flossy. She was running after her calf and
she—slipped—and she's—down. She's hooking—and—

and plunging—awfully. I—I don't know—I think her leg's broke, George——"

Mil's face was gray with fright and exhaustion. Her hair had shaken off its pins and streamed down her back, a long, thin, dark wisp. She half-sat, half-fell against the side of the hill and tried mechanically to still the shrieking baby, her eyes on George's face.

"Broke!" George snarled. "You always think the worst. You're always looking for trouble."

He hurried fast enough now, or as fast he could; he was getting too fat for speed. Mil watched him disappear, and then sat on for a minute, opening her dress to the baby. It might be he was right. She tried to forget how the brown young cow had looked there, digging up the turf with her hoofs and horns. It sometimes took a creature a long time to right herself if she fell at a disadvantage. Mil rocked the baby gently, smoothing the bib away from the damp pink chin. The sun was warm and bright and the furrows George had turned looked like good soil; he had not planted here for years; it might bring a big crop for a change. She rose, still nursing the baby, and took the reins to drive old Kate home. The crabapple tree at the corner of the wall was full of buds, she noticed as she passed; those apples made fine jelly if she could ever manage to get them cooked and strained and into glasses. Down across the flats she could see the flag waving cheerfully over Margaret's schoolhouse. She ought to get out oftener, she thought; it was bad for anybody staying in so much. As a girl, she never expected the worst, the way George said she did now. She had not expected to die when Esther was born, but before this little Vera came she had been

sure she would. Only a woman who had been shut up
in a kitchen all winter would think a cow had to
break her leg just because she fell.

George was in the shed when Mil went by, standing
on a chopping block and reaching up overhead. She
stopped.

"George—what is it—what are you after——"

"It's broke all right," said George grimly. "It's broke
all right."

Mil took a fresh grip on the baby, and on the reins.
A good cow was worth a hundred dollars, and Flossy
was the best one they had.

"Well, what can you do?" Mil asked. "What—can
you do?"

George stepped down from the chopping block with
his gun in his hand. He ran his thumb along the barrel
to wipe off the cobwebs and jammed a yellow cartridge
into the chamber.

"I can shoot her," he muttered. "She'll never amount
to nothing any more. That's the way a man gets
served, best he can manage——"

He went out. Mil stood still until she heard the re-
port of the gun. Then she had all she could do to hold
old Kate, who did not like the sound nor the sinister
smell; it almost seemed she knew what lay ahead of
horses when their teeth went bad.

"Whoa," said Mil, "whoa, girl, whoa. Whoa, whoa,
whoa."

She did not know what they would do now, what
would happen next. The three cows that were left
would not make nearly enough butter to supply her
customers, and if she lost them she would never get
them back; all the foreigners coming into the town,

the French and Polish, were too eager for butter customers and would sell too cheap. If George took
money to buy another cow he could not make this pay-
ment on the mortgage as it came due; with only three
to milk, he could not meet the next one. Anybody
could plan and plan, but there had to be something
besides plans; there had to be money, and that there
never was, not enough to use for getting more; at
least, not on the George Shaw place. The frosts came
earlier here than anywhere else, unless George's stuff
was not so forward as it ought to be; time and again
they lost cucumbers, squashes, green beans, and tomatoes before they had taken a good taste. The lightning struck their barn and if it had not been empty of
hay, it would have burned to the ground. A plague
killed off their pigs one fall and the very next spring
the hens ran in circles and died. Now the best cow had
broken her leg.

"I'm so thankful you shot her, George," she called
when she saw him, "instead of any other way." She
had not known this thought was in her head. Small,
hot tears ran down her face. "She was an awful handsome little calf. I used to hold Georgie on her back.
We've got a picture of them, Margaret took."

"Well, look out," said George. "Look out of the way.
If you can't put up the horse, I'll have to. I've got my
hands full all right, bleeding and dressing all that meat
here almost into hot weather. I guess it'll be a pretty
time of year when I get the planting done."

It always was, but Mil did not think of it. She unhitched old Kate from the plough with one hand and
led her into the barn. George must have had a feeling
for Flossy, she thought, or he would have knocked her

in the head; or maybe she had been struggling too
much for him to get near to her. Well, it did not do
for a man to have too many feelings. There had to be
the kind a man was to deal with anything like this.
She glanced gratefully at George's wide, thick shoulders bent over the tool chest in the shed, but she
moved rather faster as she passed him. The baby was
crying; she needed to be fed and have her diaper
changed. Georgie, awakened from his morning nap,
was howling, too; the gun must have frightened him.
It would be a job now to keep him from noticing
what he was too young to understand.

"What's the matter, Georgie? Stop that! You didn't
hear anything. It was a bad dream. Come downstairs
and see little sister. She's crying too. She's hungry. If
you're hungry you can have some milk. Come along
down."

But when he came she gave him a cookie instead. A
little boy ought to have all the milk he could drink;
she knew that from her magazine; but milk meant
butter, and butter was money. With only three cows
in the barn, she must be as saving as she could; not
that it would make much difference. She was tired of
working and sacrificing for weeks to save ten dollars,
and then losing ten times that in the instant that a
cow broke a leg. Drearily she began to beat up water
biscuit; the children would like them as well, for they
were crusty, but they did not have the goodness in
them.

"You stay in the sitting-room," she ordered little
George harshly. "If you come out here, I'll whip you.
Now don't you dare!"

If he came into the kitchen he would see from the

back window his father cutting a slash in Flossy's sleek yellow neck and letting her blood run out and stain the grass.

That night as Jen sat at supper she heard a car go past. Her eyes followed it, from time to time, until its headlights had crossed the swamp, disappeared in the walnut grove, and flashed out again on the hill near Ed's house. She wondered who it might be; there was not much travel over the lane at night. Later, as she sat by the window rocking, she watched it on its way back and saw it turn into the yard. By then Mark Shaw was sitting on the step in the cool of the evening.

"Hullo, pa."

"Hullo, George. Well. Nice night, ain't it?"

The car door banged. George came up and stood near his father, his foot on the step, his hands in his pockets.

"I don't know. I ain't took time to notice. I never see anything beat it the way a man has to keep going twenty hours a day to get together something to eat. I can't make out what I'm hanging around here for anyway. With all the chances there is for an able-bodied man in the cities where he can get big pay for half a day's work anybody's a fool to keep at this."

George shifted his weight from his right foot to his left.

"I just been telling Ed, we're a pair of them all right. Not another young fellow in the place that growed up the time we did but what's off somewhere getting together something without killing themselves. There ain't no money around here any more; everybody knows that. They've got to do something for the farmers or they'll be going hungry in the cities before long. Nobody's going to stay out here and drag themselves to death for nothing. Look what Fred Tarbox down at the village gets for just handling over a pound of butter. I sell it to him for thirty-two cents and he sells it out for forty. Eight cents he gets just for passing it from me to somebody else, and see what a farmer has to put into it. Buy the cow and feed and grain and milk her, and make out the butter and cart it down——"

"Steady customers is better," Mark Shaw said.

George sat down on the step beside his father.

"I lost a cow to-day," he said abruptly.

Mark Shaw turned his face toward his son.

"The brown one with the light head," George said. "Best milker I had. Three year old. Fell and broke her leg and I had to shoot her . . . Oh, that's the way it goes. I tell you they've got to do something for the farmers or there'll be trouble. We don't get paid to take these chances. They've got to make some laws. They think they know so much out there to Washington, they'd better get their heads together——"

"Where was she?" Mark Shaw asked.

"My cow? She was out in the back field. I had to turn them in there for a week or two 'til the grass got up in the pasture. I'm about out of hay. That's the way it goes. Nothing lasts over from one season to the next. They don't take account of how things are changing. It ain't like it was when men of your age was getting a start."

Mark Shaw looked straight before him, a hand on each knee.

"It's always been so that a man ain't no business turning cattle into the field," he said. "Pasture's the

place for cattle. There has to *be* hay enough to last
'til pasturing time, some way or 'nother. That's a law
they ain't got to make in Washington. It was made
before they got there. Mowing ground is soft this time
of year and cattle ain't got no business on it anyway."

"You want to lay the blame on me," George said.
"Well, I want you to know I ain't to blame for the
weather. Last year was a dry year and hay didn't grow.
You know hay didn't grow last year. And was I going
to let the animals get thin as rails waiting, just on the
chance a cow might slip and fall? I tell you, they've
got to make some allowance for things like this.
They've got to fix it so the farmer don't have to stand
his loss alone. Now, take that cow, worth a hundred
dollars. I'll get thirty for the meat, I figure. That leaves
seventy dollars, and I've got to stand it. I tell you
there's got to be some laws. It can't go on this way
with all the prices up but ours. They've got to take
account of farmers."

"A cow that's in a barnyard twice a week through
the winter never broke a leg when she was turned out
in the spring," Mark Shaw said. "It's leaving them tied
up so long that does it. And them that cut their hay
when it was ripe last summer had enough to last them
through. It wouldn't wait 'til the state road was built
to Gypsum, though, the grass wouldn't."

He did not doubt George was right that farmers
should be helped, but he knew they never would be.
There was no help but hard work and painstaking
and strength and willingness. Without these a man
was not a farmer. Mark Shaw sat with his hands on
his knees, looking out into the dark, smelling his

ground and the dressing he had spread on it and the
wet leaves and the split wood of his pile.

"You're bound to lay the blame on me," George said
sullenly.

He gathered himself up and went down to the car,
cranked it, slammed the door, and rode away. Mark
Shaw did not call him back, but sat on in the dark
with the frog-song buzzing in his ears; and Jen sat at
the kitchen window behind him, rocking quietly.

"It's too bad they'll lose their customers," Jen said at
last.

"We can spare them butter enough for that," her
father said. "I have some left over for the stores every
week."

"It wouldn't be the same," Jen said. "Mil has her
ways of making out. Customers want the same."

Mark Shaw knew this. The townspeople who
bought of George wanted butter of such a deep yellow
color it must be stained with a coloring bean, and they
wanted it strong with salt so that it had no butter taste
in their mouths. They would not like Cora Shaw's
clear, pale squares with only a dash of salt to bring out
the flavor. If George carried Cora Shaw's butter instead of Mil's, his customers would begin to buy of the
Polish and French farmers who hawked their produce
along the streets like rag-peddlers, though Doctor Mor-
rison and the Fairlees bought Cora Shaw's butter and
praised it well; it was her pride that the best people in
the village bought it and would have no one else's.
George sold mostly at the little green houses near the
shoeshop, but the money there was as good.

"And any way you look at it," Mark Shaw said, "he
can't make out on a place that size without four cows."

The others were in bed, Mrs. Shaw to rest her head and eyes, Bun for punishment, and John because it was his time. The kitchen was neat and dim. The squeak of Jen's rocker came slower and slower and stopped. She sat still with her hands folded in her lap.

"He'll have to have a cow from here," Mark Shaw said. "We can spare the one-horned one."

"It's Lois May's," said Jen. "Ma gets the money from her for Lois May. It seems too bad."

"He ought to have let them out to exercise," Mark Shaw said. "I told him often. I could have let him had some hay, too, if he'd asked. He didn't need to turn them out so early."

"She'll likely have to come home," said Jen. "She'll take it awful hard, to break off now. I don't know what ma'll say."

"It's just to tide him over," her father answered. "I'll tell him that. It's just to tide him over."

He rose, stood for a minute drawing up his shoulders, and went toward the barn. A little later he came in through the shed and sat down on the end of the couch to take off his shoes. It was full dark now. He and Jen showed in the room only as shadows against the windows. He felt his way to the chamber door and climbed the stairs slowly.

Jen stayed in her chair, rocking again. She could see the stars coming out over the silent house, a new moon down in a corner of the sky, the outline of the pump and the ash tree and the end of the barn. The frogs were still singing as if nothing had happened. It was strange that because George had worked away so much last winter, because the snow in the barnyard had been so deep it would have taken him a long time to shovel it clear, Lois May must come home from the city. Everything reached so far and touched so many people. Jen heard a stir of talk upstairs, growing higher and higher. She sighed and lit the lamp and stood by the table sorting the contents of the paper rack that hung behind the door. A knob turned. There were shuffling steps on the stairs. Mrs. Shaw came down in her white cotton nightdress, with unlaced shoes on her feet, her hair still pinned up as she wore it during the day but loose and sagging.

"Did you hear?" she asked. "Do you know what he says he's going to do? He says he's going to give that cow to George, after he give it to me for Lois May and I been counting on it. I've worked and slaved and saved to make a few pounds of butter fill out my egg money and keep her where she is . . . I want her to amount to something. I don't want her back here hanging around. Nobody else cares what happens to her. She ain't got nobody to lift a hand but her mother. Alls anybody else thinks of is farms and farming and cattle and seed and *dung* . . . It's going to drive me crazy! I've stood it as long as I can, I tell you! I've got a few rights. He may think I'll stand everything but I won't. What's George Shaw? Lazy, fat, long-tongued, empty-headed—your father says it's just to tide him over. Well, I need every cent that cow will make to get the money ready to pay the school bill for the three months that begin in June. What's going to tide me over? And you know as well as I do, he'll never manage to get him another cow, not as long's he's got this one!"

"I know it's awful hard, ma," Jen said. "I wish you wouldn't take it so. I know it's awful hard."

Mrs. Shaw leaned against the table, clutching the nightdress together over her flat breast. Her eyes were red and swollen from pain, her mouth deeply indented without the support of her teeth, her face crumpled and dark.

"What's the reason Lois May and I have got to pay for George Shaw's slovenliness?" she cried. "He's nothing to us. Why don't your father give up one of his own cows if he's so willing? What does it have to be mine for? He must think I'm awful easy——"

"You know," said Jen. "You know he can't spare but one off our own place. We have to keep our customers, too. He needs what the rest bring in to keep us going here. It's the only way. He don't want to, but George's got little young ones, ma; you've got to think of them."

"I've got to think of everything but what I want, have I? It's always been so. It's what I want don't count, for all I work my fingers to the bone. It's putting me out of my head, I tell you. I can't stand it any longer. Something will have to be done. . . . I can't *stand* it!"

She pushed by Jen and went as fast as she could through the entry and across the porch, her shoe laces catching on the rough boards, and her nightdress blowing out behind her in the dark. Her steps were heavy, blind, on the turf of the yard.

"Ma," Jen exclaimed. "Ma!"

She started after hurriedly, and then paused. Softly she closed the outside door and turned out the light. It would not do for Mrs. Janowski or another passing neighbor to stand looking up here, wondering why the lamp burned so late, and then to notice a white

figure in the orchard. She crept upstairs as quietly as
she could, not to wake the children, and crouched
by the window in her room. From there she saw her
stepmother standing by the garden fence, bent over
it, shaken with crying. Even the sound reached Jen,
a dry choking. Jen rested her forehead against the
cool sill. It seemed more than was called for to take
things so hard. Lois May would not go hungry if she
did come home; it was not so bad here, with summer
coming on, for anyone; there was nothing to cry
about. She heard Mrs. Shaw coming in slowly, dragging one foot after the other up the stairs.

"Did you get chilled through, ma?" she whispered.
"Shall I build up a little fire and fix you a hot drink?"

"No. Leave me alone," the woman said. She looked
very small in the full nightdress. "Leave me alone.
That's all I want."

She went into Mark Shaw's room and closed the
door. Jen knew her father was asleep for she heard
him snoring. She placed her clothing neatly over a
chair, one piece smooth above another, lay down on
the bed, and fell asleep herself, her hand under her
firm, round cheek.

In the morning Mark Shaw drove up to George's
place with the one-horned cow tied to the back of his
wagon.

VIII

"I hope you'll plant a good lot of them Kentucky
Wonders," Jen said. "That's the best bean, I believe,
ever I cooked."

"I'm saving seven rows for them," her father answered. "And poles all cut for them to run on, too."

"Lowe's Champion is fine, though, for a bush bean."

"You can't beat Lowe's Champion much, I always said."

Jen stopped in the shed to reach into the bags of seed potatoes her father had been quartering through the last week. They were withered and spongy, but in them she could see the hard, pinkish-brown fruit that they would bear. From this bag would come the round, red Pine Brooks Seedlings, and from those bags the Early Rose, long, crisp white potatoes with pink eyes. The Shaws liked the Early Rose the best of all. But somewhere here there was seed for the Late Rose, too, and the Green Mountain, and the Gold Coin. It made an interest in the winter to try one kind and then another, to boil this and bake that, to see which kept its flavor and texture best and made good eating in the spring. "What potatoes are these?" Mark Shaw would ask. "I got them in the arch," Jen would say. "They're the Gold Coin. Gold Coin's a good potato." But they liked the Early Rose best, for all around.

"Did you save any seed of them big potatoes ma brought down from Kezar Falls that time?" Jen asked, hearing her father behind her.

"I planted them yesterday," Mark Shaw said. "I let Ed have some, too. We don't want to let them run out. Nobody else ever raised that kind around here."

He loaded two of the bags and some wooden measures and a hoe on his wheelbarrow and called to John. Jen stood in the shed door and watched them go across the yard and through the bars and up over the hill. None of the other children had ever been so faithful as John to the spring work, not one; John had something in him. It might not be that he helped much this year, but it was good for him to get the feel of the sun on his back and the loose dirt under his feet; and next year this time he would be six, and after that, seven.

"The ground is covered with dandelions," thought Jen. "I must get me a knife and pail and dig a good mess for dinner."

She liked to walk through the grass in the morning, and reach down into the roots of things, tenderly and gratefully, to get food that cost nothing and was fresh and damp with dew. There was nothing better than wild greens in the spring.

Toward the middle of May, Margaret spent a Saturday in the field with Ed. It was not usual in Shaw women to work out-of-doors, but Margaret had insisted and Ed indulged her. Down under the hill not even the chimney tops of their house were visible to them, nor the ridgepole of their barn. It was almost as if they had no buildings, but were a peasant couple travelled out to the solitude of their own plot of land. The lilac bushes by the fence were budded and the plum trees in full bloom. Strawberries had blossomed all along the edges of the ploughed piece. A bobolink sang in the marsh. Margaret walked first, in a short plaid gingham dress with no sleeves, dropping corn, and Ed followed, dropping beans. She could feel him, tall and steady, behind her. Sometimes he spoke. "There goes a bluebird. See him? Over the hill now." After a few rows he set down his pail of beans and began covering what they had planted, with the crisp sound of metal moving the soil. "Tired, puss?" He

asked her. She shook her head but he put his arm
around her while they stood for a minute resting, and
she leaned against him. "No, Ed. Just happy." Ed
grinned. This was life as he liked it, everything simple
and in its place.

They ate their lunch in the shade of a walnut tree
on the side hill. Margaret had brought biscuit with
home-cured ham between, hard-boiled eggs, and cake,
and sweetened tea in glass bottles. When they had
finished, Ed lay with his head in Margaret's lap and
she fingered his thick, damp hair, smoothing it back
from his forehead where his hat had stuck it down.
She felt at ease with him out here, more than she did
in the house, much more than before they had been
married. She knew him now, and all his ways, and
how to please him; it was not always easy to do, but
she knew how. Ed lay relaxed, his hand unthinking
against her, his mind wandering over this which
stretched out for acres on all sides of his body and
which belonged to him. He felt the sticks and stones
under his shoulders, but they were not so hard as they
would have been to another; they were his. He felt
the softness of the grass, too, and knew that it would
grow, that he would fill his barn with it by and by
and the yellow sides of Jersey cows become sleek and
round.

"Sing me something, why don't you?" he asked.

Margaret flushed.

"Somebody might hear," she said. "I couldn't."

"Say one of your poems then."

"Oh, I couldn't."

He lifted himself on his elbows and grasped her
wrists.

"Say one!"
She said the first lines she could think of.

> *"The lark's on the wing,*
> *The snail's on the thorn——"*

At the end she added, "I'm not *sure* that's right, Ed!"

"It's good enough," Ed said. "I know what it means. That's what it's for, I guess, as much as anything else."

"I guess so," Margaret answered shyly.

It was good to have Ed speak of poetry. She sat looking down at him, feeling him heavy and hot beside her, and wondered how women told men when there were going to be children, and what men did then. She had never talked with Mil of such things, for Mil had a bitter, shame-faced way about them, and all that Margaret knew she had read in books. It did not say in the books how a woman told her husband she expected to have a child, especially when she was not sure. Except in story books where the wife whispered, "I think I'm going to have a baby, darling. Are you glad?" Margaret could not speak to Ed like that; she would feel queer. The word "baby" had too silly a sound to be said to Ed, and she never called him "darling." To Ed it would have to be told as if it did not matter; but it did, and so she could not say it at all. She did not mind. To-day she was not in the least afraid. She felt strong and capable out here. Bearing another Shaw would be a fine thing to do. If he came as she expected she could bring him into the field next spring, and let him lie on a blanket in the sun while his father planted corn and beans in hills and covered them. She felt proud now that he had happened so soon; she must be a natural mother.

"Well," said Ed. "This won't do the planting."

She walked back beside him to the piece and they worked steadily. She would be careful, she thought. She would eat the right things. She would nurse her baby and keep him pink and round. Her children would never go as Mil's went so much, with dirty hair and uncut nails and ragged stockings; she was thinking already of more than one, of a boy, and a girl, and another boy. "I can finish it Monday, if the weather's fine," Ed said. They stood looking back over what they had done. Margaret wondered if even now the kernels she had planted in the morning might be beginning to stir. If the soil was good they ought to be, she thought proudly. They went up the hill side by side, Ed pushing the wheelbarrow. The grass was tall enough to brush Margaret's ankles as she walked. Carefully they followed the track they had made coming down, not to leave two paths. The sun set in a burst of color as it had the night before and would the next night. It was a stretch of clear weather just now. A whippoorwill sang in the lilac bush.

IX

"No, now don't you leave off, ma," Jen said when a fish peddler drove into the yard. "I'll go. . . . None to-day, Mr. Robinson, but you might stop next time if you have a nice haddock just fresh caught . . . No, don't you leave off for anything, ma, if you think there's chance of getting them done."

Mrs. Shaw had been at work for days now, dyeing

sheeting yellow and binding lengths of it with orange
and white checked gingham once intended for a Sunday apron for herself. These were to be hung at the
windows of Lois May's room, and the best white
woven spread put on the bed. The room was freshly
cleaned already and a new rag rug laid before the
bureau, the pink wash bowl mended, and two sepia-
tinted pictures, one of Cupid awake and one of Cupid
asleep, hung on the walls. The pictures had been Mil's
contribution, sent over by Esther the day before, and
leaving bare-looking spots on the faded, water-streaked
walls of Mil's own bedroom. "I wish I could do something more," Mil wrote on blue-lined paper. "It's such
a shame, poor young one." Mil wore a harried,
humbled look these days whenever she saw any of the
Shaws, as if she must take the blame for the guilt
George denied.

"It's awful handsome, ma," Jen said.

"It ain't much," said Mrs. Shaw, "put up against
what she's had. She's wrote about them rooms of
Lize's, every one with curtains at the windows, and
some of them silky stuff."

"I guess it's nice," Jen said. "Must be they can't see
out much though."

She liked to see out.

"It's the way folks do now," said Mrs. Shaw. "Folks
that is anybody."

There was to be a company supper to welcome
Lois May. Ed and Margaret would come, and George
and Mil and the children. Jen had a piece of beef
already boiled, waiting to be fricasseed, and she planned
for smothered potato with onion in it, biscuit dropped
from a teaspoon to make them small and pointed on

the top, well beaten sponge cake, and ice cream full of walnut meats; and Mil would bring a can of her sweet mixed pickle, which Lois May had always fancied. It seemed too bad she must leave the school before she had finished, but there was no other way; Ed and Lize had done what they could in the beginning; a frantic letter from Mrs. Shaw to Ralph had brought no reply; so Lois May would be home now in a few days. To Jen it was as simple as a storm or falling on an icy step or catching measles; she had no capacity for resenting it; there was left only to make Lois May's coming as pleasant as possible, and so she planned for smothered potato and sponge cake and walnut ice cream, and made Lois May's room clean and bright. It was she who had suggested the yellow curtains. And she thought of taking Bun into her room from now on. Lois May would be used to a bed to herself.

Cleaning vegetables in the sinkroom, she sang cheerfully. It was the twenty-ninth of May with danger of frost past, and her tomato plants already set out in the ground. The crops were growing rank. Strawberries should ripen in another week or two; the banks of ditches would hang red. Woods berries had blossomed thick, blueberries and raspberries, and anybody willing to go into the swamps would pick a bushel of huckleberries in a day. There were "on" years and "off" years; this was an "on" year.

"So go to sleep, my ba-aby, my ba-aby," sang Jen.

From the open sinkroom window she could see the Janowskis at work on their planted piece. Stan had ploughed very nearly all of one field six weeks ago or more, and since then it seemed to Jen she never looked out without noticing three or four or five men, women, and children busy there. It was strange to see a woman and girls in the field except for a bit of cultivating or to get green stuff fresh for dinner, but with so many at work on it, the Janowski piece was not only the largest in the neighborhood, but as smooth, as straight-rowed, as well along, as tended-looking as Mark Shaw's smaller one. The Old Joe place was turning out to be a real farm after many years of lying idle; people stared at it as they rode past; Mark Shaw watched its progress with level, approving eyes.

"So go to sleep——"

Bun came in from school, bringing the mail, a letter for Mrs. Shaw, and the newspaper.

"There, this is from Lois May, poor young one. I suppose it says when we should expect her," Mrs. Shaw said fretfully. "Now I should think Mil and George would feel fine to see her back here. I should certainly think they would. Bernice, couldn't you get a pail of cool water from the well? My mouth and throat's terrible parched."

Jen sniffed the air made sweet by the drying swath of grass her father had cut to make a road to the vegetable garden. The apple trees were now in full leaf and full bloom, but Jen could still see through them the tops of two slate-colored gravestones settled at a slant into the lower corner of the field beside the lane. She could not read the names engraved on them, but she knew what they were. Joseph Watson, 1820-1891, and James Watson, son of Joseph and Hannah Watson, 1844-1863. The grave of Hannah Watson lay beside her husband's and because she had died last, she had no marker, unless the pine tree growing there might count as one. To-morrow two men would drive up and leave a basket of flowers and a flag for Joseph because he had fought in the Civil War, and for James because he had died on his way home from it, but they would not have anything for Hannah because she had only identified her son James one hot summer day on the platform of North Derwich station, and raised all the food her husband ate for the twenty years he sat in a chair in her kitchen, and done washings for Mrs. Hale to buy monuments for them at the end. But the flowers would die in the boxes; even if Jen found time to go down and set out the pansy plants in the ground, stray cows were sure to eat them off before the summer was over; and the Forrest children would take the flags to play with. Nothing would interfere with the tree.

"Well, now, here's news!" cried Mrs. Shaw. "Here's a piece of news for you, Jen!"

She came hurrying to the sinkroom door, trailing yellow cloth behind her. Her eyes were shot through with triumph, her face tight with satisfaction; she looked smaller than ever.

"Lois May's got a job!"

Jen put down her knife.

"A job!"

"Yes, ma'am, she's got a job! Now ain't that a young one, I want to know? You can't keep that kind down so easy! ... She says here she and Lize have been hunting ever since she heard I couldn't send the money, and Tuesday night she got a chance at a hotel switchboard. Fifteen dollars a week, and goes to work Monday morning. Now what do you think of that?"

"It's fine," Jen said. "My, that's fine."

"Ain't that some of it?" insisted Mrs. Shaw. "To get out and get herself a job where she won't be dependent on anybody? She'll get somewheres in this world, and you needn't think she won't. Spunk, that's what she's got, when she's put to it; all her father's folks was just the same."

"It was Lize, being mad again, got her that job," thought Jen. "Minnie Foote spunk found that job, if I don't miss my guess." Aloud she said, "I don't suppose, then, she'll get home?"

"She says here she won't," Mrs. Shaw answered, her fingers twitching at the letter. "I want to see her awfully, but I can't say I'm disappointed any. She's got now where she can show folks they can't hit out at her so easy. She'll go ahead fast, you see if she don't, and some that's took her needs so light will see the day they'll wish they hadn't . . . I'd just like to have seen her go in asking for that job!"

"I'll bet she walked airy," Jen laughed.

Bun came in out of breath, slopping water from her pail.

"What'd you say, ma? Ma, 'd you say Lois May wasn't coming home? 'D you say she wasn't coming home?"

"No, she ain't coming home," Mrs. Shaw said. "Your sister ain't so easy beat. She's got herself a job without an education——"

But Bun was not listening. She turned tragic eyes on Jen.

"Then won't we have the ice cream?" she asked mournfully. "Nor sponge cake?"

"Yes, we will," exclaimed Jen with sudden resolve. "We'll have a big supper just the same, and George and Ed will come, and their folks."

"I'm awful glad this turned out so," she thought, "for Mil's sake. It's always George gets them into trouble, and then she takes the brunt."

"I should think I could have up the curtains just the same," Bun was saying, "now they're about made. How would it *hurt?*" She put on her sweet expression. "*I* like pretty curtains, too."

Her mother looked at her in surprise, her face softened. It seemed that Bun was growing older; she might in time have nice ways like Lois May's.

"Well, there," she agreed. "You can. I don't know who's got a better right."

"Whoopee!" Bun said, relaxing. "And Jen, will you make the fricassee, just the same?"

SUMMER

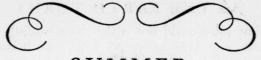

SUMMER

I

THERE were two weeks now when nothing broke the even, steady progress of the days. Every morning the cows were milked a few minutes earlier than the morning before, for Mark Shaw rose by the sun, and old Lina's sides were more distended for she had not given down for several weeks and would come in at mid-month with her seventh calf; every one so far a son, poor Lina, bound to leave her with her bag still heavy for him. The chickens had longer necks and legs and stiff, new feathers patching their bare bodies; Jen remarked it as she fed them, cracked corn instead of warm mush now. After breakfast the men found the corn each day grown taller in the fields, taking on a darker green; Mark Shaw's and Ed's, which had been planted when the white oak leaf was the size of a mouse's ear, would reach knee-high by the Fourth, which was as it should be. Peas trembled on the edge of flowering, slid into bloom and passed this stage, and pods set on. The grass was tall enough now to lodge in a rain, but no rain came, and Ed taught John how to hold a wide blade between his

hands but John could not make the whistling sound
Ed made; next year he would. The lilacs blossomed,
the syringa bush at the corner of the house, the sweet-
william and flowering almond in the garden. Every
night the air was sweet, and every night dark came
later, more birds shared the business of settling in
their nests, the leaves were bigger on the ash and
maple trees, making a stouter sound when the wind
blew through them.

In the afternoons Margaret went into the field behind the house and picked strawberries. They grew
thick there by the fence and along the ditches, places
where it did not break the grass for her to walk; in
the corner by the pasture the small, wild plants made
a bed as if they had been planted, and she could sit
down and pick quietly, holding back the leaves with
one hand and snapping off the berries with the other,
dropping them into a blue-banded lard pail.

"I wonder if I ought to eat them," she thought,
"now."

She decided against it, though she was feeling better
than since the first of April; quite well, in fact. Sometimes she wondered whether it was wise to make all
her decisions for herself, when this was her first time,
but no one else knew of her condition. She turned
away the word condition; nobody knew yet that she
was with child. Nor was that the way to say it. There
seemed to be no way. The thing itself was so sweet,
so secret, so terrifying, that human beings had no word
for it. There were no words for the grass, except to
tell its color, nor for the sun except that it was hot and
bright; and it was more than that; the berries knew,

lying here all day and all night while spring went by
and summer came on, but they had no words.

Margaret did not think all these things, but only
dimly felt them. She thought that it would be fine if
she could have her child in warm weather, and be
out here alone in the sun where nobody would know
when she cried out; if she could wash it herself in the
pool of the brook under the hill and wrap it in a little
blanket she had brought and take it out to where Ed
was at work and say laughing, "Here is something
for you." She did not pity the Indian women who only
stopped beside the trail and had their young and then
went on; she envied them; but that might be because
she did not know. In any case, there was no use in
these thoughts, for her baby would be born at Christmas time, and even Indian women, she supposed, must
have stayed by a fire in the winter. She thought of all
the things that she had sent away for and had ready,
the blankets, the silk-and-wool bands, the funny little
shirts and socks, a brush and comb and a feathery
powder puff in a blue celluloid box; and she thought
of what she would name it, if it was a girl. But she did
not believe it would be a girl. She laughed aloud, and
the sound frightened her.

Early in June came the last day of school. On that
day there was no studying. The children did not
arrive until eleven o'clock, and by then the schoolroom
had been turned into a party place, lavishly strung
with yellow and white crepe paper and decorated with
buttercups and daisies. A program of poems to be
recited and songs to be sung lay in the exact center
of each desk. The children, dressed in their best, stood
on Margaret's platform and made their contributions,

Bun's voice too loud and her manner too boisterous for the occasion, and Kathie Forrest whispering so softly of "vacation" and "summer days" and "birds" that no one could hear more than the key words. John and little George and Kathie's brother and the two smallest Janowskis had come as guests and sat in the front seats hushed with wonder at witnessing what took place in School. Margaret awarded a pocket dictionary to Manuel who had not been absent all the term, and another to Bun who had not been tardy, and a picture of two gray kittens with blue ribbons around their necks to Betty who wrote the best hand. Then they sang a closing song and went out in the yard to eat their lunches together and finish with the ice cream Margaret had made and Ed had left, packed in ice, in the woodshed on his way to market in the morning.

"Well, now, I guess that's all for this year," Margaret said. "Pick up your papers and put on your hats and get in line. Remember you're going to sing 'Vacation time is here again,' and go on singing and keeping step until by looking over your shoulders you can't even see the flag any more!"

But they were slow to do her bidding, and whispered together and ran aimlessly behind the building.

"Come, children; come."

"Well," sputtered Bun, reappearing with a package under her arm, "well—we got something for you. Here!"

She stood a little before the others, her face hot with embarrassment, her braids frowsy from being tossed about in the heat, her new teeth very large in her small mouth.

"You said we shouldn't ever give you nothing that—
that cost," she was panting, "and we didn't. It never
cost anything. Nobody even knows about it but us.
There's one from every one of us, every single one.
And I expect—I expect you'll want to keep them because—they're—very—good. They're what we thought
when we—when we—thought—about—*you!*"

She thrust the package into Margaret's hands with
energy, and because the fingers that had tied it were
not used to tying, the outside paper fell apart and
dozens of scribbled-over scraps showered to the
ground. Margaret knelt swiftly to gather them into
her hands and saw the bits of writing that she knew,
Manuel's so big and blundering, Kathie's faint and
small, Betty's even as the copybook's, Harry's with the
b's and k's all made like h's; and she felt the yellow
roughness of school paper and the crumpled stickiness
of everything children handle. "My Teacher," they
had written. "My Teacher——"

"Why, this is lovely," Margaret said. "Nothing could
have pleased me so much." She felt as if she might
cry. "Now get into line, children. 'Va-ca-a-tion ti-ime is
here again—' Mark time! . . . March!"

When one group had disappeared around the turn
and the other under the hill, she sat down on the
step in the afternoon sunshine. Around the building
ran a well-beaten path where sorrel would grow before
September when boys would come back to race along
it and girls to walk arm-in-arm and tell their secrets;
and Margaret would not be here then. Her lap was
full of the writing of children she would not teach
again. She might never turn into this yard until she

came to bring a son of her own. There was nothing of
the work left for her except with the child who was
coming and he seemed suddenly long on the way. She
opened Harry's blotted offering.

"My teacher can sing
Evrything.
She hrings
Pitures of things
For us to see.
She is very very very
Good to me."

"I got a dictionary," sang Bun, bursting into the
kitchen at home. "Lookut. Isn't it swell? That's for
never being tardy. Not even once!"

"Well, I should say," Jen agreed. "Now, that's handsome, don't you say so, ma? . . . Well, John, you old
step-and-fetch-it, how did you behave at school?"

"He was good," said Bun. "He was fine." She
beamed at her brother. "All of the rest of them talked
out loud but John never."

"They give something to Margaret," John said.
"What was it they give to Margaret, Bun?"

"Oh—nothing," Bun answered vaguely. She began
to splash at the sink, singing and snorting as she
scrubbed her face.

II

Toward the last of June Olly came home. At one
time Jen had expected him on the tenth, when his
examinations were over, but at the last minute he was

offered the chance to work about the grounds during Commencement week, and afterward to help put the buildings in order for the summer session.

"Can father spare me from the hoeing?" he wrote Jen. "I hate to ask him but this is a good-paying job; forty cents an hour for as long as I want to work."

"The weeds are not so bad as some years," Jen wrote back. "Father says if you are here in time for haying it will be all right. He thinks to cut early, the grass has shot up so, and since it come off hot it will be turning yellow. We are fine at home and hope these few lines find you just the same. Lois May writes that she likes it where she is. Lina has got a heifer calf. That makes two heifer calves this spring. Father give one to John and one to Bun. They are pretty tickled. Now you take care of yourself and don't work too hard and it will be all right as long as you get here in time for the haying."

The night he came Jen was making biscuit for supper. As she straightened from sliding them into the oven, her glance passed the window and she saw him cutting across lots through the pasture, and stopped to watch him, smiling. That was Olly. He never walked with the firm, tranquil tread of his father and George and Ed, but moved jerkily, sometimes stumbled over rough places, for his mind was preoccupied and he did not look down. Jen remembered how he had followed the cows up the lane in the days when what were now becoming John's "chores" had been his; how the young heifers would get away from him because he forgot to watch them close; how he had stubbed his bare toes until they bled. Now here he was a grown man in a neat blue suit and a stiff straw hat, coming home from college. It was a wonder what a few years would do; and yet they had not really changed him, only put him in a place where he fitted.

"Hullo, Olly! Well, I guess you're hot enough, walking all that ways in this heat! . . . No, now don't you come in here where I've got fire going. You step right into the kitchen and I'll be there in a minute."

She baked in the shed-room now, and kept the kitchen stove cold except on cool, damp mornings. The change of stoves always made a difference in what she cooked; in the shed-room she could get a quick, high heat but it never kept so regular for long, slow baking. The most that the family missed was her fruit cakes and it was probable they were too heavy for hot weather anyway.

"Look out of my way," said Olly. "This is just where I *am* coming. What you cooking—biscuit? Let's have one!"

"Oh, Olly! They're not done! . . . You'll burn your fingers! There, what did I tell you?"

For Olly had shaken open the oven door with his knee and snatched out a biscuit, a big one, still spongy and white. It was so hot that he could not hold it, but had to keep tossing it from one hand to the other; and there was no telling when he had washed his hands. He had not even taken off his hat.

"You told me I'd burn my fingers and I didn't. And you told me they weren't done but they are. Just the way I like them,—rawish and chewy!"

"Not even any butter on it, Olly——"

"I can't wait for butter. I'm starved. . . . Say, but

this is good. I haven't tasted anything like it in months, and that's the truth, Jen."

Jen laughed with pleasure. It was like Olly to be impatient and appreciative, but he talked more than he used to, and smiled more; his eyes used to be serious but now they had a glint Jen could not describe to herself.

"You've picked up a saucy look down there to college," she said at last. "I shouldn't wonder if you'd need training before the summer is over. Now you get out of this shed-room as I told you and go wash yourself and change out of your clothes, or you won't get another mite of supper. Now you mind what I say."

"Oh, Jen, I've got to have some supper," he begged her.

"Well, you march, then," she scolded contentedly. "And don't forget behind your ears and up into the edge of your hair. You're all soot off the train."

The next day he worked for twelve hours with his father in the field. He did not hold his hoe quite right, nor use it easily, but none ever set a pace that left him behind. At night he was exhausted, and could not eat much supper. Jen noticed but did not speak of it, and when she had finished the dishes she went out and sat beside him on the steps. He had a lonesome look, she thought, sitting there in shrunken overalls and a black shirt opened down his lean, white chest; he always did at home, for the children never followed him about as they did Ed, and Mark Shaw avoided the silences that fell between them when they were idle, though he liked to speak to him in passing and watch him from a distance.

"I guess you think," said Jen, "we don't make much of your coming home, after you've been away six months! Letting you work the whole first day!"

Olly lifted his head from leaning against the post of the porch and smiled.

"I have to get my hand in."

He spread his palm and even in the half-light she could see the blisters on them.

"That was no way," said Jen disapprovingly.

"I didn't think they'd do that," Olly explained, "after all the lawns I've mowed, but of course it was a different grip."

"Was that hard work down there at college?" Jen wanted to know.

"Which?" Olly asked. "Waiting on tables or tending furnaces or studying or filing cards or peddling books or drumming up ads or caddying or shovelling paths or cleaning halls or getting out evidence or putting up bunting or storing trunks?"

"I meant—whatever you've been doing since the school closed," Jen said humbly.

"Mostly putting up bunting," said Olly. "And taking it down again. And mowing lawns. No, that wasn't hard." After a minute he added, "It isn't any of it hard—when you feel you're getting somewhere."

"Do many of them have to earn their own way, like you?" Jen asked. She did not want Olly to seem less than the rest.

"A good many," Olly answered. "That's what makes jobs hard to get."

Jen wriggled herself comfortably into the crevice between the steps. Jobs were hard to get, but Olly could get them. He had earned six hundred and ten

dollars beside going to school this year, she knew
from the account book on his bureau; that was more
than George and Ed had done at his age with their
full time. He was not big like them, but he had something in him; Jen called it starch.

"I meant to have George and his folks over to
supper to-night," she said, "but Mil and two of the
children are down sick. It seems to be kind of an
epidemic going round. They had it down to Forrest's
this last week. Crampy pains in their heads and
stomachs."

"They're always having something up to George's,"
Olly said lazily, his eyes shut.

"There, I know it," sighed Jen. "I don't see what's
the reason. If it isn't stomach upset, it's sore throat
or colds or ivy poison. I was up yesterday cleaning and
baking and I told George if he'd come after me I'd
go up for a while in the morning and take some
cooked stuff."

"How is it you have to do everything?" asked Olly.
It always irked him. "What's the matter with Margaret taking a turn?"

Jen was silent. It had come dark now. She could
hear Mrs. Shaw singing to the children upstairs; she
liked to do it when she felt well enough even though
Bun chattered and would not listen, and John fell
asleep before she was well begun. The bell of the
heifer that was running wild through the summer
tinkled in the marshes.

"It isn't suitable," Jen said quietly, "for Margaret
to go where catching sickness is just now. I told Ed
so."

Olly whistled.

"They don't say anything," said Jen, "so we don't.
I just told Ed not to let her go up there 'til they're
over this and he said he wouldn't. Of course I may
be wrong, but I don't think so."

She turned her head and spoke into the dark
window.

"Father, what makes you set in there? It's real cool
where the air gets at you. Tell ma to come out, too.
It's stifling upstairs."

A little later Mark Shaw and his wife brought their
chairs and placed them on the grass before the steps.
The moon was high and the four figures showed quite
plainly, and the outline of the house and shed and
barn, and the trees of the yard and orchard. Mark
Shaw and Jen sat much alike, bent forward with their
knees apart, staring at the ground. Olly leaned, relaxed, against the post, his hands thrust into his
pockets. Mrs. Shaw yawned and stretched her feet before her, letting them rest on the heels with the toes
turned up.

"Hoo-oo, hum!" she said. "Nobody knows how the
soles of my feet burn if I stand on them any time at
all, like I did making out that butter. . . . There's
enough for your customers all right, Mark, and that's
a miracle, with one cow off the place and two calves
sucking."

Nobody answered. It did not mean they had not
heard, or were not gratified.

"I see the peas are almost full a'ready," Jen said
dreamily.

Mrs. Shaw slapped at a mosquito just as Olly did.
They both laughed.

"I got mine," said Olly. "Did you get yours?"

"I never do," his stepmother answered. "Mark says I'm too quick for 'em. Says I get there before they do."

Later Mark Shaw said, "You cal'late you and me and Ed can fill three barns this side of August, Olly?"

"*Three* barns!"

"George, he's going to work over to Freeside for the Oakeses. They've got sixty acres there of mowing land alone. It will take him six weeks anyway, he says, with favorable weather."

"What's the idea? We do his work while he goes earning?"

"Well, he's got to let his place out to halves," Mark Shaw said gently. "I thought with our crew we could do it as well as anybody. Bun, she's going to tread the loads, she says, and John there, he's going to do a lot of business, too."

Mark Shaw chuckled.

"Why, how'll George get through the winter on a half a crop of hay?" Jen exclaimed.

"He thinks to buy," her father told her.

"Oh, yes," repeated Mrs. Shaw significantly. "He *thinks* to buy!"

Mark Shaw made no reply to this. He sat on in the light of the moon, his big shoulders stooped, his thick hair standing straight up from his forehead, staring at the ground. Olly laid his cheek against the cool, painted post and sprawled along the floor of the porch, listening to the cowbell.

"Sure," he said. "We can do it all right. George hasn't got much over there to cut if it's like most years. We won't notice it, along with the rest. Ed's crop as good as yours?"

"Full," Mark Shaw said proudly. "Full as good, if

not a little mite better. He ploughed all the hill pieces over there last fall and seeded them down and rain come just the right time. He planned it good. I don't doubt there ain't no better grass anywhere in the state."

Olly remarked the change in his voice and the way Jen's eyes lifted and sought Ed's light over on Walnut Hill. He smiled wryly in the dark, thinking of speeches he had made, comments he had seen on his examination papers, the scholarship he had won, even of money he had earned, and wondered what all that together would mean to his father beside one good crop of grass that Ed grew. He did not know what either of them was thinking, nor how their minds fumbled with pleasure in his willingness to help at home and with bewilderment at what he did while he was away, wanting to ask, and not knowing how.

"Well," Olly said, "I guess I'll turn in. I'm getting stiff sitting here."

As he felt his way through the dark kitchen and up the back stairs, he told himself he should not expect approval; the greater a man was the less he got of it; that had been so all down through the ages. In a way it was good to be home, and he must not ask too much. He had his books. With Browning and Keats and Robinson on the table in his room, and Ridpath's "History of the World," Sullivan's "Turn of the Century," Ibsen's plays and a new psychology text and Shakespeare's complete works, a fellow needed nothing more except the time to read them.

"His hands are covered with blisters," said Jen softly.

"I couldn't keep him back," Mark Shaw said. "He

was bound to be even with me all the way, and he was, too. I never see such a boy."

"He ain't strong," said Mrs. Shaw. "John'll be a good deal stouter at his age."

John was her son.

"He's strong enough," Mark Shaw said. "He ought to work in easy, that's all. You let him rest in the morning, Jen."

"I'll let him rest 'til noontime if he will," said Jen.

The wind was freshening. It would be a good night to sleep. The heifer's bell tinkled more and more quietly in the marshes.

III

On Sunday the church at the fork of the road above George's place opened for the summer months. The eight families in the neighborhood could not support a minister for the year round but they could pay one five dollars a Sunday to drive up from the village through July and August, and they did. The women had cleaned the building a week before and made a kind of picnic of it, eating their lunches in the shade at the back; they had even painted steps and whitewashed fences and filled the hanging lamp with fresh oil. As Jen dressed for the two o'clock service she recalled how neat and sweet-smelling the meeting room had been when she turned the key on it, every green-painted pew shining from soap and water, the platform carpet turned and mended, the faded blue and yellow satin ribbons that marked the pulpit Bible rid of dust, the yellow wooden shutters closed to keep out the heat.

"Ma," Jen called. "Ma! You ready?"

"She's out picking flowers," Olly answered from his room. "Yes, she looks ready."

"You're going, aren't you, Olly?" Jen asked, after a minute in which she flung her bath water out of the back window, scrubbed the bowl vigorously, hung her towels to dry, and shook talcum powder over her shoulders.

Olly had not thought of going. He had just finished with a year of required church attendance and now lay on his bed reading "My Last Duchess" in such a position that he could look beyond the book to where his stepmother in a green muslin dress went back and forth in the garden and Bun and John sat sedately in a string hammock hung between two apple trees. He liked the ease and quiet of Sunday, when even Mark Shaw only walked about his land with arms folded across his back; there was time then to notice the clouds in the sky, the thinness of the maple leaves, the smell of flowers and hot grass, the sound of crickets and grasshoppers and of the brook running through the meadow; and all these things he enjoyed. It was only the slavishness of farming that had driven him away.

"Aren't you, Olly?"

"Oh—I guess not."

"Folks'll be disappointed," Jen said, buckling her white canvas slippers. "Several has spoke of seeing you this Sunday."

Olly rolled over on his back. He wanted to go, and did not want to go. It was pleasant here and his collar would be hot and the sermon would bore him. But once was the time Sunday was the day he waited for, the only time when he heard music and speaking; until he went away to college he had never missed a service; when he was seven the Elder had put his hand on his head and said, "This is the one you'll have to give to the Lord, Mark. He's got gentle ways." Olly had thought at first that being given to the Lord meant dying, and he cried in bed at night until Jen heard him and made him tell her why and explained that it only meant being like the Elder. Olly chuckled. He wondered if she remembered that . . . And the people here must not think he did not want to see them, that college had given him a big head as some of them had prophesied. He stood up and began pulling off his clothes.

"Well, don't wait for me," he called to Jen. "I'll walk. I'm not quite ready."

"In all this heat?"

"I'll like it. You go on."

When he went into the church, Margaret had just finished playing the Doxology. She sat behind the little parlor organ, facing the congregation, her head bent slightly under her wide-rimmed pink hat, waiting for the prayer. Olly slid into a vacant pew on the west side; few ever sat there, though the seats on the east were so full that people's shoulders touched. He watched them from between his eyelids and found them as he had remembered. Mil and her children occupied the front pew, the one flanking the organ, and when Margaret had finished playing, she would sit with them. A Hattie Lord and her three daughters, Flora, Annie, and Sarah Louise had taken that place when first the church was built, for Hattie sang alto, and Flora and Annie strong sopranos, and it was boasted that Sarah Louise could take any part but bass, whichever was most needed; they were sometimes called the Lord quartet. When Sarah Louise married she still sat there, and brought her two daughters, Mildred and Margaret; Flora had shared it during her lifetime, but Annie had married out of parish; it would be Mil's and Margaret's pew now as long as services were held in the church, and their children's.

Behind them were George and Ed and Jen, children of Minnie Foote, daughter of George Foote who could not sing a note, but had given the ground for the church. Olly could remember his mother herding them all into that second row of seats on the rare Sundays when she appeared at Meeting.

The third was the Mary Eliza Shaw pew, and Mark Shaw sat in it for he was her son, and Cora Shaw because she had no place of her own here, and Bun and John because it was where they belonged. The Hales had their place, and the Forrests, the Austins, the Jellisons, the Grants, the Walkers, and the Carpenters. The Janowskis sat where they might, for they were newcomers; there were seats enough. There were no rules about it. It was only that each one sat where his mother had trained him to go. The church was a matriarchy.

"I wonder if this paint still sticks," Olly thought.

As children all the Shaws had been supplied with folded papers to place at their backs as they sat down; without protection they brought home pale green stripes across their shoulders.

Elder Finnie from the village was a young man, fair-haired, hard-working, enthusiastic. He read with feeling, sang with fervor, preached with a terrible

earnestness. The congregation listened to him attentively, but kept their eyes on Elder Hobbs who sat,
sweet-faced and calm, on the horsehair chair beside the
pulpit, too old now to safely preach a sermon in hot
weather, but by whose word they had all been reared,
every one except the Janowskis and Cora Shaw. Mil
and Margaret had known the time when, as they sat in
the front pew, they watched him leaning toward them
with his arm resting on the big Bible, an old, white-
bearded man even then, with a thick gold chain
swinging across his snowy piqué vest, and distinctly
saw a halo round his head. Margaret glanced down at
Esther and Betty, wondering if they saw it now; it
must be it was visible only to little girls; she did not
believe the Elder had lost it. She was glad he had lived
to marry her and Ed; it made her feel completely
married.

They rose and sang.

"Brother Hobbs, will you pronounce the benedic-
tion?"

It was good to hear the familiar voice.

"I want first to speak a word to my Father, Who
is here . . . Lord, we thank Thee for past mercies
and ask boon for the future. Grant us hot, dry weather
for the weeks of haying. Grant us the will and
strength to labor in our vineyards, and give us to enjoy
the fruits therefrom. But if this be not Thy will, and
pests must come, and frost and storm, help us to know
it is Thy judgment and to fear not, for Thou wilt
provide."

Elder Finnie had not thought to include haying and
harvest in his prayer, for he was a village preacher.

It took old Elder Hobbs to know the first need of the parish; he had fields of his own.

"In Christ's name we ask it . . . And now may the Lord watch between thee and me while we are absent one from another."

Margaret played softly on the organ.

In the hush that followed Elder Hobbs went along the aisles, shaking hands with the women, nodding at the men, patting the children on the head. This much at least he was not yet too old to do, and the ministers from the village always left it to him.

"Well, Mildred, I'm pleased to see you out. No wonder it's hard for you sometimes with all the little ones." He spoke in a half-whisper, smiling until his forehead shone. "Hullo there, son. God bless you, children; God bless you . . . Mrs. Margaret, I enjoyed your music. Always enjoy your music . . . George. Ed. How do you do, Jennie . . . Hullo, Mark, hullo. I see your boy is home from school. That's fine, that's fine. May he use his knowledge in the service of the Lord! . . . Your flowers were beautiful, Mrs. Shaw. You enjoyed the sermon, I know . . . Amen, amen . . . Bless you, my dear . . . Ah——"

When the Elder had passed by, the service was over. People gathered into groups or leaned across the backs of pews to speak with one another. Their voices were low, as befitted the place, but they talked of weather and sickness and children and the state of the roads.

"Awful dusty, ain't it?" George said.

"We'll get a shower before night," his father told him, "and lay the dust. There's thunder in the air all right."

"It's a scorcher, that's sure," Ed agreed.

Margaret beckoned to Olly. Not only her hat was pink but her dress and a scarf she carried.

"Why haven't you been over to see us, Olly Shaw? I've looked for you every night. We have a fine place over there now and you'll say so when you see it."

"You look fine, Olly," Mil said, smiling faintly over her restless baby's head. "I guess that college down there agrees with you."

"Well, you don't, Mil. You're awfully white and your eyes look bad," Margaret said, turning toward her.

"It takes a while to get over some of these upsets that's going around, I guess."

"What do you mean, Mil? You been *sick?*"

"Didn't Ed tell you?"

"Tell me you were *sick?*"

"Why, I was flat on my back four days and Betty and Georgie had it too. There wasn't anybody to do a thing but Esther, and Jen come up twice. I sent word by George to Ed, but I thought likely you must be rushed with something so you couldn't get away."

"Ed Shaw! *Ed!* Why in the world didn't you tell me Mil was sick? I might have gone up just as well as not!"

"Say!" Ed exclaimed. "You did mention that to me, didn't you, George?"

"Ed's awful forgetful," Jen interposed. "I always noticed that about him. It's a wonder if he gets you half you send to market for."

"But in the case of sickness!" Margaret said indignantly.

"Look here," Ed told her. "You married me for better or worse, and the Elder's here to prove it. If my memory's worse you'll have to put up with it, and no fussing, mind. Won't she, Mil?"

"It's all right, anyway," Mil said. "We're coming along now. George got us something at the drug store and father sent over some of his herb tea. I've made up my mind it done the business, that pennyroyal, father, just the same!"

"There ain't nothing better," Mark Shaw said. "You want to keep it on hand."

"He always sticks up for his herb tea," smiled Mrs. Shaw. "There, I don't know. It may be as good as anything."

"Well, so you're 'round again, Olly," Doris Carpenter said, lingering near him, holding her flowered chiffon skirts against the breeze that came in at the open door.

"Yes, I'm back," Olly answered. He added, "What's new up Penny Brook way?"

Doris worked for her uncle in his general store at Penny Brook fourcorners, but came home on Sundays. For years she and Olly had recited history and geography, arithmetic and spelling together, the only two in their class. She was older than he, and looked it more than ever now that she had been earning her living during the five years he had spent in school. Her face was hard and saucy from amusing the men and boys who came to her to trade and talk. Women rarely frequented a general store.

"Nothing," she said. "Dead as dishwater. I doubt if I stay there much longer. I want to get into a city where there's something going on. Winters up there are terrible. It's worse than here."

"Don't tell me that. No place is dead where you are, Doris."

Olly himself was surprised to find how easily it came out. He had no way with girls. At college he stammered when he tried to talk with them, and though in his room he thought of light remarks like this to make, he never found a place for them. He thought it must be Doris was accountable, that without trying she put him at his best. He warmed toward her.

"Don't tell me that, Doris."

His one-sided glance, his sudden boldness made her look up quickly and down again, flushing, trying to laugh. It turned her young and helpless. Olly remembered what had been forgotten for years, the day she used his sled at recess without permission and broke the rope, and how he raged, and she stood crying. He felt a growing sense of power and mocking male gentleness.

"I'll tell you," he said. "You'd better come home often this summer."

"You think so?" she asked him, trying to go halfway, but uncertain. The men and boys who came to trade did not look like this one.

"Yes, I think so," Olly answered definitely. "It isn't going to be so dead here—now I'm home."

He did not know what he meant by that, nor where to lead the conversation next, and so he left her. Filled with a strange expansiveness he made his way through the group by the door, nodding here and there, and walked across the grass to where Stan Janowski was handing his family into a long, shabby wagon. His mother and father looked swarthy and foreign, almost grimy, and the children were too fat, too beady-eyed, too many of an age to seem natural to Derwich, but

Stan was only golden brown as if from a bright, heavy tan, and his neatly clipped hair, his blue serge suit, his quiet manner were all as smooth as Olly's.

"Well, hullo," he said, shaking hands. "You home for the summer?"

"For the haying," Olly answered. "You riding down?"

Stan laughed. His teeth were big and white.

"No, no room for me. I always walk anyway, when there's time."

"Same here," Olly said. He had never felt so thoroughly male. The sensation possessed him, made his voice for the minute heavier. "We'll walk together. How's to meet the family first, though?"

"Mother, this is Oliver Shaw," Stan said. "One of Mr. Shaw's sons. The girl who came over to the baby is his sister."

"T'at girl?" Mrs. Janowski cried. "Oh, t'at girl she one angel straight from heaven. T'at girl, I bless her every day. Some time I see her out. She always wave her hand. T'at girl she lovely one."

The introductions continued. The chatter grew. Jen, near-by, came over to pass the time of day and was surrounded. Mark Shaw bowed and spoke to any who would listen of the forwardness of the season and the fullness of the corn. The Elder paused among these new members of his flock with special greeting. The Austins, Grants, and Walkers drew near curiously, making the Janowski family the center of a considerable, not unfriendly group. From this Stan and Olly emerged a little later, two serious young men, and walked away down the sandy road, talking at first of weather and swimming, later of politics and a book they both had read.

From the church steps Doris Carpenter looked after them, unconsciously but busily arranging her short hair beneath her hat.

IV

The next day was hot and bright, as the Elder had requested.

"Well, boy," Mark Shaw said to John at breakfast, "we've got to get at this haying, but we can't do a thing 'til the scythes is ground."

John went with him to the grindstone under the ash tree and sat on a chopping block to turn the handle. Mark Shaw straddled the end of the bench and poured water on the stone, then held the scythe against it with the heels of his hands until sparks flew off. It took both John's arms to move the handle and when it stood straight up before him he threw his chest against it to make it go down. Mark Shaw paused and felt the blade with his fingers. He reached for the water can and cooled the stone again. "Well, that side's done good." They sharpened the other side, sweat standing out white on John's face. The stone moved slower and slower.

"Now you go down and count the hens," his father said. "Make sure they're all in the yard. They take to laying out in this tall grass so now I can't be sure, and I don't want any legs cut off this haying time. You speak to Bun as you go by and say she can turn for me this next scythe."

"I could, father," John said, wiping his upper lip

with the back of his hand. "I could turn for 'em all, couldn't I, if you wanted me to?"

"Well, there ain't no need," his father said. "I guess Bun can do a little something to help us out. And you're getting to be a fine counter."

Bun came importantly and turned the handle very fast, rocking on her seat.

"I bet John got tired, didn't he, father? I bet he couldn't turn for two scythes, not to save his life. I could, though. I could turn for all you've got. I'm awful strong."

"Yes, you're fine and strong for your age," Mark Shaw said, looking at her. "But you go easy now. Go easy. We'll get just as fur." And he added, feeling the blade, "Girls has to be careful."

"Girls has to be!" Bun exclaimed hotly. "*Girls* has to be! Girls are just as good as boys! . . . What do girls have to be careful for?"

As her father moved stiffly off his high seat, he said, "Well. You ask your mother." And before she reached the steps, hurrying on her curious errand, he called, "Get your cats into the house and keep the screen doors fastened. I'm going to trim out around the house and them bushes in the front yard there to-day."

All the afternoon, while Olly hoed the potato piece and Ed's mowing machine knives clicked busily on Walnut Hill, Mark Shaw patiently and carefully cut wide rings around the rose bushes at the end of the house, the syringa, the thick-leafed yucca, the fire-bush, the peonies, and the long, fenced-in garden where the pansies and sweet peas and poppies grew.

Mr. Hale, driving his cows by, said, "You got a

slow job there! I never could see what there is to flowers worth all the trouble they be."

"Well, I don't know," Mark Shaw said mildly. "Womenfolks set store by 'em."

He worked on, since Olly was there to do the milking, until supper time. Jen could hear his rifle slapping the blade as she went into the cellar for the Training Day cookies she kept on the swing shelf in a big brown crock. He must be hot, she thought. It was a sweltering day. She would make lemonade and pump up water until she had some from the very bottom of the well; it was cold as ice down there. Five years ago Mark Shaw had lowered that well to thirty feet below the surface of the ground; it was his boast now that the place would never be without water unless a greater drouth than he had ever seen came on the land.

"I'm fifty-two years old," he sometimes said, "and in that time there's never been no dry spell fit to reach that deep. Thirty feet and four inches down, it is. I guess we'll have water here as long as we want it."

The next morning, as soon as the dew was off, he rode into the field behind old Bob, shorts bags padding the seat on his machine. The blades of the knives were thin-edged and shining, and as he rode along the sides and ends of the mowing he left broad swaths behind him, lying flat and wavy on the ground. The strip that still stood in the center grew smaller and smaller, and the smell of drying grass filled the kitchen and all the upstairs rooms. Jen sniffed it as she made jam of the last of the strawberries. Bun and John waited, avid for Olly to have raked this hay and tumbled it into stacks of which one was always left for the children to play on ever since the time when George and Ed had been children here.

"Now that's yours," Olly said that night. "Don't tear down the rest."

They ran, Bun squealing, and jumped into the midst of it.

"Will you leave one for Esther to play on when you go to hay at George's?" Bun called after Olly as he walked away. "For Esther and Betty and Georgie and them to play on?"

"Oh, I suppose so," Olly said.

"'Cause George never does. Betty said so. She said he *never* does. They can't do anything up there. They never have any fun." She was singing it as she jumped. "They never have any fun. They never have any fun up there."

When Olly had gone John said, "What did you whisper? What did Jen and you whisper in the sink-room, that time?"

"When? To-day?" Bun asked, after a minute in which she chewed grass hungrily for the sweet drop at the end.

"That time when you wouldn't let me in. I tried to open the door and Jen, she held it shut with her foot. I could see her through the crack holding it shut with her foot."

"Oh . . . Well, nothing," Bun said, now staring at the sky. "Only father told me to ask ma, and she wouldn't say, so I asked Jen."

"Asked her what? Asked Jen what?"

"Nothing, I told you," screamed Bun. "Nothing. Nothing. Nothing."

She gave a great jump and landed on her stomach

on the stack with her arms spread wide. She looked at
John with gentle scorn.

"Only you needn't think," she said, "I'll tread any
more loads of hay after this than you will, even though
I could. Girls have to be careful."

One evening late in the week as Jen stood in the
sinkroom washing the supper dishes, she bent forward
until she could see Mil's light shining far up the road.
A late shower coming up and the men hustling to
get in the last load of hay on Ed's place had delayed
the meal. She knew that George had gone home late,
too, from his work at the Oakes's and supposed that
Mil was washing her dishes now. Mil had no sinkroom, and it was hot in her kitchen on a July night
to bake and eat and clear away. George ought to build
on a lean-to, Jen thought.

"There goes George down the road lickety-cut,"
said Mrs. Shaw. "He's got the back seat full of young
ones, too. I guess they'll get cooled off. My, it's getting
so we're just about the only ones don't have a car
to ride in."

Jen glanced again at Mil's light, and as she looked,
saw it go out. No other appeared, in the front room
or upstairs. As she finished her work, she considered
this. It was a lonely place up there at the edge of the
woods for a woman to sit by herself in the dark. And
by good rights Mil should be wrapping her butter
now, for to-morrow was George's market day.

"I believe I'll walk up the road a little ways," she
said, sponging her face and neck and arms with cool
water and white soap. "The mosquitoes have kind of
had their day now, so anybody can venture out once

in a while. Don't you look for me 'til I get back. There won't anything hurt me around here."

She went quietly on rubber-soled brown tennis shoes out of the yard and down the lane and padded through the pale sand of the main road. The dust from George's wheels still hung on the air and made her cough. She walked swiftly, fanning herself with her apron, past the pool her father always drove through on his way back from church to cool Bob's legs and let him drink, and across the planks that bridged the brook. In the woods it was too dark for her to see as far as her feet, but she knew every step of the way, even the ruts and the slope of the ditches; and in the clearing beyond she could distinguish the roof and chimney of George's house as it set back in the field on the left.

"Mil!" she called into the black doorway. "Mil! It's Jen! I've come a-calling!"

There was no answer but she knew Mil must be about for the door stood wide open off the stone door rock. She felt her way inside, and called again cheerfully.

"Hi! Where are you, Mrs. George Shaw?"

Then she heard Mil's voice beyond the back window.

"I'm here," it said. "Out here."

Jen pulled open the kitchen door and stepped into the fenced-in yard where Mil made the children play to keep them out of the reach of passing cars. The road past George's place was the only one leading to Mount Passy, the highest point of land in the county, and many summer people used it, driving up from the beaches in the afternoon.

"Well, cooling off?" Jen asked. "This has been a hot one."

Mil sat on the seat of the chair swing that hung from the apple tree. Her dress lay open as if to nurse, though the baby was at some distance from her on the grass.

"No," Mil said, "I don't ever expect to be cool again. I come out here to see if I could get my head together. I'm just about at the end of my rope."

Jen sat down beside the baby.

"You've got your hands full," she agreed. "I don't see how you manage as well as you do."

She had often said this to Mrs. Shaw and Lois May when they remarked on the length of Georgie's fingernails and the dingy streaks on Esther's head and the way the house looked if anybody went in unexpected. "I guess we'd have hard work to do any better than Mil, the way she's fixed."

"It makes a great difference," Mil said, "since Margaret went away."

Jen nodded.

"Margaret always takes an interest wherever she is."

"It wasn't only what she done to help," Mil said. "It was just her being here to speak a word to . . . What would you folks think if I was to leave George, Jen?"

Jen played with the baby's foot.

"Why, I guess you wouldn't do that, Mil."

"Yes," Mil said. "I guess that's what I'm going to do, Jen. I wouldn't have said it to you like that if I hadn't pretty well got my mind made up. . . . It isn't George so much. It's pretty hard to work myself to death and never get any credit, and be shut up in that kitchen washing and digging and have him come home at night and only find fault because there's no hot bread. He might help out a little instead of making everything so hard. . . . But it isn't George so much. It's me. I'm getting so I don't have any patience. It seems as if I cry more than half my time, Jen. I can't even stand to let the children have their pleasure. And I can't eat my meals. When George sets there and stuffs himself at night I can't force down a mouthful and I just sit and watch him and hate the way he does. He fair makes my stomach curl the way he grabs and gobbles——"

"There, I know it," Jen said easily. "He always had a great appetite."

"It isn't George so much, though," Mil said again. "It's me. I used to want so many things when I was growing up, and it don't seem it's right I should never have them. I used to want to go to school, off, I mean, and learn the way to do things nice. I used to like to look at pictures in the magazines, and I do now; maybe it's foolish; but people wearing good clothes and laughing together, and women driving cars, and children in real bathing suits, and houses with piazzas and curtains at the windows. I want all them things, Jen. I'm not like—some folks."

"I know it, Mil," repeated Jen. "Like me now. I'm just as contented where I am as ever the wife of a President was, so I'm no judge. Maybe if I was to think how I should feel if I had to live like Lize——"

"Oh, you're lucky," Mil said bitterly. "You're as strong as a horse and some way you can always make things go as you want them to." She left the swing and took up the baby as if she could not bear to see

Jen's firm, square hand so deftly quieting it. "Well,
I will, too. I can get along some way in a city place
and George'll have to manage the best he can. Esther
looks after Georgie as well as I do now."

"You'd have to take the baby," Jen said. "You
couldn't leave her here not weaned."

"Of course I'd take the baby," Mil exclaimed. She
rocked the child in her arms.

"And it's so hot now," said Jen. "That's what makes
it bad. And if you worked, how could you nurse her
regular? It would be a pity if your milk dried up."

"It's coming rich and good now, too," Mil said.
"But still not too rich. She's gaining on it fast."

"All of them gained on it," Jen reminded her. "Ma
said the other day she never knew a woman that fed
so many babies all so well."

"No stronger than I am," Mil said. She sat down
beside Jen and gave the child her breast.

"It's just a miracle," Jen said. " . . . Dear little young
one. She knows her mother all right."

They sat on together quietly.

"If you could only make out to stay 'til fall and
wean her," Jen said, "I'd take her over with me when
you're ready to go, and then you could have her when
you got settled in."

"Would you?" Mil asked quickly.

"I surely would," Jen told her. "You can count on
that."

Mil felt for a handkerchief and not finding any,
used the baby's dress.

"You're awful good to me, Jen," she said. "You
and all George's folks. That was one reason I wanted
to speak with you. If I left George, I wouldn't want

to think—I'd lost all of you, not having any folks but Margaret of my own, and she married to Ed; if Ed didn't want her to, I'll bet she'd never speak to me again."

"It's funny to see them," Jen laughed. "The way he likes to boss her around, and the way she is so tickled to have him."

"It's all right as long as it lasts that way," Mil said. "If only a woman don't get tied hand and foot by children before she can see how things are going to be. I'm hoping so Margaret won't have a baby for a long time."

Jen did not answer.

"But as I say," Mil was going on, "I wanted to know how you folks would feel about it—if I did."

"Well, we'd feel awful bad, of course," Jen said. "I guess it would hit father pretty hard. He's one that thinks something of a man's keeping his home together, all ways; and he's fond of you, Mil. You and Margaret both. I have means of telling. You're just as near to him as his own daughters, and if you was to go off, he'd have you on his mind, how you were getting on and if you needed anything. . . . But just the same he wouldn't hold you back from where you wanted to go, if you were sure you wanted to; he's never done that with any of them . . . No, Mil, don't worry. We'll help you all we can if in the fall you're bound to go."

She sprang up suddenly.

"I hear George. I'll cut down across the woods. Some time it might be just as well he never knew I was here to-night."

But by running she came out to the road at the

bridge before he reached it and stopped him there. Mil could not see the halted headlights from her place, and she would not be listening to the motor as Margaret would if it were Ed's.

"Well, hullo, Jen! What are you doing on the road this time of night?"

"Just walking to get cool. The young ones with you?"

"Yeah. They're all asleep. I got to talking down at the village there with Charlie Perry. He's the first one of the selectmen I ever knew to——"

"George," Jen interrupted him. She stepped up on the running board and took his arm in her stout grip. "I've got to tell you you're right on the brink of losing Mil. You'll have to take my word for it, and do everything you can to make things pleasant for her, and so'll all the rest of us. She's stood an awful lot for years now, more than she was built for. It's took it out of her. Don't you tell her you saw me; now mind what I say. Just you do what you can and I'll do what I can, everything we can think of. We've probably got 'til fall."

She disappeared into the dark and left George to stare after her, not sure how she meant he might lose his wife; which was as she had intended. Men tried to ease the last hours even of a horse, unless they were nearer brutes than she knew George to be.

v

Olly spent less and less of his evenings at home. During the day he worked steadily in the field with Ed and his father, and sat at table with the rest at supper. But by dark nearly every evening he was wandering out of the yard and up the road, sometimes stopping at George's for a minute or two, though not often, and hardly ever even glancing up as he passed the Hales' house or the Austins'. He had no friends in the neighborhood; to the people here he had always been Mark's odd one who never had a word to say when he met anybody on the road; handy with books he might be, they supposed, but unhandy with tools. He knew of prophecies that had been made concerning him, how he would never get far enough, for all his studying, but what he would be glad to come back some day to live on Ed; and these he did not forget, though he was grown now and something of a stranger and all whom he met were polite. Two Saturday nights he called in for Doris Carpenter at the big unpainted house on the hill above Austins', but he was cool, and reserved, while he waited, for Bill Carpenter, Ed's best friend, had been the loudest in his scorn of all Olly attempted as a boy; his noisy cordiality now made no impression; Olly's memory was long in these things.

"Come out and see my bus," Bill said. "I got a good buy. It may be an old model but it's got an engine like a bird, and I'm slapping on a coat of paint myself . . . Don't look bad now, does she?"

"Looks all right to me," Olly answered shortly. "I don't know anything about cars." He strolled back to sit on the steps, making a pile of broken grass between his feet, whistling softly, while Bill was left to explore alone the intricacies of his engine.

It was not until Olly had Doris to himself, sitting under the willows by the brook, or leaning over the

railing of the bridge, or walking across cut fields, that
he began to overlook the fact she was a Carpenter,
sister of Bill, one who had probably heard him laughed
at all her life. She became just any girl, and he a man,
not only a quick-witted, clever, and sophisticated person
come down out of his mysterious world to her simple
one, but a creature strong enough and ruthless enough to
take his own way. This feeling raced in Olly, a slim
boy in dark shirt and drilling trousers, whenever he
saw Doris Carpenter, though if he made up his mind
even to touch her he never quite reached the point
of doing it. He was aware that she wondered why he
did not, and even this amused him; so assured was
he; he did not care what she thought or what she
wanted; this was no girl for him except as she roused
him to a new experience; back at college in the fall
there would be others, girls who knew as much of
Greek and poetry and astronomy as he did, younger,
prettier, gentler girls than Doris Carpenter, girls not
so easily won nor held, but possessed of all Doris had
and much beside. He could wait for them.

"I love walking out like this," sighed Doris. "Say,
but that moon is swell . . . Like to hear that water
running, Olly? I do."

"Doris," Olly said mockingly, "you must be one of
those natural-born Lovers of Nature."

"Well, I sure have always had an eye for pretty
things," Doris answered with complacency.

She took everything he said as a compliment, perhaps because she was accustomed to a far less subtle
type of abuse than his. This trait sometimes made him
feel almost tender toward her, but then she would
laugh too loud or look up in the bold, provoking way

that, while it quickened his excitement, at the same
time turned him cool with distaste and seemed to
justify him in whatever he might choose to do. None
of the Shaws, not even Jen, would have known him
as he was with Doris Carpenter; he hardly knew himself; when he had left her, usually abruptly, and was
walking home in the night, with everybody sleeping
in the farmhouses that he passed, he puzzled over it.
This, he supposed, was manhood.

The only family he ever cared to see was the
Janowskis. He walked down over the hill and across
the road and into the Old Joe field nearly every night
except Saturday. Sometimes he went around to the
back of the barn where the cows and horse were kept,
and helped Stan with his chores. It was always Stan
who did the chores at night. Manuel played with his
sisters in the brook, all of them splashing and duck-
ing to wash off the mosquitoes, all naked, fat, dark
little bodies running in and out among the bushes.
Mr. and Mrs. Janowski sat on the bench before that
end of the barn in which they lived. Sometimes Olly
waited with them for Stan and listened to the long,
broken, noisy stories they told of the old days in
Poland where Stan had been born, and of later days
in New York where Mr. Janowski had owned a tailor
shop and Mrs. Janowski had helped him with the
cleaning and pressing and Stan had worked in an
American factory that turned out many million yards
of cotton cloth every single day; and where all the
younger children had been born, one after another in
rapid succession because, as Mrs. Janowski said, laughing, "I eat so much wit' nut'in' to do but set all time,
t'em kids t'ey just *come!*"

"T'at was t'e way to live," Mr. Janowski said over and over, beating his hands on the edge of the bench. "Out t'ere wit' my needle I could do good, get money. We see t'e pictures, t'em t'at move, every week, don't we, mama? We take t'em rides, high up. T'e kids, t'ey see t'e zoo and so . . . T'at was t'e way."

"What way?" Stan would ask, coming out at last to sit with the others where it was cool, nodding at Olly.

"T'e New York way," his father would cry. "T'e city way. T'is place you bring us to, you make such fuss, where we get to here? Poland, t'is might be again. Yah-h-h!"

Later in the evening, as it grew dark, the Janowskis had their music. Every pleasant night the other Shaws heard it in the distance and smiled at one another. "They're going it again!" But Olly lay stretched on the grass to listen while Mr. Janowski played tunes on his cheap, creaking fiddle, and his and Mrs. Janowski's heavy voices rollicked through big, blustering songs in their own tongue. He never tired of it, of seeing the way their bodies moved to keep the time, the man's thin and jerky, the woman's broad and swaying. Mrs. Janowski rolled her eyes and laughed as she sang. The children came from the brook, still wet and only half-dressed, and did as she did, copying every movement and giggling at the end. When they quarrelled they fought until someone gave in, shrieking, kicking, and slapping, but the elders sang on as if they noticed nothing, or as if any kind of sound was good. Often Stan sang. When he did, he became suddenly like the others, as unrestrained, as ribald, as Polish, but his voice was smoother and more flexible as even Olly could tell. When he took up the fiddle he handled it more gently than his father did and the bow brought out more delicate sounds; the songs he played were slower, quieter, sweeter, but still wild and foreign to Olly's ears. He tipped his face toward the sky and Olly could see how soft it became, merry and tender, almost childish. It seemed strange that a man could look so. Olly wondered what Ed would say if he should see Stan playing his fiddle. He did not quite like it himself, and yet he did not know why, and always stayed to listen as long as there was anything to hear. Long after the children were huddled asleep about the yard, night after night, Stan played and sang and his father and mother hummed a broad, rich accompaniment, rocking, while Olly lay with his head buried in his arms listening, feeling a half a world away from the Old Joe place; and the other Shaws, going to bed or half rousing from sleep, chuckled indulgently, "And *still* they're at it over there!"

But one night Jen was up when Olly came home. It was very warm and she sat by the open window, a lamp on the sill, knitting white yarn into a long strip. Olly slackened his pace as he crossed the yard, regarding her suspiciously. It might be she had heard about him and Doris Carpenter; the greater wonder would be if she had not, in a busy-tongued place of this size. His resentment against Derwich, against Doris, against his own restlessness grumbled in him, fused into the one violent conviction that nobody had any business waiting up for him; he was not married; a fellow had a right to his time in the evenings, he should hope.

"Been over to Ed's?" Jen asked cheerfully as he was washing. He had not gone into the kitchen where she was, but through to the sinkroom from the entry.

"No," said Olly.

"I just thought you might have happened to," Jen said. "It's some time since I saw Margaret and I wondered how she was. I wish you *would* some evening, Olly. You see so much more than Ed does. He always says she's all right, but still I wonder if he knows."

"We'll be haying up by the house beginning to-morrow," Olly yielded. "I'll see her then."

"That's so," Jen agreed, brightening. "So you will."

She smiled at Olly. He sat down tentatively on the end of the couch, watching her.

"Still at it, are you?' he asked. "Don't you ever stop?"

He had never liked it that she worked so hard.

"Of course," Jen said. "I'm through now. It *is* too hot to work on white and keep it neat, but I kind of thought it was time I got something started. It's going to be a little blanket when it's done."

She folded the strip, patted it, and stood up to lay it safely on the hanging shelf. As she sat down again, the spotted kitten climbed into her lap and paced back and forth there, purring, lapping both himself and her skirt. She stroked him. It did seem as if her hands were never idle; she wished Olly could understand it was as she would have it. She lifted her chin and drew in her lower lip to blow out the lamp.

"A lamp's a hot thing," she said.

Olly did not answer. In the dark she could not tell whether he nodded. It did not matter. A lamp certainly was a hot thing. Now the night air came in freely and cooled the room. The kitten snuggled down, his nose damp against her fingers.

"You probably wonder where I *have* been," Olly said.

Sparks darted off the kitten's fur as Jen ruffled it. "Well——"

"You think I've been after a girl!"

"Why, I don't, either," Jen declared. "I don't know who you'd bother with around here! You're not the kind that goes skylarking anyway. It was George we used to worry so about. My, the nights mother and I stayed awake listening for George! The trouble was for a while he kept taking up with the wrong kind. You can't tell what a scrape some girls will get a boy into, through no fault of his own, if he has anything to do with them. That's the worst trouble with that kind."

Olly could see her, as she sat, side to the window, plainer than she could see him. The outline of her face and figure, her hand imbedded in the kitten's fur, were serene, even complacent. The simple honesty in her voice shamed him.

"No," Jen said. "What I thought, I thought you must be off walking alone these nights, maybe planning out speeches for some of them debates. And it seemed kind of too bad you couldn't content yourself to get some rest after working hard all day. I got to thinking about it. I thought maybe—some way—we wasn't making you very happy here at home, and I kind of wondered if we couldn't, if only we just went about it right."

She sounded reasonable, willing, quietly eager. Olly

curled inside himself. Again she set him to wondering why she saw everything so straight, was so secure and capable, while he was always fighting back at life, hurting himself and those for whom he cared the most. It was not strange she could not understand him when he could not understand himself. He had no idea why it was he did not stay contentedly in and about this house, as Jen and his father always had; it was a pleasant enough place.

"It isn't that," he said awkwardly. "I'll tell you. I go over to the Janowskis'."

"Do you so!" Jen exclaimed with interest. "Well, now, you go over there! To the Janowskis'!"

She seemed surprised, but neither relieved nor annoyed. Her face turned in Olly's direction.

"They're quite a crowd," he said. He liked talking to somebody about them, especially to Jen. It made them seem more real, less like a queer dream he had over and over. "They interest me. I haven't had much chance to get used to people of another race. Come to think of it, until now there's never been anybody but Yankees around here, except the woodchoppers. That's unusual. . . . You know, Jen, I've never even yet seen a negro in my life! Nor a Chinaman nor a Jap!"

"My land!" Jen said. "I'm sure I never did either. I don't know what they've got to do with the Janowskis."

She wanted to hear what they talked about over there, what Mrs. Janowski cooked, if Olly knew. But she would ask no questions. Let him tell it as he pleased.

"Well, they're Polish," Olly reminded her. He drew

in his breath as if to say more, and then broke it off.

"Yes, but I guess Polish is different," Jen said comfortably.

The Janowskis were the people who lived on the Old Joe place now. They ploughed and planted and drove past the end of the lane every day. Their baby had the croup and their children went to school with George's and the Forrests and the rest. There was nothing in that to make anybody think of Chinamen and negroes and give himself the shivers.

Olly lay leaning against the wall behind the couch, his shoulders hunched. His thoughts seemed to be clearing before him, arranging themselves in their proper places and proportions. It was nothing new. Jen had always done this for him, all unconsciously, whenever he stayed near her long enough.

"They have their own ways, though," he said. He chuckled. "It seems as if they've never learned to hold themselves in, the way we do, and don't see any need of it. Stan does mostly; he's that much more American than his folks, and more grown-up than the kids, but I wish you could see the yard full of them scuffling over there at night, and the old folks singing for all they're worth, and smell the air that comes out of their door when its open, a clean smell, you know, but strong and heavy."

"Must be something she cooks," Jen suggested hopefully.

"Stan can really sing though," Olly told her. "And play that old fiddle, too! He's a great fellow, Stan is. You don't get to know him in a minute but there's a whole lot there. I tell him he ought to start in now and go to college, but he can't see it that way. He's

a farmer. The rest of them would pull up stakes and
move anywhere, any time, like gypsies, but Stan's a
farmer."

"Yes," Jen said. "That's what father thinks."

"He's a great fellow," Olly repeated. "There's a lot
to him."

"Seems as if you might bring him over here some
time, and let us hear him play and sing," Jen said.
"I'm sure we'd be pleased."

"Would you?" Olly exclaimed, straightening. That
was what he wanted. He knew it now. To bring Stan
Janowski over here and let him play his crazy tunes
in the Shaw yard with Mark Shaw and Jen and John
to listen, and the ash tree and the pump and the lamp
in the window looking on. Stan's music would not
sound crazy here. Nothing ever had. It would sound
good, and Olly could make his peace with it, and
definitely accept Stan as his friend. "Wouldn't you
really mind his being—Polish, Jen?"

"There, Polish!" Jen exclaimed.

Olly laughed aloud with pleasure in her, and with
relief.

"Then I will!" He stood up and stretched, elabo-
rately careless, feeling the cool air creeping up his thin,
bare arms and into his armpits. "Now I'm turning in."

"You'd better," Jen agreed. "Anybody needs their
sleep."

When he had gone she felt her way across to wind
the clock, and softly lowered the windows that faced
the southwest and might let in the damp of a night
shower.

"I don't believe there's a thing in what Ed was
telling," she thought. "That's just some of Bill Car-

penter's tongue. I suppose he thinks every fellow must be after Doris, being as she's sister to him!"

Before she put the kitten out, she stood for a minute holding him pressed against her cheek. His fur was thick and soft, his little body rocked with his song. She did not intend ever to be without a kitten in the house.

VI

Fourth of July morning George, on his way to the Oakes's, left Esther and Betty and little George to spend the day with Bun and John. They had each a package of firecrackers, two boxes of torpedoes, and a box of sparklers. And as Betty had to carry them all while Esther guided Georgie's stumbling bare feet, she staggered under the precious load coming up the lane. Bun ran to meet them, less from affection than to see the supply of fireworks increased; her crackers were gone already, having been fired off under John's window at daybreak.

"Oh, say, John! They've got an awful lot. They've got the greatest mess. Did your mother buy 'em?"

"No, sir, she never," Betty declared. "S-she never bought 'em a-t-t-tall. My daddy bought 'em! He took us down to the village with him, and he took mama too and we all went, but he went into the store his own self and got these for us. And he got mama something. He got mama a box of writing p-paper. Pink! I wisht you could see it, Bun. It's as p-pink as anything. Mama's going to write me a l-l-letter on it and send it right through the mail. She promised."

"Oh, Betty," Esther said, "you keep still. What makes you always talk so much?"

Esther's neck was spotted red. She had never seen her father give her mother anything before, and it did not seem as if it should be talked about.

"Well, here you are," Jen called from the shed-room door. "I guess there'll be racket enough now so we'll know what day it is. You girls better all take off your shoes and stockings just like John and Georgie, and be comfortable. Be awful careful not to stay too near the firecrackers when they go off, that's all; and now you have a good time."

She went back to her ironing, pleased to hear a crowd scampering round the house, to start when an explosion came without warning, to see the yard littered with ragged red tissue stamped in strange gilt Chinese characters and the wisps of white that marked where torpedoes had been. At noon she would give them biscuit and butter and bowls of new green peas and big molasses cookies and let them eat where the birds would clear away the crumbs. Children were no trouble to her; two or five or an even dozen, it was all the same.

At noon, when Ed rode by from mowing George's high ground, Mil sat beside him on the wagon seat. She waved her hand to the children but Ed did not linger. He had taken her a note from Margaret.

"Mil, dear, Ed said Jen told him when he came back from putting the milk on the train this morning that the children were coming down there to spend the Fourth. If they are, why can't you come for dinner and stay the afternoon with me? You *can*. Now come along. Every time I've asked you you've made some

excuse; and I think it's a disgrace you haven't been inside my house once yet. Now if you don't come to-day, I shan't like it. You bring the baby and if you've got any sewing, I can help you. I'm going to have a good dinner ready, and I know you wouldn't want me to go to trouble for nothing. You telephone up to Oakes's and tell George to stop here for you on his way home to-night. Now you come. Margaret."

The baby lay asleep across Mil's knees, a credit to her mother in a yellow organdie dress and bonnet, gifts from Lize at Christmas time. Ed's horse ambled gently along the clay road from cleared field to cleared field with stretches in between where the alders and birches closed in until they nearly blotted out the sky. Ed spoke to Mil politely of weather and crops and pointed out ripening berries with his whip. He said he was having a telephone put in; the linemen were setting posts as they rode past. Mil felt secure and cool, confident that she looked her best in a green linene dress Margaret had made for her in the spring; she laughed at Ed for keeping the horse so fat and asked if he fed her on butter. Years before she had teased George like this; when she had been a girl people said Mil Ross was a great one for going on. It was strange how anybody let down and kind of gave up as she grew older.

Margaret came running out.

"Well, Mil, you did come! Oh, I'm glad. If you hadn't, you'd have heard from me. Anybody that can go other places can go to see her sister. What's all this I hear about you and George gallivanting down to the village last night and sitting round talking 'til all hours, I should like to know!"

"Gracious," Mil exclaimed, flushing, "we just went down to get the young ones some fireworks——"

"Ice cream cones, too! You all had ice cream cones! ... Oh, I keep tabs on you!"

Margaret took the baby on one arm and led Mil with the other hand. Mil must see the house. She must get the view from the new roof windows, feel the mat of the overstuffed living-room set, see the linoleum in the kitchen, notice how high-posted the cellar was, how the piazza shaded the front room, in what good light the pictures hung. When they finally reached the dining-room, the table was laid with a red-and-white checked cloth and the gilt-rimmed china, and Margaret in a white apron was soon bringing in a fluffy omelette and muffins and new peas; plum sauce and cocoanut cake waited on the sideboard, and lemonade with ice and mint in it; Mil could see the green springs floating through the glass of the pitcher she had given to Margaret on the day of her marriage.

"Well, what do you think of the ranch, Mil?" Ed demanded. He pulled out her chair and pushed her into it and shoved her up against the table so close she could scarcely breathe. It was his way of showing his affection. "Is it good enough for your little sister?"

"As far as I can see, it's good enough for any woman living," Mil said. "But don't you get rough here, or I'll box your ears. I have before now and I meant it too. The way you used to chase Margaret when she was little! Until she'd screech and cry!"

"I guess you didn't box 'em hard enough," Ed grinned. "You never stopped me chasing her; did she, Peg? I'm at it yet."

"I should think you were," Margaret scolded him.

"Now haying's begun I hardly ever get a glimpse of him, Mil."

When Ed had gone, riding on his mowing machine, to finish cutting the grass on George's hill piece, Mil and Margaret sat by themselves on the porch, the house neat behind them, the fields patched green and yellow before, the baby playing on a shawl at their feet.

"Have you heard about Olly taking up some with Doris Carpenter?" Mil asked, dipping at once into the sweetness of whispering and nodding with another woman.

"Bill's had a lot to say about it to Ed," Margaret answered. "I don't believe it amounts to anything."

"I'm sure I hope not, but he'd better be careful," Mil said darkly. They had brought out lemonade in tall glasses and she sipped hers with relish. "Doris has been getting quite a name up there to Penny Brook. I only hope she ain't too smart for him."

"They have to be pretty smart to get ahead of Olly," Margaret said. Olly had been the big boy in her school the first year she taught, and she still looked upon him as a favorite. "How are the children?" she asked Mil. "It seems so long since I saw them."

"You ought to come up," Mil said. "I don't see what you have to tie you . . . Oh, they're all right, only Georgie's had the pink eye awful bad. The girls miss going to school. They'll be glad when it begins again, but I hate to send them to anybody but you. I think you're foolish not to keep your school, Marg. It's too bad to lose the chance to earn a little something of your own to do with."

"Well—Ed never liked my teaching," Margaret explained. "He thought it was too hard for me to keep the two jobs going."

"Two!" Mil exclaimed. "Most women handle a dozen! No, it's independence men won't have in women; they don't care about the jobs as long as they're at home where nobody else can see them."

"What talk!" Margaret said, wagging her finger. "I won't have it. It's a wife's business to be loyal!"

"Another job," Mil said grimly. But after a minute in which she stared at the baby she finished with, "No, but I do wonder who they'll get to take the school. First thing I know, Betty'll be trying to act just like her, whoever she is. Betty's the greatest little mimic."

"Oh, I know it," Margaret said. "She was the best actress I had in the whole school. Esther is so dependable though. I never saw a child that could take responsibility like Esther. I'd trust her as soon as I would a woman almost anywhere."

"She's a good hand with Georgie all right," her mother granted. "But then Georgie is an easy young one to get along with, Margaret. He's got far the best disposition of them all——"

They talked on, rocking, of the children and the school and the neighbors, of sealing wax and cleaning powders and pudding recipes, of prices in the catalogues and stories in the magazines and the costs of upkeep on a car. Between them they finished the baby's first pair of rompers, made of stout blue cloth with a pink rabbit appliquéed on the front. They tried it on her and found it fitted, and Margaret kissed and cuddled her and carried her over her shoulder into the garden, where Mil picked sweet peas and pansies to take home.

"I mean to have a garden of my own some time," she said, "but some way I never get to it."

"You've got a different kind of garden, Mil," said Margaret.

She kissed the baby's neck and felt its soft arms and legs through the thin romper.

"You'd think they were a garden if you had them," Mil said, smiling indulgently. "Margaret, these holly-hocks will be budding before long. And what a bed of asters you'll have here!"

Margaret was not thinking of hollyhocks nor of asters. She would keep her children as clean every hour of the day as little Vera was now, and never let their skin get chafed nor their hair dusty. She would teach them to like people, and to smile, and to wave good-by to Ed, and to say their names and where they lived very early.

"Here comes George," Mil exclaimed. "Wherever has the day gone to?"

"Where's Ed?" George asked, setting his brake with a flourish. "Get your stuff together and pile in. Jen wants everybody over there for supper."

"Oh, how nice!" Margaret exclaimed. "I wondered if she wouldn't, maybe. I think I'll take over the rest of my cocoanut cake."

They packed Mil's sewing and the baby's things. Ed came from the barn with brimming pails and Margaret hurried to strain the milk and set it in the cellar. George took the baby while Mil climbed into the back seat of the car, not looking at either of them as he did so, but saving the strain on Mil's back, however ungraciously.

"What about our milking, George?" she asked him
in an undertone.

"Oh, don't you worry about that," he told her.
"You're always worrying."

"Not to-day," she said quickly. "Not to-day, I'm not.
I just spoke of it."

Margaret came in beside her, and the men swung
into the front seat, drawing their legs after them.
George lit his pipe and the good smell of mild tobacco
drifted back. The woods and fields whizzed past;
George drove very fast for such a rough road; the
lurches made Mil and Margaret tumble against each
other. Ed called back, "You still with us?" The yard
of the old place was full of children when they drove
in. Red and white tissue still dotted the grass. The
odor of slow matches hung about the steps.

"Hullo," Jen called from the shed-room. "You go
right into the kitchen. It's nice and cool there and
we're all ready to eat."

They sat around the table and helped themselves
from platters heaped with crusty fried fresh fish,
potatoes in their skins, pork gravy thickened with
flour, peas left over from dinner, big hot biscuit, and
cold johnnycake with sugar on it and thick yellow
cream Jen had skimmed from her last night's pans.
"Have some more, Ed; you've got to keep up with
George, or nobody will." "Hey, hey, what's that?" "I
said you're getting thin, George, from not eating anything. Have another piece of fish." "Thanks, I will."
George was proud of his appetite. Mrs. Shaw held the
baby. "You don't need to toost her, ma." Jen filled
the children's plates and brought in more food from
the kitchen, tousled the boys' hair, and made Mil

taste her jam. It was not plain when she ate herself,
yet her helpings disappeared and she never hurried.
It was as it had been on other Fourth of Julys. Mark
Shaw, bent over his plate, could see out of the corner
of either eye a circular row of young and older ones
reaching around the table as far as his wife. At one
time her face blurred because of the sun but then Jen
rose and pulled down a shade. Now he could see them
clearly, fourteen of them, safe and well, eating his
food. Their voices reached him, their jokes and laughing, but he did not listen to all they said; it was
enough that they were here; he thought of Lize and
Lois May, and Ralph.

When the meal was over and the dishes were
finished, the women followed the men and children
into the yard. They sat on steps and chairs and saw-
horses from the shed, and the children lit sparklers
and set them in the grass or ran about waving them
above their heads, making fiery scrolls on the dark.
"The potato bugs are an awful pest this year," Ed
said. His father told him, "We've paris greened ours
twice already here." Margaret laid her arm across Jen's
knee. "Mil liked my garden, ma. I don't know what
she'd say to yours." Mrs. Shaw bridled. "Well, I don't
know. I wish you'd come down and spend a day with
us, Mil, and see if there's anything you like. We could
let you have some roots." Mil laughed. "I guess I'll
have to stay at home awhile to pay for this." George
thrust out his foot impatiently. "I don't know where
she gets the idea she has to stick in the house. I could
bring her down here any morning." Ed lounged on
the step and felt for Margaret's hand. Olly came up

the lane and into the yard with Stan Janowski. "Why, Olly!" Jen exclaimed. "I didn't even know you'd left. Hello, Stan. Ed, get Stan a chair." Stan said in his slow, even voice, "I'll just sit here." Mark Shaw asked him, "Bugs into your potatoes much over there?" Bun came running, her steps as heavy as a young colt's. "I made my initials. Did you see me make my initials on the air?" Olly said low to Stan as they lay together under the tree, "You know they're getting up an ice cream supper up at the church. You going?" Stan supposed he would. "We'll go together," Olly said. "It's a great place for a feed." Stan glanced at Olly sidewise. "Not taking your girl?" Olly laughed. "I should say not. I'll bet that girl would eat so much I'd have to pay double for her. She looks like a big appetite." He added, tearing up grass by the roots, "I don't see her often now anyway. Looked like she was taking it too much to heart. You know how they will." Stan said he did not know; he was no heart-breaker. "Did you bring your violin, Mr. Janowski?" Margaret asked. "The children have told me you play." Olly answered for Stan, "His father's using it to-night." As he spoke, they could all hear the faint strains of Mr. Janowski's music under the hill. Mil rocked comfortably. The last sparkler flickered out. "Well," Mark Shaw said, looking up through the leaves at the sky, "here's another Fourth of July gone by. The lightning will give us all the fireworks we'll get 'til a year from now." Margaret leaned against Ed. "Oh, I dread the thunder showers." Mark Shaw's head turned toward her. "Why, no," he said gently. "You don't want to dread them. They're a real pretty sight."

VII

Mrs. Hale, as president of the Ladies' Aid, appointed committees to take charge of the ice cream supper. She stood up in church after the service was over and the Elder had made his rounds, and read off the names she had written on a paper. A painted silk fan beat rhythmically against the breast of her black silk coat as she read, and the pulse in her throat moved in and out the black velvet ribbon that bound it.

"Solicitor, the president. Collector, Agnes Austin. Supper committee—Jennie Shaw; that's the beans and like that, Jennie. Ice cream and cake committee, Mabel Forrest; they will be sold separate, you see. Kitchen committee, Minnie Grant. Flower committee, Cora Shaw. Entertainment committee, Margaret Shaw." She folded the paper with one hand and lifted her chin higher to finish. "The committees will feel free to call on them not named to do what will be needed. The money, you remember, is to be used toward the fund for shingling the church. We have thirty-one dollars on hand at present counting, and if the love of the Lord and all His works is in us, we should make up the needed sum this summer."

She sat down, breathing hard.

"Amen," said the Elder softly. "Amen, sister Hale."

"You did good," whispered Bun across the aisle, smiling beatifically. "You did lovely, Mrs. Hale. I could hear every word."

That was what people said to her when she spoke in public.

The corn grew tall and kept as fragile and green

as the mowed fields were crisp and yellow. The
potatoes blossomed and the first cucumbers set on and
the high-bush berries ripened in the swamps, ready for
canning. Mr. Robinson, the fish man, bought huckleberries for twelve cents a quart and raspberries for
fifteen, and paid twenty-two cents a pound for all the
broilers Jen would dress and sell. It was as busy a time
as any in the year, and nothing kept the men from
their work in the fields except the dark, but the
women washed and ironed and cleaned and baked
and picked and canned and watered and nursed, and
even raked after when sudden showers were coming
up, and still somehow found time to cook extra and
fancy food, to scour their silver and the washboiler
in which the coffee would be made, to teach the children verses, and to decorate the meeting house and
grounds with evergreen and crepe paper. They were
the Ladies' Aid.

Of the men, only Olly made a contribution. Margaret asked him to give a speech for the conclusion
of her program, to talk on any subject he might
choose, and he consented. It seemed to shorten the
time he spent in the fields to be considering topics,
rejecting, choosing, organizing, and working out
figures of speech. Mark Shaw watched him turning
hay with a freer, easier motion of his fork, and thought
the boy had learned the use of tools at last, but it was
only that he was twirling words and phrases so lightly
in his mind that even his arms and hands responded.

"I'll tell them," he thought, "what a good thing it
is for everybody to find the place where he belongs;
how we ought not to expect one place to fit us all."

At night, hot as it was, he sat in his room and pored

over the outline he had made. Sweat running down his face from his forehead, he looked through his own books for suggestions; and he looked through several volumes which had been his mother's, flowery bindings with thin, finely-printed pages, and scattered through with pressed leaves and bits of ribbon and clippings from the Derwich *Democrat* which told how Miss Eliza Shaw of Rumfret had spent Christmas with her father, Mr. John Shaw and family, of Branch Road; how Edward Shaw, son of Mr. John Shaw of Branch Road, was recovering from a two months' sickness with lung fever; how Mrs. John Shaw of Branch Road passed away at her home, aged thirty-nine years and three months, a great loss to the community where her kind words and pleasant smile had endeared her to her neighbors. Jen must have put the clippings here for safe keeping. Olly smiled to himself. He had a different use for books than Jen's, or his mother's, or even Margaret's. He was a lone wolf in this family.

"I'll tell them," he thought grimly, "as parents, to look for individuals among their children."

And he wrote down, "Individ. Diff.," in his outline.

The afternoon before the church supper the last hay from the Mark Shaw meadow was housed in the barn. There was left only George's low ground to be cut. Old Bob and Ed's horse drew the loads, five of them; Ed pitched on, Mark Shaw laid the hay smooth on the cart, and Olly raked after. Their black shirts and blue overalls and sneaker shoes, the only clothes they wore, except their broad, coarse straw hats, clung wet to their skins. When the fifth load reached the barn, Ed unhitched Tommy and drove home to his own place, leaving his father to pitch off and Olly to take away. "Here she comes!" Mark Shaw said, hurling up a great forkful. After that he did not speak, but the hay came with perfect regularity like the waves of the sea, and Olly snatched and tore at it, cobwebs swinging from the beams behind his head, the air stifling with dust. He *would* not make his father stand with fork poised, or lower it unemptied once it had been raised. He could take away what any man could give him.

"That's all!" Mark Shaw said. "You'd better come out through the shed, Olly. We've built this up so you couldn't reach the ladder."

He let himself down from the cart to the barn floor and walked to the door, wiping his face on his handkerchief. As he looked out over his fields, he saw them all cut; the grass was dried, and hauled in, and put away for winter with hardly a drop of water ever having touched it. He sat down on the jutting stone of the foundation and stared straight before him, his eyes proud and content.

At last he turned his head.

"Olly! You out of there?"

"Coming," Olly said.

He had lain for ten minutes in the narrow space next to the roof, writhing with cramps, but now managed to get through the door to the shedchamber. A little later his father heard him pouring water into a zinc tub. The shedchamber was the summer bathhouse.

VIII

In the little vestry of the church Jen presided over great pots of beans, round tin cans of brown bread

still hot from the stoves of the women who had
steamed it, potato and onion salad and lettuce leaves
wrapped in damp cloths, cans of spicy pickles, and
custard pie, blueberry pie, lemon, cream, and dried
apple pie; and she kept a fire over which to make the
coffee. On the opposite side of the room Mabel Forrest cut the cakes, the fruited cake, the chocolate cake,
the angel cake, the cakes with marble frosting and
those with nuts on top; and she told Mr. Hale and
Agnes Austin where to put the ice cream freezers
when they brought them in. There was vanilla, lemon,
and banana ice cream, and Margaret had sent a
chocolate sauce with hers. "They had it that way up
to Boston," Jen explained. "Sauce on the ice cream.
According to their tell, it's very good." Agnes Austin,
who had brought the lemon, wished she had made a
sauce to be served on it; she knew a good recipe for
lemon sauce. Outside the children ran and whooped
among the tables and benches set about the yard, all
except Manuel Janowski who was upstairs reciting his
piece once more to Margaret; his big voice boomed
down through the register in the ceiling of the vestry.
Mrs. Janowski, leaning against the sink, ready in a
white all-over apron to wash any dishes that might be
brought to her, listened in rapt satisfaction. He had a
fine voice, Manny did. Mrs. Shaw sat on the stairs leading up to the church, making buttonhole bouquets of
pansies, lilies of the valley, and one zinnia for each,
and thinking Margaret must be deafened by this time.
She said as much to Mil, who was helping with the
flowers, and Mil smiled and shrugged her shoulders.
Mrs. Hale hurried from one to another, indoors and
out, upstairs and down, considering this, explaining

that. Her small old face worked with eagerness and
elation. She was the president. The thought and the
duties were joys that never lessened, though she had
been president for twenty years continually. She knew
what should be done, and who should do it, and the
church would be shingled by fall; the love of the
Lord and all his works was in her; and her skirts
rustled busily through the doorways of his house.

"My," Jen whispered admiringly to Mabel Forrest,
"don't the years rest light on Mrs. Hale? She's never
changed a mite since I can remember."

"She's never changed a mite since she married
Aaron," Mabel answered. "Always up and going it,
any place like this. She started Ladies' Aid, you know."

"Yes," Jen said respectfully. "She's a religious
woman."

Jen put wood on the fire and began dipping beans
into the thick white vestry dishes with a blue enamel
spoon. Her own beans were rich with slitted lumps of
sweet salt pork and ruddy with mustard and molasses
and long cooking, but Mil's were pale and harder
and meant to be sweetened with sugar; some liked
them one way, and some another. Men's voices sounded
about the yard. The children lingered at the door and
sniffed. The sun was going down. Jen dipped faster
and faster, her face pink with pleasure and excitement.
By the time she had filled a bowl for each table, and
sliced the brownbread, and turned out potfuls of the
coffee, Mil and Margaret and Doris Carpenter and the
two Grant girls, who waited on the tables, were back
for more beans. Jen attended to them again and again,
and all she saw of the supper was a glimpse now and
then, as she passed the door, of men and children eating

heartily and laughing, sitting at long, heaped tables in the twilight. She ate only a taste now and then, as the other women did, a spoonful of Mil's beans, a crumb of Mrs. Hale's angel cake, a bit of Margaret's sauce caught before it dripped off the spoon; she would not have had it any other way.

"Mr. Hale wants another plateful of your beans, Jen. He says that's all he ever comes to a church supper for, to get some of Jen Shaw's beans."

"Well, they're all gone, but you tell him to try some of my custard pie. It's just as good as my beans, you tell him."

The supper over, orders began to come in for ice cream and cake. Doris held the lamp by which Mabel Forrest looked down into the freezers and chose vanilla, or lemon, or banana. Jen's fingers grew numb with packing and unpacking cracked ice. Mrs. Janow-ski attacked a mountain of dishes, humming as she worked, her huge body filling the alcove where the sink stood until nobody could find room to help her.

"You go 'long," she laughed. "Oh, I do t'at. Oh, sure. T'at ain't nut'in'."

All the ice cream was bought and paid for, and nearly all the cake, for the children were hungry, and a crowd of young men and boys had come down from Penny Brook way with big appetites and with Satur-day night wages in their pockets. By the time every one had finished it was black dark, and the women had to feel over the tables for the dishes; two of Mrs. Hale's teaspoons were not found. They might have fallen on the grass or been carried away as a joke by the Penny Brook boys who, as everybody knew, had no idea of manners, but Mrs. Hale held her head high and said it did not matter; she had twenty-four dollars and seventy cents in the plate she had passed among the tables, a better sum than she had expected. Now they must go to hear the speaking, all of them, for it was fitting; they could finish the work in the vestry later on. Mrs. Hale went up the stairway first and the others followed, except Margaret who had gone long before to prepare the children. Mrs. Janowski creakingly brought up the rear, smoothing the damp spot over her stomach, and smiling a proud, broad, dark smile. They sat in two rows at the back, the Ladies' Aid.

"They've fixed it up nice, ain't they?" Agnes Austin whispered.

Margaret heard her as she twined Betty's shoulders with a chain of ox-eyed daisies, behind a sheet hung across the front of the platform as a curtain, and worked yet more carefully. The church did look pretty with the flowers and evergreen and braided crepe paper. Now if the children would remember their poetry and not be frightened and if they would bow low enough so that the bow would show—then if she should be kept from taking charge of the next concert in the parish, people might speak of this and say how good it was. She gave a daisy chain to Esther and one to Bun and one to Kathie Forrest; they were to sing the welcome song together.

"Now, I'll play for you. You sing good and loud, won't you? You especially, Esther. You've got a nice voice . . ."

Margaret stepped out between the curtains and down from the platform. The Penny Brook boys applauded her. She flushed and tried to hide herself be-

hind the organ, though she thought she did look
rather well. She was surprisingly healthy, and kept
her color, and her eyes looked bright. Her wedding
dress was still as crisp and snowy as before it had ever
been washed, and the cape collar ruffled softly over her
bare arms, but she could not wear it again after this;
at least not for months. She should not pump the
organ, either, she supposed, but just this once it would
not matter. She wondered if Ed, slouching in a dark
corner, was looking at her, if he was proud he had
married her, what he would say if he knew what she
knew; it was beginning to frighten her that she had
not told him yet; sometimes she even thought he
guessed it. Her hands touched the cracked keys gently.

"De-ear friends, we're glad you've come——"

She heard the curtain swishing back and the footsteps of the children, even their breathlessness.

"De-ear friends——"

All the children were joining in bravely. Everything
was begun. Manuel would come next, and he *had*
known his piece an hour ago.

"Gee, I was scared," Bun told Esther as they scuttled
off the platform. "Weren't you scared? Gee, I'm always scared."

The other children clapped, and the fathers of the
children, and the Ladies' Aid and the boys from Penny
Brook way. There were not many entertainments to
be enjoyed; the audience was not critical. The doors
and windows stood open and the air felt cool; outside
in the dark the fields had been cut and the second
crop was growing; in places corn was setting on.
Harvest would soon be here and crops promised to
be good as well as early. They all clapped until their

hands stung, and settled back to await what would come next. Margaret Ross could always get up a good concert; it was born in her; Sarah Louise and old Hattie Lord had been just the same.

Manuel recited "Under the Spreading Chestnut Tree" with only one prompting. Betty Shaw danced the "Summer Wind" to a sprightly tune that Margaret played, and as far as Margaret could tell nobody objected even if it was in the church, Betty's slim body and small feet and the yellow curls that Mil had made of naturally straight hair blew so lightly about the place where the pulpit usually stood; it could not be wrong, for the Lord Himself made dandelions and turned them into balls of fuzz. Norma Austin and her little brother did a dialogue. Bun spoke a long poem with bombast and great good humor. John followed her without warning and stood, and bowed, and solemnly spoke the same piece as perfectly as she had. "Why, nobody ever taught it to him!" his mother gasped. He went back to her and she held him close. Mark Shaw's eyes dwelt on him from a dim corner. Esther sang alone in a high sweet voice, and Betty pirouetted in to join her in the chorus with many airs and graces.

Then the fourth Shaw boy went down the aisle. It had been announced that he would talk to-night on what he had learned at college about the new ways of education. Reading and writing and arithmetic were not enough these days, it seemed; new-fangled ideas about the schools were going around. The women bent forward. He was a fine-appearing boy in his dark suit with the trousers creased and his white shirt and neat-fitting collar; he seemed used to his

clothes, too, and everything about him was very clean.
Nobody could say that he was handsome; he took after
his mother, and all the Footes had big noses and long,
narrow heads, but he had their smart look and a way
of his own. The men observed him curiously; this was
Mark's odd one.

"My sisters think," said Olly evenly, "that you
would like to hear something about the difference that
scientists find in very young children, not the simple
differences in height and weight, but the differences
in intelligence, character, disposition and special gifts.
It is a mistake to believe that any child can be made
as ambitious as any other child, or as honorable, or as
brilliant. Parents are given certain materials, and their
part must be to make of these materials the most and
best that can be made of them; you cannot do more,
you must not do less."

He spoke clearly, easily, and forcefully. Though he
held himself rigidly within bounds, it was plain that
emotion colored much of his thought. He was too
young, too intense yet to keep it out altogether; the
problems of the world seemed too vital to him, not
only mathematical formulae. He knew this and
crooked his lip, but eagerness still flooded his voice;
and if it had not, the audience would have ceased to
listen; none of his cold-blooded professors could have
kept the Derwich farmers and their wives awake for
thirty minutes after a long hay day and an ice cream
supper.

"It is important," Olly said in concluding, "to look
into your children, to recognize and use the differences
among them, not to try to make them all the same,
all like the one that happens to give you the most per-

sonal satisfaction. Parents should realize that children are not children long, but individuals always. And when they do grow up, don't hold them back. Help them to understand themselves, and then let them go in whatever direction they choose; even if it seems the wrong direction it is too late to teach them, then, and they must find it out . . ."

Olly glanced at the floor and up, half-smiling.

"That is one good thing," he said, "I grew up with —not the only one. But at our house, nobody is held back . . . And if the stuff is in us, we shall prove some day that—Mark Shaw was a good father."

He had not intended to say this. The next instant, as he turned to leave the platform, he was wishing bitterly that he had not said it. The personal had no place in a public speech; moreover the Shaws did not speak even in private of such things. But people said he was more Foote than Shaw. Perhaps it was the Foote in him that had seen his father standing alone on the edge of the meeting, a silent man, well thought of but little known, and remembered the kind, puzzled, patient face with which he had watched four of his children go into a world he did not understand. For Mark Shaw the country outside of Derwich was shut off by hills he could never see over, and the language there was one he could not use; unless the children were at home they were "away," and more than that, switchboards, airports, colleges, bosses, salaries, courses, he could not grasp; thinking of it bewildered him. But he had not held them back. And Olly, probably because he was a Foote, had suddenly felt obliged to say so. It was something no Shaw would have done. He slid almost miserably into his seat.

"That was great," Bun told him, seizing him around the neck from the back. "I could hear every word."

"Why, it was fine, Olly," Mil said. She was wiping her eyes unashamedly. "I declare, I'd never have guessed that you could speak so. Shows how little we know our own, don't it, ma?"

"There, I should say," Mrs. Shaw answered admiringly. "I bet he has done a world of good by that talk."

"Olly," Margaret said, touching his arm, "I—I can't tell you how splendid that was. And what you said about father! . . . I'm so *glad* you did, Olly."

He realized then that they had honestly liked it, that he had not embarrassed them, that the whole family was touched and proud, even George and Ed, grinning over their wives' heads, but still he could not meet his father's eyes. The little group broke away from him to let the neighbors in. "They're making quite a piece of work over you all of a sudden, Olly," Mabel Forrest said in her hearty voice, "but I always knew you'd 'mount to something from the time you was a little whoppet." Even two of the Penny Brook boys shook hands with him, hastily, sheepishly, without speaking, as if they did not want to do it, but would not like to think that they had not. "That was a good talk," Aaron Hale said. He had once told Olly he drove a horse the poorest of any twelve-year-old boy he had ever seen, but that opinion did not deter him now. "Good talk as ever I heard." And Mrs. Janowski with the tears still streaming down her face said, "I sure am glad my man he hear t'at. He t'ink our kids t'ey never care what a lot we do. I sure am proud my kids t'ey see you. Kids, t'ey need somebody

to look up to, I always tell." For the minute Olly
stood on a pinnacle, but he was well aware how short a
time he would stay, let him but start to mow a field at
George's place, or even to build a yard for Jen's chickens. He knew that each profession remembers its own
heroes and forgets the rest; here the need was for
straight rows and swaths and truly driven nails, skill-
ful muscles, a weather eye and a patient spirit; this
kingdom was Ed's. Some other, if any, must be his.

The women drifted back into the vestry.

"Well, Jen, I guess you're proud to-night," Agnes
Austin said. "You've got reason to be."

"Yes," said Jen, her dish towel flying, "it was a nice
concert, wasn't it?"

"But I meant Olly," Agnes said. "How he's changing! I don't doubt he'll be a great man some day. And
the way he spoke about your father. It ain't many
young men has such respect. Look at them Penny
Brook boys, chasing everywhere and stealing teaspoons——"

"Well, I should hope," said Jen with dignity, "he
has his manners."

Bun shouted through the screen door, "Jen! Come!
You 'most ready? Father wants to get started home."

"Goodness, no," Jen answered. "We're nowheres
near through here. You tell father to take the rest of
you and go along. I'll come when I can."

"Ain't you scared to go alone at night?" Agnes
Austin asked.

"Goodness, no," said Jen again. "What would I be
scared of? And anyway, Olly's somewheres around.
He's walking too. There isn't room for so many in
one wagon."

Upstairs Olly helped Margaret to take down the curtains and put up the pulpit and carry away a litter of paper and daisies and cheesecloth. Margaret wished Ed were as thoughtful as Olly, as deft with little jobs, as attentive and appreciative. Now that it was all over she felt tired and heavy, all she wanted was to get home as soon as possible and take off the tight dress. It seemed like hours that she sat in the wagon, while Olly looked for Ed among the groups of men standing talking and smoking about the yard; she tried to curl up on the seat but it was hard and her feet felt swollen in her shoes. She even envied Mil when she heard her climbing into the car and George's voice saying gruffly, "You done enough before. Let the rest of them clean up." But when Ed came he was tall and broad and swung himself in beside her carelessly. His shoulder felt and smelled familiar, and a little way down the road she could snuggle into it; even if he did not think to suggest her doing so, he would ease himself back to make her comfortable. Ed was her man.

"Good night, Olly," she said. "And thank you."

Olly was a dear boy, she thought, and forgot him. With skill Ed guided his horse through the crowd and along the edge of a steep bank, Margaret clinging to his arm.

Olly became suddenly aware of someone beside him in the streaked dark and knew without looking down who it must be.

"I guess you're in awful demand here to-night. Poor little me, I don't get as much as a look from you. Anybody'd think we didn't know each other!"

"Well, we don't, do we?"

"Why, Oliver Shaw!"

"I mean," Olly explained, with an effort, "a fellow couldn't get to know you in the little I've seen of you, Doris. You're too deep, you know."

Doris giggled.

"Oh, yeah? So that's what you think, is it?"

Suddenly she slid her hand into his pocket beside his. He could feel the long, pointed nails and the grate of the multitudinous thread-like creases that covered her palm. It set his teeth on edge. He knew now why he had never touched her of his own accord; she was not really clean, although she looked so. Not only this discovery annoyed him, but the consciousness that her eyes had clung to him all during supper and the evening, begging him to acknowledge her before the neighbors.

"I'm not so deep," she was saying. "Honest, I'm pretty nice . . . If you're going to take me home, let's start. The sooner we leave, the longer we'll have on the way, you know. Ever hear that before?"

She pressed her chin hard against his arm, and then he felt her look up.

"Did you ever, Olly?"

"Look here," he told her heavily. "I didn't think about you. Stan Janowski's waiting somewhere for me to go down with him. We came together."

"Stan Janowski! . . . You can just tell him, Olly. Tell him you've got to take your girl home."

"Look here, I——"

" 'Cause you have, Olly. I'm all alone. Bill's gone long ago. I'd be scared to death up through the pines. Honest I would."

"All right," Olly gave in. "Come along then."

"I've just got to get my hat. You wait a minute."

While he waited, Olly took no time to look for Stan. He was too busy making plans of his own. When Doris returned, skipping playfully over the wet grass, his mouth was grim, his mind set. Even his words were chosen. He took her firmly by the elbow and guided her through the shadows behind the church and along the bank of the river that ran past her house.

"Oh, Olly, this is the *quickest* way!"

"Well, I have to get back. Stan'll be waiting for me."

"Stan! . . . And the grass is so wet! My slippers are awful thin."

"You can change them as soon as you get home. It won't hurt."

After a minute she said softly, "Gosh, you've got a swell hold, Olly. I bet you're a swell dancer."

"I don't dance at all."

Nor did he. But he would learn this fall. He would have learned before the date of the sophomore tea-dance. He believed that usually came between Thanksgiving and Christmas.

"Say, Olly! I'll teach you!"

"No. Look here, Doris." He slackened his pace. "I think I ought to tell you. I've decided we'd better not see each other any more."

She gave a gasp. She stopped and faced him and cried out what did he think he was talking about, he couldn't shake her like that, a girl he had been out with four Saturday nights running, and more than one knew of it too. Her voice was shrill, vicious. Olly hoped it would not carry as far back as the church. He hated her.

"Now listen, Doris. You don't understand." He spoke very gently and put his arm across her shoulders, urging her by the pressure to walk beside him, to lean against him. He had been right; there was even a slight odor about her, other than the perfume. "You don't understand. It's you I'm thinking about. I'm determined not to ruin your life, Doris."

He told her she was lovely. He said there was no reason why she should not marry a man who could give her everything, furs and jewels and motors. He explained that he might never have enough money and a high enough position to be worthy of her, that if he ever did, it would be many years from now and she could not afford to risk her youth and beauty in waiting. He told her that what she should do was to keep herself from the small-time men she met here and go to the city, as she had once suggested; the city was the place for her; the city would be her element. All this he said in a tender, reluctant, generous voice, his arm adding reassurance, and Doris listened. She softened, and wept, and brightened. When they stopped before her dark house she flung her arms about his neck and laid her head on his shoulder.

"Oh, Olly," she declared, "I guess you're right. But whoever I get, I bet I'll never get one that's as *sweet* as you!"

"I know I'm right," Olly said. "And you'll get one much better than I am, Doris."

It was just like the magazines. Doris caught her breath with the wonder of it. Slowly he set her away from him, holding her wrists while he kissed her hair, and then turned and marched away into the dark.

He hated himself now as much as he had hated her.

But as he walked, his distaste fell away from him. If he had sacrificed something of straightforwardness, he had won a new freedom, a new confidence with girls, which would add to both his comfort and his pleasure; and the tact with which he had extricated himself had served Doris well. His might not be the way of a minister or a Boy Scout, but it was the way of an intelligent man, an intercollegiate debater, a fellow who moved sure-footed in a slippery world.

He reached the church and finding it deserted, strode on whistling. His legs felt long, his shoulders broad, his lungs strong, his mind facile. Lights in the windows that he passed reminded him of the ice cream supper and his speech; he wondered if any were speaking of it now; individual differences, that was an important fact to recognize.

"Well, Jen! You up still? I thought father left early!"

"He did, but I stayed cleaning up."

"Walked home then?"

"Yes."

"Alone? That's too bad. Probably you thought I'd be around."

"I thought you might. And Stan did, too. We were both hunting for you, and when we didn't find you, we walked down along together."

"He came over here, then, with you?"

"Yes, he was bound to. I told him he didn't need to bother."

"Well, that's decent of him. I appreciate it."

Stan was a splendid fellow, a real friend. Jen looked pretty in the new blue voile dress that crossed over her round breasts and tied in a bow at the back; her braids

were pinned smooth and shone with life and cleanliness; Jen was always very clean. The kitchen was clean, too, and cool, and cheerful with the checkered tablecloth and the lamp with the white shade and the almanac hanging under the ticking clock. Olly felt all in a glow.

"You gave as fine a talk," Jen said, "as ever I heard in my life."

"Oh, that!" said Olly.

IX

A little before daybreak the next morning Jen was awakened suddenly. She stirred and listened, and the sound came again. Pound, pound, pound on the front door. She sprang out of bed and snatched at her dress, holding it before her as she hurried sleepily down the stairs and fumbled with the key. "It's one of the Grants," she thought. Mrs. Grant had come there in the night several times during the last few years, panting, calling, knocking under Jen's window. (*"Jen! Jen! Will you send somebody to telephone for the doctor? The doctor! And can you come over to the house? Charlie is took bad."*) But this time no one spoke, and the knock had been repeated only twice. Jen felt thankful. The noise always terrified the children. Wide awake now, she shook the door until the key gave in the lock, and peered out into the silvery dark.

It was Ed who stood there.

"What is it?" Jen asked. "What's the matter, Ed?" She thought of Margaret.

"I got a telephone call a few minutes ago," Ed said.

His voice was deep and sober. The birds on the apple tree behind him sang shrilly. Jen could not see his features. "Kind of bad news, Jen."

"What is it?" Jen asked again.

"It's Ralph," Ed said.

"What's he done?" Jen asked. "Where is he?"

She could not have explained, even to herself, what was in her head to lead to those questions, and she did not need to; she never remembered afterward that she had asked them.

"He's down there in Hartford," Ed said. "There's been an accident. He's hurt."

Margaret had told him how to break the news. "Say first that he's hurt, Ed. It won't be such a shock."

"Do you know how bad?"

"He's dead," Ed said. He doubted now if Margaret's way had helped very much. "He was killed. It happened last night. He and two other fellows he took up as passengers."

After a minute Jen asked, "He was in a plane then?"

"Yes, in a plane. They said it happened last night in the evening. It was a nurse from a hospital telephoned. She said they had been trying all night to find out who to get in touch with. She said it wasn't his fault, any way. Everybody was satisfied of that, she made it plain."

"Well," Jen said slowly, "that's good."

She had forgotten to hold her dress before her. It hung from her hand as she stood in her white cotton nightgown, barefooted, her hair in braids down her back.

"I suppose you'll tell father," Ed suggested. He only

glanced at her, and then back toward his team waiting
in the road. "Won't you?"

"Yes," Jen said. "I'll tell him."

"I'll wait out here," Ed said. "I've got my milk to
put on the train. If he wanted to go down to see about
anything, or to send word——"

"Yes," Jen said. "You wait. I'll speak to him."

She went back up the stairs. Ed heard her open a
door and say gently, "Father! Father, you awake?"
Then he sought his cart, and sat hunched on the seat
of it in the gathering light, the reins buckled and un-
buckled between his hands, until his father, fully
dressed even to his hat, came out of the back door and
along beside the house.

Mark Shaw stopped at the fence and rested his
hands on it.

"You tell them," he said, "to send the boy home."

"Anything else?" Ed asked awkwardly. He changed
the position of the milk cans.

"No," Mark Shaw said. "I don't see as there is anything else. You can tell them to send the boy home."
He turned away and then turned back as Ed clucked
to his horse. "You tell them," he said, for the first time
unsteadily, "we're expecting of him."

The next few days were hushed and strange and
very busy. Jen tore the paper off the parlor walls and
washed the ivory paint and put on new paper that had
been waiting in the shedchamber since the spring, buff
color with a neat gray figure. She sponged the carpet
and rehung the pictures, one a crayon drawing of
Ralph when he was four, and one of Lize; they were
twins and both wore wide, white collars stiff with
starch. She washed and mended the lace curtains and

they hung very full and rich. When the men brought in a big cedar box and placed it on a table between the windows she thought it was a fine, clean room for anybody to come into. She stood watching, quietly wiping away tears with the corner of her apron.

"You're certain you want it here?" the undertaker asked in his soft, considerate voice. "It isn't usual to put a coffin before windows, Miss Shaw."

"That's where we have it, though," said Jen. "That's where we had mother."

"You know it doesn't seem best to open the coffin?"

"Yes," said Jen. "We know about that. It's all right." She touched one of the silver handles and said smiling, crying, "It's a fine one, ain't it? It's as good as any?"

"It's plenty good enough. It's neat and tasty," the undertaker assured her. "It's what you selected," he added.

"Yes," Jen said. "That's the way it seems to me. Kind of tasty." She stood looking at it.

"Now," the undertaker suggested, "won't you set down a minute, Miss Shaw? There's a number of things we have to see to."

He wanted to know how many would come to the funeral, how many chairs he should bring, who would preach the sermon, whether she wanted singers, what floral pieces he should order for the family, who was to dig the grave, whether there would be a second service at the cemetery. Jen listened and answered carefully. No one doubted that it was her place. Mrs. Shaw was busy making over the black clothes she had worn when her first husband died and cutting new things for Jen who had never worn mourning. Mark Shaw said, "You see Jen. She's tending to it." He went into the field with his hoe as usual. There was no impropriety in this, only the furore of ploughing or mowing would have surprised his neighbors; nothing new could be begun, but what was started must go on. And he was of no use in the house where Jen cleaned and baked and Mrs. Shaw sewed and the cedar box in the parlor had its cover fastened down.

"What is it?" John asked Bun, peeking fearfully through a crack of the door into the still room.

"It's Ralph."

"Is Ralph in there?"

"Why, sure he is," loftily.

"Why don't he come out?"

"He's dead."

"Can't you come out if you're dead, Bun?"

"'Course you can't; what do you think!"

"Can't he *ever* come out?"

"Of *course* not. You're awful silly, John."

That night when Jen put John to bed he would not let her go. He kept calling her back to bring him a drink, to turn the light higher, to listen while he whispered to her; he clutched her tight.

"I *wisht* Ralph could come out," he said.

"Come out!"

"Come out of that box."

Jen thought swiftly, tired as she was.

"Ralph isn't in any box," she said. "Foolish!"

"Bun said he was."

"Well, he isn't. He's off up in the sky somewhere. Don't you remember the way he went the last time he was home? Up in his airplane?"

"Ed and Margaret went, too," John said.

"Yes," said Jen. "And they came back. But Ralph

didn't. He kept on going. Why, you couldn't get Ralph into any box. He's too big!"

"Then what we got the box for?" John pressed her.

"It's," Jen began bravely, "well, I guess it's kind of something to say good-by to. Because he went so quick and we didn't have time to say it to him. We wouldn't want not to say it at all, would we? Father especially wouldn't. You see, once Ralph was a little boy like you, and father's going to miss him; of course he's been away a long time but father could always look ahead to his coming back, and now we know he won't come back any more. So we'll have to be awful good to father for a while, you see, John. We'll have to——"

She sat on the edge of the bed, rocking him in her arms, her tears wetting his hair, and already he was sound asleep. She smiled down at his eyelashes. The days were full of crying and smiling, but it would not do for babies to share it; and to-night John was a baby; he was all the Shaw babies, from George down, and she rocked him tenderly.

Downstairs Mark Shaw and Olly sat alone in the kitchen. Mrs. Shaw was stitching in the sitting-room.

"You been in?" Mark Shaw asked out of the silence. Olly glanced up and shook his head.

"We might go in," Mark Shaw said.

He went with slow steps past his wife, through the long front entry, and into the parlor, holding a hand-lamp. Olly followed him. They stood looking down into the blank, shining surface of the coffin. Behind it the white lace curtains stirred in the air from the open door.

"Seems strange," Mark Shaw said, "it's so that we can't look at him." He cleared his throat. "Seems as if it would kind of help to look at him. Wouldn't it, Olly?"

Olly could not answer. His father stood there with the lamp in his big hand, his eyes trying to pierce polished cedar, his voice patient, puzzled.

"He was a good boy when he was a young one," Mark Shaw said. "I guess he was quite a flier, too. I don't know much about such things, but I guess he was a good one. He had a knack with anything he tackled. Sometimes I get to thinking, of course, what if I had made him come home. I guess I could have."

Olly muttered something and moved toward the door. His father's voice made him stop. It broke twice, humbly.

"That's what you said, though, wasn't it, Olly? You said—they hadn't ought to—be held back——"

"God, father!" Olly said.

He went out and walked in the fields for hours, and the second crop of grass was drenched with dew.

The next day Lize and Lois May came home. Two cousins from Haverhill came down, and a friend of Ralph's from Hartford. The Hales, the Forrests, the Austins, the Carpenters, and the Grants came. The yard was full of automobiles and carriages. The Shaws sat in the parlor, and the others in the sitting-room. The old Elder took his place in the doorway between to preach his sermon; "—for it is soon cut off," was his text; and Margaret and Mil sang two hymns as they stood in the alcove under the stairs. After the singing the undertaker in his black coat read names, two by two. The Carpenters first, then the Forrests, then the Austins, and so on up to Mark Shaw and his wife last. It had been Jen's wish to have the neighbors'

names read. "It isn't usual," Mr. Anderson had told
her, "to call any but the relatives." But Jen had insisted. "We did for mother," she said. "They're 'most
all some connection, one way or another, them that
has lived here a long time. It won't hurt to read them
all." She sat watching them as they passed by her to
the front door, her face serene; this was no time to
cry, before so many; the house looked neat and good
and she felt proud of it; the coffin was nearly covered
in hothouse flowers, roses and delphinium and lilies
and carnations; they made a handsome sight.

The undertaker read her name with Olly's and she
went out in her black dress and hat. The line had
formed and she and Olly took their place at the head
of it. Mark Shaw and his wife came and stood before
them. Four men brought out the cedar box with all its
flowers. The procession walked slowly down through
the field to the little cemetery on the hill in the pasture. As the old Elder prayed beside the open grave,
Jen could hear the children playing over in the grove
where they had been sent. She hoped John was playing with the rest.

"And so it is with Thee," the Elder said, "we leave
him, knowing Thy ways are best. Amen."

They walked back, disorganized. At the house Jen
and Mrs. Shaw and Olly talked with the men and
women, and shook hands. Lize and Lois May set out
sandwiches and pie and cake that Jen had ready, and
asked the guests to refresh themselves; they would be
late home to their suppers. But Mark Shaw had
stopped at the shed for his hoe and gone, still in his
best suit, to the field. His head barely reached above the

rim of the hill, jerking with the movement of his shoulders as he worked.

"You'll have to excuse father," Jen said quietly. "He isn't just himself to-day."

X

Through August the sweet corn ripened and string beans were ready for picking. Mark Shaw and Ed and Olly finished the haying in George's marshes, and three barns were full. Fall apples hung red and greenish-yellow on the trees. At night the yards and lanes were powdery with evening primroses, and poppy petals travelled on every wind. The air lost its early summer sweetness and hung heavy, fruity. John learned how to bring a stream of milk from a cow's full bag. "That's the youngest," his father said, "that ever one of mine has done it." One day the Shaws drove to tide water, and the children waded and the men caught alewives while the women sat in the shade and talked and spread out lunches. The fields were green again, the corn grew tall enough for children to hide in, the house smelled of sugar and spice, and early potatoes ripened. This was August like last August and like other Augusts that had gone before. Whatever else might change, the seasons kept their course.

FALL

FALL

"DON'T you have an idea," said Jen, "it'll take itself out in talk?"

Stan shook his head.

"No. I think they'll go .... My father's going to Boston next week to look around. My mother's brother lives there; he may know of something. The papers say business is improving everywhere . . . He might as well. He's no good here. He doesn't do a thing but argue from morning until night. He swears if he doesn't get hold of a needle again before winter, he'll have rheumatism in his finger joints . . . He heard about a tailor once that did. It's always worried him."

"Well, I could give him hold of a needle," Jen said, "if that's all."

She shook her mending bag and a heap of riddled stockings, torn overalls, shrunken petticoats and buttonless undershirts came tumbling into her lap. She laughed across it, and Stan laughed back, but did not speak. He sat quietly at the end of the stove, watching her hands feel through the pile to sort out what would be needed first. She took up a darner from which nearly all the varnish had been worn away and which had some time been split and nailed together again; it slid into her father's brown sock with a rasping sound and could not have been used with silk, but she had no silk in her bag. Now, as she worked, Stan could see only her braided hair, the round end of her nose, her shoulders and upper arms, one hand arched above a yawning hole, and her feet in their shabby, broad-toed shoes, each set firmly on the floor a little apart from the other, making a hollow between her knees to cup the heap of clothing. Beyond her, rain beat against the window. Otherwise there was no sound during the long pauses in their conversation. Jen's fingers flew evenly at their weaving, and Stan watched them, stroking his soft wet hat with one hand as he held it in the other.

"My land, I should think your mother'd hate to go," said Jen. "With so many young ones. Up to Boston. This time of year."

"She's crazy to," Stan said. "It's what she wants. She's lonesome here. She always has been. It doesn't suit her . . . It doesn't suit either one of them."

Jen took scissors by the points and pounded her darn smooth with the handle.

"It suits you, don't it?" she asked.

"Yes, it suits me fine. I always knew it would. I've wanted to get onto a farm ever since I could remember. I like this town, too. I like the people. At first, you know, I thought they were going to hold out against us, but almost everybody acts all right now . . . I know it's due a good deal to you folks here. I appreciate it . . . Yes, this suits me fine."

"Well, it's something," said Jen, "if *one* is satisfied."

She took up a small pair of overalls and snipped the frayed edges of a hole in the knee. The threads caught on her skirt and clung, Stan noticed. She reached into a basket on the table for a piece of blue drilling, lifting her arm so high that Stan could see the under side of it; that side was softer and whiter than the top. She settled back in her chair and set swift, not too small stitches around the patch; it was the wearing quality she thought of, not beauty.

"I don't quite see, though," Stan said, "how I'd manage alone. If I stayed here after they went."

"Oh, yes," said Jen. "You could. Father did. He shifted for himself a year or more before he married mother. It's wonderful what men can do if they have to."

"It isn't that so much. Not the house. It's not much of a house to keep . . . That's one thing, of course. If I could get up a better place to live in, my mother might stay. I've been promising her, but I can't do it. I'm not going to get much for my potatoes."

"No. Potatoes are so plenty everywhere."

"She wants a lot. She wants a bathroom."

Jen dropped her hands.

"A bathroom!"

"She wants furnace heat and linoleum on the floors . . . You see, she had it in the city. She wants a car to ride in."

"It isn't reasonable," Jen told him. "You just getting started."

She went back to her sewing. Stan watched her. He had never talked with anybody else who let his mind travel its careful way, did not hurry him or excite him;

for he could be excited and then he did foolish things. He liked the sound of her voice. He liked the way her hair shone and her hands moved. He sat watching her.

"One man alone can't get ahead fast, though, on a place like mine that needs so much done to it."

"Not fast," Jen agreed.

He pondered this.

"You've got neighbors," Jen added. "They could help out in a pinch."

"I've got fine neighbors."

It was raining harder than ever. Jen thought of the children coming home from school. Bun would be drenched. But it was a warm rain, and the shallow wells needed it.

"I get to thinking, too," Stan said, "they're my family, after all. I got them to come up here. I took father away from his own shop. Some of what he sold out for is invested in the place. They haven't much to start out new on. They're not young any longer, and the children cost something."

"Didn't they want to come?" Jen asked, folding and patting. "Did you force it on them?"

"Oh, they wanted to come. But they thought I'd make more money. They thought we could live easier than we do."

"You're doing the best you can," Jen said. "You're doing well . . . I don't believe myself it's best to follow after them that's always hunting easier living." She shut her lips together and then opened them to add, "You'll have to pay back what you owe as soon as you can. So it'll all belong to you. Potatoes won't always be this cheap."

She put back into the bag what mending was left

to be done, and crossed the floor to start the fire. It had
gone out since noon and she meant to stew beans and
bake a johnnycake for supper; that dish always went
well on a stormy night. She sprinkled shavings over
the ashes in the stove, laid two dry sticks on them, and
dropped in a match; she never needed oil. She stood
very near Stan. Her skirts brushed his hand. The flame
must be kindling in the stove, he thought, for he could
see a yellow light on her face. She replaced the cover,
shaking it into its groove.

"I hear father coming now," she said. "He's through,
then. He never leaves a horse in the spare floor."

Mark Shaw came into the kitchen, his overalls hanging loose on him for he always lost weight in the haying, his hat pushed off his forehead out of his way.
His eyes changed when he saw Stan but he did not
smile.

"Well. Hullo," he said. "What's this storm? Line
Gale?"

"If it is, it's early, isn't it?" Stan asked.

"Might be," Mark Shaw said. "May last. I see your
smoke beating right down to the ground yesterday
morning. I knew then there'd be weather." He stood
by the window, his hand on the middle sash. "Still
travelling west, I see. Won't be much change until the
wind turns . . . Well, we needed it. But not too much
of it."

John followed his father in and stood looking at
Stan.

"Having quite a rainy spell," he said.

"Pretty wet," Stan agreed. He never laughed at
John. John liked him. "I came over to see if I could
get you to tighten up my horses' shoes, Mr. Shaw. And

one's lost off. I know you do your own shoeing but I don't have the knack of it yet; and it isn't very convenient to drive them to the village right now."

"No," Mark Shaw answered. "No, I wouldn't say so . . . Yes, I guess I can fix them up. They out here?"

"In the barnyard," Stan said. "I didn't want to stop to hitch them, it was coming down so then."

"I just finished shoeing mine, it happens. My tools is still out."

"So Jen said. I'll make it right with you, Mr. Shaw. I'll be much obliged."

"It ain't nothing much to shoe a horse. You'll get onto it yourself. It's best not to have to depend on getting to the village any time. I never can."

Jen glanced up at them as they passed her on their way through the sinkroom toward the barn. Her father led the way, a figure so familiar to her that she hardly saw him, though she could have listed every detail of his face and clothes; and John, growing taller even as he passed, it seemed to her, held to the hand of Stan Janowski, a blue-eyed, brown-skinned young neighbor whose horses needed shoeing. They did not latch the shed-room door securely and she attended to it, then went on looking over her beans; now and then she found a wormy or a withered one, but for the most part they were good; about two hours would be right for the stewing; she believed she would use the time to tuin out the sitting-room cupboard; that would be a fine start on the fall cleaning. She sang quietly, thinking of Olly gone back to college for his second year, of whether Bun had worn her rubbers, of people who could never be contented anywhere but must needs always be wandering like gypsies, of her stepmother gone with such pride and anticipation on a visit to Lois May and Lize, of the flowers she had left on Ralph's grave and which the rain would have destroyed by now, of shelf paper and how dust collects on dishes not in use, of rain and beans and fire and soap and meal and whether clove or cinnamon should flavor an apple pie.

At supper her father said, "House seems quiet."

"Quiet, yes!" said Jen. "It fair makes my ears ring."

"I got a letter from ma," suggested Bun.

"Yes," said Jen. "Bun got a letter from ma."

Mark Shaw passed his plate for more beans.

"She well?" he asked.

"She went to the pictures," Bun said. "It was about a millionaire's daughter that tried being poor. Lize's boy friend took them all. Gee, I'll bet he's nice. I wish I could ever go anywheres and see anything."

Her tone of voice turned very like her mother's. Jen looked amused.

"I thought you'd been to school and seen your new teacher . . . John, finish up your milk."

"Oh, I did," Bun exclaimed. "She's the handsomest thing! She's so little and thin and her hair curls. It curls itself. I asked her. I just love the way she looks in the back of her neck."

"Who have they got?" Mark Shaw asked.

"A Harris girl from up to Milton Mills," Jen answered.

"Gloria Harris," Bun amended that. "Her name's Gloria." She sighed enviously, adoringly.

Jen could see John's tongue trying over the new word. Getting up to clear the table, she hugged him to her as she helped him down from his perch. In one

way it seemed a pity that he grew so fast. He no
longer needed the high chair young Mark Shaw had
built for his first-born, George, but when John let it
go, there would be no further use for it; it must go up
into the shedchamber under the eaves, only brought
down for George's children when they came here for
a meal, and Ed's and Margaret's in time. By another
summer, Jen estimated, one of Ed's and Margaret's
should be sitting up and drinking from the mug with
the picture of the kittens on the side. She smiled wisely
to herself.

"Stan was saying his folks don't think to stay another winter," her father remarked from where he sat
now by the back window.

"He talked that way to me," said Jen, the dishes
passing quietly through her hands.

"That didn't last long, with them."

"No."

"I figure he'll stay."

"He can't make up his mind."

"I figure he'll stay."

"You can't tell. You can't tell how a man is going
to turn until you know him pretty well."

"I told him he'd better."

"I shan't say anything. Not any more."

"As I see it, it'll show what he is. What he does."

"Yes. It's a matter for judgment."

Jen began hanging her towels behind the stove to
dry. Her mouth was firm.

"Bun," John said, edging close. "Bun, what did you
say her name was? That teacher?"

"Gloria Harris, I said."

"Geo—ya——"

"Gloria Harris! Can't you understand anything?
Here."

Bun took a pencil and wrote the name large on the
margin of the newspaper. John stared gravely and
made nothing of it, but to Bun it represented all the
wonder of soft voices and silk dresses and curved white
nails and millionaires' daughters who pretend they are
poor.

Jen blew out the lamp in the sinkroom and pro-
duced her mending bag again with energy. She was
accomplishing a good deal to-day.

II

When the sky cleared, the road and lower fields
were spotted with blue pools but the sun came
out so hot that within a few hours dust was blowing
again after every passing wheel. The dull thud of falling apples—Red Astrachans, snowflakes, sweetings—
reached the kitchens; it must have reached the outhouses, too, for hens had nearly always been and left
their marks and gone again before a woman or a child
could get to the trees with basin or looped apron.
There were no longer any services at the church.
Mark Shaw went into the woods of a Sunday and
found wild grapes growing over old stone walls that
had once encircled the homes of people whom he
knew; green grapes along the road where he had
driven his father's cows as a little boy, blue grapes in
the underbrush of the yard of the Hampliton young
ones, Bill and Annie and Gus, who had been his
schoolmates; he took both green and blue home to Jen
and she made jelly and preserve of them, setting the

glasses along the window sills among her ripening
tomatoes. Bun and John and George's children
searched George's pasture for walnut trees and dug
patiently with teeth and nails at thick green burrs the
frost had not yet humbled; returning, spotted with
brown, they found by the fence the long, wide new
grave where old Kate had been buried. George, Esther
knew, had dug the grave first and led Kate out to it
and shot her there; she told about it as soberly as the
others listened. They picked goldenrod and wild asters
by the armful and placed them with dignity and
tenderness at both ends of the grave, going home the
quieter; Jen, they knew, did this for Ralph, and came
home so. Kate had been a fine horse; they all had
ridden on her sharp old back; George had a new one
now, a big, fat black one by the name of Prince,
bought with money he had earned by haying for the
Oakes's, but the children thought Kate had been as
fine a horse as anybody could wish. Jen, after canning
and pickling since early August, still canned and
pickled; the air of her kitchen stung the throat with
the strong smell of vinegar and sugar and spices cooking; huckleberries, raspberries, strawberries, grapes,
corn, peas, beans, greens, chopped pickle, mustard
pickle, sweet pickle she had already on her cellar
shelves, and great stone jars of whole, sour pickles
covered with old white plates, and still there was much
of many varieties to be found in woods and fields—
tomatoes and mushrooms and high blackberries; all
these must be taken care of before barberry and cranberry time; she hastened to store her wealth, glad that
her father was one who bought sugar, as well as flour,
by the barrel, or she would have been sending for it
every week. Mrs. Shaw came back from Rumfret with

tilted chin and much to tell and many new ideas to
incorporate into old dress patterns; she took back the
job of butter-making graciously. "The customers will
be as glad as we are that you're back, ma," Jen said.
"I never could get the balls so smooth and pretty."
Mark Shaw went into the field and for the first time
in many years finished digging his whole potato crop
without a son to take the row next his; last fall Ed
had been here, but now he was busy with his own, and
Mark Shaw dug and shook the stalks, bent, picked up
into baskets and turned into bags every potato he had
grown, with no one near but John, who fell on his
knees and burrowed into the loose dirt until he was
as covered with it as woodchucks and field mice are,
looking for one brown root his father might have
missed; each one was precious to him. Only Mark and
John were there, and sometimes John lay asleep in the
sun, but still the long ranks of full bags grew, and
Mark Shaw went at dusk to haul them in with horse
and cart, as he always had, until at last his cellar was
full, and one end of his shed, and even John could
not, with all his digging, find one potato in the whole
length of the piece. It was time now to think of the
corn.

One night when Ed came back from a day in the
woods, tracing the boundaries of a lot he thought of
buying, he brought a note for Margaret and gave it
to her as he passed the flower garden where she was at
work.

"Mil sent it down," he said. "I stopped there to
speak to George and she come running out with it.
Mil's looking well for her."

"I'm glad of that," Margaret answered. She stood
leaning against the fence, looking at Ed, smiling.

Under an old sweater of his—she never went out now without a coat or sweater—her heart beat so excitedly it seemed to choke her, she was so relieved to have him back where she could see him, touch him, speak to him. It left her limp and languid to be alone, although she tried to fight the feeling off, sure Ed would be quick to show impatience with it if he knew. "I hope things are straightening out with her and George. Jen thinks they are."

Ed drove on to the barn. Margaret laid her trowel on the gate and unfolded the paper Mil had written on. Automatically she remarked it was the same blue-lined scratch paper Mil had always used for notes, not the festive pink George had bought for her; Mil must be saving that for real occasions; but Margaret's ears were for the steady, solid steps of Ed's horse on the barn floor, and Ed's voice saying "Whoa" once, and not again. Everything had changed in the last few minutes, even the chill September air that reddened and stiffened her fingers, even the smell of the plants and the sound of the wind in the maples and the outline of the house against the pinkish-yellow sky; it was as if her senses had been asleep all day until now. She drew a long breath, snuggling into the corner of the fence, curving one arm comfortingly under the weight of the child that, as she relaxed, never failed to stir.

"—overheard Ed saying to George that he is called to serve on the jury up to Alfred, and I run right in to scribble this to you. When he goes, you'll come up here and stay with me, won't you? I've got the open chamber cleaned up for the children to sleep in now, so you could have the parlor. George got me a brand-

new bed couch for it when he finished haying for the
Oakes's, one of them that shoves underneath, you
know, one side. I'm crazy for you to see it, and we can
have a good visit together, just like old times. You'll
be sure to come, won't you? I'd be worried to death
about you staying way off over there, one woman
alone. There's such works going on now every-
wheres——"

Margaret stopped reading. She could not leave this
place, this yard where she crossed the driveway to
come to her garden, this house with the high, clean
old rooms, her own bed and clock and rugs, and the
hills and trees she saw here every day the same as
before she had thought of a child and the same as she
would see when her body should again be her own.
Above all, she could not let Ed stay away from her for
days, for nights, for weeks. She heard a small sound
and knew that she had made it.

"What?" Ed asked, coming through the half-dark.

His voice gripped her, though it was careless and
changed by the chatter of leaves under his feet. She
could not hold back what she wanted to say but because of him she could say it quietly.

"Mil says you're drawn to serve on the jury."

"She gets news quick, don't she? They notify her
before they did me?"

He always resented having his affairs discussed.
Margaret knew this, but could not stop for it.

"When did you hear?"

"Got a letter this morning when I passed the box."
He came into the garden and stood looking down at
the pink and purple and white asters beating about
in the wind. "Frost kill these, will it?"

"Will you have to go up to Alfred?" Margaret asked.

Ed looked at her curiously.

"They don't say anything about having jury meet down here on my doorstep so as to be handy."

Margaret held to the fence, looking back at him.

"When—will you have to go?"

She could not keep him. She saw that now. It was Ed Shaw she had married. He had concerns of his own and was attending to them; having this baby was her business. She could beg him and perhaps he would give in to her if she told him why, but he would never forget it; she would not beg him. She waited to hear what he would say.

"Oh, I ain't going up there," Ed said.

"Not going——"

"I don't have to. Maybe they can get *some* farmers off their places this time of year to earn a few dollars a day. They can't get me. George, now, he says he'd jump at the chance. Let them take him then. I've got my crops to think of——"

"Not going——"

She felt the easy tears coming and bit them back. Her hand with Mil's note inside went out to Ed and he took it in a great, sudden, awkward, knowing pressure. All the way to the house he held her arm stiff and hard against his. He said nothing more, only that he was not going because he had his crops to think of, but their supper together was different from any other supper they had ever had, though they ate the same foods. And when the dishes were done, Margaret brought out her sewing openly for the first time, white outing flannel that she was making into gertrudes, white nainsook that would be a dress, pink yarn for crocheting sacques. She could not work on it all at once, but she spread it out along her side of the table, and now and then she saw Ed glance across. At last, when he had done with his daily paper, he even reached over to put one big brown finger into a sheer neckband.

"They come that small?" he asked, grinning.

III

Bun brought in the four Janowski girls from school one afternoon. They stood in a row along the kitchen wall, each one a half-head taller than the next, all dressed alike in black challie dresses with black velvet Eton jackets trimmed with gold braid, all with fat, dark, shining faces and big, eager, watchful shoe-button eyes. Bun put them through their paces as if she were their trainer.

"This is Maria, you know it, ma?" she asked, pointing. "And Ellena and Louise and Marian. See, they've got dresses just alike. Their father made them, sewed them up himself. Ain't—isn't that funny? Don't they look good, though? Turn around, Ellena, so she can see the back. Don't that look good, ma? See the buttons. Did you know Louise had got curls? Take off that cap and let her see your curls. There, see, ma?"

"Very nice," said Mrs. Shaw with reserve. These Poles might be all right; most folks seemed to think so now; but she was not certain she wanted her children too much with them. It was a queer twist to dress young ones in black. "Pretty, I'm sure."

Bun faced her belligerently, her legs well apart. Her

face looked hot and determined. Her breast heaved.

"Why don't you say they're handsome?" she demanded. "You just say they're handsome now!"

"Why, Bernice Shaw!"

"You go ahead! You say they're handsome! You—you——"

Mrs. Shaw sprang up and stood in a sudden fury over her child, her hand raised.

"Another word out of you——"

Jen came in from the sinkroom.

"Ma! Ma! . . . Sssh! The Grants are going by!"

"There won't be any noise if she stops these actions," Mrs. Shaw said. She lowered her voice but not her hand. Her face had taken on the vicious look it always had in anger. "I never heard such talk——"

Bun turned and flung herself bodily upon Jen, burrowing her head into Jen's stomach.

"They said—they said at sch—school—they said their dresses was—was homely. The other kids." She was sobbing now, and screaming. It would take more than the passing of the Grants to hush Bun. "Tom—Tom Austin called them—he called them NIGGERS! I guess—I guess—I guess if my father made *me* dresses —they said he was a—was a SISSY . . . He—he ain't —isn't a sissy, is he—Jen? They—they ain't NIGGERS, are they—are they, Jen?"

"My land, no!" Jen said easily. "What foolishness!" She smiled at the little girls cowering by the wall. "That's just young ones' running on. Some at school always has to show their mean streak."

"Well," Bun cried, drawing a little away, braver now, ignoring her mother. "Well, I—I lit into Tom

Austin! . . . And I slapped Evelyn Carpenter's face!
I *pasted* her good!"

"That," said Jen, "was no way to do."

"No," Bun agreed, "but I done it . . . And—and
then, Evelyn—she said it was—it was just like the
Shaws to take up for Poles. She said—she said probably
I was just like—like *you;* probably I'd—I'd let *Manuel*
walk home with *me!* . . . She said we didn't have any
—any pride; that was the way we acted any—anyway,
taking up with anybody that—that came along. . . .
And I hit her again, and I—I got her down, and I told
her Poles was—was just as good as—as any Carpenters
—or even any Shaws——"

Here Bun broke off short and stood back to regard
Jen with eyes full of a tremendous need for reassurance. The four little Polish girls behind her also
looked fearfully at Jen.

"*Be* they?" Bun asked.

Jen's face had not changed, though she had heard
every word and understood its significance, but remained still young, smooth, pleasant, unshaken, as if,
having taken her stand, she could no more be moved
from it while still alive than the ash tree from the corner of the yard, and out of the same security of position
looked around her with indulgence at lesser things
making a stir. She took Bun's cheeks between her
fingers as she would have to give her a sailor kiss, but
did not stoop.

"Yes, Bun," she said, looking down. "Yes, yes, yes.
Just as good as any of us. Just exactly. You did all
right—except the fighting."

She hesitated over that and let it go, releasing Bun
at the same time.

"Now you'd better all go out and play and forget about it. You can take the pole and knock you off some porters. I guess the Astrachans and sweetings are all gone by, but there's some porters. Just you remember young ones at school have got to spit out spite sometimes; it don't mean anything."

She opened the door, giving each little Janowski a pat on the shoulder as she scuttled past, and Bun a cheerful, sisterly spank. She smiled, watching them fill the yard with sudden life. Two of them clutched the pole and shook a branch until eight or ten long, green apples came tumbling down, striking at them, making them shriek with excited laughter. Jen laughed too. They were all right now. Beyond them in the field Mark Shaw was picking corn. John, seeing the children about the tree, came running, but Mark Shaw set on the stubble beside his piece a basket full of yellow ears and stooped to fill another. Beyond him the sun was going down very clear and red, and the moon was coming up pale in a still, blue sky.

"Everything looks just right for a frost to-night," Jen said. "I believe I'll get out some blankets and newspapers and cover up my tomatoes anyway. It'll be late when we get back from supper up to Mil's, and I don't want to lose them yet."

Mrs. Shaw said nothing but when she heard the door close on Jen, crossed to the window and watched her go down the pasture lane and climb the fence into the lower field, a broad, short, energetic figure in a dark print dress and ragged man's sweater, with a bundle of coverings on her arm.

All the anger was gone now from Mrs. Shaw's face and figure. She looked only startled, curious, and faintly frightened. Her fingers pinned and unpinned the bib of her apron.

"Sometimes I wonder," she said aloud, "if it could be she's really thinking some of——"

Jen was thinking just then of the feel of the air, and nothing else. It had a tang to it, a chill, a smell, a threat. Frost would come, if not to-night, then soon. It was close to October. It was time the leaves turned red and yellow. She could feel the change coming, she had lived so long with the seasons. Contentedly she crouched to tie a shorts bag carefully around a tomato vine, to lay a paper over a cucumber plant and weight it down with sand and small stones, satisfied that she knew when to expect a frost and how to meet it. And all that filtered through this which was less thought than sensation was awareness of a letter which had that morning come from Olly, and a bold, white, triumphant pride in him.

Up the road at George's house all was bustle and confusion. It was not often that Mil entertained. Pots and kettles and frying pans of many shapes and sizes crowded her stove, iron and enamel and aluminum and tin; cookie dough and a rolling pin and basin balanced on the edge of a table heaped with pushed-back papers, dishes, water pails, recipe books, and stove cloths; the door stood open into the little dining-room which had once been a downstairs bedroom, and another from that into the parlor where the new couch and fresh bunches of paper flowers stood on display; these openings let out of the kitchen not only warmth to take off the evening chill, but all the smells of cellarway and cooking. It was not as Margaret would have done, or Jen, but it was Mil's way and for once, also in her way, she was enjoying herself. Her steps fell hurried and heavy, her voice sharp as she gave directions to the children, but she took pleasure in laying her big table with a clean cloth and the bluebird china, in hovering over Esther as she painstakingly filled a glass dish with the India relish all the Shaws professed to like so much, in snatching cookies from the oven, with a grunt and a gasp, at the last minute before they would have burned. Saved again, she thought. Without the cookies, her tapioca pudding and the apple pie would have been all the dessert she had to serve, and the others were not to think that the George Shaws went hungry, whatever else they might lack. She whipped white of egg for the top of the tapioca, holding the bowl in one hand because there was no place to set it down, and gave the scrapings to Georgie, but caught them away from him just in time to keep him from smearing himself. She lived by snatches, by fits and starts, by spurts of desperate effort, and had for years; sometimes it seemed she could not stand the strain of it; but lately it was different; she could manage. She hurried in to place the pudding in the center of the table, the cookies at one end, the pie at the other, to arrange two plates of fresh baker's bread, two pats of butter, two jellies, two pickles, two great dishes of cold, sliced beef, leaving barely room enough for the hot foods which must be brought on at the last minute. She even thought of the oranges George had brought Saturday night, and ringed the pudding with them as a centerpiece. The table now looked to her very festive, and, above all and most to be desired, lavishly spread. She would have liked to pause and survey it but she had no way of knowing that the milk for the white sauce might not be boiling over by now and so went at a half-run into the kitchen, her shoulders reaching ahead of her feet.

"Here's Uncle Ed and Aunt Margaret," the children cried. They turned from the windows, eyeing her, as anxious as she that everything should be right to-night. None of George's children was growing up without a sense of responsibility. "They're driving right into the yard now——"

"So soon! Oh, dear, I don't see how I can—well, there, it's only Margaret."

The children breathed again. It was only Aunt Margaret. It was all right. They rushed to the door and threw it open, their mother behind them.

"Hullo, Aunt Margaret! Hullo, Uncle Ed!"

"Hullo, Ed! You can hitch to the fence if you want to . . . There, Margaret, I'm in a mess here as usual. You'll have to shut your eyes and come right through into the parlor. If you can get by the table, that is; it's lucky you're slim . . . Here, let me take your coat. Is it cold out? . . . Why,—Margaret! You're—you're not—why, Margaret!"

"Why, Mil!" Margaret returned, holding her head high, laughing.

"You're not going to—have——"

"Have a baby? Of course I am!" She faced the gilt-framed mirror to arrange her hair and saw that her cheeks were blazing. It was Mil's fault, she thought; it was because of the look in Mil's eyes. "Any reason why I shouldn't?"

"But—so soon?"

"Oh, not until the last of December. It's *proper* enough, Mil——"

"I didn't mean that, Margaret. I just meant—oh, I don't know . . . I hate so to see you starting in, that's all." Mil chewed at the lining of her cheek. Her eyes grew narrow with what she had been through and now remembered, the days, the nights, the long summers, the longer winters, the weight, the pain, the shame, the sickness, and with it all the rest of life, nothing made easier by what she bore, only harder, more complicated, more impossible, and she each time less capable of coping with it. She took up a corner of a drapery that needed to be washed and pinched it between her fingers. "I been hoping you'd have it different—than I did——"

Margaret continued to smile, with confidence she thought, with defiance it seemed to Mil.

"Well, I don't want it different, if you mean not having children. I couldn't *stand* it not to have children. I'm just as pleased as I can be—and so is Ed! We think it's *lovely!* . . . And we shan't have it a bit hard. There's so much room at our place we could house an orphanage, I guess! Why, I *need* a baby, Mil, to take up my time! Now I'm not teaching, I don't have half enough to do. . . . And Mil, he—" She laughed apologetically, though eager to share her experience with another woman. "He's so cunning already! I mean—he's so full of business night and day! I just know it'll be a boy! Isn't that what they say it means, when the child's active?"

"Yes, that's what they say," Mil answered. "But I don't know. I believe Vera was the hardest of any I carried."

"Hardest! Oh, Mil, it isn't *hard!* It's sweet."

Something gave way in Mil, as if for the time she

stopped fighting, as if the effort to cling to reality in the face of the magic Margaret was seeing became too great. Faintly she remembered a sweetness that even she had found now and then in bearing children, especially at first. And surely it was better to hold on to that as long as a woman could; without it she had nothing. Mil smiled.

"There, I know it," she said. "It is. That's right." She pulled Margaret against her and kissed her on the cheek.

"Dear old Mil!"

"Ed's got to see you get good care," Mil said. "You take it easy from now on, and don't you hurry afterwards to get up. You look after yourself."

"Ed says I can have Mrs. Norris from the village," Margaret answered proudly. No other woman in the place had ever been cared for by a real trained nurse. "And he says she can stay just as long as the doctor wants her to. Ed's more thoughtful than anybody might suppose."

"You take care of yourself, and you'll be all right," Mil repeated. She had no faith in the thoughtfulness of men. At best it came and went, never there when a woman needed it most. "Maybe," she added suddenly, "if you like that Mrs. Norris, I'll have her in the spring."

"Oh, Mil. You, too?"

"Me, too." Mil laughed. This was neither the time nor the place to show her fierce resentment. In fact, she scarcely felt it just now. "In April. I'm feeling fine, too. I don't know when I've had so much ambition or could get so much done in a day."

"Why, Mil, that's fine. They'll—be almost the same

age, won't they? I know what we'll do, Mil! We'll make some little suits some time and dress them up alike!"

"All right. We will."

They hugged each other. It was dark now, and they hugged as they had when they were little girls shivering in bed on a cold night.

"Ma! Ma, something's boiling over out here!"

"Oh, dear," Mil cried, "it must be my white sauce. I thought I'd set it well enough back . . . Oh, look how dark! That supper'll never be ready——"

"I'll help you, Mil——"

When the other Shaws came a few minutes later, they found the two busy in the kitchen, their faces flushed with the heat, their voices quiet and cordial, towels pinned about their waists; and Mark Shaw and Jen, recalling when the two had been "the Ross sisters," could not see that they had greatly changed. Esther and Betty ran back and forth importantly with spoons and laden dishes, and even little George attended to his special task of picking up the toys that Vera flung away from her. Ed came in with George from the milking.

"You folks lay off your things in there in the parlor. Or, wait a minute—Margaret, did you light the lamp?"

"Yes, Mil. It's lit."

"Well, then, you go right in. Here, John, give Mil a kiss. That's the boy. My, ma, how he——"

"Where'll we set this milk, Mil?"

"Oh—wherever you can find a place. On the floor there. It'll be all right. Now, Georgie, you watch where you're going! Betty, is the sugar on?"

"Yes, Mil, I put that on myself. Everything's ready but your fish."

"Well, pour the sauce over it, Esther. It didn't lump, did it?"

"No, I guess not . . . It's kind of thick, mama——"

"Oh, that's just right, Esther. Mil, here's my compact; put a little powder on your nose. Betty, you tell the rest of them to come . . . No, Mil, that's too much. There. Now you're pretty."

"Yes, I'm a picture!"

"We're both pictures." They giggled. "Come on."

During supper the meal itself was the center of interest. Everybody must eat heartily of everything; more must be brought on; appreciation must be expressed and recipes given above the confusion that six children, however well-behaved, will make around any table. The talking was the women's share, the eating mostly the men's, until toward the last when the men had contented themselves and the women realized that there were still jellies, a meat, a bread, or a pudding they had not tasted; then Mrs. Shaw bent to her plate, furtively greedy with an appetite born of excitement and companionship. Jen and Margaret spread jelly with their knives for themselves and the children; it was not often they had baker's bread; they liked the fine grain of it.

"Well, father," George exclaimed expansively, "you ain't done?" He would have liked to see the family here often for meals, and the neighbors; the unfamiliar sense of generosity warmed him through. "You try that pie!"

"No," Mark Shaw said. "No, I've eat a big supper, for me."

"He has, too, Mil," Jen added. "Everything seems to taste awful good to him over here. I've noticed it before."

"Well, I'm sure I'm glad," Mil said modestly, "if he finds anything——"

"You'll have something else, Ed?" George urged, waving an arm over the table. "Another dish of pudding. Mil, give Ed some——"

"Not here," Ed said. "I'm stuffed."

The three leaned back in their chairs, George feeling in his pockets for his pipe, Ed staring at his plate, Mark Shaw looking meditatively about the room.

"Well," George sent out on a long, satisfied breath, "they seem to think the Democrats have got a chance this fall."

"Say, it'll be presidential election pretty soon now, won't it?" Ed contributed.

"You bet. You bet it will. And this time the rest of the country is going as Maine does and going Democratic at that; you wait and see if it don't. 'As Maine goes, so goes the nation.' I tell you, the Republicans have had their chance and what have they done with it? Look where potatoes went to this fall. Look at grain down the lowest it's been in three hundred years. Yes, sir! I was reading that this morning,—three hundred years! Now that's quite a while, I tell you. Sometimes I get to thinking I don't know what times are coming to. There ain't no work in the cities, according to the papers, and there ain't no money on a farm. Things are at a terrible pass, as anybody could see except them setting down in Washington, going to balls and parading around and wasting their time. They don't care what happens to the farmers. What

do they care? They're comfortable. It's the rich ones
they're doing business for. Why, I see some of them
farmers out west is letting grain rot in the fields. They
can't afford to cut it. Now what way is that to live?
Driving to raise stuff that ain't worth cutting?"

Mark Shaw moved in his chair and cleared his
throat. The others fell quiet, looking at him, knowing
that he was about to speak.

"I suppose," he said. He began again. "I suppose
we'll be getting first-hand knowledge of how it is out
west. We won't have to be depending on the papers."

He paused, placing his knife and fork yet more
precisely across his plate.

"What's up?" Ed asked. "You going out?"

Nobody laughed.

"No," Mark Shaw said mildly. "It's Olly. Olly, he's
going out."

Now they all straightened, leaning forward. It was
strange how a hush or a movement ran so quickly
and evenly around the table. Only Jen sat as she had
been, Mil's baby on her arm. She saw her brothers who
had so long thought theirs the only skill, the women
who had married into the family and been kind to
the thin, dark boy nobody liked, the children who had
plainly never admired Olly as they did other men.
Now they would hear something that would surprise
them, all of them.

"Olly!" Margaret exclaimed.

"Yes," Mark Shaw said. "Yes, just for a spell. The
college down there is sending him. It's speaking he's
got to do, that—debating, ain't it, Jen?"

Jen nodded.

"Yes," Mark Shaw said, reassured. "Debating. Jen

got a letter to-day. He's going clear through to Californy before he gets back."

"Good lord," said Ed. "Where'll he get the money?"

"They're sending of him," Mark Shaw repeated.
"It's on business for them, as I take it. It don't cost him
a cent. It's—I guess it's quite a thing. He's starting on
the cars to-morrow night, but he stops off some few
places on the way. He's going to send back postcards
when he can."

"Gosh," Ed said. "What do you know about that?"
He thought of mentioning it to Bill Carpenter in the
morning. "That kid!"

George's pipe had gone out, and still he chewed the
stem of it, staring. California, without its costing a
cent; he turned this thought over and over in his
mind.

"Oh," Mark Shaw said complacently, "I guess Olly's
about man-grown. He's going to make a lawyer of
himself. He's got it fixed."

"A lawyer!" Margaret exclaimed softly. "Oh, *isn't*
that fine?"

"His mother's Uncle Jeff," Mark Shaw said, "he was
a lawyer. I always heard he made a pile of money. He
got his start in Californy, too."

Now he had finished. He relaxed in his chair,
satisfied that at last he understood what way one who
was gone had turned his head. Seeing through it all
had not been easy, but Jen had done her best, and he
had squinted and labored to read the letter through a
dozen times out by the back barn door until he knew
that Olly would go to California now and it would
cost him nothing, that when the right time came he

would be a lawyer, like Minnie's Uncle Jeff; but Olly's
name was not Foote; it was Shaw.

"Why," Mil marvelled. "Why, it just don't seem as
if you could believe it, does it?"

"Well, I guess it's so," Jen said, laughing. "I know
I had to make him up two new pairs of pajamas in
a dreadful hurry. He'll need a lot of clothes with no
chance to get them washed . . . Come, Mil. Let's hustle
through these dishes."

"There, Jen, for once you leave the work alone——"

"No, now, we'll all duff right in and all be through
in no time."

"Well—then you menfolks go into the parlor and
keep out from under foot."

There was little further mention of Olly that night.
In squeezing past the kitchen table Georgie knocked
off a butcher knife and tripped and cut his wrist. The
gash was deep for the blade had been made razor sharp
to slice the cold meat before supper, and he seemed
covered with blood by the time his mother could get to
him. Jen thought at once of Margaret.

"You put on this coat and run out to the well,"
she said, "for some cold water. Don't look so scared.
It's nothing."

Mil rocked Georgie on her knees, groaning. George
came and stood by, helpless, fearful; this was his son.
Mark Shaw and Ed seemed to fill the shadows. The
little girls' eyes grew large with terror. Jen and Mrs.
Shaw hurried about with cloths and basins and a bottle
from the cellarway.

"Oh, George," Mil cried. "You'll have to call the
doctor. Why do you *stand* there so? See how white

he is! . . . Georgie, dear, don't—don't cry! Poor baby——"

George looked at Jen.

"No," Jen said. "You don't need a doctor . . . Here, Georgie, let Aunt Jen see your arm. (Mil, don't act so; you're scaring him.) Georgie! *Georgie!* There, that's the boy. Now let Aunt Jen see . . . Well, what a cut! We'll have to wash it off clean and put this on it—it won't hurt! There! Now we'll do it up, like this . . . Hullo, Aunt Margaret. Georgie wants you to see what a cut he got. And he ain't even crying— much."

"It bleeded," Georgie explained ruefully. He looked down with regret at the floor which he had seen washed *t*hat morning, his mother on her knees to it, her mouth grim and twisted. "It left spots, mama. Big spots."

"Well, don't you care," Mil cried tearfully, laughing, kissing him, "about any old floor. As long as you're all right."

She tucked him into the rocking chair and gave him a cookie. The little girls were told to amuse him. The women went back to clearing away the dishes but cast him affectionate glances and left pats as they passed. "I never see a worse cut on a young one in my life," Mrs. Shaw declared. It was Georgie's hour.

"Once I split my head open," Bun suggested hopefully. "You said, ma. Up in Kezar Falls."

"Yes," her mother agreed. "That was an awful time. I don't believe it bled so though. Not as I remember. But we was all awful scared."

"John," Mark Shaw said. "John, you come in here and set. Out of the way."

In the parlor he found a chair for John and placed it beside his own, where he could rest his arm across the back. It was as well not to leave a child free in Mil's kitchen, or about George's place. At home no butcher knives ever lay within short reach, a high shelf was the place for matches, axes, when not in use, were riveted as deep into chopping blocks as a man's full strength could drive them, and children, as well as chickens and cats, were kept inside the house during the mowing; but here one never knew; here, too, much was left to Providence in more ways than one.

"John," Mark Shaw said, reaching for a book, "you want to look at this?"

John took the book and held it carefully but did not open it. He liked sitting with the men. He looked from one to another with gravity as they spoke of this year's crops and next year's, of roads and weather and stock. By the time the kitchen work was done all George's children had fallen asleep and even Bun was drowsy, but John still sat straight and attentive in the shadow of his father's arm.

"Well," Ed asked Margaret, stirring, stretching, "you about ready to go?"

"Now listen to that!" Mil exclaimed. "Ain't that just like a man? No, she's not ready, Ed Shaw. She hasn't had a minute since she got here for anything but work. You make me sick!"

"I think Mil's going to hit me," Ed said, grinning. "I'm scared."

"I might at that," Mil returned with spirit. She made a pass at him and he dodged. George watched appreciatively. It made him feel for once as good as Ed to see the way his wife stood up to him; Mil had a streak of fun in her when she would show it. "I don't doubt it would do you good!"

Margaret spun the organ stool.

"There!" Mrs. Shaw said, settling herself. "That's what I want to hear. A little music. Play something, Margaret, and everybody sing."

"What'll I play?"

"Oh, Margaret, play that one you were learning when you left here. 'My Blue Heaven.' Play it. Here's your music sheet."

"I don't believe I can, I'm so out of practice. And nobody knows it to sing."

"It's awful pretty though. Well, here. Play 'When It's Apple Blossom Time.' I always liked that."

"I'll feel safer on hymns."

They always came to hymns in the end, either because they were easy to play or because the words of the favorites were to be found somewhere in every one of the half-dozen hymn books in the house.

"Play 'Sunshine and Rain' then. That's always nice. It goes along so light."

"All right. That's in all the books . . . Here's one for you, ma. Here, George, here's yours . . . Here, Ed; where my finger is. Don't lose the place now, Clumsy! . . . Oh, you'd better sing, father. You can't do any worse than the rest of us."

But Mark Shaw would not sing. He sat big and silent in the corner with John next to him, while Margaret bent tenderly over the worn white keys she had not touched for months, her back to him, her pale neck and dark head outlined against the brown wood of the towering, filigreed top on the modest little organ. She would have a child, he saw; Ed's child;

the first. Mil sang, reading over Margaret's shoulder,
her hands clasped in front of her, her mouth opened
wide and her under lip puckered and drawn in; all
the Lords had looked so, singing. Cora rocked in the
rhythm; her voice rose shrill and sweet above Mil's
alto; she held her head high, her chin quivering; this
was the kind of time she liked. George had a voice
for singing and boomed out the words, holding his
pipe in one hand, "Give me, Lord, the sunshine and
the rain"; but whichever came, or both, he could not
make the best use of it; George either did not calcu-
late, or calculated wrong, it was always so, and one
way as bad as the other; still he might turn out all
right, you never knew. Though Ed and Jen had books
and Jen's lips were moving, Mark Shaw heard no
sound of them. Ed, his father made his guess, had
thoughts of harvest, or else of that lot up in the woods
that he would buy, the Pickering lot; it was good
growth, well situated; Ed would make no mistake; Ed
and George were not alike and never had been. Jen,
now, nobody knew what she was thinking; Jen was
the quiet kind, a good girl. Mark Shaw thought of
Olly. The others sang "Bringing in the Sheaves," "Blest
Be the Tie," "Shall We Gather at the River," and "Will
There Be Any Stars in My Crown," while Mark Shaw
thought of Olly; the boy would go to California then,
starting to-morrow night; he would cross the Mississippi, see the Rocky Mountains, pass the Great Lakes;
there was a big map up chamber that would show
where he went. Olly would be a lawyer; but he had
better not stay in California as Jeff Foote had; California was a place to see but not to stay in; there was
work enough for lawyers nearer home.

"Well, there," said Mrs. Shaw reluctantly. "I hate to but I suppose we'll have to go. I know well enough your father's getting fidgety."

"Morning's coming right along," Jen agreed. "It'll be Saturday morning too."

They stood up.

"Oh, dear," Mil said, "it seems as if you had just come——"

But she brought their coats, stifling a yawn.

"You'd better button it right up, ma—it's pretty snappy out."

"I suppose it is, this late. Why, I don't know when I've ever been out anywheres after dark. It's quite a treat, I tell you. That supper was just as nice as it could be. Wasn't it, Mark?"

"Supper was fine."

"I'm glad I got that recipe wrote down, Mil. It beats any of mine for using molasses as a sweetening. We all like molasses, too."

"Well, I'm sure I'm glad if you found anything you liked. I wouldn't want you going away hungry, that's all. I wish I could have done more——"

"You did enough, Mil. You did plenty. It was all lovely. Now to-morrow you rest up."

"Well, *you* take care of *yourself*. Oh, Margaret! . . . I didn't think, but I don't know about your pushing on them pedals so long——"

The women were on the steps now, the men unhitching their horses.

"Oh, that's all right. I had a good time. I feel fine. Now you come over!"

"Yes, and you come up here."

"Is Bun in all right? She's 'most asleep. Look out

for John, father . . . Well, you folks all come down!"

"Yes, and you come up again whenever you can."

"It'll be winter before we know it now, and we won't get anywheres."

"There, I know it. Feels real chilly, don't it?"

"Well, good night."

It was still, clear, starry. The wagons were loaded with shadows. Light fell only on Mil and George as they stood together before their door. A train whistled in the distance.

"Say, I suppose this time to-morrow Olly'll be starting."

"There, just think of it!"

"It seems an awful ways, don't it?"

"I guess it is. How far is it, Margaret?"

"Where?"

"Out to California. Where Olly's going."

"Thirty-six hundred miles, I think."

"My, that's an awful ways."

"I wonder if he'll see roses blooming out there this time of year, the way they tell for."

"There, it don't seem possible. I hope he'll send us home some postcard pictures."

"He said he would. I guess he will. Olly's thoughtful like that."

"Well, good night."

"Good night, and you all come up again."

"And you come down now. I hope Georgie'll be all right. Good night."

"Good night."

"Good night."

Mil wrapped her arms in her apron as she ran back into the house, and that night the first frost came.

IV

In sheltered places the leaves were untouched a few
days longer, but elsewhere the green went suddenly
and before the week was out red and yellow took
everything, the sharp, bold colors that come too late
to last. Mark Shaw cut the stripped stalks of his corn
with long, slow, even motions of his hook, tied them
into bundles and stood them on end, like wigwams,
here and there among the yellow pumpkins and
squashes of his piece. The days were warm and bright,
the nights crisp and strong with the smell of vines that
curled and blackened; every morning the fields and
buildings and even the latches of outside doors and
the buckles of harnesses were coated white, so that a
damp finger laid on a bit of iron at daybreak might
be expected to leave skin behind it when it came away.
Mark Shaw drove into the woods for cartloads of wild
apples, some of which he took to the cider mill to be
ground, leaving the best for Jen to pare and quarter
and core and string and hang on a rack in the sun to
dry; she liked wild apples for drying because of the
tang they had, though they were small and it took
many quarters to make a string. Sometimes Bun stole
a strand from the rack and wore it as beads, playing
with John by the cornstalks, calling herself an Indian
princess; once she even browned her cheeks with walnut juice, for the frosts were now opening stubborn
burrs and putting the little creased gray shells at the
mercy of children and squirrels. But walnut juice is
hard to scrub away and very ugly to wear, and apples,
unless quite dry, may stain a dress; Bun had lately
begun to think on these things. It was no less fun,

she found, to ride up to Cherry Camps with her father and John and jump again and again from the crest into the pit of the sawdust heap the mill had left when it moved on, and come back seated high on the red load that Mark Shaw would later use for banking the house and bedding down the creatures; if this filled her shoes and underclothing with square, gritty kernels she could shake them out or brush them off; they would not be there to shame her when next she came before the clear blue eyes of Miss Harris, christened Gloria, from Milton Mills.

"My," Jen said, "potatoes this year are a handsome lot."

Mark Shaw sat sorting them in the shed, day after day, the large and smooth to be sold to the market, the medium grade in size and quality for the home table, the small and gnarly for the pigs. The palm of his hand passed over each fair one caressingly. He had three baskets set in a row before him, and always that which should go to market was filled first.

"The mean ones is scarce," he answered Jen. "I don't know what the pigs will live on, hardly."

"On the best you've got, it seems like enough," his wife flung at him. "Or else they'll rot. Prices down to little or nothing and nobody needing them at any price."

She and Jen were on their way to the cellar with gladiola and dahlia bulbs that must be kept from freezing if they could find a space next to the chimney, but there was scarcely room for anything, potatoes filled up so.

"I figure," Mark Shaw said, "there'll be a change after a while. It's time now to hold onto them. There's always some will glut the market in the early fall, a-hankering after ready money."

His son George was one of these. George had dug before his crop was fairly ripe and sold a hundred bushels at sixty cents. The wonder was that he had raised so many. Ed, though, had five times that in his field, and Ed was storing his away until a better time; by spring the city folks would come to it; by spring Mark Shaw and Ed would get what they earned; that young Janowski over there the same; no man starved that could see ahead. Mark Shaw was still sorting patiently, thoughtfully, touching each potato with the palm of his hand.

"Well, I don't know what you think," Jen said to her mother, "but it seems to me it's time to get at the potting of them plants."

"There, yes," Cora Shaw agreed. "The quicker now they're into the house the better off they'll be."

One brought sand from the bottom of the potato hills and mixed it with fine, dry manure left over from planting in the spring. The other dug with her trowel into the hollow of an apple tree and brought pailful after pailful of a rich, black soil that smelled of rotted wood and a long dampness. These two they stirred together, putting a little above the stones in the bottom of the pots they had scrubbed until, bricky rough as they were, they shone. Tenderly Jen set in a plant taken from the garden; gently Mrs. Shaw filled in around it with the good soil; carefully and firmly they pressed this soil down and watered it.

"That one's thrifty. It will do well," Jen prophesied.

"If it stays in a dark place until it gets a start," Mrs. Shaw agreed.

When they had finished, twenty-four pots were filled, and still the garden was not empty. Geraniums were left in the ground, all colors, and petunias, hyacinths, Wandering Jews, Stars of Bethlehem, and ferns of three kinds, as well as asters and tough little pansy plants and the perennials.

"It seems a pity," said Mrs. Shaw, "to leave them out to freeze, so many of them."

She leaned regretfully against the fence. Summer had gone. Fall was passing fast. The garden had been the prettiest that ever she had kept, but before it was green again there must come storms and bellowing winds, blocking snows, and ice, bitter cold, and sickness. She had rheumatism in the winter; her blood was poor; her feet were never warm even when she wore on them more than she could well drag around. This winter, for the first time, Lois May would not be here, to talk and plan and need things, smiling in her pretty way; she might not even get home for a week-end after Christmas if the storms came on as bad as they had some years. It was a hard thing raising up a child to go away, and plants that must be left to freeze and die.

"Well, we've got all we can attend to," Jen said briskly, starting in with her first load of pots. "As many as we can keep the sun on in one room."

Jen had no regrets for anything her back was turned upon.

A little later George and Mil drove in with a rumble and a clatter. Bun and John came running from the field to see what had so suddenly disturbed the quiet of the evening.

"Oh," Bun exclaimed with bitter envy, "you've been to the Fair!"

Mil carried three balloons, one red, one blue, one yellow, and her hat was all awry from being brushed so often by them. In the seat between her and George there lay an Indian blanket and some paper parcels and two little whips, a red one and a green one, with long, striped, silken lashes. Mil looked cold, tired, proud, and travel-stained, and even George had taken on an expression of having at last been somewhere and come back, a restlessness and bustle.

"Well, we have," Mil said triumphantly. "Now we have. I let Betty take Georgie to school and kept Esther home to see to the baby, and we just up and went."

"I said this morning when I got up," George explained, hunching forward over his steering wheel to see past the balloons, "I said to myself this was as good a Fair Day as I ever see and I was going to have a look at them cattle if I swung for it."

"I told him I couldn't see as we'd ever get a better chance," Mil said, "and we never let a thing trig our wheels. We've had a great day of it."

"I'll bet you did," Mrs. Shaw cried. "Near as that Fair is, I ain't so much as set foot on the fairgrounds since I come here. They all say it's fine."

Jen and her father stood by with pleasant faces, non-committal. They had neither time nor money for a Fair, nor wish to mix themselves with crowds and noise and skin-games going on.

"Oh, it's wonderful," Mil said. "I just wish you could see the flowers, ma. They're a handsome sight. There's a great court crowded full of them, more kinds than you could name."

"Cattle is handsome this year," George told his father. "They got some prize Holsteins I should like to own. It's Holsteins give the milk."

"Thin, though," Mark Shaw said. "Their milk is poor, Holsteins."

"Jen, you'd have been interested in the canned stuff. Every kind of thing they had, even to canned chicken. Now I tell you it looked pretty, all arranged so nice. They had fancy work too, and the rugs and quilts! I just wished you could see them!"

"They're probably nice to see," Jen agreed politely.

"And George had his usual stroke of luck," Mil laughed. The Shaws should see that the day had brought its gain. "Shake out your blanket, George."

He bent his arm and laid back a brown fold modestly. It was thick and warm and marked all over with white triangles on the brown background.

"They had little monkeys in cars on a track," Mil said. "And they sold tickets with numbers printed on them. George bought one—just on the chance—and the man struck a bell and the cars went around and around until he struck the bell again and then they stopped. The car that stopped nearest a number won. You see they had numbers every here and there along the track. And the one that had that number on his ticket got a blanket. And it was George's number! I never was more surprised in all my life."

"That so," Mark Shaw said.

Jen reached in and felt the blanket.

"I bet there was forty other ones," George said, "had tickets on that race."

"You know he's always lucky like that," Mil insisted, though she could not now remember exactly what else he had ever won.

"Must be worth two or three dollars," calculated George, "at the inside." He chuckled. "Not a bad job."

Neither told of the other tickets they had bought, or of the sideshows they had stolen into so guiltily, so eagerly, the bearded lady they had seen, the boy with the crocodile skin, the little black wild man from Africa, and the girl born with three legs. "We shan't think of every dime to-day," George had said grandly. "We're at the Fair!" And sharing his recklessness, holding tight to his arm in her excitement, Mil had thrown to the winds her fear of marking her child by what she saw; she could not always be thinking of young ones; this was her life that she was living. They had sat at a counter for a dinner of frankfort rolls and root beer, and eaten pink spun sugar as dessert, three rolls and two mugs of beer and two sugar cones apiece, and it had not hurt her; she felt fine to-night; she felt kinder toward George than she had in years; George was well enough.

"Jen!" she said impulsively. She whispered in Jen's ear, her neck spotted red with embarrassment. "So now you forget I ever said it, won't you? I was all strung up that night."

Jen nodded.

"I forgot that long ago," she answered. "My memory is awful short sometimes."

Mil laughed in confusion.

"Well, George, we'll have to go along. No knowing what them young ones may be up to."

"The cows want milking, too, I guess," George said. "If they don't give so much as some."

He grinned at the little group that he was leaving, started his noisy engine and drove away, feeling himself the first-born of this place, the one who had experiences and luck. The balloons bobbed gaily at the car window, as they rode down the lane.

"It's like them to have everything that way," scolded Mrs. Shaw. "I don't see how they do it, but they do. . . . Well, yes, I can, too, see. They sponge off other ones that won't afford nothing for themselves. That's how they get along."

She went with jerky, resentful steps toward the dark house. A minute afterwards lights were shining out from every window, high, bright lights, as if she would at least spend oil, as long as she could hear the wash of any when she shook the can.

"It's potatoes went for that," Mark Shaw said. "Them green potatoes he sold off."

"Yes," Jen said. "Like enough."

"Was that much of a blanket, would you say, or wasn't it?"

"It'll be pretty sleazy after washing, I mistrust."

"I thought's likely."

Mark Shaw sighed as he turned away but Jen's eyes watching his broad, bent back were humorous, indulgent, satisfied. She saw a secret side of this. Sometimes an ounce of foolishness went farther with a woman than a pound of sense, and Fair time came only once a year.

"You might have thought," Bun said to John, walking disconsolate between the pump and the tree, "just one of all them things they brought could have been for us. I never had a balloon."

"I never had a little whip," John realized.

"They must have bought Fair candy, too," Bun said, walking faster. "Everybody always brings Fair candy home when they go up there."

John panted to keep step with her.

"Tom Austin went, himself, last year," Bun said. "And Kitty's been. They rode on the merry-go-round; they had five rides apiece. I'm 'most too big now, I guess, to ride on merry-go-rounds, and I never did."

"I never either," John said. "I ain't too big. I could ride on them if I could just get where they be."

They wandered wistfully back and forth, back and forth, between the pump and the tree, for one was nine and the other was six and neither had been to the Fair.

v

Every few nights now Stan Janowski came to sit for a while in Mark Shaw's kitchen. He always asked what word had reached home from Olly and, if there were postcards, leaned close to the lamp to study them, a picture of the new bridge across the Hudson just above New York, a Michigan lake boat at the pier in a little town named Grand Haven, a street scene in Minneapolis where the Hathorn team had met and defeated the University of Minnesota; on the back of this last Olly had written in a jubilant hand, and word of the achievement of the little down-east college reached and stirred the Boston papers; the *Globe* ran a picture of the team. Stan helped Mark Shaw to find the Minnesota city on the cracked pink map that now covered nearly all of one wall in the kitchen, the space between the window and the cellar door; the map was one which had been Minnie Foote's the year that she taught school in District Number Nine; it was a long time now since it had been in use, but the lines and lettering still showed plain. "Why, that's right on the bank of the Mississippi, ain't it?" Mark Shaw exclaimed in wonder. He traced the course of the river all the way down to New Orleans, and Jen came to watch the progress of his thumb. "From there," she said, "from Minneapolis he thinks to go to Spokane, Washington." Stan's glance travelled on until he had found and indicated this. "Due west," Mark Shaw said with deliberation. "Due west, that'll be." Stan stood with his hands in his hip pockets, his eyes warm. "It's a great trip," he said. "It'll be a great thing for him. It'll mean a lot. Now he's got his start he'll be climbing fast." Jen liked to hear the way Stan spoke. "Yes," Mark Shaw said contentedly. "Yes. He's going to make a lawyer of himself . . . Well, I'd better see if I can't trace a few more ears of corn."

Many nights Stan helped with the tracing. He brought a chair and sat across from Mark, beyond the row of baskets full of corn, to braid the husks of each ear firmly with two others as Mark had taught him weeks ago. Even at this time in the evening Jen was hardly ever idle; if Mrs. Shaw did the mending, then Jen must be packing away dried apples in paper bags or stirring cider applesauce or barberries in a big kettle on the stove; when the children had gone to bed she sometimes knit on the third white blanket for Ed's baby, or on the red, ribbed stockings she always gave to men and boys at Christmas. Whatever Jen did, she did it quietly, and had eyes still for the way Stan's hands moved among the yellow ears and pale brown husks.

"Here, try my barberry sauce," she said.

She brought it to him in a saucer, a rich, reddish mass of sweet and sour tempered with cubes of pumpkin meat which she had cooked in such a way that it remained still firm and clear. She passed him a buttered biscuit and a teaspoon and stood there waiting, her hands on her hips, intent on his opinion.

Stan's eyes, too, missed little. Even as he searched the map, he still knew where Jen was, what she was doing, what way her steps were taking her. The tracing of the corn made use only of his hands. At work there by the baskets he always saw whether she sat with ankles crossed or knees, how she stirred what she was stewing with an even, circular, free swing of wrist and shoulder; he saw her sitting or standing, walking or halting, coming or going, speaking or listening, and whichever it was it never failed to please him. He thought of Jen as he thought of music, a peace, a release, a tune already finished and perfected, not to be questioned, only to be sung. He went so far as to think of her in words like these, and wrote them down on paper in the night or early morning or while he was by himself in the fields or woods. It would have puzzled Jen to know it, it would scarcely have delighted her, and this Stan understood.

"Tastes fine," he said of the barberry sauce, "to me."

He did not say he noticed the color of what she had brought him on the saucer, the gold of pumpkin, red of barberries, white of beaten biscuit, nor that the thought of her picking these berries among the junipers of pasture land, a basket on her arm, her feet in

broken shoes, her face chapped by the fall wind, laid
a mist before his eyes; that was a Polish way, perhaps;
he would be Yankee now for fear of frightening this
girl with any of his strangeness.

"Sweet enough?" Jen pressed him.

"Plenty sweet," Stan answered. He finished heartily
and handed her the saucer. "You're a fine cook, Jen.
I never saw your equal at anything you make, and
that's the truth."

"Yes, I guess so," Jen said derisively. She took a taste
herself from the big stirring spoon. "Well, it'll have to
do. Nobody eats it much anyway but father and he's
satisfied however it comes out."

"It always goes good in the woods," Mark Shaw
said. "I don't know why it is but in the winter when
I'm off I'll take that barberry sauce between my bread
the first of anything." He added, braiding, "When you
hang up your corn to your rafters, Stan, be sure it's
anyways two feet from off the floor."

"Two feet," Stan repeated. He was seeing Jen as she
stood between him and the lamp, turning down the
flame before a gust of wind should smoke the chimney.
"Mice, I suppose."

"Mice will get it if they can," Mark Shaw said.

"You want to save your traces, too, when the ears
have been pulled off," Mrs. Shaw contributed. She
could tell this young man a thing or two, since he was
so eager to learn. "Traces make a good, stout mat to go
before the door."

"Say, they would, wouldn't they?" Stan exclaimed.
"I never should have thought of that. It would be
pretty too, if the traces had been braided even."

Mrs. Shaw looked on him with a reluctant new approval. Here was a man who thought of how a rug would look.

"My, hear that wind," Jen said, sitting down, at last, to her knitting. "Old Betty's bones are on the rack to-night, all right."

The small Janowskis had news to tell nearly every day they came to school. The other children could see it in their faces as they took their seats, and marched down front for recitation, and worked their problems on the board, even as they joined with lowered eyes and folded hands in the Lord's Prayer. Curiosity, as well as Bun's violent and persistent championship, con-trived to make Manuel and his sisters the center of the group at every recess. It was better than playing Haley-Over, or using colored chalk, to hear of the wonders these five looked forward to; it was like one of Miss Harris's Friday stories coming true before your eyes; even Miss Harris herself, it was plain, could not for-bear to listen.

"Ellena! Ellena!—did your father go up to Boston yesterday?"

"Yes, and he didn't get back until late last night. He brought me this ring."

"Oh, ain't—isn't that lovely! Teacher, see Ellena's ring. Did it really come from Boston?"

"Yes, and the other kids have got some, too."

So they had, and every ring with a different colored stone.

"Well, did he get a job?"

It was always Manuel who told about the job. It seemed to him it was a man's concern. He braced back and looked as solemn as he could, saying at one time that Mr. Janowski had found nothing to his liking, and at another that a friend of his had prospects for him; for Mr. Janowski, through the fall, made several trips. But one day Manuel's voice could hardly keep the pitch and pace that he required of it.

"Yes, sir," he said. "He got a job all right. He got a job, a swell one. It starts two weeks from yesterday. In Lynn, it is. He's going to get big pay."

"What pay?" his audience asked with no misgivings.

"Thirty dollars every week! It's a swell, big tailor shop."

Thirty dollars every week. It was something to think on how so much could possibly be spent.

"I suppose," said Bun, "he'll put it in the bank."

"Some of it," Manuel agreed easily. "First he's going to get us a good place to live."

Marian added airily, "We've got on like we are so long as we intend to. That's what mother says. We're going to have a bathroom and carpets on the floor."

The Shaws, the Austins, the Jellisons, the Grant, the Carpenter could think of nothing to reply to this. They stood awed, awaiting further revelation.

"We're going to have a piano, very first thing," Marian declared. "We're all going to take up playing lessons and learn to do it right."

"I've got to go to dancing school," put in Ellena, "before my muscles get all stiff, Dad says."

"I hope the zoo in Boston is some good," Manuel said, "even if it can't come up to that one at the Bronx. Up at the Bronx they had every kind of thing. You ought to see the lions they had there, enormous great ones——"

The other boys could never hear enough of what

Manuel had seen at the zoo in the past and expected
to see in the future, though sometimes it seemed best
to act as if they would not climb a fence to own it all.
Manuel was not deceived and if he stopped talking
when they turned away, he cheerfully began again
when they came straggling back to ask how zebras
were, compared to horses, and if apes and monkeys
looked the same except for size.

One day Louise brought in a big china doll. It had
a flowered dress and velvet cape and sat like another
child beside her until school was dismissed. Then without a lingering touch or glance she held it out at arm's
length toward Betty Shaw.

"Here," she said. "You can have her, Betty. She's a
present to you."

Betty had not even seen such a doll before to-day,
much less possessed one. She took it reverently.

"To keep?" she asked.

Here Gloria Harris interfered.

"Are you sure about this, Louise? Are you sure you
want to give your doll away? Did your mother say
you might?"

Louise nodded vehemently.

"Mother said that I was *to*. She said we had enough
to pack without a doll to get breaked up."

And all her sisters nodded with her.

"But," Miss Harris was insisting, "it's a lovely doll.
You're not through playing with dolls yet. I think
you'll find you want her."

Betty stood looking from one to the other, clutching
the doll against her stomach but convinced she must
let it go. She felt velvet along her arms, smelled the
good smell of stiff yellow curls beneath her chin, and

heard the strong new joints creak as the thumping of her heart shook her and what she held.

"No," Louise said negligently. "I don't want her. I'll have a new one that'll walk and talk when I get up to Lynn." They were all to understand that the Janowskis would not leave as they had come. "A much bigger one."

That night Bun described the scene at home.

"They'll be awful rich, won't they?" she asked. "They go to moving pictures every week when they're in the city. The school they're going to has got hundreds of kids in it, Manuel said." After a minute she added, "But I shouldn't think Louise would want another doll, however nice it is, as much as that doll; one she's had. You know how you feel when you're young enough to play with dolls at all. You like the ones you got."

"Some don't," Jen told her quietly. "That's just the difference that there is in folks. Some don't like anything they've got. They never think anything that is can quite come up to what is going to be, if they can only work it."

That night when Stan came he had neither shaved nor changed his shirt. He was restless while Mark Shaw talked to him, kept his mind with difficulty on the map, though now Olly had seen the Golden Gate and the Spanish Missions and was travelling east again by way of the Grand Canyon of the Colorado. "He didn't stop there long," Mark Shaw said with satisfaction. "No longer than he had to, there in Californy. He says the Pacific Ocean ain't no ways as good as the Atlantic. I guess he's got the old state of Maine ground well into him, for 'tain't likely one ocean's much dif-

ferent from another when you look at them alike."
Stan seemed to listen but said little in reply. He did
not offer to help with the tracing of the corn.

"It's a fine night," he said to Jen. "You might come
out and have a breath of air."

"I suppose I might," Jen said, "when I can get the
milk out of the way."

They went through the yard and over the lane in
the direction of Ed's light, walking briskly because the
air was cold, and the wind blew high and harsh. Every
clod of loosened clay and cluster of pebbles was as
plain to be seen as in broad daylight for the moon had
fulled and hung almost directly overhead. The sky
looked pale behind the bare, waving twigs of the lilac
bushes and young willows that grew along the Flats.
Jen walked in the center of the road, the horses' path,
leaving the side for Stan, with only a wheelrut between
them, but still they had to shout to make themselves
heard against the wind.

"My father's got a job in Lynn."

"I heard he had."

"He's going back to-morrow to look up a rent."
"He is?"

"They mean to leave the last of this week."
"Do they?"

The two went on in silence until Jen thought they
had gone far enough. She stopped and turned, holding
her wool scarf against her cheek with one hand, the
other tucked deep inside the old gray coat that Lois
May had left behind. She had a calm, substantial look
against the noisy, brilliant night. Stan touched her
elbow.

"Jen, what do you think I'd better do?"

She looked at him, seeing the outline of his figure plainly, and the familiar concerned, uncertain expression on his face. She remembered his hands as they traced the corn, the admiration with which he spoke of Olly to her father, his voice the few times he had sung his songs to her and the rest at home, the field he ploughed and the care he gave it, the crop he raised from run-out ground, the sleekness of his creatures, the sureness of his hammer blows, the patience of his ways. She knew his mind hung balanced between two wills, one of them to stay and one to go, and that what she told him he would do.

"It's as you think," she said.

"I can't think," he told her desperately. "I've had it back and forth until I can't go straight either way. I want to stay here, but the folks want me to go. It may be as they say; it may be I can't get ahead as I should want to; there's some good reason so few men are staying on the farms; I want to make a living anyway . . . I don't know. What do you think is best?"

"It's not my say-so," she insisted.

"Sure it is, Jen." He had taken both her elbows now, his shadow blotting out hers. "Would you like it in a city? If I was earning money enough to get a good place with all the things in it to make it easy taken care of? I was going ahead all right when I came up here."

Jen stood looking back at him steadfastly. She saw his need, and was aware she could supply it, and Jen was used to giving when she could. It would be easier to give than to hold back for she felt strong and her mind was free, looking in only one direction. But this was not the time to speak. Hard as it was, let him make his own choice whether it seemed his place to finish what he had begun or to be forever following after them with gypsy ways. Let him show once and for all which kind of man he was; then she would know, and he would never be a wonder to her. No, it was best that he decide of his own accord; not by word or sign would she attempt to guide him, nor let him see that by one choice he might have her, and by the other she would become as much a stranger as if he had never lived here and walked with her in the evenings but only, perhaps, stopped in one day as he was going by to inquire the way up to Mount Passy.

"I'll tell you, Stan," she said, "it seems to me we'd better not be thinking on these things just now. There's time enough for them. What you've got to settle first is what's best for *you* to do. Then we can see."

When he still did not let her go, she pushed him gently away from her, smiling cheerfully, and started walking back across the Flats. She did not feel afraid. It would turn out one way or the other, just as the clouds scudding across the sky might bring either rain or snow or be blown away and leave fair weather. What came would come; she had only to wait.

"If I don't miss my guess," she said as they climbed the hill, "there'll be a freeze to-night."

"It's cold enough," Stan said.

He was walking now behind her, his eyes on her back. She puzzled him. He had never made any claim to understanding her. "Not to be questioned," he thought, "but to be sung." He hooked one finger over the belt of her coat. All his advances toward her were like that, tentative, inquiring, almost impersonal, and

though she did not repulse she seemed to take no
friendly notice of them; he asked for nothing; to be
near her quite contented him. Still he sometimes felt
an urge to make her show the tenderness he had not
for some weeks doubted that she felt.

"I'll tell you this," he said. "If I stay, I stay. And
if I go, I go. Whichever I do will be the end of it,
once and for all."

"That's right," Jen answered evenly. "I should have
it so myself, and not be any longer dwelling over it.
That's just so much time wasted, once you've made
up your mind."

Whichever he did would be the end of it.

She said good night and went hurrying through her
yard, soundly beating her ear, while Stan took the
other way across the field. She did not see him again
for several nights and when, as she hung her dish
towels on the line in the evening, she heard violin
music carried on the crisp air, she could not tell
whether it was Stan or his father who played the soft,
wandering, thoughtful tunes.

On Friday the Shaws saw the Janowskis going down
the road, two teams of them. In the first, a wagon,
rode Mr. and Mrs. Janowski and the six children; the
second was a cart loaded with crates and bags and
boxes and Stan drove it. This was the middle of the
morning, with the weekly cleaning to be done and
squashes to be hauled in from the field. Nobody had
time to watch the road to see what travelled it in either
direction from then on.

But early in the evening Mrs. Shaw cried, coming
down from upstairs, "As I'm alive, there's a light burning up in the Old Joe barn. What will you bet Stan

never went with the rest of them? If he didn't, he's an awful fool, if I must say so. What way is that for a young man to be laying out his life?"

Jen did not answer, but she met Mark Shaw's eyes. He had seen Stan's light a full hour ago, from the back barn door, and she from the sinkroom window; she had heard his music, too, and smiled in pity to think of him sitting over there alone, stirring up the echoes, for she had no idea what music meant to him and never would have. The glance that passed between her and her father was rich in satisfaction; what Stan had done, they thought, showed what he was; it had been a matter for judgment.

When they heard his step in the dry grass at the door a little later, Jen went to open it, though he could have let himself in, as usual, if she had kept her chair.

VI

"—if that," Mark Shaw said, "is a way you wouldn't have no objection to my doing."

"Why, no," Jen answered. "No. It sounds reasonable enough to me."

"Well, then," Mark Shaw said.

He left her picking up dry wood in the shed and went out of his yard and down the lane. It was a Sunday well along into November. Beneath his sheepskin-lined brown corduroy coat he wore his store suit, a black necktie tied in a bow-knot under his chin, a white handkerchief in his pocket; and his feet were lightly dressed in black shoes and rubbers. He walked easily and purposefully, one arm across his back to grip the elbow of the other, going to have a word with the men

who lived near, to make the rounds of his neighbors'
barns before the snows set in. He stopped at George's,
speaking to the children and to Mil, eating a piece of
Mil's pumpkin pie, and then went out with George.
They stood in the yard looking at the maple tree,
estimating whether it would outlive another icestorm.
They looked at each one of George's creatures, feeling
their flanks, slapping their sides, going busily in and
out of the stalls. Mark Shaw put up his hand to the
window, feeling a cold wind that should have been
kept out, and spoke of what putty and rags would do
toward making a place tight when sills had warped.
He noticed George had not yet brought in sawdust for
the bedding, and all the cows were caked with filth.
It was no way.

"I can let you have the one-horn back 'most any
time," George said. "I've spoke for one that Henry
Plaisted's got."

"I don't hold to getting much from dealers," Mark
Shaw said. "They're sharp."

"Well, so am I," George promised him. "They can't
fool me on cows. Henry Plaisted knows it's no use trying out his tricks on me. She's fat and good, this cow,
a striped one. I made him fix it so what butter she
makes will have to pay for her."

George would still be paying Plaisted for this cow
long after she was dead.

"I'm going up along," his father said. "You come
down when you can."

He went to Hales', and Austins', and on up to Carpenters', not knocking at the houses but going to barn
doors, trying them, and if they were open, walking in.
It was to be expected the men would be here or would

come out; only women visited in kitchens. Aaron Hale appeared at once, and Harry Austin with his boy, but nobody stirred from Carpenters', though Mark had seen Bill by a window when he went through the yard. He did not resent not being greeted. It might be they had company, or corn was on to pop. It was, after all, the cattle he had come to see, and if the barns were snug for winter. Aaron Hale's was like his own, and the Austins' well enough, but the Carpenters' was worse than George's, clapboards off both ends until the light of day came through the cracks, and cows and horses all thin and sick-looking with no grain in the chest; Mark Shaw raked down some fodder and put a handful in each crib but it was poor stuff, marsh grass housed too quick and getting moldy; it would be small wonder if a barn filled with such hay blazed up and burned some night; Bill was a poor hand at his work, not like his father before him. Once this place had been a county pride. He swung his hand toward Bill when he went out, a recognition of him, nothing more. It was hard to say what would become of any place when the old died off.

The sun was still high when he crossed into the Old Joe field over the culvert he had helped to lay in the spring; he struck this now with his heel to see if it still held firm when the ground had frozen. Smoke poured out of Stan's two chimneys but the glass in the small panes by the door were thick with frost; it was not easy keeping any barn warm enough for a man to live in it. Stan started up from one of the beds when he heard a step in the room.

"Guess I woke you up," Mark Shaw said.

"I guess it was time," Stan answered. His face was

red, his eyes still heavy. He yawned and stretched and placed a chair. "I don't know how I happened to drop off, only I was up late last night, at my fiddle."

"I just stopped in," Mark Shaw said, "to see your barn stock. I been up the road."

"Well, that's easy," Stan grinned. "We don't have far to go."

He opened a door and they went together into the end of the building which had been left to the cows and horses. There was no fire burning here, but neither were there any draughts, for every board and every shingle was secure, and shorts bag curtains hung over the two windows that stood open. Stan's new floor was smooth and swept and had been washed that day as if it were a house floor. His five cows stood well apart from one another, all fat and round and curried clean. Mark Shaw knew Stan washed their bags before he milked them. The mows were full of good sweet hay. One end of the barn was as well kept as the other and Mark Shaw thought a creature that could not pass the winter here would be wanting somewhat in her beginnings. It almost embarrassed him to see a barn so like a house. He thought it would mean more to Jen than he could see in it. He thought the same of Stan, and yet he liked the boy; he even liked his tunes, strange as it seemed to know a man that set great store by such as music.

"It looks clean enough to cook in," Mark Shaw said at last.

Stan laughed.

"Well, come in now and sit down a while."

"Oh, I got to be going home."

"No, you come in. It's not chore time yet."

They went back into the kitchen, a place that seemed as bleak for its purpose, to Mark Shaw, as the other end did snug as a barn. Mark Shaw laid back his coat but kept his cap on to ward off the chill. Stan sat on a cot bed, wearing his wool shirt and lumberjack and high boots as if he were outside.

"Your folks," Mark Shaw said, "they all settled in up there to Lynn?"

Stan nodded.

"Yes, they've found a rent. I've got to get some of this stuff packed up and sent to them. They're finding that furniture costs a lot to buy outright. Our place was mostly furnished in New York."

He glanced about him.

"They want the beds," he said, "except mine here. And one of the stoves. My mother can't get food to suit her over gas."

"Yes," Mark Shaw observed. "Well. That won't leave you much."

"A stove, a bed, and a table," Stan smiled. "And a kettle or two. I'm camping out." He added grimly, "I owe them that and more in straight money value. I've got a thousand dollars to scare up before my father's all paid back for what he put in here last spring."

"Yes," Mark Shaw said. "Well . . . I been thinking . . . I been thinking if you might want to give me four days of your time a week this winter. I've bought the firewood from two lots that's been cut over and I can use a man to help me haul. There'll be a market for it at the village when it's dry . . . I had it kind of figured out if you could give me four days, I could give you two of mine and your board and let you have my horse for any work you might be doing over here.

. . . Or maybe you wouldn't see way clear to planning so."

"Board over at your place?" Stan asked.

"We always have enough to eat," Mark Shaw said. "Such as it is. And there is rooms enough with so many gone. And I could let you have two days of my time and horse. I kind of thought it might put us both ahead before another spring."

"Why—yes," Stan said. He laughed with some embarrassment. "It would be an awful stroke of luck for me. I can't help thinking, though, it's just a favor on your part. Did Jen——"

"I just now spoke of it to Jen, as I was leaving," Mark Shaw told him. "She seemed to think it wouldn't make no extra work. She said she hadn't no objections to it. And I need another hand. There's things one man alone can't do with as two could . . . I've had a boy about the place so long I've got used to planning out that way, but they're all off now. John, he needs a spell to grow."

"Well," Stan said. He saw Jen's kitchen taking the place of this one, her food instead of his, her and her family replacing his solitude, and he filled up with an emotion he did not care to show to this grave man with the colorless eyes and the black necktie fastened loosely under his chin. "If Jen's willing, and you think I can be of any use——"

"You come," Mark Shaw said, rising. "That's all. As soon as you can get around to it. We'll look for you any time. You bring what you need."

"I'll do *you* a favor, Mr. Shaw," laughed Stan, following to the door. "I'll leave my fiddle over here and when I feel a need to play it I'll get off by myself."

Mark Shaw stood outside, shrugging into his coat. Finished with that, he looked out levelly at Stan, seeing him a man with a different build than that of any other man he knew, with different hair and eyes, and different voice, and a different manner of speaking.

"No," he said. "No, you bring your fiddle along with you. We're quiet folks at our house but a little touch of music won't do us any harm."

What he meant was, "We're Yankee folks at our house but a little touch of Polish won't do us any harm."

And he turned and walked away with tranquil tread.

Before another week went by Jen saw Stan Janowski established in her house. He occupied Ed's bed, read books from Olly's room, washed at the sink, and hung his coat next to Mark Shaw's in the entry. He had his place at the table, his taste as to salt and pepper, his step to be recognized as he came through the shed. He rose early to go over to do the barn work on his own place and sent his milk to the train by Ed; then all day he worked with Mark Shaw hauling in the frozen cornstalks, painting and puttying and putting on storm windows, banking the house with troughs full of sawdust and hemlock boughs. One night snow fell and in the morning he went with Mark Shaw to do the butchering. From behind the barn came the first shrill scream and fainter cryings that Mrs. Shaw had learned to dread, but Jen worked on cheerfully, clearing tables for the dressing down, thinking of fat she must try out and hogshead cheese and minces she must make against the winter. By night the fire was out in the brick oven in the cellar where scalding water had been heated, and the hog hung in the shed, the sides propped apart with short, straight sticks, the lining of the body bright and clean, the color the pale pink and white of well-bled meat. The men's share of the job was done, and Stan sat at his ease and whittled toys for Bun and John from soft pine wood; he had a way with children. He had a way with women, too, to humor them, as Jen observed; he saw much that other men had never seen; he did not hesitate to lift a chair or fill the stove or even set a table if he saw the plates about; Jen thought he would have washed the dishes some nights, if she would have let him; he seemed to know no difference between men's and women's places and was neither awkward nor ashamed to be heard speaking of such things as the colors in the sky. All this Jen overlooked in him indulgently, but by the same means he won Cora Shaw against her will, until she became his champion at every turn.

"Ain't you going to play?" she asked, night after night. "John, go get Stan's fiddle. Careful with it now. . . . There, I've been looking forward all day long to hear you play."

She sat with folded hands to listen to him, and often quite forgot the howling wind, the weak spot in her back, the cold air creeping in about the floor, even that this man was Polish and how she had fought against his coming when she first heard of it. For the minute her face was softer and younger. Even Mark Shaw noticed this. He noticed too that she forgot to take her drug store tonic two meals out of three and seemed no worse for it; if this kept up he would be saved seventy-five cents a week. He figured, moving his lips. But he heard the music, too, and sometimes when it

was gay he bent forward in his chair, smiling, tapping
his feet, remembering the nights when he and Minnie
Foote had danced at parties, the two-steps and the reels.

"I don't suppose," he said, "you know that one about
'It rains and it hails'? . . . No, you wouldn't know it.
That was an old-timer; they used to get it going at
the serenades. It had quite a swing to it, I tell you."

"How did it go?" Stan asked.

"Oh, I don't know as I could say."

"If I could hear the air, I could play it."

"Try it over, Mark," his wife said eagerly.

And Jen, peeling apples for her mincemeat, heard
for the first time in her life her father's voice in song;
not a good, nor a true, nor a young voice but he let
it out for once as if it were all three.

"It rains and it hails and it's cold, stormy weather;
Along comes the farmer, drinking cider!
I'll be the reaper, who'll be the binder?
Looking for my true love,—where shall I find her?
La-di-da-di dum!"

"Say, that's a keen tune!" Stan cried. "Listen. Is this
it?" He played, his bow dancing over the strings, his
face intent and interested. "There. Was that it?"

"It was, wasn't it, Mark?" exclaimed Mrs. Shaw in
delight. "I remember hearing that when I was a little
girl. And didn't he catch it up just right?"

"That was how it went," Mark Shaw said.

He had withdrawn again into his silence and his
half-memories, seeing in the heat waves from the stove
Aaron Hale as he had played that piece and others,
Hen Joy's dancing school in a big upstairs chamber,

Minnie Foote as she had looked coming down to him
when he called for her at ten o'clock on Friday nights;
she had had a quick, light foot for dancing, Minnie
had.

"—Along comes the farmer, drinking cider," Stan
played impudently, looking straight at Jen with a grin
made one-sided to hold his instrument in place. "I'll
be the reaper. Who'll be the binder? Looking for my
true love——"

"He's looking at you, Jen," Bun giggled. Little
escaped Bun. "He's looking right *at* you!"

Cora Shaw, too, glanced at Jen with teasing eyes.

"Well, let him look," Jen said good-humoredly. "He
won't see much."

But when she passed him next she rumpled his hair
until it stood up from his face in a dark peak. She
liked his odd, black hair, feeling so crisp and thick
to her fingers.

VII

At Thanksgiving Lois May and Lize drove home
from Rumfret in an old Ford runabout lately painted
a bright greenish-blue. The Shaws came running from
house and barn to look at it.

"My land! You girls got a car?"

"I'll say we have." They were noisy and excited,
very proud of having actually arrived. Both hopped
out and ran about in their patent leather slippers over
the frozen ground, pointing with small muffs at the
hood, the tires, the steering gear. Their skirts were
long, their jackets short, their hats tight to their heads
and tilted. Lois May looked as tall as Lize, as smart,

and not much younger. "Don't you think it's quite a bus?"

"I guess likely," Jen said, "but come along into the house before you freeze. You ain't got hardly a thing on, either of you."

"No, but how do you like the paint job, father?" Lize persisted. Lois May laughed loudly and Lize glared at her. "Pretty good, isn't it?"

Mark Shaw touched a door with his finger.

"Fair," he said. "Do it yourselves?"

"Do it ourselves!" scoffed Lois May. "Nothing like it! Bobby did it. Bobby does all our odd jobs now. Bobby's Lize's new man. You ought to see him. You ought to hear him talk. He's from the South, you know, one of *the* Montgomerys of Arkansas, and everything——"

"Oh, shut up," Lize suggested mildly.

"Ah'm gwine ter see she brings him home fo' Christmas," promised Lois May, hugging her mother as much for warmth as for any other reason, and all the time looking at Lize. "Ah'm raht fond of her Bobby——"

"Well, now *I'm* going to see that you two get into the house," Jen declared. She clapped her hands and waved her shawl as if they were chickens. "You can talk all this over while I'm getting dinner on."

Lois May and Lize in the kitchen were like two of Lize as she had always been when she came home, both bony-thin, both busy-tongued and restless, staying only a minute with any one topic or any one chair. Mrs. Shaw kept up with every word and movement, her eyes bright from the effort it cost her, touching Lois May or catching her eye as often as she could.

"Well, which one of you is it drives your car?"

"Oh, we both do. I drove my half this morning, didn't I, Lize?"

"Yes, and almost slewed us into the ditch twice or three times."

"Lize Shaw, you liar!"

"Sh-h-h-h! What are you saying, Lois May!"

"Well, she is, ma. I'm a better driver than she is. The garage man told her so. Didn't he, Lize?"

"There, yes, honey, yes——"

"Hear that? Honey! She gets *that* from Bobby! Everything is 'honey' and 'mah chile'——"

"Well, what's become of that boy that took us to the pictures when I was down there with you? He was a nice boy, I thought——"

"Oh, that Melville Baker! Don't mention *him* to Lize!"

"No, don't! . . . One, two, three—only eight plates, Jen?"

"Yes, just us and Stan."

"Stan?"

"Oh, yes," said Mrs. Shaw significantly. "Stan's one of the family now."

Lize and Lois May raised their eyebrows.

"I asked George and Mil but they didn't quite see fit to come," Jen said, taking up a roast of pork. "And Olly thought best not to use the carfare money with Christmas so close on. He's had expenses."

"Oh," sighed Lois May, "I'm dying to see him. I'll bet he's *changed!*"

"Not Ed and Margaret either?" Lize inquired.

Jen shook her head.

"What do they, think it's romantic,—Thanksgiving in their own love nest?"

"Well," Jen said. "That, maybe. And it would be bad getting here with the ground so rough."

Lize looked around quickly.

Mrs. Shaw nodded. "I wrote you how that was, Lois May——"

"Oh, Lord!" said Lize. She let her shoulders sag in a gesture of giving up. "Rough ground bad for sister Mildred, too?"

"I don't know," Jen replied, making room on the table for cranberry sauce and smoking biscuit. "I don't hear anything."

"I shouldn't be a bit surprised," said Mrs. Shaw. "That's my idea of it exactly." She rocked. "Of course I may be wrong——"

"I don't believe you are," Lois May put in. Her small, hard face did not betray how her heart beat as she shared such a conversation. "That's always the safe side—with Mil!"

"I guess I wrote you," Mrs. Shaw said, "that Doris Carpenter is married to a man up there at Penny Brook. The wedding was only two weeks back and people say she's a good three months along. Mrs. Hale was telling me."

"There!" Jen exclaimed. "Here comes the young ones and menfolks. Lois May, you pull up the chairs."

She went into the entry to get napkins from the drawer of a black bureau that stood there, and Lize followed her, whispering.

"Jen, I *like* this Stan. I don't think he looks much Polish. Just enough to be exciting. I could get crazy about a foreigner, I know. . . . Do you think you'll really—I mean, would you *marry* him?"

"There," Jen said. "Now what a question. If ever I get married, Lize, I'll see you know about it soon enough, don't worry." She counted the napkins and got up from her knees, pushing the drawer shut with her foot. "How about you and this Bobby that Lois May runs on about? *You* going to marry *him?*"

"Oh, I don't know," Lize answered. Jen thought she colored. "I would quick enough if he asked me," she whispered suddenly. "He's darling, Jen; he's——"

"Jen!" Lois May called. "Shall we begin?"

"I guess we can't stop now to talk," Jen said. She did not wish to stop. She had no confidences to be shared with this thin girl from Rumfret, or with anyone else. It was not her way to reveal how she felt or dwell upon it. "My chicken fricassee still wants dishing up."

Lize caught at her arm and held her back.

"Well, I'm going to say this much while I've got a chance. If you *do* get married, Jen, don't you go and have a raft of children, like most country women do. There's no sense in it."

"And don't you worry about that," Jen said again. "About me having anything I can't well take care of."

"Oh, Jen," sighed Lize, letting her go. "I never *could* get anywhere with you!"

Jen laughed, not without a certain pride in her independence, and went on to take up the fricasseed chicken, to set her steamed spice and suet pudding where it would keep hot but not go dry, to pin John's napkin and glance once more about the table, to start everybody eating while the food was at its best. She liked Thanksgiving. She liked any excuse for bringing the family together in this kitchen where she could feed and wait on them. It was a pleasure to her that such a large proportion of what she had laid out came from their own place; the fresh pork, the chicken, the crisp fried fat scraps, the potatoes, the squash, the turnip; even the cranberries had come from no farther away than the marshes, and the onions and celery from Stan's piece.

"Stan raised this celery himself," said Mrs. Shaw. "The onions too. He seems to have fine luck with vegetables."

"He's going to try tobacco next spring," Mark Shaw added. "Thinks there ain't no reason why you couldn't grow it in that valley over there. Nobody in these parts has ever raised tobacco."

"You must be a fancy farmer," Lois May said to Stan with a flicker of her eyelashes. "All most men raise is corn and hay and potatoes."

"I raise them too," Stan told her, smiling.

"And that's where he's right," Mark Shaw interposed again. "You got to raise the main things. Corn and hay and potatoes a man has got to raise. Then if he can go beyond it he's that much better off."

There had not been so much talk of farming in the house since Ed went away, and never such accord as lately.

"You'll have another piece of pork," Jen said to Lize. "Did you try my stuffing? . . . Well, then, which will you have first, the pie or pudding? It's pumpkin and mince pie and suet pudding."

"*I* can't eat much more," Bun said, "until I shake this down."

She flung a shawl over her head and ran out to gallop around and around the house, her steps determined and heavy. When she came back, she was so refreshed that she began again with pork and chicken, mashed potato and squash, celery and cranberry sauce. No one attempted to dissuade her. Thanksgiving dinner never hurt a child. John's head nodded over his full plate.

"I remember," Lize said thoughtfully, "when I used to eat until I fell asleep. Then mother would put me on the sitting-room couch and spread a quilt over me. I'd lay looking at the patchwork squares when I woke up."

Lize always was remembering. She would not have gone back to times as they had been when she and Ralph and George and Ed were the children of this house, with Jen and Olly the babies, and Minnie Foote dragging herself from room to room. The unpleasant stayed with her as well as the pleasant—the mice who had nested under her bed before the chambers were finished off, the draughty floors and the heavy colds, the nauseating homemade remedies, the weeks in winter when there was nothing to eat but biscuit and potatoes and fried salt pork and pie. She did not know how Jen and the others still endured the life, even though she realized it was somewhat easier now than it had been in her mother's time and hers. She took a satisfaction none of her city-born friends would ever know in swept streets, hissing radiators, gas and electricity and perfumed soap, silk stockings, manicures, and upholstered seats in moving-picture theaters. And yet she was driven to come back every now and then—would never go very far away from Derwich

—because of the pictures in her mind and a fierce loyalty to those whom she had left here.

Lois May was different. She remembered very little and imagined much. Whatever had passed seemed hazy to her; whatever lay ahead, or might lie ahead, was clear and bright. She had lived in this house last year, of course, but already it had grown rather strange. The family, too, was strange; only Lize seemed natural and right; unless Lize was in the room, Lois May felt insecure. She and Lize lived in Rumfret; they had an apartment, jobs, and friends; they gave parties, washed their underwear at night, read *Vogue* and *Vanity Fair* and bought or made their clothes from these suggestions, kept up with popular music, slang, and cigarettes, were trim and stylish, punctual, gay and disillusioned. This was life as Lois May knew it. It had been difficult at first, but now she knew it and was hardly aware of ever having lived any other.

But it was not enough. It might do for Lize, but not for Lois May. Lois May would never spend all her days before a switchboard, nor all her evenings at picture shows or public dancing palaces, nor all her nights in a two-room apartment that smelled of the last meal which had been cooked and the last bath which had been taken, in a peculiar blend. She saw with a great distinctness the type of man who would some day check into the Madison Hotel, the way he would look at her and speak to her, the dress she would wear while she dined with him in the Dutch Room to which, as a hotel employee, she had never been admitted. She caught the tilt of her head in the gilded mirrors, heard herself speak and laugh, saw his fingers reaching for hers across the tablecloth. She saw herself

on a train with him, in a church with him, in New
York and Washington and Los Angeles, on shipboard
with him; and though he was not in the least like
stubbed Alfred Peters who took her to moving-picture
theaters now, or Len Morganstein from the office who
hopped when he danced and was growing bald, she
saw him plainer than she had ever seen either of them,
and knew him better. She was still not eighteen.

"Lois May!" shrieked Lize. "Can't you hear anything? Ma's speaking to you."

Lois May's glance travelled back complacently to the
wrinkled little woman in the blue dress slightly soiled
at the neck, spotted on the skirt; her mother it was.

"I heard her the first time," she said. "I was just
thinking what to say. Yes, I like it, ma. Anyway, it
isn't hard, when you've learned not to get fussed when
people rage at you. Nobody in a hotel can wait a
minute for anything, you know, especially a number.
But the job's smooth enough—for now."

Mrs. Shaw craved more enthusiasm.

"I guess," she said, "it would have been a great sight
easier for you to get along if you could have finished
up your schooling like you ought to."

"Lord, no," answered Lois May, grimacing at Lize.
"Not that place! *That* was just about as lively as a
convent. I was glad enough to get out of *there*."

This was confusing, for once her faith had been
pinned as securely upon school as upon heaven. Nearly
everything she said was confusing, seeming always ad-
dressed to Lize who alone appeared to understand it.
For Mrs. Shaw it was pleasanter just to look at her.
Lois May was pretty, almost prettier than anybody
could believe. In these fine new clothes, with her fine

new airs, she was lovelier than any other girl who had ever gone out of Derwich, so slim, so dark, so graceful and vivacious and quick with shrugs and winks and movements of her hands. Secretly Mrs. Shaw wondered what the directors of the moving pictures out there to Hollywood would say if they could see this child of Cora Frederick and Charlie Webster. She would have been surprised to know that this one thought she shared with Lois May, surprised and delighted to share anything with her. But Hollywood was not mentioned and the afternoon wore away until both girls sprang up in haste and ran for their coats, gasping of distances, road repairs, and bad tires. The other Shaws hurried them off, more afraid than they of that long trip back for it was less familiar to them. It seemed a wonder that two girls alone could drive so far and still be driving after dark. Mrs. Shaw waved her handkerchief at the window as long as she could see them, and then sat down and cried, but after the tears felt relieved and better. She and Mark and Jen and Stan and the children ate pork sandwiches and milk and pumpkin pie for supper, the leftovers, not even setting the table, but standing about the sink and stove with the food in their hands; things were back again as they had been, with nothing to live up to; Stan played his violin for hours in the evening, quiet old pieces that everybody knew, while Mark Shaw peeled apples at the table, passing around quarters on the point of his knife.

The last days of November wore away. George went past every morning, a gun carried under his arm, taking full advantage of the open season. As a boy he had once shot a deer and this one triumph teased his memory in the fall until he left everything to try again, though deer were few and his aim not of the best. Coming back at night, cold and hungry, he often stopped in at his father's to warm his hands and get something to eat. Sometimes he carried a rabbit or a partridge; never more than that; and he longed for a light snow to show where game had passed, and for the luck of Andy Grant and Bill Carpenter who had brought in two-point bucks, forgetting the blanket he had won at the Fair. He looked forward to the winter in the hope that trapping would be good.

"How are all the folks," Jen always asked him, "up your way?"

"Oh, well enough. Only Georgie, he's got the chickenpox on him."

"The chickenpox!"

"He's all of a spatter. He don't seem sick much, though."

"But I suppose the rest will have to get it, and it will drag on."

"No. The girls, they had it, Mil says, back when Esther started in to school. If the baby gets it, she won't have it hard, Mil says, being light complected so."

"No. That's right. Well, you tell Mil to keep up her courage. Anybody gets into these holes and then gets out of them. It don't do to give up."

One noon Mr. Keele drove in, white horse, blue cart, high reins and all. The children ran to meet him and crowded back with him and his suitcases through the door. He showed his wares and talked as fast as ever, but his eyes looked larger in his small dark face and he had a hunted way with him, glancing into the fields and along the road between every word or two.

"You'll stay to dinner, Mr. Keele?" Jen asked him, having thought of enough and good enough that she had to offer.

"Oh, my, no. No, I got a little box of bread and cheese by me. I be all right. I got to hurry now. It get dark quick, these days so short."

"Well, now, it won't take me any time to get it on. You'd better wait and have a hot mouthful. It will do you good. I'll start right in. Here are the menfolks coming now——"

"Coming, the men, are they? No. Oh, my, no. I must be getting on. Business, you know, business. Here's that cotton batting, Miz Shaw, and the percale, and the two dozen buttons. I guess that all you said to-day. Good-by, good-by. Take care yourselves. I see you in the spring. I bring some nice stuff in the spring. Good-by, good-by."

He went, his red pasteboard cases only partly strapped, his coat tails flying. A cut of the whip sent the old horse romping out of the yard. Jen had never seen him use the whip before, and this was the shortest call he had ever made. She wondered at it as she watched him go, wishing she might at least have had a cup of coffee ready to warm his poor old stomach through.

Stan came in from the shed.

"Who was that?" he asked. "Was that Manuel Keele?"

"It was Mr. Keele," Jen said. "Is that his first name —Manuel? We never heard."

Stan stood beside her, watching too, as the back end of the blue cart disappeared over the hill by his place.

"He was in an awful rush," he said. "I tried to get here before he left but I couldn't make it."

"Did you need something of him?" Jen asked. "You might have spoke to me. I could have got it for you."

"All I wanted was to speak to him," Stan said slowly. He saw that they were alone and put his arm about Jen's waist but did not look at her. They were both watching the road. "I'm going to tell you something, Jen," he said. "I'm not supposed to tell it but I want you to know. Manuel Keele is a great friend of my father's. He was the one that got us over here from Poland; he came first and sent the money back. . . . He's done a lot for me. He helped me get through high school and he lent me some of the money I've put in up here."

"Well, is he afraid that you won't pay him back?" Jen asked. "Or what makes him so offish, then, that he don't even speak to you? He never said to us he was a friend of yours."

Stan shook his head.

"He don't want you to know," he said. "That's why."

"Don't want me to know!"

"Not you—nor anybody here. He thinks it's—well, kind of a disgrace to be a peddler. And he thinks it's fine to be a farmer. . . . He was pretty proud when we came up here. You see, he's got no family of his own. . . . It broke him all up when my father made up his mind he wouldn't stay. You see, Manuel is getting old. He wanted to know we'd got a place and were settled in."

Jen pondered this.

"Well, *you've* got a place," she said, smiling. *"You're* settled in."

This was enough for her, she thought. It ought to be enough for Mr. Keele. She hoped it seemed so to him, as he rode now along the frozen road, eating his bread and cheese from his left hand, holding the reins with his right.

One more caller was to come before the winter. Mark and Stan were in the barn when they saw his car turn into the yard. Between them lay a long, wide strip of dry beanpods on the clean-swept floor, and they were beating it with flails, Mark at one end of the barn, Stan at the other; their blows were sharp and regular, like clockwork. John leaned against a ladder, watching them.

"A man is coming out this way," Stan said. "Must be to see you."

Mark Shaw stood looking out through the crack of the door, the flail hanging at his side. The man in the yard was short and stout with a round, pink face and a close-clipped white mustache. He wore a gray fur coat and a black derby hat and limped as he walked. Mark Shaw gave the door a push that sent it rolling back, and waited. The stranger did not speak until he had stepped in, though he was smiling cordially.

"You're never Mark Shaw," he said then.

"Yes, I think 's likely I am."

"Well, you don't know me, Mark!"

"I guess I do. It's Gus Hampliton, ain't it?"

The stranger beamed. He shook Mark's hand and studied him.

"Say, you're right. I don't know how you guessed it.

I'd never have known you out of here, Mark. Never in
God's world. Time puts a stamp right on us, don't it?
Yes, sir, we don't get away with anything. Why, *that*
looks more like Mark Shaw to me than you do. I guess
you was some older than him, though, the last I saw
of you."

"Yes. That's John. He ain't seven yet. He's my
youngest boy."

"That so? Well, he's a chip right off the old block,
I see that. You was just about as big as him when your
mother used to bring you up to the old place and
spend the day."

Mark Shaw remembered those times. His mother
and Gus Hampliton's had been great friends. They
used to sit and knit in the front yard while he and
Gus and Bell and Annie played with a cosset lamb
beside the barn. Nabby Hampliton would always ask
what Jerusha Shaw would like best for her dinner, and
Jerusha always said, as the young ones gathered near
to listen, "Well, Nabby, there's no dish more to my
taste than fish 'n' 'taters. And if you had a mite of your
spice cake a-laying about the house——"

"I was up there early in the fall," Mark Shaw said,
"to get some grapes. It's all growed up wild."

"I suppose it must be. I kind of hate to go up there,
don't know as I will . . . I haven't been this way since
Annie's funeral, and then the house was rotting
down."

"That must have been around twenty years ago.
Annie, she's been gone some time. . . . You took Bell
back with you, as I remember. She's living still, I
suppose?"

"Bell? No, no, Bell died last summer. She'd been

staying out there in Illinois with us for ten years or
more. You know, Mark, I kind of think she fretted to
get back this way. We was always planning on the
trip, but some way we never got to it while she was
living. . . . The Hamplitons never was a very long-
lived bunch, you know, Mark. I thought this year I'd
better come out and be sure of it."

Gus Hampliton grinned cheerfully at Mark. They
stood together, one with a round, pink face, one hard
and brown, Gus in fur, Mark in blue drilling; they
were past their fiftieth years, Gus nearer sixty, and yet
they were the same people who had played with the
cosset lamb where junipers and bayberry bushes now
grew, and who had been called in to finish the fish-
and-potatoes and spice cake when Nabby and Jerusha
had eaten all they could.

"Well, I'm glad you did. You must come in the
house. You bring your wife?"

"No, no, Mark, I can't stop. I've got a man from
the village driving me out and I've got to catch a train.
I'm in Boston on some business this week, how I happened down. No, my wife didn't make the trip. She
was here when Annie died and she didn't take much
to this part of the country. She was born and brought
up out there in Springfield, Illinois, you know. It's
home to her. . . . Somebody told me down along that
you got married again, Mark, after Minnie died."

"Yes. Yes, I married Cora Webster up to Kezar
Falls."

"That so? This big fellow one of Minnie's boys?"

"No. He's working for me. My boys are all away
but John."

"In city places somewhere, I suppose?"

"Only Olly. He's in college. George and Ed, they've got farms around. That's Ed's barn you can see up on the hill. He's on the old Searles place——"

Here Gus Hampliton chuckled, taking off his hat and smoothing his bald head.

"You don't mean it, Mark? You don't mean there's younger ones will stay stuck here the way you did? It don't seem possible. . . . Why, Mark, since we was twenty years old I've been around the world. I've been to the Klondike after gold. I've set up steam shovels in a dozen places in every state of the Union, I suppose. And here you've been!"

"Yes," Mark Shaw agreed. "I've been right here."

Gus suddenly grew eloquent, feeling Stan's and John's young eyes and ears on him.

"And haven't ever got sick of it?" he demanded. "Never wanted to get off down south to where they burn up? Why, Mark, I tell you, I've sat dressing my feet on the side of the bed down there in Texas and heard a rattler sing behind my heels! . . . And the gold rush didn't get you either? Say, I went into Alaska like I was chased." He jerked up his trouser leg and showed a wooden member. "I made room for this fellow while I was up there. Got off the trail and was lost there for three days and nights with nothing but snow and the timber wolves to ask questions of. It wasn't much like here, I tell you, up there to the Klondike."

Mark Shaw shook his head, looking down at the wooden foot, feeling his own feet warm inside his boots.

"No," he said mildly. "Well. I never was one to hanker much for making changes."

Gus struck him jovially on the back, playing still to Stan and John.

"Well, where would this country have got to with only men like you around, Mark? Nobody'd ever have landed on it in the first place, and if they had they'd have set on that Plymouth Rock until they sunk it into the ground. Where's your old pioneering spirit, Mark? I don't see how it happened you got born on this side. I don't see how your ancestors ever managed to get across the ocean!"

Mark Shaw considered this.

"Well, I don't know," he said. "Not unless the pioneering ones brought them along just so's to have somebody to leave behind when their kind went a-traipsing off again. I guess this pioneering don't amount to much without somebody stays to home and does the work."

"He's got you there, sir," Stan exclaimed with some delight.

Gus Hampliton turned to look at him and as Stan looked back, he seemed to see only the two bright, restless eyes and a wooden foot which now had been covered. And he heard again scraps of the conversation. " . . . I suppose it must be growed up wild. I'd kind of hate to go up there. . . . We was always planning on the trip . . . The Hamplitons never was a very long-lived bunch. I thought this year I'd better come out and be sure of it. . . . No, I can't stop. I've got to catch a train. . . . My wife didn't come . . . She didn't take much to this part of the country. She was born and brought up out there to Springfield, Illinois. It's home to her. . . . " All that he had seen

and heard used his mind as he used violin strings,
touching it truly in the right places.

"We need both kinds," Stan said, "to make a
country."

"Yes," Mark Shaw added, to conclude. "I guess
there's use enough for all of us as long as we can keep
a-going." He smiled. "You'd better stay to dinner, Gus,
and lay off your coat and give a hand to thrashing out
these beans. You was used to thrashing when you lived
around here, I guess."

"Oh, yes," Gus said. "I've thrashed barrels of them.
Pea beans, these are, ain't they? . . . No, Mark, I
can't stay. I wanted to ride up the road a little farther
and see once more how the land lays . . . You still use
flails here then? I've read there wasn't one anywhere
to be found."

Mark Shaw drew his through his hand.

"Yes, everybody uses flails. Everybody that raises
any amount of beans. It's slow work shelling out by
hand."

"Oh, there's machinery now, you know."

"Is?" Mark asked indulgently. "Well, then Ed'll be
a-getting it. Ed, he's the one that's all for new-fangled
ways. We can get our beans out of the pods by the old
notions, can't we, Stan?"

"They're about out now," Stan answered, kicking
into the crisp heap.

"Well, Mark, I've got to go. How is that road down
into the old place? Could we get over it with a car if
I should take it into my head I wanted to——"

Gus Hampliton and Mark Shaw went out of the
barn together. John took his father's flail and beat
valiantly along with Stan. Then Mark came back and

he and Stan raked off the pods and swept up what was left. They carried out two flour barrels to the yard where a brisk wind blew and turned the beans from baskets through a wire sieve into the barrels. Whatever chaff did not blow across their arms and into the field was caught in the sieve and could be shaken out; the beans were left very clean and white, needing only Jen's quick eyes and fingers to run them through and wash them, a quart at a time, on Friday nights in winter. She liked to soak them well, and parboil them, and let them bake in a slow oven for ten hours or more. Jen's recipe had once been Jerusha Shaw's, known in her time and afterwards as a great hand with beans.

WINTER AGAIN

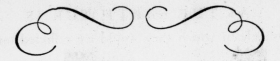

WINTER AGAIN

I

IT HAD been snowing since noon and the high wind had not died down at sunset but still spit and growled past doors and chimneys and swept deep drifts into every place where they could catch and cling. There was no light anywhere except in Mark Shaw's kitchen and another in his parlor with a stretch of dark that was the long front entry lying between.

"I'd better go out again," Ed said, "and see the lane's still clear."

"All right," Stan agreed. "It blows in fast. I'll go along."

They yawned and stretched, both half asleep, and pulled on boots and coats and caps. The shovels made a heavy, metallic sound as the men dragged them off the steps where they had been left an hour or two before. The yard was clear and icy, but at two points in the lane new drifts were already some feet deep. Ed and Stan bent to them, fighting in the dark against the storm and the wind to keep the road open. Behind them the drawn shades in the parlor let out a dim, reddish gleam which they would see reflected on the snow ahead.

The kitchen, left to itself, seemed to be waiting. The air was hot and cold in gusts with the unsteady heat of a nearly dead fire not long ago rebuilt. Table, couch, and floor were very neat as Jen always left them when she went to bed. The children's clothes —stockings, garters, and long-legged underwear—hung on nails behind the stove, and Mark Shaw's shoes set side by side beneath his chair. Minnie Foote's clock read half-past one. Jen glanced at it as she tiptoed out of the parlor with a hot water bottle to be filled, and went back quietly, not to waken those who slept.

Ed and Stan came in, leaving the shovels on the steps, hanging their coats over the oven door, and took their places, Ed by the back window where he could look down the road, Stan in the dark corner by the stairs. Their cheeks were blood red from the beating of fine particles of ice, their eyes bloodshot from the wind; they looked tired and sober.

Ed made an effort.

"I'm much obliged to you, Stan," he said, "for what you've done. Now you might as well go turn in and get some sleep."

"That's all right," Stan answered. "I'll stay up. We may have to dig the doctor out when he gets along."

"I didn't mean to rout anybody up," Ed said. "It wasn't as we planned, you can be sure. I had a nurse all fixed to come next week, but it's away ahead of time . . . I wasn't taking any chances of being blocked in over there alone, while we could still get out. I guess I can't be blamed for that."

"No. Well, it's all right. As it happened, you see, we hadn't even gone to bed, Jen and I. We were just sitting here and Jen was saying not a minute before you folks drove in, 'My land, it's 'most morning!' "

"It's a lot to put on Jen," Ed felt bound to say to Stan. "It wasn't as we planned."

"No," Stan repeated. "It's all right. I know she thinks so. Women hang together at a time like this."

They had finished the proprieties now and fell silent. Jen came out once or twice and went quickly back again. Stan rose once in a while to put wood on the fire. Otherwise the room was very still. Ed watched the road and the sky. It was clearing now; big blue clouds raced before the wind and there was a light spot where the moon should be. The doctor came at last and went through with his bag into the parlor, but Ed still stared out of the window at the clouds and the snow and the bare, bending trees. Sometimes a star shot into sight and was immediately buried by the clouds like a daisy by a gathering windrow of hay.

A cry from Margaret came all the way along the entry to the two men. Another followed it. A bitter, shamed color spotted Ed's neck and cheeks. Sitting there he shouldered the blame he felt fairly belonged on him as the male, and made resolutions he could never keep, or even see the need of keeping once all this was past. Stan's pulses still stung with pleasure at having been spoken to by Jen's brother as if she were his wife already. He thought of Jen shut away in the other end of the house and found he had no dread of what she must do to-night, though she had not yet borne a child herself, or so much as been married, or even felt a man's hand at her breast. Jen seemed to

him equal to whatever might be asked of her, to-night
or afterward. He doubted if when her own time came,
perhaps a year from now, he should be frightened, as it
was plain to him that Ed was frightened. Stan sat
thinking of goddesses and found no humor in the
thought, though Jen was short and stocky with a broad,
contented face.

"I guess it won't be long now," he said to Ed. "It
must be almost time."

Ed did not answer.

The doctor came out later for a cup of tea. Stan
poured it for him from an earthenware pot on the
back of the stove, and he stood drinking it, warming
his hands, a tall, gray-headed figure with a shadow
that crossed the room and bent up at the baseboard to
climb the wall, an easy voice speaking of the storm
and the roads until Jen opened the door and called
him back. Jen herself went in and out. Once she wore
a more secret and excited look than Stan had ever seen
on her, and hurried to place two chairs before the stove,
on one of them a big white washbowl from her room.
She caught up the men's coats and threw them on the
couch, replacing them over the oven door by a blanket
on which she spread some small white garments from
the suitcase Ed had brought. To Ed she said, "Don't
you worry now. Margaret's all right. She's doing fine."
To Stan, "Fill up the kettle, will you? And set it on the
hot end." Still she seemed hardly aware of either man
and went away with her secret look, closing the doors
behind her.

With all the activity the house was hushed. The
wind, the crackle of the fire, the small singing of the
kettle, and the snapping of clapboard nails broken by

the frost were sounds to be reckoned with. The tick
of Minnie Foote's clock had an echo. Nobody stirred
upstairs. The house was waiting.

Suddenly Jen came into the room again and stopped,
outlined against the door. She looked now to Stan as
if she might have been running for some distance
through the night, as if it were the wind that had
blown her hair into ruffles and the cold reddened her
face, as if she were glad to see them after being away
a long time; he wondered if anybody else ever had
such thoughts as his. She carried a bundle wrapped in
a gray shawl on her arm.

"Well, here we are," she said triumphantly. "Ed!
Here's your baby!"

Ed stood up then. Stan saw how his legs shook; he
would always remember this in Ed.

"She all right?" Ed asked, not looking at the bundle.

"She's fine," Jen said. "She's a brave girl, Ed. Ma
heard us and came down an hour or so back. She
said she never see the beat of Margaret. The doctor
said so too. . . . You might go in a minute now, if
you want to."

Ed reached for the doorknob.

"You could just peek at us," Jen said reproachfully.
She turned back a corner of the blanket. "We're quite
a big little boy. We guess we weigh a good eight
pounds or so."

Ed paused as if with reluctance, looking down. Then
his expression began to change and lighten. He cast a
quick glance at Stan, flushing again but not so deeply.

"A boy, is it?"

"Eight solid pounds of boy. Maybe a little more."

"Well—I'll be right back."

He went on toward the parlor, leaving the kitchen to Jen and Stan and the bundle. Jen sat down close by the oven and tested the water she had left in the bowl, finding it too cool. She reached for the kettle but Stan took it off the stove for her and poured in from it until she nodded that she had enough and began softening a washcloth with a new bar of castile soap. She held the shawl so high, to keep off draughts, that Stan could not see the baby she was bathing but he could hear the whimpering, bird-like noises it made. He watched Jen's fingers and bare arms and shining hair.

"There!" she was saying. "There now!" She smiled at Stan. "I'm leaving his eyes and ears and nose 'til last. And then he'll holler good!"

"How do you know so much?" Stan asked. He leaned forward, his elbows on his knees, as near to her as he could get, not to be in the way.

Jen laughed softly.

"Oh, there's been babies washed before now in this old kitchen!"

"You wash them?"

"John I did. The first time and always afterwards. He wouldn't stand it from anybody else. . . . Sometimes it seems to me as if I'd tended to them all when they was this one's bigness . . . That must sound funny——"

"No," Stan told her. Then he said, "You'd want your own here, would you, Jen? In this same house where you've had the rest?"

Jen sat looking back at him, her head higher than his as he leaned toward her, her eyes grave.

"I guess I would, Stan. I've done some thinking on

it. I didn't know how you'd feel . . . But I can't make
it seem I'd get along so well in any other place."

"No," Stan said again. "Well, that's all right. It'll be
just as you say, you know, Jen, anything like that."

Jen stooped suddenly over the baby, attacking the
last, most delicate task of eyes and ears and nose. The
lusty shriek that she had promised ran into the depths
of the oven and out again. It hardly seemed that so
much sound could have come from under the blanket
on her lap. Jen looked up at Stan, laughing, but he
saw her eyes were full of tears and her cheeks were
wet. He wondered why he had waited so long to say
what she wanted most to hear. He liked living with
the Shaws, and they all liked having him, he knew.
He and Mark would do well to farm together. He
could not imagine Jen in a new house.

"I see somebody's fist," he said.

"We've got big fists," said Jen. "We'll have a lot of
use for them. You see, we're another Shaw."

II

After supper, on Christmas Eve, Mark Shaw went
into the yard for the full-branched balsam which had
been left for good keeping in a snowbank by the shed
since the day a week ago when he brought it from the
woods on the top of his load. Coming back, he stopped
by the steps, shaking the snow off the tree, and looked
through the window at the family.

They were all at home, every one. George sat smoking and talking to Stan who had a bit of white wood
in his hand and was cutting notches in it with his
knife. It was a thing to notice how even George, as

well as all the rest, had changed as time went on in
his unfriendly feeling about this man with a dark skin
and a long name. Now he was Stan. Ed stood at the
tank end of the stove shelling popping corn, grinding
two ears together between his palms. Ed was strong
for all he was so lean and lank, and strength grew in
him every day now he had a son to think of, another
Ed come after him. Olly shook the popper harder and
faster than there was any need, and jerked his head a
little with the motion of his arm. But he was steadier
than he had once been, more easy in his ways; it was
not so hard to manage to make talk with him, and he
had more to say himself; he knew about the mountains and the lakes, even deserts and the prairie country, and he would be a lawyer in good time, like
Minnie's Uncle Jeff. A strange way to do it might
seem, but his way and reasonable enough when looked
at from all sides; not everybody laid his plan like
everybody else. Lize and Lois May were wrapping
boxes at the table. They had fine clothes and curly hair
and shining fingernails, and the paper they used was
gold-color and the ribbon wide and red; it looked ex-
travagant but they were doing well and made good
pay, both of them. Mil and Cora Shaw sat by stringing
popcorn and cranberries, talking fast as women will,
with quick changes on their faces every word or two;
Cora looked brighter and more cheerful than she had
in years, but Mil was going gray again and getting big;
there would be another mouth for George to see to;
he must learn to think less of that pipe and more of
working; five was too many for a laggard and this
George would come to understand; he was a young
man yet. Margaret, out of her room for the first time,

sat in a sheltered corner by the stove holding the baby on her lap; young Ed was a likely child; he took a stout grip on a finger; he would do. Jen went back and forth between the pan of hot molasses for the pop-corn balls and the children undressing on the rug be-fore the stove; she had planned beds for everyone to-night and when Mark Shaw lay down in his he could be thinking that they were all asleep beneath his roof and so would be safe until morning. All who had ever lived in this house were here; all who could come; and even Minnie Foote and Ralph slept not far away, in-side as stout a stone and iron fence as any man could build; they were safe too, at last, not flying high nor sick with wanting to.

Mark Shaw took up the balsam tree and carried it inside.

"Now ain't that a handsome one?" Jen cried. "My, that's handsome, father. You put it in the sitting-room. You'll find the base is there, and Lize and Lois May will be right in to trim it. My, I'll bet that'll hit the ceiling, won't it?"

She turned back to the children.

"You young ones hustle up. It's full time some folks got to bed in case Santa comes around early! Come now, see which one is undressed first."

"Esther," Mil called. "You help Georgie with his shoestrings and his buttons."

"Say, you know, they're sweet," Lize said, watching them. "Esther makes me think so much of Jen as she used to be."

"When are you going to get married, Lize," asked Cora Shaw, "and bring home some of yours? And where's that Bobby you was telling for?"

"Bobby's been given the air," said Lois May. "Bobby was a gay deceiver, wasn't he, Lize?"

"Bobby was a mess," Lize answered briefly.

Jen heard this and remembered how differently Lize had spoken of him that day not a month ago out in the entry. Lize was not the marrying kind, she thought. Lize would still be a trim, smart office girl when she was fifty. It would not be so with Lois May.

"Look, Ed," said Margaret. "He's waking up a little."

"He'd better go back to sleep," said Ed, "or Santa Claus won't bring him anything. . . . There, that ought to be enough corn, Ob. Did you go through the corn belt on that trip you took? Iowa, and them places?"

"Yes," Olly told him. "Just after harvest. It was stacks as far as you could see in all directions."

"I guess they use it mostly for their hogs," George said. "It must be a big job to raise up all that stuff and feed it out and like as not get nothing for it in the end. From all I hear they cover a lot more territory out that way but most of them don't get ahead much faster——"

The children stood, a row of six, Mil's Vera wavering between her older sisters, all in their striped outing flannel nightgowns, each holding a stocking he had just taken off. Jen did not approve the hanging of stockings from a drawer. Let each child hang his own, with the imprint of his foot still in it, a bigger foot each year. She had always done so, and Olly had, and Lize and Ed and George and Ralph.

"Now then, father! Where's your nails? We're needing six this year. No, seven, it is."

Mark Shaw brought his hammer and leaned across

the woodbox to nail each stocking in place from the shelf behind the stove. He took Bun's first because she was the oldest; it hung long and wide; then Esther's, Betty's, John's, Georgie's, Vera's, and young Ed's. The children watched with solemn eyes, each breathlessly waiting for his turn to come, and Margaret held up her baby's small white sock until Mark Shaw came to it in his due course and fastened it as carefully as the others next to the funnel.

"Mine's most as big as John's," cried Georgie. "Next year it will be; won't it, daddy?"

"I guess you'll have to hyper," chuckled George.

"It won't," John retorted doubtfully. "I guess. Will it, Bun?"

"Course not," Bun answered. "It'll just be longer than it is, and so will yours, and so'll the baby's." She eyed her own.

"There!" Jen exclaimed. "And now you're going to bed, as fast as you can scoot. Lois May'll take up the hot rocks for us."

"It don't seem as if I'd go to sleep," objected Betty. She was all blue eyes and yellow curls to-night, unreal beside the others.

"No," laughed Jen, "but you'll find you will."

She had seen wide eyes before on Christmas Eve.

With the children gone, the elders had their brief turn at being young again. Filling the stockings and decorating the tree with strung popcorn and cranberries and tying little packages for one another on the boughs, they talked and laughed, remembering what had been in the past and hoping for the future. Lize curled up on the floor like a kitten, wearing an old plaid dress Jen had brought down for her from the attic, and leaned against her father's knee as she had years before; he kept looking down at the top of her head. Jen and Margaret worked fast at pressing corn-balls into shape and heaping them on platters here and there about the sitting-room and kitchen. There were bowls of candied popcorn too, and sugared orange peel, and pans of polished apples. Lois May kept tasting first one and then another, daintily, but still her glance would travel in the direction of the tree; she wondered what it bore for her, especially what Lize had put there. Mil was in high spirits, with much to say to tease Ed and Stan and Olly, and even George. Jen listened to her with amusement; this was like the old Mil who had come here for Christmases while she was still the oldest Ross girl, and sometimes brought her younger sister with her, the grave, sweet one who went to normal school.

It was close to midnight when Mrs. Shaw broke in with, "We going to hear that new machine of yours before we go to bed, Stan?"

"His new machine!"

"Shall I?" Stan asked Jen.

"He got his Christmas present from his folks this morning," Jen explained. "It's an accordion. . . . Why, yes, Stan, play it, if you think you can."

He brought it out and it was a strange thing to see in the Shaw kitchen, but still it looked like Christmas for it was red and black with squares of mother-of-pearl set in the ends. Stan lifted it tenderly, his eyes intent, his mouth smiling, and tried a note or two, pushing it in and out from the ends, an odd way to make music. Suddenly he straightened, throwing back his head, and began to play a Christmas tune, "Hark,

the Herald Angels Sing." He played it no more like a
hymn than like a dance, and no less; his shoulders
swayed with every note; he sang with it, laughing as
he sang.

"Hark, the herald angels sing
Glory to the new-born King—"

Olly saw the strange, wild look in Stan's eyes that
he had seen there in the summer but none of the other
Shaws seemed to notice it, or be afraid. They were
laughing, too, and singing; even Mark Shaw smiled,
watching Stan.

"Now wasn't that fine?" asked Mrs. Shaw. "You
can't imagine the pleasure we've took with his music
all the fall. And I declare I think I like the way this
works full better than the fiddle."

"It's just lovely," Margaret said. She was tired and
leaned against Ed's arm but her face was bright from
the singing. "I don't see how you knew how to play
it, Stan!"

"Oh, I've tried one a few times before," Stan said
modestly.

"It seems to come awful natural to him some way,
playing tunes," Jen said. "Now I think *we'd* better go
to bed and get ready for to-morrow, like the young
ones. It's almost to-morrow now."

They yawned and nodded, wandering off, one alone,
two at a time, as Jen told them where they were to
sleep.

"Good night."
"Good night, everybody."
"Good night."

When twelve o'clock came, it found only Jen and her father in the kitchen, she clearing away the litter of paper and string and cooking dishes, he taking a lantern from the shelf and going toward the barn. She wondered if he would find the cattle restless, having heard they were so on Christmas Eve. Quietly she carried her plants away from the windows, wound the clock, and set the chairs in order. Her father's step was slow and steady coming back.

"Everything all right out there, father?"

"Yes. All right."

He hung the lantern in its place and sat down to take off his shoes.

"Cold night," he said. "Clear as a bell."

"I see the stars are all out bright."

She closed the draughts of the stove and turned down the light.

"You put this out when you come up, won't you?"

"Yes. I'll put it out."

As she opened the stairway door he looked up at her. She smiled.

"We got a full house, father."

"Running over, ain't it?"

"Just the way it ought to be. For Christmas anyway."

Alone Mark Shaw sat for some time on the end of the couch, looking down at his feet in their brown cotton stockings. Then he rose deliberately and with his thumbs stretched his suspenders until he could ease his shoulders out of them. Now he was more comfortable, and he stood idly by the window looking out at the snow and the woods and the blue, starred sky overhead. The glass was already frosting over, but the

room felt warm. He turned back into it, hearing
Minnie Foote's steeple clock ticking, smelling the
apples and the molasses and the green life of the tree.
Yawning, he went over to where the stockings hung
behind the stove, seven in a row. His face, as he sur-
veyed them, was serene, proud, meditating. Thoughtfully he slid his fingers into his overalls pocket and
withdrew a handful of change, selecting several small
silver coins and dropping one into each stretched top.
He had done so every Christmas Eve for nearly thirty
years now. It was his part.